FORGIVE ME

KATE EMBERS

To Franny, I wish you were here to read it

Trigger Warnings:
- Sexual Assault
- Violence
- Stalking
- Kidnapping
- Blood & Gore
- Alcohol Abuse
- Panic Attacks
- Anxiety
- Death

1

ANDREW

"Andrew," the barista called.

"Thanks," Andrew murmured to the young girl with a slight dip of his head as he picked up the cup of coffee. Sliding a sleeve onto the cup, Andrew made a hasty retreat to the door of the on-campus coffee shop. He didn't frequent the coffee shop on campus often due to the number of students that typically hung out there as if it was their home away from home, but he had been running late that morning and hadn't had time to make his coffee before heading to work.

As he opened the door to make his escape, a blur of a woman fell past him to his feet, letting out a small yelp. A pair of big brown eyes blinked up at him as a bashful grin slowly formed on the woman's face.

"Sorry," she said, meekly with a small shrug. Andrew gave her a slight smile and offered her his hand. Her small hand slid into his and firmly gripped it as he hauled her to her feet. The woman was shorter than him by almost a good foot and was currently looking up at him from underneath her green baseball cap with those beautiful brown eyes.

"Well, that was embarrassing," the woman declared in a tone that sounded as if she were more amused by the situation than embarrassed. They stared at one another for a few seconds longer than what would have been considered proper and polite, but neither of them moved to look away or continue with their day. Andrew felt frozen in time and was sure he was losing his mind.

Why? Why are we standing here staring at one another?
Should I say something?

He swallowed, hoping she would say something and put him out of his misery.

Her eyes slid from his to their still clasped hands.

"Oh, sorry," she exclaimed, slowly sliding her fingers from his. Andrew continued to stare at her, lacking the ability to look away. Any minute now, he was officially going to be labeled a creep by anyone witnessing this embarrassing exchange.

The silence was growing awkward, but he could not for the life of himself conjure up anything to say.

"Okay, well, thanks again," the woman told him, breaking the silence as she stepped aside to pick up the backpack she had dropped.

With a nod of her head, she began to move past him but paused as Andrew opened his mouth to say something; however, silence only filled the air between them. The words continued to remain absent.

How did this become an embarrassing moment for me instead of her?

He snapped his mouth shut, dipped his head, and started for the door. As he opened the door, he gave her one last look over his shoulder and mentally kicked himself for not being able to say a single word to her.

There seemed to be nothing special about her, but for some reason, she had rendered him utterly speechless as she had fallen to his feet. Andrew may have been a man of few words, but he'd certainly never been devoid of them. His own wife had never made him feel incapable of words. Unable to decide how to feel or what to do with this new realization, he continued out the door, heading across campus to his office.

Andrew had always been partial to the start of the Fall semester. The world was beginning to enter its dying period, but academia was starting anew. It had always served as a reminder that life coexisted with death. Time never rested, even if the heart requested it, and joy could not live without sorrow. This was what kept Andrew going some days, knowing he could survive in the grief of the closing chapters of his life.

Opening the door to his office, he let out a small sigh of contentedness at the familiarity of the small room. The room was basic and square, like most university offices. His was filled with bookshelves, brimming with books and two big leather chairs that took up most of the floor space in front of his desk.

Classes didn't officially begin for two more days, but he had more work than he would like to admit to, which was the only reason he'd reluctantly allowed the head of the English department, Dr. Hayesworth, to assign him a graduate assistant for the semester. Andrew didn't particularly care to train someone or have someone working closely with him, but he was swamped with work since returning from his trip to Wyoming. Three months in the mountains of Wyoming might be restoring for the soul, but it was rough on reality.

Lost in thought and concentration of setting up his classes in the university's online system, Andrew failed to hear the knock on his open door or notice the woman now standing in his office staring at him.

"Dr. Brant?" A sweet angelic voice called his name.

His head snapped up from the computer to find the woman from the coffee shop, standing in the middle of his office, grinning at him.

"Hi, Dr. Brant, I'm Evie. Your graduate assistant." A bright smile lit her face as she greeted him.

This must be a twisted joke.

Andrew felt as though he was being pranked. He had just spent the last twenty minutes wanting to crawl into a hole over not being able to utter a single word to the woman now standing before him but had finally concluded that it was okay because he would most likely never have to encounter her ever again. He could live with the embarrassment of being stricken wordless if he knew their paths were to never cross. However, she now stood in the middle of his office, smiling at him with the cutest pair of dimples.

That alluring, enchanting smile was causing his stomach to twist into a knot, silently threatening to kill him. First, no words. Now, a strange feeling akin to butterflies. This semester may prove to be the death of him.

Realizing the seconds were ticking by and the room was becoming awkward, Andrew cleared his throat preparing for the words to let him down for the second time that morning. "Welcome, Miss James. I am just finishing uploading the first week's assignments for a few of the online classes. Let me get this finished, and then we can discuss what to expect for the semester."

He was surprised he had managed to get all the words out. Mentally, he crossed his fingers, hoping she would leave his office and wait somewhere else to give him time to figure out what to say next. However, the day didn't seem to be his day.

She simply replied, "Okay, sounds good," slid the black backpack off her shoulders and plopped into one of the big, comfy leather chairs in front of his desk. He watched as she opened her backpack and pulled a book out, clearly with no intention of leaving his office for the foreseeable future. Settling into the chair, she opened the book and began to read. Ever so slowly, Andrew pulled his gaze from her and forced himself to get back to work.

After about ten minutes into working, Andrew heard Evie quietly giggle to herself. His heart caught him off guard by taking a noticeable leap at the sound of her. Looking up, he found her smiling at the book, amused by something she was reading. She had also all but curled herself into the chair, looking as if she were completely at home there in his office.

Something in Andrew's chest relaxed just a bit, and he felt as if he could spend the rest of his life just watching her read. It was rare that a student looked comfortable in his office, and none of them had certainly ever relaxed enough to curl up in that leather chair. He knew the reputation he had around campus of being the rigid and cynical professor, but he'd never really minded it until Evie had walked into his office that morning and announced she was his graduate assistant. Maybe she hadn't heard the rumors about him or maybe she didn't believe them, but either way, he hoped she would forever remain this relaxed around him.

Now, his own thoughts were catching him off guard.

What is happening to me?

Shaking off the unwanted thoughts and feelings, he interrupted her reading, calling her name.

"Hmm?" She absentmindedly responded, dragging her eyes unhurriedly from her book to look at him. Those brown eyes of hers might be his undoing. Before he spoke, a reminder to keep breathing and using words flittered through this mind.

"I'm almost finished with this if you want to take a look at the syllabus to get an idea of what to expect out of the English 101 class. Since it's a basic requirement, there isn't anything special or unexpected about it. Should be fairly, straightforward." Picking up one of the copies, he held it out to her.

Setting aside her book, she leaned forward and grabbed the syllabus from him. "Thanks."

He watched as she sat back in the chair, casually tossing her long brown ponytail over her shoulder as she leaned forward to rest her elbows on her knees. Her eyebrows furrowed in concentration as she began to read over the syllabus. The newfound butterflies fluttered in his stomach, once again.

She looks quite endearing with her eyebrows scrunched together like that.

His thought caused him to pause.

Where are these thoughts coming from?

After a while, Andrew realized Evie was quiet and should have finished looking over the syllabus by then. He peered around his computer at her and found her with a slight frown on her face.

"Is something wrong?" An uneasiness filled his deep voice.

Evie's head popped up. "What?"

"You're frowning. Is there something wrong with the syllabus?"

"Oh, um, no. Not quite," she replied, somewhat hesitantly. She started to say something else but seemed to decide against.

"What is it?" Andrew asked her, hoping to elicit a straightforward answer from her.

"Nothing. It's fine."

"Your face suggests otherwise." Sitting back in his chair, he crossed his arms and waited for her to tell him what she really thought about it. "Come on. Out with it."

Evie studied him as if she were judging how much truth she could reveal to him before she hastily asked, "When was the last time you taught a 101 class?"

Andrew was caught off guard by the question and stammered out, "It has been a few years. Why?"

"Because," she hesitated again.

He hated that she kept hesitating and questioning everything she wanted to say to him. For some reason, it was important to him that she felt at ease around him. It was evident she'd heard the rumors about him, and regardless of whatever fleeting feelings possessed him, it was going to be a long semester working together if she couldn't speak freely with him.

Before she could hesitate again, he leaned forward and said, "Let's go ahead and get something straight between us, Miss James. Here in my office, you are permitted to speak freely and openly to me. The semester is long, and it will be even longer if you do not feel comfortable enough to tell me what you're thinking. If there is something that I can change or do differently to the benefit of my students, then I am all ears." Vulnerability was woven throughout his words. There was a rawness in the way he spoke to her. It was clear as day in his tone, and something that was rarely there. He really hoped he'd kept the desperation building up inside of him out of it.

Quickly, he cleared his throat, erasing any sign of susceptibility in his voice. Normally, he wouldn't care too much about what a student thought about him, but for whatever reason, with Evie, it mattered. It was beginning to drive him mad as to why. However, the answer was already in the back of his mind, waiting to be acknowledged, and that scared him more than anything.

Evie's mouth was slightly slacked as she stared at him, but she quickly snapped back to attention. "Alright, Dr. Brant." There was a challenging note in her tone that didn't go unnoticed by him.

Andrew couldn't see anything that confirmed his thoughts, but he knew in his gut something had just shifted between them. Somehow, a certain level of trust had just been solidified between them, and Andrew felt the tightness in chest begin to relax even more.

Before he could give anymore thought to what had just occurred between them, Evie took him up on his offer to speak freely. "First of all, I would swap up some of these assignments, and there are way too many essays." She leaned forward and plucked one of the pens from his "Take a Hike" mug.

Maybe, I made the wrong choice. She seems to have a lot of thoughts on the subject.

Andrew watched as she began scribbling all over the copy of the syllabus. He became impressed when she stood while writing and walked around the side of his desk, never looking up or breaking from her scribbling. It was as if she had been in his office a thousand times and knew exactly where she was going—how to get to him.

"There." She proudly set the syllabus down on the desk. He looked at the paper on the desk before shifting his gaze to her. Her face was full of pride and confidence at the revisions she'd made to his syllabus.

Looking back at it, he realized she'd marked and written all over the page. "That isn't a suggestion. It's a complete redo," he all but shrieked at her. Never in his life had he made such a caterwaul of a noise, but this girl was prompting all sorts of new reactions from him.

She put her hands on her hips and gave him a pointed look. "You're the one who asked. If you don't like my suggestions, then it's your own fault."

Andrew could see the fire simmering in her eyes. If they weren't in his office, he would've liked to push her further to see what would happen if he were able to set those eyes ablaze. Quickly, he shoved the thought away and focused on the problem at hand.

Rubbing a hand down his face, he looked back at the syllabus. "Okay, I did ask, but I wasn't expecting this. I honestly didn't think it was that bad." Evie quirked an eyebrow at him. "I have taught a 101 class before," he protested.

Evie let her hands fall from her hips. "Yes, but you said it has been a while and things have changed a little bit. You know that. I'm just trying to assist you in my official assistant duties." A little sarcasm lined the last thing she said. He was sure she was going to give him a run for his money before the semester was out.

Andrew smiled up at her and conceded the point. "Fine, but I am not redoing this entire class; therefore, we will compromise. You said there were too many essays, so I will cut it back to six."

"Six? There are seven on there! You can't be serious."

She eyed him like he had just grown horns and several more eyeballs on his head.

He twisted in his chair to face her and crossed his arms. "I most certainly am serious." His voice came out cool and defiant, but there was a thread of humor woven throughout. He waited for her to respond, hoping she would challenge him on it. This was the most fun he'd had at school in a long time, and he was going to make the most of it.

Delight filled Andrew when he saw that simmering fire in her eyes spark. "Four essays," she contested, narrowing her eyes and mirroring him by crossing her arms.

"Five."

"Five, but you get rid of the research paper." They stared one another down as he contemplated her request.

"Five essays, no research paper, but the paired essay stays." Andrew watched as she mulled over his offer.

Finally, she stuck her hand out and said, "Deal."

He grasped her hand and shook it, savoring in the warmth of it. "Pleasure doing business with you, Miss James."

As she stepped back around his desk, her voice turned back to its bubbly nature as she said, "You can call me Evie if you want."

"Alright. Evie it is." He replied, smiling at the feel of her name on his lips.

Andrew knew he was getting into dangerous territory, but he heard himself saying, "Like I said, you are open to speak freely here in my office with me. If you like, you can call me Andrew. However, in the classroom or around other faculty or students, it's Dr. Brant. Deal?"

Evie thought for a second before grinning and shaking her head yes. "Deal."

"Good." A smile appeared on his face, matching hers.

Andrew and Evie spent the next couple of hours going over and discussing each of his classes. Her insight and creativity impressed him. By noon, Andrew had almost changed each one of his classes. Although the work had been tedious, he found all the classes had been improved upon in ways he'd never considered, and each class now held a small touch of Evie.

"Well, it appears my job is done for the day," Evie announced, handing him a stack of new assignments and exercises for first year students.

"What? You don't want to stay and finish uploading all of these documents for every section? I am both shocked and hurt." Evie laughed at his dramatic tone, filling his office with its sweet sound. Andrew thought his heart might actually burst at the sound of it. He hadn't felt that way since he'd first laid eyes on his wife, and that particular thought made him want to vomit.

The mixture of emotions was almost enough to undo him.

"I would love to, but I must go back to the real world and go to my actual job. Are you going to be here in the morning?"

"Yes, I will be finalizing everything for the first day and probably making thousands of copies of everything." Annoyance filled his tone. There was nothing he hated more than making copies, but he'd found students tended to actually look at the syllabus and other information when it was in their hands.

She stooped to pick up her backpack and slung it over her shoulder. "Well, I'll see you then."

As she reached the door, Andrew said, "Have a good rest of your day, Evie."

She turned around, smiling at him one last time. "You too, Andrew."

Andrew finally turned the computer off at 8pm. Sitting back, he stretched his arms and let out a sigh as he loosened his tie. He'd spent the last several hours working and hadn't realized how late it'd grown.

It'd been hard to ignore the apparent absence of Evie though. One morning with her had been enough to change the entire dynamic of his typically quiet and broody office. Normally, he didn't like the distraction of someone talking and interrupting him while working, but surprisingly enough, Evie had been a welcome distraction. She'd not only helped with organizing his classes but also with clearing his mind. With his mind cleared, he'd been able to focus solely on his work and not the lingering nightmarish thoughts of what his life had become over the past year.

Shutting off his desk lamp, Andrew stood, grabbing his worn leather messenger bag and headed for the door. The bag had become his closest companion over the past year. It had seen him through the good, bad, and ugly as he had slowly navigated the new normal of his life; however, he didn't know where the bag had come from. It had appeared in his office one day with a note that had read, "I noticed your briefcase had broken. I hope this helps." The note had been signed "EJ," but he didn't know anyone who went by EJ. Initially, he had wanted to track down the person and return the bag. Given the quality of leather and craftsmanship, it had to be expensive, and he didn't know why anyone would have wanted to gift it to him.

While heading towards the door, Andrew noticed Evie had left her book on the table next to the chair. He smiled to himself at the sight of it sitting there like it belonged;

however, he pushed the thought from his mind and headed home for the night.

2

ANDREW

Andrew sat at his desk the next morning, trying to work but was having trouble focusing due to the lack of sleep and caffeine. He'd woken up late again that morning and hadn't had time to make or stop for coffee. The inability to sleep was beginning to become a legitimate problem now that the semester was beginning, and if he was going to survive the school year, he would need to make a change.

Lost in thought, Andrew once again didn't hear Evie enter his office and was startled when a cup of coffee was set down on the desk in front of him. He looked up to find Evie smiling, holding her own cup of coffee. She was wearing jeans and a dark green blouse with her long brown hair flowing over her shoulders, which was a very different look from the leggings and hoodie with a ponytail and ballcap she'd worn yesterday; however, he noted both were very good looks on her petite fit body.

Great. A new day of ridiculous thoughts and desires.

"Good morning, I thought you might need this, this morning." She gestured to the cup of coffee in front of him.

How did she know I needed coffee?

She shrugged, seeing the questioning look on his face. "I saw you get out of your truck this morning with a glazed over look that suggested you weren't quite awake yet. I didn't see you with coffee cup, so I assumed you didn't have any. Thus, the coffee." She stepped over to the leather chair and sat down.

"Ah, thank you." Andrew picked up the cup, inhaling the bitter scent.

"No problem." She smiled brightly at him. "So, what is on the agenda for today?"

"Well, all we really need to do is go back over everything to make sure we didn't miss anything and make copies of the syllabi for each class. Then, we need to discuss how much teaching you would like to do," he explained.

"Teaching?" she asked anxiously.

"Mhm," he answered, taking a sip of the coffee. She'd gotten his coffee order correct. It wasn't hard to get wrong given it was only black coffee, but she hadn't brought packets of sugar or creamer.

How does she know how I take my coffee?

He was eyeing the drink, attempting to figure out how she knew his order when he heard her quizzically ask, "What are you doing?"

"Oh, um," he hesitated. "Trying to figure out how you know how I take my coffee." He looked over at Evie, finding her with her head cocked to the side with an amused look on her face.

"I asked the barista what you ordered yesterday. No stalking or criminal activity involved." She held up both hands, displaying her innocence. "I also thought knowing your order might come in handy as the semester goes on."

"Now, Evie, you cannot buy my good opinion with

coffee." A smirk formed on his face as he teased her. He took another sip of his coffee, watching her settle into the chair.

"A girl can always try," she responded with a wink. Andrew nearly sputtered his coffee and quickly, looked away from her to regain his manly composure.

Clearing his throat, he hastily changed the topic to not do something stupid—like flirt mercilessly with her. "So, you don't want to teach?"

"It's not that I don't want to teach," she answered, trailing off and fidgeting with her jeans. She seemed nervous by the idea of teaching, and to his shock, he found her reaction cute.

He suppressed the smile beginning to form on his face and gently asked, "Then what is it?"

"I don't." She stopped speaking, looking away.

"Don't what?" He prodded. There was something about teaching she didn't like, and he wanted to know the answer. It was also strange that she'd sign up to be a graduate assistant if she didn't want to teach. While not all grad assistants taught, most did teach a class here or there, so she must've known it was a possibility.

"I don't like talking in front of others." She blurted out. "It makes me overly nervous, and I feel like I am going to choke and die from the words getting stuck in my throat. It has only gotten worse as I have gotten older, so the idea of teaching makes me want to be sick and puke all over this chair."

She let out a breath and looked at him. She did look a little green—like she may very well vomit on his chair. "Please don't puke on my chair. It's my favorite, and I'd be very upset to have to get rid of it," he teased, hoping to ease her anxiety.

Her eyes were full of amusement unlike her timid tone, "I make no promises."

"Evie, I can help you get over your stage fright, but the only way to fully get over it is to just do it, to get up and speak." The more he spoke, the paler she grew until it seemed as though she was no longer breathing.

"Evie?" Concern flooded his voice. He waited, but she didn't respond or move. "Evie," he said a little louder. Now, he really was concerned she wasn't breathing.

He leapt from his chair and rounded his desk to her. "Evie, breathe." He commanded as he knelt in front of her. She looked like she may pass out from fear, and he wasn't sure how to help her. He grabbed ahold of her fisted hands. They were shaking, so he tightened his hold on them. "Evie, look at me," he said, keeping his voice soft but firm. When she still didn't move, he let go of one of her hands and gently cradled her face, adjusting it to look at him. "Look at me."

Slowly, her eyes moved in his direction. A small breath of relief left him as their eyes me. "Good. You're okay. It's just you and me. Okay? Just you and me. No one else." He brushed aside a strand of hair that had fallen in her face. "It's just you and me. Breathe. Take a breath for me."

She followed his command. "Good, take another." She continued to take slow deep breaths until the color began to return to her face.

The corners of her mouth turned up into a small apologetic smile as she whispered, "Sorry."

"No, there is nothing to be sorry for. I wouldn't have brought it up if I had known you were this terrified of speaking in front of people." He felt twinge of guilt at having caused her a mild panic attack. "How about this? You can handle my online classes. You won't have to speak in front of anyone, but it'll still count as teaching experi-ence." She slowly nodded her agreement. There was no way he would ever force her to teach if it was going to cause her this much discomfort.

"Are you okay?" The office faded away at his hushed tone, keeping them in a bubble of solace—a moment in time for only them.

She nodded again. "Yes, thank you." Her voice trembled but sounded stronger.

Andrew could feel the tension growing as she held his gaze. Quickly, he stood up and backed away, putting some distance between them. "Well, now that, that is settled we should get to work." He made his way back around his desk and sat down, squeezing his hands into fists underneath the desk. Maybe if he squeezed hard enough, it would keep him from touching her again. "I'll grant you access to my online classes, so you'll be able to work on them from your laptop."

They spent the next two hours in silence, working. Andrew found himself glancing at her more than anyone should, especially someone they barely knew. Evie was in full concentration, and he was sure she hadn't looked up from her work for the entire two hours. She'd pulled over the too small side table and had perched her laptop upon it. She needed a better workspace, which would be difficult to provide. Even though the office was one of the bigger ones in the department, it was still relatively small.

A shrill filled the air, causing Evie to jump as her phone started ringing. Without looking away from her laptop, she reached over and absentmindedly answered, "Hello?" There was a slight pause before she demanded, "How did you get this number?" Fear and indignation suddenly filled her voice.

Andrew snapped to attention at the sound of her tone. Her body went still and rigid as the other person began speaking. Every inch of him went on alert.

Something is very, very wrong.

"I told you not to contact me," she bit off, getting up and heading to the door. Evie froze as she reached the door. She shook her head as if to clear it and continued walking out. "No, you don't get to run me out of this city too. I'm done with your games." Her voice trailed off as she made her way down the hall.

Andrew was once again left speechless because of this woman. A fierce urgent need to protect her pulsed through his veins. His jaw clenched at the thought of someone wanting to harm her. Blowing out a breath, he tried to calm his racing heart.

What is wrong with me? I barely know this woman.

Before he could think about it, Andrew shoved away from his desk and made his way down the hall in the direction Evie had gone. He looked in each room, but there was no sign of her. As he neared the end of the hall, he peered into the stairwell and found her at the bottom of the stairs, curled tightly into a ball. The sight of her caused his heart to squeeze tightly in his chest.

Andrew slowly opened the door and made his way down the stairs to her. She didn't move or look up. Not wanting to startle her, he kept his voice soft. "Evie, are you okay?"

"I'm fine," she sneered at him, quickly scrambling to her feet. He blocked her as she tried to push by him.

"You're not fine. You were balled up on the floor, crying. Who was that on the phone?"

She raised her head to look him in the eye with that fire blazing in them. "I'm fine, and it's none of your business."

The fear was quickly replaced with unrelenting anger. "Move out of my way," she slowly and unyieldingly growled at him like a cornered animal.

Andrew reluctantly stepped to the side and let her pass. All he could do was stare after her as she quickly brushed past him and hurtled up the stairs. He felt glued to the spot at the bottom of the stairs, wondering who had hurt her and had been the cause of that vicious, scared tone she'd used on him. Andrew had only known Evie for two days, and it was definitely not enough time to know someone; however, he was certain the cheerful and optimistic Evie in his office had been born, but the ferocious caged Evie he just witnessed had been made.

The thought made his stomach churn because only hurt and devastation created emotions like that.

Andrew returned to his office to find Evie and all of her things gone. He knew he'd overstepped in the stairwell, but something had propelled him down there. He barely knew her, but he felt as though he had somehow known her for forever. He had no right to pry into her life, but the thought of someone threatening or hurting her made him want to set fire to the world, even if he was already too late to stop the damage.

How is it possible to feel this way after knowing her for only two days?

The urge to destroy had never been there for his wife, but then again, there had never really been a cause to stand between her and a threat. Lily had been simple and uncomplicated. The first time he'd seen her still felt like yesterday to him. He'd been walking through the mall trying to shop for a birthday present for his niece when he saw her looking through the window of a store.

She had been wearing a yellow sundress with her long

blonde hair cascading over her shoulders. He'd been so captivated by her he had walked directly into a display and knocked it over, causing an embarrassingly loud crash. She had rushed over to help him up, and he'd asked her to coffee. That was that.

They began dating and married two years later. Andrew wasn't sure he'd ever truly been in love with Lily, but he'd been committed to her, nevertheless. He knew if he kept thinking about his marriage, he would find himself wandering down a path he didn't want to be on, so he forced his thoughts back to the present.

Andrew had planned to work for the rest of the day but decided to go ahead and call it quits. Tomorrow would take care of itself, and after everything that had occurred, Andrew could use some time to calm down and make sure he was good to go for the first day of classes. After stepping across the line that he hadn't even known was there, he wondered if Evie would even show up tomorrow or continue to be his grad assistant.

He whispered to himself, "Let tomorrow worry about itself." Slipping his messenger bag on his shoulder, he flipped the light off and closed the door behind him.

EVIE

Evie hadn't meant to snap at Andrew the way she had. She'd felt betrayed and cornered with nowhere to go, causing her to lash out at him. He was only trying to be nice; she knew that. Andrew wasn't the type of man to bombard or bully his way into a person's life, and she believed that deep within her heart. There was a distinct difference between a man wanting to protect and one wanting to possess, and she knew the difference well.

Sitting at a table in the corner of the coffee shop on campus, Evie stared out the window, contemplating what she was going to do about the fact Dylan had found her. She'd made the decision almost three years ago to stop running, so, she'd applied for graduate school, packed up her car, moved several hours away from the sanctuary of her family's farm, deciding to begin living again.

The last time she'd seen or heard from her ex had been over a year ago in Kentucky. She didn't know how he'd tracked her to North Carolina or why.

Does a psycho really need a reason?

Taking a sip of her cappuccino, she sighed and began to

feel guilty again about how she'd treated Andrew. "I will worry about it tomorrow," she whispered to herself as she pulled her laptop from her backpack. She still had work to do before classes began tomorrow. She refused to let herself stress about how she was going to balance being a graduate assistant, her own classes, and work. It would get done one way or the other, and there was no sense in worrying about it.

Evie spent the next ten minutes attempting to focus on her work, but her thoughts kept drifting back to Andrew. She'd seen him from the corner of her eye when she'd begun talking to Dylan. He'd gone stiff and unmoving, watching and assessing through those dark green eyes of his.

Those eyes.

She internally sighed, thinking about them. They looked like a cool lake nestled in a deep forest, and she just wanted to dive in and see what lurked beneath.

His eyes were only the starting point. She couldn't see them, but she knew a number of well-defined muscles were hidden beneath his clothing.

That man is built rock solid. I just know it.

She wanted to run her hands through his short brown hair. It was always pushed up in the front as if he spent his time running his hand through it. It was a good look on him. Evie didn't know how anyone was focused on how he was as a professor when he looked like that.

You can't beat his jawline. Does no one see the jawline?

What about the muscles?

People around here are foolish for overlooking that specimen of a man.

It's a real shame.

Evie realized she was shaking her head and hastily shut the thoughts down.

Reacting to your thoughts in public is not a good look, Evie. Get it together.

She hadn't made it a foot in the Language Arts building two years ago before hearing the rumors about him, but she'd never witnessed anything to make her believe them. Evie knew the difference between a person who was a monster and one who was reserved. Dr. Brant was a strict professor who required the best from his students, but most students failed to see how that was only helping them to improve because his ability to be quiet and brooding stood out stronger than the rest of his attributes.

That was exactly why Evie had jumped on the chance to be his graduate assistant, but if she was being honest, there hadn't been much of a fight for the position.

Evie exited out of her work and opened her email. Her fingers began to move on the keyboard before her mind could catch up.

"Dear Andrew,

I am sorry about today. The last thing I meant to do was take out my anger on you. I have a lot going on that I am not quite ready to talk to anyone about. I hope you can forgive me for how I behaved towards you.

See you tomorrow,

Evie

With the email sent, Evie felt the guilt subside and went back to work, trying and failing to keep her thoughts from the very attractive professor.

ANDREW

Andrew had just stepped into his truck when his phone pinged with an alert and was surprised to find an email from Evie in his inbox. His heart began to pound as he read her email.

She's sorry?

He had been the one to overstep and push her too far for the second time that morning. She had nothing to be sorry for. He tapped the reply button and rapidly, began typing out a reply.

Evie,

You have nothing to apologize for. It is I who should be apologizing. I overstepped, and I had no right to do so. I look forward to seeing you tomorrow.

If you ever need anything, here is my number (xxx-xxx-xxxx).

Yours,

Andrew

Andrew was glad she had reached out to him and cleared the air between them. He'd only known her for two days, but he was growing quite fond of Evie James.

Andrew pulled into his driveway twenty minutes later. Before running off to Wyoming, he'd made the decision to move closer to campus and away from the memories his house with Lily held.

Andrew loved this house. It was a small two-bedroom cottage tucked at the edge of the mountains. A small shop was off to the side of the cottage—where he was able to work on his old ford pickup truck and woodworking. On the back of the property, there was a small trail, weaving itself through the wooded hillside that connected to the main mountain trail. He hoped to hike on the weekends once the semester got underway.

Andrew unlocked the front door and went inside to change into his work clothes. Evie needed a bigger workspace, and he could easily build her something that was bigger and also functionable.

Ten minutes later, he was dressed and headed downstairs to get to work on the table. Grabbing an apple from the fruit bowl on the island in the kitchen, he headed for the shop. As he opened the garage door, his phone pinged with a text. The message was from a strange number.

What time is your first class tomorrow?

Before Andrew had time to question who was messaging him, another text popped up.

E: This is Evie, btw

Andrew smiled. Taking a bite out of his apple, he texted her back.

A: 7:30. You don't have to be there.

His phone pinged again before he could put it down.

E: It's the first day. I'll be there.

E: If only for moral support

A: I appreciate your support

E: Oh, I meant support for the students ;)

A: What? You wound me

E: Somehow, I think you'll survive

A: I guess we will find out

Andrew set his phone down and got to work, framing the new table for Evie. He didn't stop working until the alarm he had set for himself went off at 11pm. Reluctantly, he stepped away from the small table and went inside to get ready for bed. If he didn't get some sleep tonight, he really wouldn't survive tomorrow.

Sleep had been hard to come by since returning to North Carolina. Guilt constantly ate at him over his wife. Regret was always lurking, enticing him to wonder if he could've done things differently. When he did manage to fall asleep, the nightmares drug him right back to the surface.

Time. I just need time.

3
EVIE

Evie's alarm went off bright and early Wednesday morning. Rolling over with a groan, she slapped the snooze button.

Five more minutes. I just need five more minutes.

She'd stayed up late, watching a romcom with her roommate and best friend, Lucy. With school starting, they wouldn't have much time to spend together, so they tried to squeeze in as much time as possible, which came as a detriment to Evie's sleep schedule.

Before she could even open her eyes, her door burst open, and Lucy sashayed inside. "Wake up, sleepy head. It's the first day of school with the broody professor."

"He isn't broody," Evie mumbled. Lucy stopped and stared at her like she was clearly losing her mind. "Fine. He's a little broody, but he's not what everyone makes him out to be."

"A brooding, egotistical, stick up his butt professor?" She arched a perfectly tweezed eyebrow at her.

"Yes, he's not even close."

"EJ, I've taken his class, and he *is* exactly those things. I barely made it through the semester, and it was only a basic class," Lucy replied, opening the curtains in Evie's room. Sunlight flooded the room, causing Evie to let out a shriek.

"A little warning would be great next time, Luce!"

In typical Lucy fashion, she responded with a half shrug.

Lucy was the only person to call Evie, EJ. She'd met Lucy during her first semester at Beaumont University, and they had instantly clicked. Lucy was Evie's opposite in every possible way, but that seemed to be what made the relationship work. It'd been like two pieces of a puzzle coming together, and Evie had never been more thankful for a friendship before.

Three months after meeting, they moved into an apartment together and had been best friends ever since.

Lucy had a more eclectic sense of style than Evie. She was always well dressed and never afraid to play with colors and patterns. Evie admired Lucy for making almost anything look professional. Being a law student, Lucy had to maintain a certain level of professionalism, unlike Evie—who mostly wore leggings and a hoodie.

Envy had never been Evie's thing until she'd come face-to-face with Lucy's curly hair. Unlike Lucy, Evie struggled to do anything with her long, slightly wavy hair; she'd give anything for her hair to have even half of a curl.

If grace and elegance were a person, they'd be Lucy. She was also very quick-witted and smart on her feet. While Lucy studied cases and law books, Evie read novels and wrote about them. They were different on every level but loved each other all the same.

"Come on," Lucy pleaded, yanking on Evie's foot. After a few seconds of trying, she gave up. A sigh escaped Evie's lips. Now, she could get back to sleeping. "Fine. I'm going to pick you an outfit for your first day."

"No!" Evie yelled as she sat straight up. Lucy turned and gave her a smirk but continued towards the closet. "I don't want to wear a dress or something fancy and be uncomfortable all day." Her voice came out whiny, but she didn't care. There was a reason she mainly wore leggings. Being uncomfortable in her clothes was a for sure way for her to have a terrible day.

"I'm insulted you think I'd want you to be uncomfortable all day, but I'm even more insulted you think I don't know you well enough to pick an outfit you would enjoy and feel powerful wearing." Lucy turned her attention back to Evie's clothes. "Besides, it's not like you own anything uncomfortable or fancy."

Evie rolled out of bed and stumbled to the bathroom. Emerging five minutes later with an empty bladder and fresh breath, Evie found Lucy standing in front of her freshly made bed with the outfit she'd chosen laid upon it.

"Thanks for making the bed."

"Well, I knew you never would," Lucy smirked. "Get dressed. I'm going to fix you breakfast."

"You don't have to do that," she told her, but Lucy had already disappeared through the bedroom door just as quickly as she'd appeared.

Turning her attention back to the bed, Evie had to admit she was impressed with Lucy's choice of outfit. She would be comfortable but also feel powerful. Thirty minutes later, Evie emerged from her room with clothes on, hair fixed, and makeup done. The outfit of choice was black skinny jeans paired with a black fitted shirt and gray plaid blazer. The look was completed with black and white sneakers.

"Wow! Slay girl! Yas!" Lucy shouted from the kitchen. Evie could always count on Lucy to hype her up. She could be wearing a trash bag, and Lucy would make her believe she was worth walking the runway at fashion week.

"I really don't have time to eat Lucy," Evie said apologetically.

"I know. That's why I only made toast," Lucy replied from the kitchen. Of course, she'd only made toast. Lucy was always thinking three steps ahead.

Evie finished shoving her things into the new leather tote her dad had sent her over the weekend. According to him, her well-loved backpack wasn't going to cut it as a graduate assistant, so he'd sent her the most beautiful, dark brown, leather tote bag, complete with her initials. Sliding the straps onto her shoulder, she pulled her phone out of her back pocket and snapped a quick selfie to send to her dad.

She captioned the photo, "Proof of Life."

"Here you go," Lucy said, handing her the piece of toast.

"Thanks, Luce! I don't know what I'd do without you." She planted a kiss on Lucy's cheek and headed out the door.

"Good luck," Lucy hollered as the door shut behind her.

ANDREW

Andrew liked to arrive early to class on the first day to make sure everything was set up and good to go before students arrived. Campus was just beginning to wake as he'd arrived that morning. Not many students had 7:30am lectures, but he had around sixty students in this first class. Most of those were probably dreading having to sit through a class that early.

As he was getting his laptop set up, he heard the door of the lecture hall open. Glancing up, his breath caught as Evie strolled into the room.

"Good morning, Dr. Brant," she greeted him with a cheerful smile. He couldn't stop the grin from forming on his face as she made her way over to him.

She looks stunning this morning.

"Morning," he smiled down at her as she came up beside him.

"I didn't know if you'd have coffee this morning or not, but to be on the safe side, I brought you one anyways," she told him as she held the cup out to him.

"Thank you, Evie," he responded, taking the cup. Their

fingers brushed as he took the cup, and he could've sworn he heard her breath catch just as his did.

He swallowed and attempted to pry his eyes away from hers. He was failing miserably to look away from those charming brown eyes of hers, so he simply said, "I'm surprised you showed up."

Her eyes lit up. "And miss this? I don't think so."

"Miss what? Moral support for the students," he grunted, pretending to be offended.

"Is the cynical professor feeling unsupported this morning?" she teased as she wandered over to the little table for graduate assistants.

He froze.

She's heard the rumors. Does she believe them?

Maybe, not.

Hopefully, not.

He must've been silent for longer than he thought because when he turned towards her, she was at his side. "You know, if I believed half of what I heard, I wouldn't be in here." Truth echoed in her words, making him believe them.

The thing that'd been tight in his chest since before his wife's diagnosis began to relax just a little bit more. "Oh really?" he asked, letting out an inner breath of relief.

Crossing her arms, she leaned against the table. "Mhm, and I didn't want to miss *your* first day. I'm your grad assistant, and I'm here for *you*. If you need copies, I've got you. If you need moral support, I'm your girl."

"And if I need coffee?" he asked, gesturing to the cup sitting on the table.

She straightened a little bit, looking down. "No, the coffee isn't an assistant thing. It's," her voice trailed off. Their eyes met as she confessed, "Well, it's a friend thing."

He just stared at her taken aback. She'd probably heard every horrible thing about him, but here she was going above and beyond her duties as a graduate assistant, offering him friendship. He cocked his head to the side and sized her up. "So, we are friends?"

Determination filled her eyes as she replied, "Yes. If you want to be."

He narrowed his eyes just a bit at her as he held his hand out. "Deal." The door at the back of the lecture hall opened, but neither of them looked to it. He waited for her to take his hand and solidify their new friendship in their own special way.

She grasped his hand and shook it. "Deal." Then quickly added, "No take backs."

Andrew let out a small laugh. "Okay, no take backs." Reluctantly, he released her hand, hating the coolness that replaced it.

He wanted nothing more than to hold her hand for the rest of his days.

Maybe, one day, he'd get the chance to hold it again.

EVIE

Evie walked over to her bag and pulled out copies of the class syllabus. Somehow, she knew Andrew had forgotten to make some, so she'd gotten to campus early to make a bunch of copies. Most professors did everything online, but she appreciated Andrew's preference of a paper copy.

Pen and paper were always going to be her preferred method—just like her preference of physical books to eBooks. In her opinion, electronics stole the magic out of things.

Walking back over to Andrew, she found herself slightly slack-jawed from the sight of him. He had on a dark green, plaid button down with sleeves that hugged his biceps. If she stared hard enough, she could see the muscles in his arms ripple as he moved.

I think it's safe to assume my theory is correct.

He is built rock solid.

The chino pants he was wearing had a blush creeping up her cheeks; they were tight in all the right areas and thoroughly, accentuated those areas. The combination was enough to send someone into cardiac arrest.

Thankfully, a group of girls walked through the door talking loudly, drawing her concentration elsewhere. Her mind had started to drift into unknown and dangerous waters. Not to mention, she was pretty much drooling over Andrew.

Get it together, girl.

Subtly, she tried to fan herself with the papers she was holding to ease the heat in her cheeks, but unfortunately for her, it wasn't helping because Andrew was still there, looking gorgeous.

Evie was fairly sure professors weren't allowed to date their grad assistants. None of that mattered anyways because she knew he'd never return her feelings. Someone like him would never go for the farm girl like her. Not to mention, he was her boss and had lost his wife a year ago.

It would just be too complicated.

And unrealistic.

He's out of my league.

It's fine. I'll look from afar.

Farther than I am now though. This is too close.

Why is it so hot in here?

She set the copies on the table next to his laptop and tried to escape his captivating presence.

Before she could turn to go back to her seat, he said, "Thank you."

Those dark green eyes met hers, and it felt as if the earth was trembling beneath her feet. It wasn't possible for many different reasons, so she was clearly just losing her mind.

I need to put some space between us.

What is this feeling?

What is happening?

Quickly, she retreated to her little table in the corner of the room.

This is a safe distance. Surely.

The room began to fill up, and Evie was very impressed by the number of students willing to be up so early for class. She'd never scheduled 7:30am classes as an undergrad, unless she had no other choice. It required a level of dedication she just wasn't willing to give.

Peering over her laptop to Andrew, she found him fidgeting with his laptop and papers.

Is he nervous? There's no way.

He was the professor students feared not the one who feared them. Before she thought about it, Evie picked up her phone and began typing out a text.

E: You're going to do great!

She watched him peer down at his phone as it pinged with her text. Her heart felt like it might beat straight through her chest as she saw the smile on his face grow as he read her text. He threw her a glance, and she was sure she'd melt right there in the chair.

"Get it together," she whispered to herself.

Her phone pinged with an alert.

A: I thought you were here to give the students moral support ;) but I do appreciate it

A: You look very nice today, btw

Evie's eyes shot to him and discovered him watching her with an intensity she'd never seen or experienced before. Her cheeks quickly began to warm under his gaze. Biting her bottom lip and averting her eyes, she quickly typed out a reply.

E: Thank you :)

Setting his phone down, Andrew cleared his throat, calling the class to attention. "Good morning, class.

Welcome back. I hope you all had a great summer and are ready to get down to business." There was a slight collective groan.

Evie smiled, remembering the days of undergrad and sympathized with their struggle to come off summer break and begin working again.

After a few minutes of introducing the class and expectations for the semester, Andrew gestured to her. "Everyone, say hello to Miss James." The class gave their hellos to her; however, there were a few male voices that seemed a little more enthusiastic than she would've preferred. It was going to be a long semester if she had to spend it fending off young adult males.

Evie gave a small wave to the class and a smile to Andrew as he continued. "Miss James is my graduate assistant for the semester. She will be joining us on and off throughout the next several months, and she will also be around to assist you with whatever needs you might have for the class. If you cannot get ahold of me, need a question answered quickly, or need help with something, your best bet is to contact her." Evie nodded her agreement.

Andrew went over the syllabus and a few other things and to her surprise, let the class go early. She assumed he'd be one of the professors that lectured on the first day.

As Evie began to pack up her things, she noticed a group of guys had begun to form around her small table. "Um, hi. Can I help y'all?" she asked.

None of the guys answered. They only stared at her with goofy grins on their faces. Evie was growing uncomfortable by the second. "Well, if none of y'all need anything, I have somewhere I need to be," she told them, hoping they'd leave.

A young male voice rang out from the back of the group.

"Do you make house calls? I may need some extra help."
The guys started to snicker and murmur their agreements.

"That's enough." Andrew's deep voice sliced through
the group. The guys immediately stiffened at his presence.
Clearly, in their lustful state of being, they'd forgotten Dr.
Brant was still in the room. "I want each and every one of
you to look at me and hear me when I say Miss James is to
be treated with respect. The next time I hear a comment
like that come from one you, you will automatically receive
a failing grade and not be allowed back in my classroom. Do
we understand one another?"

"Yes sir." The group mumbled before finally filing out of
the room.

When the last student disappeared through the door,
Evie let out the breath she'd been holding. "Thank you for
that," she said, walking over to Andrew.

"Are you okay?" he asked, pausing to look at her. His
eyes scanned her face.

"Yeah, it's not the first time something like that has
happened, and it'll probably not be the last." Andrew
slowly nodded in response. "However, that was the first
time an entire group of guys decided to approach me, and if
I'm being honest, it was a little unnerving," she quietly
admitted.

Andrew's voice was gruff as he said, "I will not tolerate
behavior like that towards you in my classroom or elsewhere. I meant it. I will fail them if they are disrespectful
towards you."

"I appreciate it, but don't you think that's a little
much?"

While she knew they should all be able to control themselves better, they were also just harmless freshman boys
still in need of some maturing. Failing and kicking them out

of class for some off-putting comments seemed a bit much to her, but she did appreciate Andrew's intolerance toward their behavior.

Andrew picked up his bag and stepped towards her, placing a hand on her shoulder. His eyes darkened as he told her, "If it's a choice between an F and your safety or peace, I will always choose to give the F. Besides, they can always retake the class. There's no need for you to spend months being uneasy or uncomfortable."

Evie's mouth opened but quickly, shut. She was too stunned to speak. This should be the norm of all men, but unfortunately, for her, it wasn't.

With a light squeeze, Andrew let his hand slide from her shoulder and backed up a step. "Come on, let's go prepare for the next class."

ANDREW

As they walked back to his office, Andrew's thoughts kept drifting back to the guy asking Evie if she made house calls. He'd never wanted to throttle someone so much in his life. He refused to let anyone speak to her that way. Not just her, he wouldn't tolerate that behavior towards any female in his class.

Andrew glanced down at Evie walking beside him and found himself completely content in just being near her. It was one of the first times he'd ever felt completely comfortable and happy walking down the hallway. He listened to her rattle on nonstop about a movie she'd watched the night before. Usually, he wasn't one for idle chit chat, but with Evie, it was agreeable.

As they came to a stop in front of his closed office door, Evie was still talking. He wasn't sure she had taken a breath the entire walk there. A smile crawled across his lips as he listened to her. The sound of her voice did something to him. It was like a soothing salve to his frayed emotions.

The smile instantly dropped from his face as he caught the tail end of what she'd said. "You ran over a rabbit?"

With a sad sigh, she mumbled, "Yeah."

When did she change topics? I can't keep up with this girl.

Unlocking the door, he stepped aside to let her go before him. The subtle scent of her perfume caught his nose as she passed by him. The scent was intoxicating, and he wanted to get lost in it. He trailed behind her, following the scent as she walked over to her chair and plopped down in it.

"What you want to do now, boss?"

One of Andrew's eyebrows shot up. "Boss?" He set his bag down, tossing his keys on the desk.

"Mhm," was her only response. This woman was going to be his undoing.

"Well, I have some emails to answer before my next class. I don't have anything for you to do at the moment, so I guess you are free to go." Her face dropped a little when he mentioned her leaving. He hoped it was because she wanted to spend more time with him like he did with her. "Of course, you're welcome to hang out in here," he quickly added before she could get up and leave.

"Good," she replied firmly with smile, settling back into the chair. She grabbed her book off the table and flipped to the page she had dogeared. Andrew was strictly a book-mark person, but Evie seemed to use whatever was nearby to mark the page or simply dogeared it.

Even though they were different, he found her quite endearing.

"Good," he echoed softly. It was as if she'd always been a part of his office, his life.

After a little while, Andrew heard Evie rummaging through her bag. He glanced over right as she pulled a smushed chocolate bar from the bag. With a triumphant smile, she let out a quiet, "Yes!"

Andrew cringed at the crumpled chocolate bar. "How old is that?" She jumped at the sound of his voice and looked like a kid who'd just been caught with a hand in the cookie jar. He couldn't help but laugh at her expression, finding it very adorable.

"Oh, um. I'm not sure." Evie turned the chocolate bar over and examined it. "I'm sure it's fine, though." False confidence filled her voice.

"I'm sure," he mused, sitting back in his chair and folding his arms across his chest. "And how long has it been in your bag?"

"Only since this morning." She gave him a very innocent look, which he didn't buy for a moment.

"There is no way that has only been in your bag since this morning."

"Ye of little faith," she retorted.

"That thing looks like it has been run over several times and lived several lives." He grimaced as she waved it in the air at him, making her laugh. His stomach twisted at the sound of her laughter, filling his office. Evie made his office come to life, and it felt more like home than it ever had before.

"Well, it may look like that, but I swear it has only been in my bag since this morning."

"That is not possible."

"Well, I didn't say it hadn't been in another bag before entering this one." A mischievous look crossed her face.

"Ah, well, that explains things."

"Look, we all can't be big shot professors and afford fancy foods like apples and oranges." The sarcasm and humor melded together in her voice, forcing Andrew to suppress a grin.

His eyebrows rose. "Big shot professor? That's what you think of me?"

"Not the point," she swiftly replied.

Deciding to let it drop, he checked the time. "Well, if you will give me another hour and a half, this big shot professor will take you to get some lunch."

"Normally, I would object, but I didn't have time to pack a lunch this morning." She frowned at her chocolate bar.

"Here," he said, pulling an apple from the basket on top of the mini fridge next to his desk. Standing, he walked the apple over to her. He extended his empty hand to her. "Trade. Chocolate for the apple."

Evie suspiciously eyed the apple. "What happens if I refuse this trade?"

"Come on. I can't let you eat that older than dust chocolate."

"Aw, Andrew, I didn't know you cared about me," she teased.

"I care about my rug. You eat that, and you will be puking your guts up on it."

"I think that might be a bit dramatic but fine," she said, handing him the chocolate bar and taking the apple. Andrew turned to head back to his desk when she added, "I knew you were a big shot professor with apples."

Shaking his head, he smiled and sat back down, watching as she took a bite and settled back into the chair with her book. Too bad he had to go to a meeting, he would've enjoyed spending the next hour or so hanging out with her.

Walking back into his office an hour later, he found Evie still reading in what was quickly becoming "her" chair.

"You ready for lunch?" he asked, walking into the office to put his things down.

"Yes," she replied enthusiastically, snapping her book shut. "Where are we going?"

"What about Mexican?" She scrunched her face up at his suggestion, causing him to let out a small laugh. "Okay, that's a no."

"I didn't say that."

"No, but your face did," he grinned. "Come on. Let's go." He turned, heading towards the door. He let her pass through the door before him and turned around to lock it. This wasn't a date, but this was as close as he'd ever get to one. He kept reminding himself she was his graduate assistant, and it would not be advisable for a professor and grad assistant to date.

Why?

Why am I so drawn to her?

Why do I want to throw myself at her mercy and be whatever and whoever she needs me to be?

He'd never felt like this before, and it scared him.

Lily had never made him feel this way, nor had she had this kind of hold over him. It was a bit unnerving, but he wanted nothing more than to lean into it.

He wanted her.

4
EVIE

Evie knew Andrew's truck. She'd seen him numerous times in the black F250, driving across campus. She knew it was big, but standing next to it, she was shocked. It wasn't raised high in a gaudy way or jacked up like some of the more country boys did their trucks. It was simply big, especially compared to her small frame.

She must've made a sound as they made their way to the passenger side door because she heard Andrew ask, "What?"

"Andrew?" she asked, drawing his name out.

"Yes?" he drawled back.

She thought it was cute when he mimicked her.

"Why are there no side steps on your truck?"

Opening the passenger door for her, he explained, "I ordered a new set and am waiting for them to ship. I decided to take the old ones off in the meantime."

"Sounds reasonable," she replied, stepping up to the truck. "However," she started, turning back to look at him. "How do you expect a 5'3 woman to get in?"

He smiled at her, scratching his brow. "Well, I wasn't planning on having a 5'3 woman in my truck, so I guess I never really thought of it."

"Clearly." She smarted off to him.

He chuckled, causing her blood to hum at the sound. Evie knew she'd never heard anything more lovely in her life. The sound brought comfort to her chaotic nervous system. She liked knowing she could make the brooding professor laugh and smile. Turning to face the truck again, she hid the blush beginning to bloom on her face.

"Here, I'll give you a boost." He said from behind her. She felt him suddenly draw near, sliding his hands onto her hips. His fingers flexed before settling on her hips. His touch seared into her skin, branding her.

She could've sworn she heard herself sigh from his touch, and she really hoped she'd imagined it.

Pull it together, girl.

Evie put a foot on the side of the truck, and Andrew hoisted her up like she was nothing more than a mere feather.

He must workout with some serious weights.

Shutting the door for her, he made his way around to the driver's side. Evie took the time to admire how his shoulder muscles and biceps slightly bulged through his form fitting shirt.

Yep. He definitely works out.

Noticing her mouth was slightly agape, she quickly shut it, clearing her throat as he climbed into the truck.

Ten minutes later, Evie and Andrew were seated at her favorite pizza place. It was a cute little place off the square in the middle of town. The cute little brick building was inviting with its red and white striped canopy over the door. Decals of pizza and cannoli decorated the windows, overlooking Main St. The air surrounding the restaurant always smelled of pizza, eliciting watery mouths and grumbling stomachs.

"Have you ever been here?" she asked Andrew as they sat down at one of the tables by the window.

"Yeah, but it's been a while. You?"

"Same," she replied nonchalantly.

"Evie," a loud voice hollered from across the small restaurant. "Girl, what are you doing here in the middle of the day? Aren't you supposed to be starting your assistant job today?" Looking up, she saw Suzanne excitedly running over to greet her, smiling broadly. She all but pulled Evie out of her chair with a massive hug.

Suzanne was a loud, exuberant older woman. Her gray hair was twisted into a bun on her head, and there was flour coating her lavender apron. She and her husband Ed owned, "Beaumont Pizzeria."

Suzanna turned and hollered over her shoulder to her husband. "Hey, Ed, look who came to see us today." Evie glanced over at the bar to Ed and gave a small wave.

Ed came around the bar, speaking every bit as loud as his wife. He wiped his hands on his apron before bending down to give Evie a hug and kiss on the cheek. "Evie, what are you doing here? Don't you have classes today? You better not be skipping class." Ed's voice was stern, but his eyes glimmered with affection.

"I'm on lunch break at the moment," she answered, gesturing to the table as if that were an obvious explanation.

Suzanne and Ed had been a part of Evie's life for as long as she could remember. Her dad and Ed had served in the military together for several years before Ed retired. Having them there in Beaumont was like having a home away from home.

She looked at Andrew to see how he was handling the situation and noticed him studying her with an amused look on his face. Evie realized Suzanne and Ed had gone quiet. Turning her attention back to them, she was almost mortified to see them quietly observing Andrew.

"Who do we have here? Friend, foe, or both?" Suzanne asked, eyeing Andrew—ready to defend or befriend based upon Evie's next words.

Evie tilted her head to the side as she gazed at Andrew. She quickly smiled at him before she looked up at Suzanne with her answer. "Friend."

Suzanne and Ed watched Andrew for a moment longer before launching into loud conversation again. "I'll bring you two the usual," Suzanne told them, snatching the menus and heading toward the kitchen behind Ed.

Evie turned to face Andrew and his amused expression.

"So, you haven't been here in a while?" His tone was slightly accusatory but also full of curiosity.

"What is a while?" She spread her hands in question.

"A month or longer," he answered. The amusement danced in his eyes. He was clearly enjoying himself, which relieved Evie. She knew Suzanne and Ed could be a bit much, but she loved them dearly. They meant the world to her, and if someone in her life didn't like them, then they couldn't remain in hers.

"Oh. Well, if that's the case, then I change my answer."

"When *was* the last time you were here?"

"Last night," she answered, looking out the window to view the traffic on the street. She'd always loved downtown Beaumont. It had the feel of a small town without the feel of being smothered by knowing everyone.

Her eyes drifted back to Andrew. She could tell he was still trying to put the pieces together.

"I work here sometimes. I also come here to study if Lucy has people over at the apartment or something. It's kind of my home away from home," she explained.

He slowly nodded, taking in her words. "Yeah, you definitely have the wrong definition of in a while," he teased.

"Well, you would know, Mr. Big Hot Shot Professor," she teased back. He laughed, and the butterflies in her stomach tried to take flight.

"So, what is the usual?" he asked a bit warily.

"I have no clue. It's different every time." She leaned forward and put her arms on the table. "You know, I've never actually read the menu. Suzanne or Ed just brings me whatever." She leaned a little closer and lowered her voice. Andrew leaned closer too, and she hoped he couldn't hear her heart pounding. "I think there might be magic involved because I have never had anything bad from here. Ever," she whispered, eyeing the kitchen.

"Maybe, they have a secret magical oven that can read the minds of customers," he whispered back.

Andrew's ability to play and be conspiratory with her excited her.

"You think? I'm pretty sure the FBI is looking into it."

Evie didn't realize how close they were to one another until she turned her head back to him. To her, it felt like a movie moment—that moment when the world seemed to stop as the main characters felt their otherworldly connection snap into place. His eyes left hers, drifting to her mouth. Evie didn't think she was breathing.

Suzanne came out the kitchen carrying pizza and yelling something to Ed, breaking the spell. Evie and

Andrew sat back in their seats, awaiting their mystery pizza.

Suzanne set the pizza on the table, and Ed showed up a moment later with two sweet teas. "Let me know if you two need anything," Suzanne told them before walking back to the kitchen. That was what Evie admired most about Suzanne and Ed. They could be loud and overbearing, but they knew how to not hover.

She loved talking to them, but in that moment, she only wanted Andrew's undivided attention.

ANDREW

They'd finished eating, leaving Andrew thoroughly impressed and full. "You're right. I don't like sausage on my pizza, but I want to eat this for the rest of my life. And, this sweet tea is amazing," he admitted, taking another sip of his tea.

"I told you." A smug look sat on her face.

Adorable.

"Magic," they whispered at the same time, sparking laughter at their new inside joke.

"This has been one of the best first days of school I've had in a long time," he genuinely told her as their laughter died down.

"Me too." A smile lit her face as her brown eyes sparkled in the light of the noon sun.

"Do we pay here or up at the counter?"

Evie started to shake her head. "Suzanne won't let me pay."

"Seriously? Or are you trying to get me in trouble?" He accused her, narrowing his eyes ever so slightly at her. He wouldn't put it past her to mess with him. Evie had a playful side to her that he quite enjoyed.

She just smiled at him with a smile that made him feel like his heart was going double in size before it exploded and left him bleeding out on the floor.

"Suzanne, how much do I owe you," she yelled across the restaurant. Evie didn't bother to look over at Suzanne but instead, held his gaze with a look that said she was about to prove him wrong once again.

Suzanne's boisterous voice filled the restaurant as she yelled back, "Your money is no good here, Honey. You know that. Get back to school and make us proud."

"Thank you!" Evie smirked at him. "Satisfied?"

"I guess so." That smirk of hers was going to get him into trouble.

Evie started muttering about how she couldn't believe he thought she'd try to get him in trouble. Andrew couldn't do anything but smile. Evie James was very unexpectedly capturing his heart, and he was enjoying every second of it, even though there was no hope of anything more between them.

Their lunch break was coming to an end, but he wasn't ready to get back to reality just yet. Desperate for more time, he asked, "How do you know Suzanne and Ed?"

"My dad. He and Ed served together for a little while and remained friends after leaving the military."

"So, home away from home is somewhat literal?"

A soft smile of adoration appeared on her face. With the sun rays beaming on her, Evie looked almost angelic, and the image of her stole his breath.

"Yeah, they're like my second family. It's nice having them close since my family is so far away."

"Not from around here, then?"

She shook her head. "No, my family has a farm in Kentucky."

"Do you get to see them much?"

"Aren't you so full of questions?" Evie teased him, but the humor didn't quite reach her eyes.

Something about his words bothered her, but he brushed it off.

Letting out a soft chuckle, he answered, "Just trying to get to know my graduate assistant."

Evie picked up her phone from where it'd been lying on the table. "Well, it looks like we are all out of time for questions today. We will have to pick this up later." Even though her voice was light, there was something definitive about it. He knew he wouldn't be getting anymore answers from her, which only left him with more questions.

"Are you okay?"

Alert entered her eyes but was gone before she responded with, "Yeah."

Disappointment filled him as their time together ended. He wished there was more, but luckily, they had an entire semester to spend together.

There's plenty of time to get to know her better.

Although he knew he had months with her and hopefully, longer, he couldn't shake the feeling he was racing against time.

The hour he'd spent talking to Evie had relaxed him more than three months alone in the mountains.

"As long as there is a later."

"You bet," she said with a wink.

Heaven, help me.

EVIE

After they returned, Evie bid farewell to Andrew and headed to the on-campus coffee shop. As she walked in, she couldn't help but smile to herself as she remembered when she'd fallen to Andrew's feet. It should've been more embarrassing than it had been, but there was something about Andrew that put her at ease. At least, that had been the case until he began asking her a lot of questions during their lunch, inducing her anxiety.

Thankfully, it had ended up fine, and to be honest, she hadn't minded answering his questions. She liked talking to him. It was easy, and lunch had been amazing and fun. It had been a while since she'd had that, and she wasn't about to let her anxiety ruin it.

Picking a corner table, she pulled out her laptop and checked to see if they'd chosen a professor for her literature class, starting that afternoon. She really hoped it wasn't Dr. Burg. Bless that woman, but she was old as time itself, deaf as a bat, and had about 99 cats. Evie blew out a breath as she saw there was no update.

"Hey, EJ!" Evie looked up to see Lucy making her way

towards her with a coffee in hand. "How's first day going?" she cheerily asked, taking a seat.

"It's going well. Although, it started out by me getting harassed by a group of freshman boys."

"I can't with the audacity of the boys around here. If you need a restraining order, I've got you."

Evie couldn't help but smile. Lucy was so spunky and made to be a lawyer. She was always ready and willing to sue or restrain on Evie's behalf, and Evie loved her all the more for it.

"I appreciate it, Luce. Other than that, it's been good. I've spent most of the day with Dr. Brant. We just got back from lunch at Suzanne's."

Lucy's eyes widened. "You took Dr. Egotistical to your sacred place?" Mock horror lined her voice.

Evie rolled her eyes. "It's not my sacred place but yes. I was hungry and wanted pizza, and he wanted to tag alone." It may have not been the whole truth, but she wasn't quite ready to explain what she was feeling to Lucy. She knew she didn't have the answers to the questions Lucy would ask.

Heck, I don't have the answers for myself.

Lucy sat back in her chair eyeing her carefully. "If you say so."

Evie was relieved Lucy was willing to let it drop. Deciding it was best to change the topic, she asked, "What does the rest of your day look like?"

"Not much. I'm done with classes for today, but I have a study group session tonight. I won't be at the apartment for dinner, so you're on your own for that. What about you?"

"I have my first class in about thirty minutes, but then, I should be done for the day."

"Is this the lit class without a teacher?" Lucy asked.

"Yep. The class starts in thirty minutes, and they still

haven't posted who is teaching it." Frustration and anxiety were beginning to gnaw at her. Her foot started bouncing uncontrollably with extra energy.

Lucy put a firm hand on her knee, stopping it. "It'll be fine, EJ. I'm sure they're not giving many classes to Dr. Burg anymore, especially not this late in the afternoon."

"What are you talking about? It's barely the afternoon yet."

"Well, it is for old people," Lucy stated matter-of-factly.

"If you say so, Luce." No use in arguing with a future attorney. Evie stuffed her laptop back into her bag and pushed away from the table. "Walk me to class?"

"Sure." Lucy looped her arm through Evie's and led her out.

They'd barely made it to the door of the lecture hall when Evie came to an abrupt halt and grabbed ahold of Lucy's arm with a grip of unyielding steel. "I'm freaking out. Will you peek in there and see who it is?"

Lucy eyed her as she pried Evie's death grip from her arm. "Seriously? Come on, girl. It's not that big of deal."

"Just do it," Evie all but demanded.

"Fine," Lucy huffed.

As Lucy stuck her head into the door to see, Evie closed her eyes and silently sent up a prayer for Dr. Burg to not be standing there. A moment later, Evie heard, "What are you doing?"

"Praying." When Lucy didn't respond, she cracked an eye open. "Well?"

"Well, there's no professor in there."

"What do you mean? Are you sure?" Evie asked, stepping around her to look for herself.

"Yes, unless one of the grad students has been assigned

the class, which isn't likely to happen since it's a graduate level class."

"Maybe they haven't assigned a professor, and the class will be canceled." That seemed like a better alternative to Dr. Burg. A miniscule of guilt rippled through her. It wasn't that she hated Dr. Burg.

We just have creative differences.

Brushing the guilt away along with her thoughts, she turned her attention to what Lucy was saying.

"Either way, it's going to be okay. Just go find a seat and be patient. If it is Dr. Burg, you can drop the class." Lucy firmly gripped her shoulders, turning and pushing her towards the door.

"Fine, but if it is, I am for real dropping it," Evie warned, stepping into the door and waving goodbye to Lucy. As she walked into the room, she took a second to survey it to see who was there. That's when she saw a giant warm waving at her.

"Hey, Evie, up here!" David yelled to her from the middle of the lecture hall. David was devastatingly handsome with his chiseled features, blonde hair, and blue eyes. Whenever he was around, Evie couldn't help but notice the girls drooling over him. Even she had drooled a little when they'd first met, but the initial attraction had quickly faded, resulting in a genuine friendship.

"Hey," she said, taking a seat in the empty chair next to him.

"Hey, Evie, David," a female voice called from behind her. She turned to see Lizzie taking the seat on her other side.

"Hey! How are you?" David, Lizzie, and Evie had met their first day of grad school and had managed to take almost every class together. They were a big reason she hadn't failed within the first semester. The three of them tried to study together once a week and kept each other on track with a reading schedule for the insane amount of required reading. "Do y'all know who is teaching this class?"

"No, but I heard a rumor it was Dr. Burg," David replied with a cringe.

"I will drop this class so fast if it's her," Lizzie said with a cringe of her own.

"We should make a pact. If its Dr. Burg, we all drop the class." David and Lizzie echoed their agreements.

Evie was pulling her things out of her bag when she heard David and Lizzie both let out a collective, "Oh, No."

"What? Dr. Burg?" she asked, too scared to look.

"Maybe worse," David told her, letting out a breath.

"Possibly a lot worse." Lizzie's face held a grimace, flooding Evie with concern.

Dread filled her. "Who?" Evie's voice trailed off when she saw who was standing at the front of the room.

"Good afternoon class. I'm sorry I am late. I just received this class about an hour ago and am playing catchup," he said, scanning the room. His eyes met hers, and they both froze. He flashed her a half grin and continued addressing the class.

Lizzie was right.

It was worse.

A lot worse.

5
ANDREW

ndrew was rushing to class—the one he was now late for.

Thank you, Dr. Hayesworth.

She'd dropped another graduate level class in his lap last minute.

As he walked into the room, he could've sworn he heard quiet groans from some of the students, but he'd grown accustomed to hearing them and knew what they all thought of him. However, he didn't let it bother him and let it slide right off his shoulders. He had a job to do, and it was to ensure these students came out of his class with more knowledge and ability than when they'd started.

Setting his stuff down, Andrew turned to address the perturbed graduate students. "Good afternoon, class. I'm sorry I am late. I just received this class about an hour ago and am playing catchup." As he was talking, he scanned the room to get a feel for the students and an idea of who was in the class, when his eyes landed on the last person he thought would be in there.

After a quick double take, Andrew hastily covered his

surprise. He should've known this might happen, considering he knew she had a class scheduled for that afternoon. Evie didn't so much as blink as their eyes met. Teasing and flirting as professor to graduate assistant was one thing—professor to student was something else entirely. Shooting her a quick smile, Andrew forced his eyes to keep moving as he finished up what he was saying.

How did this day start out so well only for it to be turned into a nightmare within a few minutes?

Since he'd only gotten the class an hour ago, Andrew went over a few important details and let the class go. He took his time gathering his things in hopes Evie would come talk to him, but everyone seemed to stop and talk to her. He wasn't surprised though. She had an ease to her that made her easy to talk to and approach. However, something gnawed at his gut as he watched her laugh at something the tall blonde guy said, and when the same guy bent down and whispered something in her ear, it annoyed him to no end. Whatever the guy said made her blush, and Andrew felt a roaring jealousy, pulsating throughout his body. He went eerily still, like a predator sizing up its prey. As the jealousy began to take root, he knew lingering was no longer an option.

I'm clearly losing my mind.

What is wrong with me?

Huffing out a small breath and giving Evie one last look, he left the room.

EVIE

Evie had hoped she might be able to speak to Andrew before he left, but when she'd turned back to where he'd been standing, he was gone. After agreeing to a study group next week, Evie said her goodbyes to Lizzie and David and found herself wandering the halls toward Andrew's office.

She lightly knocked on his open door, leaning against the door frame. "Hello, Dr. Brant," she said, quirking an eyebrow at him as she emphasized his name.

"Hey, yourself," he replied somewhat stiffly.

Evie took that as an invitation and strolled inside. "So, that was a surprise," she told him, as she stepped up to the front of his desk.

"Yes, it certainly was." His reply was quiet and clipped. For whatever reason, he wouldn't meet her eyes.

Something is definitely wrong. I'm not going to assume, but what if it's the same as my wrong?

It couldn't be.

Could it?

No. Maybe.

She didn't say anything as she waited for him to look up

at her. When he still wouldn't look at her, she asked, "Are you okay?"

"Mhm," he grunted, keeping his eyes on the papers in front of him.

"You sure?"

"Just busy, Evie." Her heart stumbled at his aggravated and dismissive tone.

Did this class just ruin everything?

Please don't do this.

Please.

She hesitated for a moment, willing him to look up. When he didn't, she softly said, "I'll leave you to it then."

Confusion and defeat overtook her as she headed for the door. He'd never treated her this way before, but then again, she'd only known him for less than a week. Maybe, he was a little more like what people said. She quickly pushed the thought away because there was no way, and she knew deep in her bones Andrew wasn't those things. She'd bet her life on him not being anything like the rumors about him.

Just as she stepped out the door, she heard, "Evie."

Slowly, she turned to find him looking at her. He stood up and came around his desk, leaving several feet of distance between them. "I'm sorry," he started. "I was really caught off guard this afternoon, and I don't quite know what to do with it. However, that doesn't excuse my behavior towards you." He paused before adding, "I know you were just as caught off guard as me."

Relief threatened to sweep Evie off her feet.

I knew it.

She knew he wasn't the guy made up by rumors, and there was the proof.

A slow smile started to spread across her face, and she

knew it was the most inappropriate time to be smiling; however, she was beyond thrilled to be proven right.

He stopped talking as he noticed her smile. "Why are you smiling?" A quizzical expression lit his face.

"Because of you," she replied, smiling even bigger.

"Me?" He was confused, which only caused a giggle to bubble to the surface.

"Yes, you." She was full on grinning now, and nothing could wipe it from her face.

"Why? Have I said something amusing?" he asked, clearly baffled by her inappropriately timed smile.

"No, you just proved me right once again today."

"I have?" His brows wrinkled in confusion.

"Yes," she said, turning to leave.

"About what?" he asked before she could leave. "And where are you going?"

"About you being the man, I always believed you to be," she told him. "And I'm going to work. We'll figure it out later."

"Figure out what?"

"Us."

ANDREW

Andrew was left speechless once again because of this woman. He just stood there, staring at the space she'd just occupied. He'd always tried to live his life in a way that would show honor and integrity, but for some reason, he never came off that way to others. His quiet demeanor and straight to the point attitude always came across wrong; however, Evie had managed to see all the way to his core. They still barely knew one another, but he knew the connection went deeper than anything on the surface. He also knew she felt it too. He didn't know how he knew, but he would stake his life on the fact she felt it too.

Us.

His hand slid to his chest just above his heart.

You feel it too. Don't you?

In that moment, he knew his heart was hers. He didn't know how long it would take, but he knew without a doubt, one day, their hearts would entwine, creating something inseparable.

6

ANDREW

The next morning, Andrew walked into the language arts building with a new confidence—one he hadn't had before yesterday. There was a surety to every step he took. A resolve within him, refusing to quit.

While he didn't know what the future held, he knew who he was going to take with him, but it was going to take time.

He'd almost made it to his office when he heard Evie's voice, echoing down the empty hallway.

"Please, Dr. Langston. There has to be something you can do," she pleaded.

"Evie, I'm sorry. I've looked through every possibility, and there is no other option if you want to graduate on time," he heard Carl tell her.

"You asked Dr. Burg if she would open a seat in her class?"

"Yes, and she said no."

"Are you sure she heard you?" Exasperated sarcasm laced her words.

Andrew laughed to himself. The woman had a sense of humor even when upset, even if it was a bit inappropriate.

"Evie," Carl warned.

"Sorry," she muttered. He knew he shouldn't be eavesdropping, but he was curious why she was so upset.

"Again, I'm sorry. Really and truly. I know it's not what you want to hear. If anything opens up in the next couple of weeks, I will let you know, but for now, you're stuck with Dr. Brant."

A heaviness slammed into his chest as he heard his name. If she was feeling half of what he was feeling for her, he knew why she didn't want to be in his class. The situation was far from ideal. Guilt embedded itself deep within him. Although he knew the situation was out of his control, he still felt responsible for Evie's discomfort.

"Fine," she huffed and walked out.

Thankfully, she didn't spot him as she walked out of Carl's office. He waited until she was out of sight before going to question Carl.

"Why are you upsetting my grad assistant, Carl?" Andrew asked, stepping into the office. He kept his voice light and humorous. He felt anything but those things; however, he wasn't about to let Carl know that.

"Oh, you heard that?"

"I caught the end of it as I walked up. What is Evie upset about?"

"She was waiting for me this morning when I got here and begged me to drop her from your class and to find her another one," he explained.

"Did she say why she wanted to drop my class?"

"Just that she thought it would be a conflict of interest due to being your graduate assistant." He added, "There aren't any classes available. She can drop your class, but she won't graduate on time. Maybe you can convince her to stay in the class. This isn't the first time a graduate assistant had to take their professor's class. Just keep it professional and don't discuss your class outside of the classroom."

Andrew nodded. "Thanks, Carl. I'll speak with her about it."

Walking down the quiet hallway, Andrew pondered on what it all meant. He was encroaching on a boundary he wasn't completely sure he needed to cross. Everything he felt for her was very sudden and extremely unexpected. If he ended up being wrong about what he was feeling, then he might ruin them both.

Maybe it's just lust.

Maybe she doesn't even feel the same way or think of me in that way.

Maybe I made all of this up in my head.

He knew in the pit of his stomach he was lying to himself.

This was real, and she felt it too.

Us.

Andrew found Evie waiting outside of his office. Neither of them greeted the other. A heaviness filled the air between them.

Opening the door, they silently went inside. Evie plopped down in her chair and was unnaturally quiet. It was unusual for her to be this silent. He was hoping she'd bring up what happened in Carl's office. It was clearly weighing heavy on her mind.

Instead of sitting in his chair, he leaned against the front of his desk and waited, trying to determine what to say.

"Carl told me you want to drop my class," he finally

said, breaking the silence between them. He waited for her to say something or to look at him, but she did neither. "Evie, look at me," he urged her. Very slowly, she looked up at him. "What's wrong? I thought everything was fine when you left yesterday."

"It was. Is. Everything was more than fine when I left yesterday."

"So, what's the problem?" He gently prodded.

She hesitated for a moment before softly telling him, "The problem is everything is more than fine." Her eyes slid to him, pleading and questioning. "Right? Everything is turning out to be a little too fine?" The question held more meaning to it than the words she spoke. The real questions were there in her eyes, staring at him—waiting to be voiced and answered.

"Yes. Yes, it is."

If she was going to lay the truth on the table, then he would too.

"To be honest, it's all a little too much. I was fine with being your grad assistant and spending time around you as professor and grad assistant, but with me as your student, it makes things a lot more complicated. Not just because you will be grading me, but there's the other thing. Right?" Once again, she looked up at him with eyes that seemed to be pleading with him to confirm what she was thinking, to read between the lines of what she was saying.

"Right. I," he started but noticed the door open. "Hold on." Quickly, he shut the door and returned to his spot at the desk. "Evie, if you are referring to this strange connection between us, then yes, you would be right that things would become more complicated." He paused, waiting for her to affirm what he was saying.

She looked away and nodded. They were both quiet for

a moment as he swiftly thought things through. He hoped what he was about to say was right and didn't come back to haunt them.

"I have a proposal for you if you are willing to hear it."

"Alright," she responded, looking at him again.

"I propose you stay in my class and as my graduate assistant. No running from either. You need to graduate on time, and this shouldn't be a reason you don't. What is between us can go no further for now, but we can spend the next several months getting to know one another. I'd like to think we are already friends." A sheepish grin creeped onto her face. "We can continue in this friendship until the end of the semester."

His heart started to pound as he took a step across the unspoken boundary. "Then, we can reevaluate things between us and see if this connection between us is worth pursuing. I like you, Evie. You bring a joy that I desperately need." He watched as her eyes brightened at his reluctant confession. "I would hate to lose you all together, which is why I would really like for you to remain as my student and grad assistant."

The cards were now on the table, and it felt kind of good to have them there. The decision would ultimately be hers, but he really hoped she would choose to be his friend for the foreseeable future.

A smile grew on her face. The one that threatened to bring him to his knees every time it appeared. "I like the sound of that. I don't want to lose you either. The past couple of days spent with you have been very refreshing for me. Plus, I really like being your friend."

A genuine smile lit his face. "Good. So, we have a deal?" Hope filled him for the first time in a very long time.

She reached her hand out and clasped his. "Deal."

Andrew absentmindedly rubbed his thumb over the back of her hand and quietly echoed her, "Deal." It was going to be a long semester, especially when he just decided he really enjoyed holding her hand. "So, just to be clear. No running, continue to be friends, and reassess at the end of the semester."

She nodded. "No running, friends, and reassess."

He gripped her hand a little tighter and took a breath before telling her, "Because I'm willing to wait for you, Evie James. No matter how long it takes." He didn't wait for her reply as he dropped her hand and went to open the door.

That's probably enough truth for one day.

Their bubble of privacy burst as the sounds of the hallway spilled into the room.

Andrew was sure his heart might beat its way out of his chest, but despite that, he felt more at peace than he had in a long time. There was no better feeling than knowing you were right where you were supposed to be, and he was there.

After a year of grief, he finally felt like he was surfacing from underneath the water. There was air to be breathed, and he was going to take every breath he could.

Andrew went over to his desk to begin his workday as Evie pulled out her book.

Together, they began their new normal and friendship.

The first week of school had been one of the best Andrew had ever experienced. That Friday afternoon, he headed home excited about the promise of a chance at a future with Evie. For the first time in a long time, he felt happy. The thing in his chest that had tightened and threatened to strangle him after his wife's death had all but disappeared, and he only had Evie to thank for it. She was his most unexpected blessing and treasure.

Andrew spent his weekend finishing the table for Evie. By Saturday night, he had it completely finished. It was big enough for her to comfortably set her laptop on it and still have a small amount of room to work. There was a spacious drawer built into it for her books, and if he knew her well enough, there would also be chocolate kept in there. Andrew had attached small wheels on the legs, so she could easily move it around as needed.

Now, he just had to get it in his office.

7

ANDREW

"You must really like this girl if you're going through this much trouble," Zack grunted under the weight of the huge leather chair.

"Just hush and keep moving," Andrew grunted back to him.

Zack had been Andrew's best friend since they'd met in little league baseball. They'd been by each other's side for everything life had thrown at them since. Zack was the one person who knew Andrew better than anyone else. He'd seen the good, the bad, and the ugly of his life.

They managed to wrangle the leather chair down the stairs and out of the building to his truck. Both were panting by the time they got the chair in the back of the truck. "I forgot how heavy this chair was," Andrew said, shutting the tailgate.

"I didn't. I remember when I helped you move that thing in there," Zack said between gasps.

Andrew huffed a laugh. "Come on, man. I thought you were in shape. It wasn't that bad."

"I thought I was in shape too." Zack shot him a smile.

They stood in companionable silence, catching their breaths. Turning serious, he said, "She must be one heck of a woman."

Andrew looked over to see Zack watching him intently. "She is."

"Okay, then." That was one of the many things Andrew appreciated about Zack. He was great at knowing when Andrew was ready to talk about something and when he wasn't.

Zack had, had a front row seat to the disaster of his marriage and to the hard year that had followed. Andrew knew he would have a lot more to say about Evie later, but for now, Zack would give him the space to sort it out.

Andrew still felt as if he were imagining things when he thought about her. The connection he felt to her seemed unreal. It seemed straight out of a novel, and he'd read enough to know those weren't real. A connection like he felt was something rare, and to be honest, he didn't think he deserved something so sacred. Part of him was scared he'd wake up to find out it'd all been a dream, but Evie had acknowledged the connection and confirmed what he was feeling.

It's real.

The only people he knew that had that fictional kind of love were his parents. They'd always said it was love at first sight when they'd met. Growing up, Andrew had often caught his dad gazing at his mom like she was the most beautiful and precious thing he had ever possessed. Even after thirty years of marriage, they'd been head-over-heels for one another. The only good thing about their deaths had been them not having to live without the other.

Andrew knew what it meant to have to live after the

death of a spouse, but for him, it hadn't been earth shattering. His love for Lily hadn't run deep enough.

Andrew had this sinking feeling that if he let himself completely fall for Evie, it would be an all-consuming, earth-shattering kind of love.

The kind of love that would ruin him in the end.

Andrew pondered on everything while he and Zack finished rearranging and organizing his office.

"Looks good, man," Zack said, clapping him on the shoulder.

"Thanks for your help. I really appreciate it."

"Anytime." They took a minute to survey the work they'd done. "You did a great job on that table," Zack told him, gesturing towards the table Andrew had made for Evie.

"Thanks. It wasn't as bad to make as I thought it would be," he replied, straightening up some of the things on his desk.

"Are you ever going to finish making that end table for me?" Zack was referring to the table Andrew had promised to make him over a year ago but never got around to.

"Eventually."

Zack laughed. "I guess it would help if I were a pretty girl."

Andrew didn't take the bait and instead said, "If you were a girl, you definitely wouldn't be described as pretty."

Zack put a hand to his chest as if hurt by his words. "I'm offended."

"As you should be," Andrew laughed.

"You ready? I am starving."

"Yeah, I'm ready," Andrew answered, grabbing his keys. As he locked the door, he asked, "Want to get pizza?"

Twenty minutes later, Andrew and Zack walked into

The Beaumont Pizzeria. It was quite a bit busier than it'd been when he and Evie had come for lunch on Wednesday, but even with the crowd, it still had a welcoming and warm atmosphere. They found an open table along the exposed brick wall with a large pizza mural hanging on it.

After they gave the waitress their drink orders, she asked if they wanted to order from the menu or wanted the usual. Before Zack could answer, Andrew told her, "The usual."

As she walked away, Zack asked, "What's the usual?"

"It's the owners pick, and it will be delicious no matter what it is. Trust me."

"Alright," Zack replied, looking around. "I can't believe I've never been in here before."

Andrew was about to respond when a group of kids sitting at the bar began to chant, "We want Evie." His head snapped in their direction. Suzanne stood behind the bar, laughing at their chant for Evie.

"Okay, Okay," she told them. Turning towards the kitchen, she hollered, "Evie, you've got some customers."

A moment later, Evie appeared from out of the kitchen. She began laughing when she heard the kids chanting. Andrew watched as she made her way over, giving them a stern look before firmly saying, "No." The chanting then turned to a chorus of pleads. "No," she told them again. Several people in the restaurant had begun to watch the exchange between Evie and the kids. "I'm not doing it."

Andrew hadn't noticed the waitress had returned with their drinks until he heard Zack ask, "What's that all about?"

"Oh, that is a weekly special. Every Sunday evening, this family comes in and sits at the bar, and their kids always beg for Evie to make their pizza. It's become a running thing, and most of the customers join in on the fun too. The bar is reserved for the kids on Sunday evenings." Andrew and Zack noticed the room had quieted down as everyone turned their attention to Evie and the kids.

"Why did it just get quiet?" Zack asked her.

"You'll see" was all she said before walking off.

EVIE

The Colson twins were giving Evie their best puppy dog eyes. She didn't know how long she could hold out against the six-year-old twins. As she put her hair up in a ponytail, all the kids seated at the bar began cheering. She even heard a couple of claps and cheers around the room. How this had become a weekly occurrence she would never know, but she enjoyed it a lot.

She finished with her hair and put her hands on her hips. "Well, you know the drill," she said with mock impatience. The kids snapped to attention, but it was the Colson twins who gave the orders. Ethan's hand shot to his head in salute and with a big toothy grin yelled, "Pepperoni." Abigail did the same, but her grin was missing it's two front teeth. "Cheese."

Evie did her best not to smile and commanded, "At ease, Team Pineapple."

She and the twins had dubbed themselves, Team Pineapple. After a long debate on a slow night at the pizzeria, they'd unanimously decided pineapple belonged on pizza. Since then, whenever she made their pizza, pineapple was always the main topping.

She looked to the twins, picked up the ball of dough, and very slowly began to flatten it out into a disk. As she was focused on her work, a slow rumble began to spread throughout the restaurant. She couldn't help the smile that spread across her face. The kids banged on the bar and chanted her name until she started tossing the dough, but they always started off very slow and low, giving her enough time to prep the dough. By the time she was finished flattening the dough into a disk, everyone was pounding wildly and yelling her name at the top of their lungs.

Evie picked up the dough and began to toss it around. The chants turned to squeals and cheers as she tossed the dough in the air. Evie knew she wasn't an expert dough tosser by any means, but she wasn't half bad. It'd taken a lot of practice and a lot of mistakes to get the hang of it, but Ethan and Abigail had been her biggest supporters. They'd cheered her on through every drop and mishap.

After the dough was thoroughly tossed, Evie sat it down, and the room filled with applause.

Now, it was time for Evie's favorite part of the night.

Evie yelled to the restaurant, "Democrat." In response the twins and most of the restaurant yelled back, "Republican." This meant it was time to vote before the rest of the pizza making could begin. Evie ran to the end of the bar where Ed was waiting with the step ladder. Suzanne rang the small bell hanging on the wall, signaling for everyone to quiet down.

She quickly climbed the small step ladder and stood on the edge of the bar, and shouted, "Election Day! Pineapple. Yay or Nay?" A chorus of "yay's" and "nay's" wrang out across the restaurant. Evie looked to Ed and Suzanne for the deciding vote. They both shook their head yes, and Evie called, "They yay's have it!" Cheers erupted throughout the restaurant, and Evie grinned broadly at the crowd.

As she went to climb down, her eyes fell on a familiar sight. There he was, sitting with a man she'd never seen before, grinning at her. The butterflies in her stomach took flight at the sight of him and almost sent her soaring straight towards him. However, she remained grounded and forced herself to go back to making the twin's pizza. Evie put the twin's pizza in the oven and set the time on Suzanne's old hand timer.

"Let me know when it dings," she told the twins, placing the timer on the bar in front of them.

Before she could walk into the kitchen, Ed came out and handed her a pizza. "This is for your friend," he told her with a wink.

Evie looked down to find a pepperoni pizza with pineapple. "Really? Don't you think that's a bit over assuming?"

"Don't question the process, Evie."

Evie shook her head as Ed turned to go back in the kitchen.

As Evie made her way over to Andrew, she felt the butterflies in her stomach taking flight once more. She could feel Andrew's eyes on her before she turned the corner of the bar. They always seemed to track her, and if she were being honest, she didn't mind one bit. Knowing Andrew Brant watched her, filled her with a warm fuzzy feeling. It was a mixture of satisfaction and belonging, and for the first time in a very long time, Evie knew she was right where she was meant to be.

A smile danced across her face as she reached the table.

"I hope you two were part of the "yay's." As she set the pizza on the table, the man she didn't know let out a low chuckle. "I'll take that as a no."

"Yeah, we've both never been fans of pineapple on pizza," Andrew answered, grinning up at her.

"Well, I would apologize, but you know this is out of my hands."

"Oh. I do, which is why I am not complaining." His green eyes gleamed with amusement.

"Well, I might have to complain," Zack mumbled.

"Evie, this is Zack. Zack, this is Evie," Andrew said, introducing her to the mystery man. Evie turned to Zack, who's eyes had widened slightly at the mention of her name.

Has Andrew talked to him about me?

Aw! What if he's telling his friends about me?

"Hi," Evie greeted, reaching her hand out.

"Nice to meet you," Zack replied shaking her hand.

"Yeah, you too."

Evie heard a ding from behind her, and then, the twins' loud yells for her. Evie smiled over her shoulder at them. "I've got to get back to the twins but let me know if y'all need," her voice trailed off as she caught a glimpse of something outside. A wave of terror slammed hard into her, and she quickly stumbled back away from the table. There'd been no hiding her fear or time to cover it.

She heard Andrew call her name, but his voice sounded far away. She could tell by the tone of his voice he was worried and confused, but the only thing she could do was turn and run for the kitchen.

Bursting through the kitchen doors, she gasped for breath as the panic took hold.

He found me. He found me. He found me.

Her heart thrummed in her ears but not loud enough to drown out the repetitive thoughts.

He's here. He's here. He's here.

One look at her had Ed asking, "Where?"

"Outside," she rasped between breaths. Suzanne had an arm around her, helping her to the stool in the corner as Ed rushed out of the kitchen.

"Try to take a breath, Honey. You're safe in here," Suzanne said gently. Evie tried to take a deep breath, but it was a pitiful attempt. Her lungs were struggling to take in air. "That's it. Take another one." Suzanne's voice was a soothing caress to her frayed nerves.

It was comforting to have someone to act as a secondary mother while hers was hours away. With Suzanne and Ed here, she would always have a home away from home, but nothing could replace the real thing. Thoughts of home and her parents drifted through her mind, shoving at the panic. As the warm thoughts wrapped their way around the terrifying thoughts, Evie's mind began to quiet, and her breathing slowly evened out.

Evie gasped again as she remembered the twin's pizza. "I'll take care of it," Suzanne told her as if reading her mind. She poked her head out of the kitchen doors and yelled, "Hey, Tony. Will ya take the twin's pizza out of the oven. Evie is taking a break."

"Sure thing." Tony yell back. Everyone that worked at the pizzeria tended to be very loud. Sometimes, Evie found it comforting, but right then, she needed quiet.

"Thanks, Suzanne." Evie's voice was calm but shaking slightly.

"No problem, Honey. Take as long as you need." Evie took another deep breath and let it out just as Ed returned.

"I didn't see any sign of him." Ed's face was serious and

a picture of stone. Despite the gray hair and aging appearance, the man could scare a bear when he was in "fight"
mode.

"I swear he was there." Cold dread passed over her.
Nervously, she twisted her hands together as thoughts
blurred together in her mind.

Where did he go? Did he see me? Will he find me again?

Is it all about to start again? Will I survive it again?

*How much more can I take before I can no longer come back
to myself?*

"I believe you, Hon. I don't doubt he was there, but he's
gone for now. He'll be back though. You need to be on alert
since we know he's in town," Ed said gravely. A weight fell
upon her at his words.

History was coming to repeat itself just as everything
was going right and wonderful.

Her shoulders slumped in defeat. Ed was right. She was
going to have to go back on high alert, and the thought
made her want to scream; however, the only thing that
came out was a quiet, "Yes, sir."

"Come on, I'll take you home and make sure everything
is secure before I go," Ed told her, gesturing for her to follow
him to the door.

"Thank you, I appreciate it."

Evie bid Suzanne goodnight, gathering her things, and
left out the back door with Ed. Thankfully, his truck was
parked next to the back door. She was in the truck and
buckled before she could even worry about what might be
lurking in the shadows.

Ed walked her to her apartment door and checked all
the windows and locks before leaving. She fell into bed that
night full of anxiety and worry.

How did he find me?

How much does he know about my current life?

How long did he see me talking to Andrew?

Despite the apprehension, she made a mental side note about Andrew and Zack being friends. In the two years she had been at Beaumont University, she had never seen Andrew with a friend. It was a nice surprise. She liked seeing a new side of him and wanted to know more. However, it wouldn't matter if she ended up caught again because she had a feeling, she wouldn't be able to come back from it this time.

I'm so tired.

I don't have it in me to do this again.

To survive.

Evie was deep in thought when her phone pinged with an alert, causing her to jolt and nearly fall out of the bed. Andrew's name filled the top of her phone screen. Even though everything was going wrong, she couldn't help but smile at his name.

A: Hey, I just wanted to check and see if you were okay

E: I'm fine. Sorry for being weird

A: As long as you're okay, I can forgive the weirdness

She hoped he wouldn't press the subject any further, because it wasn't something she was ready to talk to anyone about, let alone Andrew. Just to be safe, she changed the subject.

E: How was your pineapple pizza?

A: Surprisingly, delicious.

E: The magical oven wins again

A: I might be disappointed if the FBI discovers its powers

A: Btw, you were impressive tonight

E: Thank you. You came on a good night. The twins always make it fun

E: I was very surprised to find out the grumpy professor has a friend

A: LOL It helps that Zack knew me before I became the grumpy professor

E: When was that? The rock ages?

A: Wow! Someone is sassy tonight

A: And since little league

E: You played baseball?

A: Yep. All the way through college

E: Pics or it didn't happen

A few minutes later Evie's phone dinged again with a picture of Andrew in a college baseball uniform.

That is hotter than it should be

E: Look at you, Dr. Brant! I never would've believed it.

A: Lol that was a long time before the Dr.

E: You'll have to tell me all about it one day

A: I will. I'll see you in the morning. Night, Evie

E: Night, Andrew.

Evie set her phone on the little table next to the bed. Her thoughts drifted back to the deal she and Andrew had made in his office. Evie had known something was different about him the first time she'd laid eyes on him in the hallway of the English department.

She knew deep in her gut, in her bones, that he was a part of her future. When he told her she was worth waiting for, she thought she was going melt right into the floor of his office. Right now, they could be nothing more than friends, and even though that wasn't what she wanted, she was surprisingly okay with it. Perhaps, it was due to his promise of one day.

Unable to keep her eyes open any longer, Evie slipped into sleep.

The idea of something and someone better than what awaited her in the darkness lulled her to sleep.

8

EVIE

The next morning, Evie woke up exhausted and late from a night of restless sleep. Nightmares had plagued her all night long, chasing her from her sleep.

Snatching up her black leggings and oversized t-shirt from the chair in the corner of her room, she stumbled to the bathroom and hurriedly got ready. Five minutes later, she was out the door.

As she approached her black SUV, she noticed a note on the windshield. Her name was written in an all too familiar handwriting, freezing her in her tracks. Frantically looking around, she tried to survey the area. Everything seemed in its place, and nothing out of the ordinary grabbed her attention. Deciding it was all clear for the moment, Evie carefully walked to the side of car and with shaking hands, grabbed the note. Bile rose in the back of her throat as she opened it and read.

"I found you, Little Genny. See you soon. XO"

Evie quickly got in her car and locked the doors. Her hands were shaking too hard to get the key into the ignition, and the tears started falling before she could stop them. A cry of frustration and anguish left her as she slammed her palms on the steering wheel as a mixture of exhaustion and fear pumped through her, causing warm tears to cascade down her cheeks.

Why did he hunt me down again?

Why can't he just leave me alone?

Before she could start spiraling completely out of control, Evie began to use the breathing techniques her dad had taught her. After a couple of rounds of breathing, she had enough control to pull out her phone and send a picture of the note to her dad. If there was anyone who would know what to do, it was him. Her dad had always been her safe place, her rock and shelter.

She did one more round of the breathing exercises, wiped her face, and started the car. She refused to let him win. He didn't get to push her around anymore.

No more.

I can't.

Evie was very late by the time she parked on campus. She rushed up the stairs and down the hallway to Andrew's office. She was out of breath by the time she got there. His head popped up as she stumbled through the door, breathing heavily.

"Wow, what happened in here?" she rasped between breaths.

Andrew didn't answer. Instead, he studied her face for a second before asking, "What's wrong?"

Her eyes drifted around his office until they landed on Andrew. "Nothing," she answered, trying to keep her voice casual and even. Although, the heavy breathing wasn't exactly helping her case.

"You've been crying." His voice was gentle as he pointed

out the obvious. Getting up from his chair, he came around the desk towards her, approaching her cautiously.

She casually shrugged. "It happens from time to time."

"You're also late."

"Yeah, I'm sorry. I didn't mean to be." Evie looked around the office again, avoiding eye contact with Andrew.

"Evie."

"Yeah?"

"What happened?" He was standing close to her now. The scent of him was like the antidote to her fear. The events of the morning began to fade away with every breath she took of him. Instinctively, she took a small step closer to him, longing to cure herself of it all.

"I just. It. I." She started and stopped not knowing how to explain things. She also wasn't sure she was ready to explain things just yet.

His face was so full of concern and worry for her that she thought her heart might physically break at the sight of it. The look on his face was so vastly different from that of her ex—who had nothing but hate written on his.

"Evie, you can trust me. I won't force you to tell me if you don't want to, but I'd like to know if something is wrong." His voice was so sincere, so tender. No one outside of her family had ever spoken to her like that before. Evie's eyes filled with tears all over again but for a very different reason. One of Andrew's hands caressed her shoulder as the other gently gripped her chin, tilting her face up to look at him. "You can trust me." His voice adamant but soft. "We are friends after all."

"I know," she told him. "I'm just not quite ready to talk about it, but I promise I will tell you about it one day." Emotion flooded her voice as she added, "Because I trust you."

His eyes darkened ever so slightly at her words. She could feel the desire emanating from him, but it slowly faded as the wall of propriety began to slide back into place. "I'm going to hold you to that."

"Deal," she smiled up at him.

"Deal," he echoed as his hand slid from her chin to cup her cheek. His hand was warm and somewhat rough against her face from the callouses on his hands. His thumb gently scraped across her skin as he wiped away a lone tear. Evie admired that he had callouses on his hands from working with them.

She also found her thoughts trying to imagine what else his hands were capable of doing. Her cheeks began to heat at her wayward thoughts, and quickly, she doused the flame by changing the subject. "So, what happened in here?"

He smiled at her as he let his hand fall away from her face. "I have a surprise for you."

"You do?" The skepticism was evident in her voice.

"I do," he replied firmly, walking to far corner of his office. Evie followed behind him, stopping next to his desk. When Andrew stepped out of the way, she saw that he'd moved the leather chair into the corner of the room behind his desk and next to it was the cutest little table.

"You got me table?"

"I made you a table." A shyness crept over his features.

She stared at him in disbelief. "You made me a table." The words were barely a whisper from the disbelief and awe. She walked over to it and reverently ran her fingers over the smooth wooden surface.

Evie set her backpack in the chair and turned to look at him. "I love it. Thank you." A heavy emotion flooded into her chest, making her a little uncomfortable. She didn't know what it was, but it was very overwhelming.

"I knew you needed something bigger than the little table you have been using. I also built a drawer into it, so you have a place to store your questionable chocolate bars," he teased, eliciting a smirk from her. "I also moved your chair and table back here behind my desk to keep anyone from using them."

"My chair?"

He stuck his hands in his pockets and shrugged. "I decided it was your chair the first time I saw you curl up in it." He hesitated before continuing. "No one has ever been that relaxed around me, especially not in this office."

Evie's heart cracked just a bit at his admittance. She hated the thought of no one taking the time to see through the broody façade to the man underneath.

Evie looked between him and the table and realized, despite everything, her heart was slipping from her grasp. It wanted him. If she wasn't careful, she would lose her heart to him, and she couldn't afford it.

I won't risk him.

He was constantly surprising her with how caring he was, and it was a very welcome surprise. "Thank you, Andrew. I really love it." A genuine smile lit her face. Even in the darkest of moments, Andrew could cause her to smile, and it meant everything to her.

Andrew glanced at his watch. "I've got class in a little bit. Do you want to come with me or stay here?"

"I'll go with you. I don't have much to do today, especially since one of my professors hadn't been entirely prepared for our first week of class," she teased.

"Yeah, well, that all changes today. I spent the weekend

getting the class together," he replied, turning to get his things.

"I thought you spent the weekend building me a table," she challenged. Sass lined her tone, and his face said he understood every bit of her sass. He slid the strap of his bag over his shoulder and stepped closer to her.

"Do you think you consume all of my time, Miss James?" His voice dropped dangerously low, causing a shiver to run along her skin.

He was so close to her, she had to tip her head back to look up at him. They were almost touching. Her heart thumped loudly in her ears. His dark eyes slid from hers down to her mouth. She watched intently as he licked his bottom lip. Heat spread throughout every inch of her body.

A slow predatory grin slid across his face as he told her, "I may not have sass like you, but I do know other tricks." Evie bit her bottom lip, and his eyes flared in delight. He leaned closer to her, lips lightly grazing her cheek. His breath caressed her ear, causing her to shiver again. His voice came out deep and thick. "You should be careful, Miss James, before that sass of yours gets you into trouble."

Without another word or glance, he walked towards the door, giving her the space to let out the breath she'd been holding.

"You coming?" he asked as if nothing had just occurred.

Breathe, Evie. Breathe.

Air! I need air!

Why is it so hot in here?

I'm in massive trouble.

"Mhm," she murmured, grabbing her backpack.

He chuckled, and she knew he knew exactly what he'd just done to her.

It's going to be a long semester.

Evie started ranting under her breath about him being a smart butt professor. He must have heard her because he looked at her with amusement dancing in those dark green eyes and smiled. Evie shook her head and stalked off towards the classroom, leaving Andrew to follow.

9
ANDREW

ndrew laughed to himself as he trailed behind Evie, listening to her rant on and on about how he was a smart butt professor. He probably shouldn't have gotten as close to her as he did, but he couldn't help himself.

The real mistake had been looking down at those full lips of hers. The desire to press his mouth to hers and to finally taste her had almost overpowered every sense of control within him. The want had been in her eyes. He knew she would've let him kiss her if he'd tried, and he'd wanted nothing more; however, the first time he kissed her wasn't going to be in his office.

He needed somewhere he could take his time and savor her, if she would have him. He wasn't against dropping to his knees before her and begging her for one taste. For one moment to run his tongue over those lovely pink lips of hers before finally sliding inside and experiencing her.

He'd clean all the sass out of her beautiful mouth.

The thought was enough to nearly undo him.

Andrew blew out a hard breath, trying to clear his mind.

It's going to be a long semester.

He shoved the thoughts of her away and tried to focus on his class. He needed to be the smart butt professor she was still ranting about and not the love smitten fool he was becoming. Although, it seemed a too late. There was no returning to the man he was before Evie.

As class got started, Andrew decided he liked having Evie in his classes as his grad assistant. She was very perceptive at knowing what he needed before he had time to think about it. If he needed a new pen, she had one waiting. One time he'd forgotten the copies of an assignment, and she had them in her bag. It was as if she anticipated his every need. She didn't have to do it, but it was certainly making his life a lot easier.

The classes also passed by a lot faster with her there. Sometimes, the classes felt as if they would never end, but when that feeling set in, he would look over at her. Sometimes, she would be focusing on her work and not notice him watching her, but other times, she would see him and give him one of her stunning smiles.

Evie's smile was like a surge of energy for him.

Every smile propelled him forward.

Andrew also just enjoyed her company. It was nice to have her close. One of his favorite moments was when class was over, and she'd decide to stay and hang out in his office.

Today was no exception. Evie was currently curled up in her chair, reading a book. He'd told her she didn't have to stay since he didn't have anything for her to do, but she'd wanted to stay and hang out. He'd never admit it aloud, but the joy of her choosing to stay with him was enough to make his chest hurt.

Feelings aside, it was also the first time Andrew felt like he had a true friend at Beaumont, and that felt amazing.

Andrew was reading over notes for his upcoming class when a shadow fell across the doorway of his office. He looked up to find a rather large man, standing at the threshold of his office with his arms folded, staring keenly at Evie.

"Can I help you?" Andrew demanded. The tone of his voice caught him off guard. A primal urge to protect arose within him.

He'd fight every demon from hell for Evie, and that included the stone wall of a man in his doorway. The man's eyes flickered to him but before he could respond, a loud squeal reverberated throughout the small office.

Andrew's head whipped around to see Evie leap out of her chair and rush to the door. He was stunned as he watched her fling herself into the man's arms. The man chuckled and wrapped his huge arms around her, lifting her off the ground.

Jealously flared through Andrew, leaving him with the feeling of having swallowed a brick.

"What are you doing here?" she asked very excitedly.

"What do you mean what am I doing here? You sent me that text and expected me not come?" The man set her gently on the floor.

"Well, I guess I didn't really think about it."

"You've got to start using this noggin of yours more often, kiddo," he teased, rubbing her head like she was a child.

"Stop that." She giggled, provoking Andrew's gut to twist into a knot.

The man smiled at her affectionately before checking

the black watch on his wrist. "Can you break away for a little bit? I'll take you to lunch."

"I think I can make that happen," she told the man, spinning around to face him. Andrew didn't know what look was on his face, but obviously, it wasn't great given Evie's reaction.

"Oh," she paused as she locked eyes with him. "Sorry, Andrew. This is my dad, Aiden," she said, gesturing to the large man, standing behind her. "Dad, this is Dr. Andrew Brant."

Andrew stood up and walked around his desk. "It's a pleasure to meet you, sir," he said, holding his hand out to her father.

"Likewise," Aiden replied, gripping Andrew's hand.

Aiden maintained solid eye contact with him, but Andrew held it right back. He noted Aiden's grip on his hand tightened ever so slightly.

So, not a threat. Just a very protective father.

"My daughter has told me a lot about you. She speaks very highly of you," Aiden told him, his deep voice filling the room.

Andrew knew her father was sizing him up. It was only natural for him to do so, but he was now wondering what exactly Evie had told him.

"I think highly of her too, sir," he replied.

Her father nodded his agreement and let go of his hand.

Andrew slid his attention from Aiden to Evie. "I don't have anything else for you to do today, so you are free until class this afternoon."

"Great," she said, going to grab her things.

"Where is the bag I made for you?" Aiden asked her accusingly.

"It didn't really go with my outfit today," she replied, waving a hand at her leggings and oversized t-shirt.

"So? What does that have to do with anything?"

Evie rolled her eyes. "It's just a thing. I'll use your bag tomorrow if I wake up on time to put on something nice."

Andrew watched Aiden lightly touch Evie's chin and tilt her head up to him, examining her face. "Have you not been sleeping?" Concern was etched on his face.

Evie pulled her chin out of his hand and avoided eye contact with her father. "I'm fine."

She'd acted the same with Andrew earlier.

There's definitely something wrong.

"You should've called me sooner."

"I said I was fine, and I mean it." Her voice was unyielding as she raised her chin in defiance to her father's accusations.

"I know you are, Buttercup." Aiden's soft tone contradicted everything about him. "Come on. Let's go get some food."

As Evie picked up her backpack, Andrew said, "Don't be late. The real work begins at two."

She snorted and rolled her eyes. "Yeah, whatever you say Dr. Brant."

"Oh, she likes you," Aiden observed in a curious tone.

Evie shoved her dad towards the door. "I do not." Turning her attention to Andrew, she said, "Don't believe a word out of his mouth. I definitely do *not* like you." With a wink, she disappeared through the door behind her dad.

Andrew stared with his mouth slightly agape at the space Evie had just inhabited.

Did she just flirt with me in front of her dad?

The woman left him flabbergasted most of the time.

10

EVIE

E vie and her dad strolled across campus to the Café. It was still quite warm outside, but there was a cool breeze, floating through the air. The day was beautiful, and Evie was thankful to be spending part of it with her dad. She hadn't seen him much since returning to Beaumont for the semester, and she had to admit she'd missed their daily conversations.

She'd only had her dad around fulltime for about six years. Growing up, he'd been gone a lot on deployment, so she hadn't gotten to spend a lot of time with him. After he'd retired, things became rocky between them, but they'd eventually found their way into a close relationship.

Her dad's voice broke through her thoughts. "How are classes going?"

"They're fine, for now. We haven't really gotten into much work yet."

"What did Dr. Boss Man mean by the real work begins at two?"

Evie rolled her eyes at her dad and smirked. "I keep messing with him about not being prepared for the first day of class and not having anything set up. Granted, he was given the class about an hour before the class started, but he swears today is the day he gives us the work that lives up to his egotistical, hard butt professor status."

Her dad looked at her with those assessing eyes of his and was silent as he pondered on something. Evie always knew when he was thinking something over because he got this far away look in his eyes, as if he were digging deep into the storage files of his brain for the answer.

She was glad he was there. Peace had a way of following him around, and it was something she desperately needed. Glancing up at him, she realized the years were just beginning to show on him. The little lines and wrinkles on his face were more pronounced than they used to be. Some of those she knew were because of her. No apology would ever be enough. No matter how old she got, her father would always be her guardian, towering over her.

He'd always been and would always be her shadow.

Evie had always thought his broad shoulders seemed to carry the weight of the world on them, and even though he bore the weight of many, including her, he would never admit to it. To admit to it, would be to admit to weakness, and he'd never allow it. Her dad rarely showed cracks in his armor, and the one time it did crack in front of her, she'd been the reason for it. It'd left her broken in more ways than one, and she swore she'd never break her dad in that way again.

Like any good dad, he'd always made her feel safe and secure. Even now, at the age of twenty-seven, he was the one she ran to when things were overwhelming or troubling. She knew she was lucky to have him. There were too many girls without good fathers to be there for them. Her dad had always been her rock, keeping her rooted whenever she felt she was beginning to flail about.

"You love him," her dad stated, breaking through her thoughts.

Huh?

Her eyebrows knit together in confusion. "Love who? What are you talking about?"

Aiden shot her a look. "You know who." When she continued to stare at him, he finally answered, "Andrew."

Shock hit her hard.

Is he insane?

Her mouth opened and shut several times. Feeling like a fish, she clamped her mouth shut before finally stammering out, "That's a bit of an assumption, don't you think?"

"Is it?"

Is it?

The question was casual enough, but it sent Evie spiraling. Her mind raced as she hastily analyzed every feeling and interaction with Andrew. She felt foolish for even entertaining the idea of love because they hardly knew one another.

They hadn't even been on a date yet. It wasn't even allowed. At the very most, they were friends.

She didn't even know his favorite color.

Wait. Yes, I do.

It's blue. To be exact, blue like the lake in front of his house.

Oh, boy.

Evie could feel her dad's eyes on her as they meandered down the small path through the campus square. He'd give her the space to answer, but she knew if she didn't answer now, he'd circle back to it at some point. Even though she didn't really have an answer, she decided to at least talk about it and get her dad's advice. He was probably the only person that could help her figure out what was going on in her mind and heart. Even if it wasn't love, she was still confused about how she'd been feeling.

"Is it even possible?" she asked, glancing at her father—who was now staring straight ahead. "I mean, I haven't known him for that long. We haven't even been on a date, which we can't by the way. Nothing can happen until the semester is over, but besides that, love goes beyond just liking someone. Love is the "till death do us part" emotion." Rambling had taken over. It always happened when she got nervous and didn't have a concrete answer to something. Everything was becoming jumbled and falling out of her, but she continued anyway. The answer had to be in there somewhere.

"It can't be possible. Can it? It seems rather impossible to me. Besides, let's just say that I did. Hypothetically, of course."

"Of course," her dad quietly murmured, keeping his eyes on the path. Amusement and a touch of sarcasm lined his words, sending alarm bells off in Evie's head.

She ignored his comment and kept going because it scared her. It could only mean one thing—he was sure of his earlier statement. He was merely waiting for her to confirm what he already knew.

Surely, not. How could he possibly know before me?

He doesn't even know Andrew and saw us together for all of two minutes.

Her heart began to race as she started her rambling again.

"None of it would really matter anyways if he doesn't feel the same way. Although, he did seem to hint at the fact that he did have some sort of feeling for me. He did say he was willing to wait for me, but that could just mean that he's interested and nothing more. All of that to say the whole thing is highly improbable." Evie paused for a moment, considering all the things she admired about Andrew and their time together.

"However, he is amazing and easy to talk to. He also made me this beautiful side table to use in his office. Made it, Dad." Aiden looked over at her. "Made it." Her eyes got big as she enunciated each word, causing her dad to smile. "Who makes someone they barely know a table?"

"A man in love," her dad said under his breath.

Evie stumbled as she caught his words. Once again ignoring her dad's commentary, she began to tick things off with her fingers as she spoke. "One, we don't know each other. Two, we aren't dating. Three, he's older and my boss." She faltered on number four.

What else is there? There has to be something?

That's all I got? Seriously?

It can't be possible. It doesn't make any sense.

She took a big breath, walking faster. The feelings were too much. A hand on her arm prompted her to stop walking before she made an all-out run for it. Her dad pulled her into his arms, softly chuckling.

After a moment, he pulled back, keeping his hands on her arms as he said, "Evie, love isn't something that can be rationalized. It either is or isn't. It doesn't have to make sense for it to be." She slowly nodded, chewing on her bottom lip and thinking over her dad's words. They were simple and to the point—like everything he said.

He was quietly watching her, assessing, and waiting for her response.

"Well, it seems you might be correct once again," she faintly confessed. Her vision blurred as tears began to well up. Once again, she found herself wrapped tightly in her dad's arms.

The tears spilled over as the realization hit her.

She loved Andrew Brant.

I love him. I really and truly love him.

She didn't know if she was "in love," but she knew she loved him with a love that was deeply rooted somewhere within her in a place she hadn't known existed.

Aiden kissed the top of her head and said, "It's a good thing, Evie. Even if it takes a while for it to materialize, it's good. You deserve it, Buttercup. And, for what it's worth, I think I like Dr. Boss Man." Evie laughed into her dad's chest. "Come on, let's eat before I starve to death," he said very melodramatically.

Thankfully, lunch passed uneventfully. She was grateful for the quality time with her dad. She'd missed him more than she'd realized. Peace settled over her as they walked back across campus, chatting about nothing and everything.

Evie walked into class with her dad, trailing behind her. He'd insisted on coming with her. She thought it was completely unnecessary and slightly embarrassing, and she was fairly certain her dad just wanted to spy on Andrew; however, given the note on her car that morning, she hadn't objected too much. They hadn't talked about the note yet, but she knew that conversation was coming.

Her dad waited in the back of the room as she made her way down to the front to where Andrew was setting up his laptop. "Hey, Dr. Brant."

"Hello, yourself." Andrew smiled at her with a smile that triggered the butterflies in her stomach.

He is too good looking for his own good.

"Do you mind if my dad sits in the back? He insisted on coming, but say the word, and I'll kick him out."

Andrew gave her a pointed look before saying, "Evie, I am touched that you think I have the gall to tell your father to get out of my class."

She smirked at him. "Well, technically, it would be me telling him to get out."

"Well," he said, mimicking her. "It's fine if he stays, but why does he want to?"

"He, um, just wants to keep an eye on things," she hesitantly told him. There wasn't really a good answer. Andrew turned serious and gave her a leveled look. "Everything is fine. For now."

"For now? Does that mean it has previously not been fine or that it might not be fine in the future?" He sounded very concerned, and it only made her love him more.

"Both," she replied lightheartedly. The situation with her ex was anything but amusing; however, she wasn't about to cause Andrew a drop of worry over it, especially with class starting.

"Evie," Andrew started.

Reaching out, she placed a hand over the one he had resting on the table, not caring if anyone saw. "I'm fine. Everything is fine. I promised you I would tell you about it, and I will," she said in a soft but adamant voice. She squeezed his hand before letting go.

"Fine, but I am still going to worry," he conceded.

"Good."

Andrew's eyes drifted to the back of the room. "I don't know how I am supposed to get through the next hour with your dad staring at me." Nervousness etched his voice.

Evie let out a little laugh. "You'll be just fine."

"That's what you think," he replied nervously, causing her to laugh again.

"It's not funny. He's intimidating." Even though he sounded anxious, there was a smile on his face and amusement dancing in his eyes. "If you don't stop laughing, I am going to lose my grumpy professor status."

"Sorry," she said, trying her best to stop. His green eyes crinkled with laughter. He was failing miserably to conceal the smile on his face. A giggle erupted from her as she pointed an accusing finger at him. "You know you want to laugh."

"I do not. Now, go sit down so I can start class," he commanded, trying to sound stern.

"Whatever you say, Dr. Brant." Sass filled her voice.

As she turned to go, she heard him whisper, "Smart butt."

Evie gave her dad a thumbs up as she made her way to her seat next to David and Lizzie.

"What was that?" David asked her as she sat down. His eyes were slightly wide in disbelief.

"What was what?"

"You were laughing with Brant," Lizzie answered for David.

"We were just talking."

"I've never seen anyone laugh while talking to him or smile for that matter," Lizzie stated.

David nodded in agreement before saying, "I've never seen him smile while talking to anyone."

"He's not as bad as everyone makes him out to be," Evie told them. This rhetoric of Andrew being a mean and terrible person was beginning to get old.

"Oh, please. He made at least two freshman girls cry just this morning. He's as bad as they say," David told her.

"I heard about that too," Lizzie said to David.

"I don't know what happened this morning, but he truly isn't like what people say about him." Evie's tone was becoming defensive. The rumors hadn't escaped Evie, but to hear the words from two of her friends was almost too much.

"Do you have a crush on him or something?" David's tone was accusing, and she didn't appreciate it.

"What? Have y'all forgotten that I am his grad assistant? I spend one-on-one time with him almost every day. He can be nice. He *is* nice," she snapped, growing irritated by the second. She hated how people believed the worst about Andrew. He was a genuinely good guy, and she didn't know why people couldn't see it.

"Okay," Lizzie said. Thankfully, she and David both dropped the subject. She didn't want to hear any more about it.

However, by the end of class, Evie was beginning to question her own thoughts about Andrew.

"Still think he's such a nice guy?" Lizzie sardonically whispered to her.

"I don't know," Evie whispered back in reply.

"This is ridiculous," David whispered to them.

"Quiet in the back," Andrew announced from the front of the room. All three of their heads popped up to find him eyeing them.

Evie stared him down, trying to find the man that she supposedly loved because the man standing there was a borderline tyrant. He was lecturing faster than she could take notes, and he'd given them more work than could possibly be done in a semester, especially with all the extra work she was doing as his graduate assistant and at the pizzeria. She ran a hand down her face and groaned inwardly.

Her phone vibrated on the table next to her notebook. Andrew's name popped up on the phone screen.

A: Believe me now?

When did he have time to send a text?

She never heard a break in his lecturing. Evie wasn't prepared for this side of Andrew. She knew his reputation and had seen him teach before, but she'd never been on the receiving end. And, quite frankly, it sucked.

Now, he was sending her taunting messages.

Rude.

Who is this man?

E: (Crying emoji)

Evie looked up just in time to see Andrew glance at his phone as it pinged with her text. A grin formed on his face as he saw her message. The man didn't falter his words as he checked his phone. Not even a misstep. Even though she was thoroughly intimidated at this point, she had to admit she was very impressed with him.

Her phone vibrated again.

Dad: Quit texting your professor and pay attention

Evie turned around in her seat to see her dad, smiling at her with a very amused look on his face. She snapped back around in her seat and listened as Andrew gave out the homework assignment for the week.

"I don't know how I am going to get any of this done," David told them after class was finished.

"Me either," she replied.

"Study group this week?" Lizzie asked. She and David agreed.

David stood up, slinging his backpack on his shoulder,

clearly upset. "This had to be the class standing between me and graduation," he mumbled as he stormed off.

"I'll see you later," Lizzie told her before walking off, shaking her head.

Evie stuffed her notebook and pens into her backpack, feeling defeated. She stood up and found her dad at the end of the row, waiting on her. He started to laugh when he saw her face.

"Not a word," Evie warned.

"I think he's a fantastic professor," her dad amusingly stated. He was clearly enjoying her torture. Tossing an arm around her shoulders as they walked out of the lecture hall, he said, "You'll be just fine, Buttercup. You always are." He bid her goodbye with a kiss on the head and promised to see her later.

Evie walked into Andrew's office without looking at him and dropped into her chair. She let out a huff. Andrew swiveled in his chair to look at her. She waited for him to say something, but he just sat silently, watching and waiting.

After what seemed like forever, she heard him ask, "Do you want to talk about it?"

"No," she grumbled, crossing her arms and sinking further into the chair.

"You sure?"

She shot her eyes to him. "How am I supposed to complain to you about you?"

"Evie, is it really that bad?" She could've sworn hurt flashed in his eyes.

"Yes! I don't know how I'm going to get everything done," she practically yelled at him. She could feel the anger rising within her. She stared him down as he rolled his chair closer to her.

In a gentle voice, he said, "When I started organizing this class, I knew your schedule. Do you really think I would overload you until you broke?"

She looked into those dark green eyes that were pleading with her to see him and his heart. Not that she wanted to admit it, but he was right. She knew he'd never do anything to intentionally hurt or sabotage her. He was tough but fair.

"No. No, you wouldn't do that to me." Relief flooded his eyes, and Evie immediately felt bad for ever thinking that he would purposefully sabotage her in that way.

"No, but I am going to push you. I want to make sure you excel. That is my job as your professor, but it's also my job as your friend. I'm on your side. I'm team Evie."

The anger in her completely dissolved at his words. "Team Evie?"

Nodding his head, he asked, "Will you trust me, Evie? Trust that I am not going to push you over the educational cliff, and that I truly have your best interest at heart in all regards?"

"Deal," she softly replied.

"Good."

Evie loved the grin that formed on his face.

They'd both needed that reassurance. Evie had forgotten that Andrew had to also be her professor, and that they were both in the situation together.

"However, it's not official unless we shake hands," she coyly stated.

"If I didn't know any better, Miss James, I would say you wanted to hold my hand," he teased with a seductive smile.

"And, what if I did?" She challenged. If he could use seduction, so could she. Or, at least, she could try. She'd never actually been good at the art of seduction, and Andrew was clearly a master.

He rolled his chair little closer to her until their knees were touching. Her heart started beating rapidly at his nearness. "Then, I'd say I would like nothing more than for you to hold my hand." To her surprise, his response was unexpectedly real and serious, but she sensed a bit of hesitation in his tone.

"But?"

"But, we are in my office, and we both know the rules."

"Stupid rules," she huffed.

"Well, the rules are there to keep," he started, but she cut him off.

"No, no more. I can't handle any more of your lecturing today," she said dramatically.

He rolled his chair back to his desk, putting some distance between them. "Smart butt."

"Not the first time I've been called that today," she smirked at him.

There was a knock on the open office door, and they both turned to look. Andrew switched back into professor mode as two students came in to ask about an assignment. Evie pulled out the table Andrew had made for her and got to work, sorting through student emails.

She liked this part of her day, working side-by-side with Andrew. She really hoped it would be a "till death do us part" kind of thing.

11

ANDREW

Andrew heard Evie packing up her things and glanced at the clock on the wall. He'd been so absorbed in his work that he'd hardly noticed the time passing. "Calling it a day?"

"Yeah, I told my dad I would have dinner with him tonight," she answered, zipping up her backpack.

"You and your dad are close, I take it."

"We are," she smiled. "He's my best friend."

Andrew loved that Evie was close to her father. He wished he'd had more time with his own, and he couldn't help but be a little bit jealous of Evie and her dad.

"Can I walk you out?" he heard himself ask without thinking.

What am I doing?

Treading into dangerous waters, Brant.

A genuine and gorgeous smile appeared on her face. "Yeah, I'd like that."

As they headed down the hallway, Andrew wondered about the situation that'd brought her dad to town. He didn't want to push her to talk about it if she didn't want to, but at the same time, he needed to know she was safe.

"How long is your dad in town for," he asked as they reached the lobby of the building.

"I'm not sure. I think he's for sure staying for a couple of days though," she nonchalantly told him.

Evie seemed very calm, considering she was in a situation that warranted her dad's presence in his classroom. Andrew couldn't tell if she didn't think the situation was a big deal or if she was trying to keep him from worrying about her. If it was the latter, he really wished she would let him worry.

"Is he going to be staying nearby?" he asked, prodding just a little further.

"He has an apartment in the same complex as mine."

"He lives here?"

"No, he and my mom have a farm outside Lexington, Kentucky. He got an apartment here, so they could stay close to me if they needed or if their stay in town was prolonged," she answered.

Everything she was telling him seemed logical and normal, but he knew there was a big piece of information she was leaving out. "Is his stay prolonged this time?"

He knew he was beginning to push his luck, but he had to know.

She stopped walking in the middle of the lobby and turned to face him. Those brown eyes of hers were assessing him, and he held his breath, hoping she'd choose to trust him. He really wanted their relationship to grow, but that would never happen, under any circumstance, if she didn't trust him.

After letting out a quick breath, she said, "My ex is stalking me." He stilled, waiting for her to continue. "Not in the "please call me, I can't get over you" kind of way. Not that there is a good way of stalking someone, but my ex, is entirely too possessive and dangerous." She glanced to the front doors of the building. The sun was beginning to make its nightly descent and was casting shadows along the front of the building.

Turning back to him, she admitted, "I want to tell you the full story, but I don't have time right now."

Andrew's blood ran cold at what he was hearing, and it also filled him full of rage. He could feel his jaw clenching and tried to relax. It wouldn't help to get upset. Besides, she wasn't officially his to worry about.

Inconsequential.

"I'm so sorry, Evie. Is your ex in town?"

They started walking again as she told him, "Yes, I found a note on my car this morning. That's why my dad showed up at your office."

Andrew had never felt the amount of rage that was coursing through him before, and he wasn't sure what to do with it. The fact that some guy thought he had a claim to Evie and was threatening her was enough to make him want to hunt the guy down and take him out into the woods behind his house where no one could hear.

Calm down before you do something stupid.

Andrew felt Evie briefly touch his arm. "It's okay." Her voice was gentle, as if she could sense his anger. "This has been going on for years now, so I'm used to it."

"Years?" He nearly choked on the word.

He was beyond shocked and sick to his stomach. There should be no world in which Evie's normal was to be stalked by her ex-boyfriend.

"Yes." Her voice was grave.

They continued walking out of the building. In the

distance, he could see Aiden, waiting by Evie's SUV. He felt a bit of relief at knowing Aiden was currently there. If her ex was around, he didn't want her to be alone more than she had to be, and he had no doubt Aiden possessed the ability to become a person's nightmare and own personal hell.

"Evie, I am so sorry. If you ever need someone, especially if your dad isn't around, please call me. I don't care what time it is. I will come, no matter the time or place."

"Thank you. I will. I promise," she replied. "Thanks for walking me out." Despite the grimness of their conversation, she smiled up at him. Small flecks of gold sparkled in her brown eyes in the afternoon sunlight. "I really appreciate it, Andrew."

Hearing her say his name did something to him. Her voice was the only one he wanted saying it.

"Thank you for trusting me with all of this."

"Always," she said with one last smile as she walked off to meet her father.

Andrew was utterly sick to his stomach.

How could someone want to harm her?

He could fully understand someone not wanting to let her go but not someone trying to keep her against her will. He wished there was something more he could do for her, but for now, he would just be there for her if and when she ever needed him.

EVIE

Evie walked into Andrew's office the next morning only to find it empty. He was normally there before she arrived but was nowhere to be seen. As she approached her chair, she noticed a coffee cup, bar of chocolate, and a note on her table. Picking up the note, she read,

Evie,

I have a meeting this morning, or I would've given you this in person. I took care of everything this morning, so please spend your time sipping coffee, eating chocolate, and reading.

PS: This chocolate bar is safe for consumption.

Yours,

Andrew

She couldn't help but smile as she sat down in her chair. Evie was filled with so much happiness she thought she might burst. No guy had ever treated her this way before.

If this is him when we aren't dating, I wonder what it'd be like if were to actually date.

She tried to imagine it as she picked up the still warm

cup of coffee. Before taking a sip, she inhaled the delightful aroma of the coffee. Not that she would care because she was sincerely grateful, but she was curious as to what kind of liquid filled the cup. As she took a sip, the liquid from a warm, delicious vanilla cappuccino flowed over her tongue. A couple of sips later, she was immensely satisfied. It was the perfect start to the day.

"He is a keeper," she murmured to herself.

She decided to follow his suggestion and pulled out her book. Despite being a required reading, she was enjoying the novel about forbidden love. If a book had a love story, she'd read it. She was a sucker for a good love story and a hopeless romantic in every way, even though her actual love life was a disaster and a little psychotic.

Andrew would make a fantastic book boyfriend.

Evie hadn't realized how tired she was, but after the events of the past couple of days, she should've known. Sleep had barely found her the past two nights, and after becoming warm and cozy thanks to her drink and comfy chair, she managed to drift off to sleep.

A while later, a deep voice beckoned her back to reality. "Evie." A soft whine sounded from her. The low voice tried to sweetly coax her out of her slumber again, but she didn't want to give up the safe confines of her sleep. It'd been several days since she'd had any real sleep and having to give it up so soon seemed unfair.

The voice quietly chuckled at her whine. "Evie." The voice called again. "You have to wake up." She whined a little louder in protest this time.

"I'd love to let you keep sleeping, but I can't. You have class in ten minutes." Andrew's voice was closer this time. She felt the back of his fingers gently brushing up and down her cheek, persuading her to wake.

"Then, I definitely don't want to wake up," she grumbled.

A deep laugh sounded beside her. "I wouldn't want to wake up either if I had Shakespeare, but you didn't hear me tell you that." She rolled her head towards him and cracked her eyes open to find him crouched beside her chair. "Hey, there you are." His voice was soothing to her still sluggish brain.

"Hey," she replied groggily.

"Sleeping was not in my note."

"It's your fault though," she protested.

"How is it my fault?" His face twisted in amusement as he awaited her answer, and Evie thought it was the cutest thing ever.

"You filled me with warm goodness and left me this comfy chair. How was I not to fall asleep?"

He grinned at her, and it made her hope for a day when she might wake up to his face every morning. She didn't allow herself to think that far into the future, because they were still a long way from the semester being over, but she found herself longing for that day.

"Well, I apologize for causing you to fall asleep."

"I forgive you," she retorted. Her reply got a small laugh out of him.

I wonder how often he laughs at school.

As she thought about it, she noticed the hand that'd been on her face was now resting comfortably on her knee. There was an ease between them that couldn't be made or forced. It was rare for her to be so connected and completely at ease with someone. Even if there was no future for them, Evie was glad to have Andrew as a friend.

"Thank you for this," she told him, gesturing to the empty coffee cup and candy wrapper on her table.

"You're welcome. Anytime you want coffee or chocolate or both, just say the word, and I'll make it happen."

"Andrew, you can't go around providing women with coffee and chocolate. You'll make them fall in love with you," she teased.

"Not women. Only you. And if coffee and chocolate is what it takes to make you fall in love with me, then I will bring it to you every day for the rest of my life." Suddenly, all the amusement was gone from his eyes. Evie swallowed hard, heart pounding in her ears.

"I don't know what to say to that," she whispered.

"You don't have to say anything," he whispered back. His eyes flicked towards the open door and back to her. As he stood up from his crouched position, he leaned forward and pressed a soft kiss to her forehead, causing her heart to try to pry itself out of her chest. Everything around her faded into nothing. The only thing she saw was Andrew, and that's when she knew.

I'm in love with this man.

"You better hurry. Class starts in five minutes."

The spell was broken. Back to reality.

"Oh, crap," she exclaimed. She'd have to sprint across the building to make it on time. Snatching up her backpack, she ran out the door to the sound of Andrew's laughter.

The world could be exploding all around her, and she wouldn't even give a care because Dr. Andrew Brant had all but declared his love through coffee, chocolate, and a kiss to the forehead.

What more could a girl want or need?

Ah, bliss! This is bliss!

Evie struggled to focus during her Shakespeare class. It'd been an hour, and she still felt the warmth of Andrew's lips on her forehead. She tried to push down the hope that kept trying to rise to surface, but it seemed like a fool's errand at that point. Andrew had already told her he would wait. Now, he'd kissed her and confessed he wanted her to fall in love with him.

What else is there besides dating?
Are we in a relationship?
Whoa, girl. Slow your roll.

Everything was happening so much faster than she'd anticipated. Most love stories never developed this quickly. It made her nervous but also excited. Maybe, it was okay for things to happen this fast, and perhaps, this was how her story was meant to be written.

Class finally ended, but Evie's mind was too chaotic to return to Andrew's office after class. She needed to clear her mind before anything else could happen. Instead, she decided to go home to change clothes and go for a run. Running usually cleared her mind just enough to let her gain some perspective.

It'd been a long time since she'd enjoyed something as simple as running. Growing up, she'd ran the tree line of her parent's farm almost every morning. Even though it wasn't the same, Evie decided to go to the park to run the trail because it often reminded her of home. She enjoyed living in town, but she missed the quiet of the farm.

Rolling down the windows of her SUV, she turned the music up and headed to the park.

Today is a great day! Sun, music, and running!
What more could I want?
Andrew.

12

EVIE

Pulling into a parking spot, she sent a quick text to Lucy to let her know she was going for a run at the park. Hopping out of the SUV, she put her head-phones on and turned on her favorite running playlist. The songs were a mix of different genres. She tended to listen to a little bit of everything, but the songs were all upbeat. If she ran to slow songs, she tended to lose motivation and would stop her run in favor of something else.

After a quick stretch, Evie set out on the trail at a brisk pace and tried to clear her mind. The music was loud enough to block out her breathing and footsteps. It helped her to focus solely on the trail in front of her. There was nothing but the music in her ears and the nature surrounding her.

About halfway through her run, the trail widened as the creek came into view. Breathing heavily, she slowed her pace to take a quick breather before finishing her run. The creek was one of her favorite spots on the trail. The water was almost always clear and running peacefully over the rocks, and the birds were always welcoming with their songs. This was as close to home as she could get. Taking a deep breath, she tried to relish in her surroundings.

It was normally calm and peaceful, but today, she couldn't help but feel anxious. To be on the safe side, Evie scanned her surroundings for any potential threats. She didn't see anything, and the animals were scurrying about unbothered.

Pulling her headphones off, she took a minute to just listen. The birds were chirping, meaning nothing sinister should be nearby. Everything that'd happened over the past couple of days had her on edge, so it didn't surprise her that she felt anxious, running alone.

However, growing up with a Navy Seal as a father, she'd been taught to trust her instincts and be wary of anything that seemed "off." Everything seemed to be okay, but she still couldn't shake the feeling. Deciding it was best to keep moving, she slipped her headphones back on and took off. The faster she got done, the faster she could go home and relax.

And eat. I am starving.

Using food as her motivator to finish quickly, she pushed herself to go faster. The pace was faster than she'd normally run, but she didn't have much farther to go. As she neared the end of the trail, she began to relax a little as the anxiety subsided a smidge. She had one more bend to clear, and then, she'd be at the parking lot.

It's nothing. I'm being silly.

Almost done, and then, I can go home and eat dinner.

As she rounded the last curve into the straightaway, the world went askew as something hard and solid slammed into her chest, causing her feet to leave the ground and body to fly backwards. Her back hit the rocky trail with a thud, forcing all the breath in her body to vacate.

As she tried to gasp for air, a shadow slowly fell across her. Her eyes widened as she looked up and found the source.

Horror filled every inch her. If she hadn't been gasping for air, she would've screamed.

Standing above her was her ex, Dylan.

No!

Please, no!

Please!

A hand roughly ripped the headphones from her head, eliciting a cry as it ripped some of her hair out.

"I've been waiting for you, Kitten." His sinister voice washed over her. As she attempted to move, a fist collided with her face. Her vision blurred as bright spots flashed in her eyes. A cry of pain worked its way out of her throat. She prayed someone would hear it, but her hopes were quickly shattered as Dylan dropped on top of her, knees on either side of her hips.

His large hand wrapped around her throat, cutting her off mid scream. "That'll teach you to not keep me waiting, Little Genny," Dylan said in a low threatening voice that set off every warning bell within her. "I thought I'd already taught you not to keep me waiting." His face was beginning to fade in and out of view as he kept a firm grip on her throat.

Evie wasn't ready to die.

This can't be how it ends. I can't die like this.

Not here.

Not by him.

Her hands were frantically searching for a grip on the earth to keep her grounded.

To keep her there.

The hand on her throat loosened its grip enough to let a

little slip of air in as the heavy weight on her abdomen left. The relief that began to flood in was quickly replaced with pain as Dylan stomped his steel toed boot on her left hand.

"What have I told you about fighting back?" The pain was enough to make her stomach turn over, but she immediately stilled. "You still have a lot to learn, Kitten." Dylan's voice sounded far away, but she knew he was close because the weight on him settled back on her. His hand tightened around her throat again as he pulled her face up to his.

"I've missed you." His voice was thick with need. Evie's stomach threatened to lose its contents as his lips slammed onto hers. Instincts kicked in, and she began to limply push at him, forgetting to be still. A growl erupted from his throat.

"No fighting," he ground out. There was no warning as his hand slapped her cheek. The only thing that kept her upright was the hand on her throat, which began choking her with a crazed ferocity. The hand didn't relent until everything had faded to black, leaving her in the void.

Everything was quiet and cold.

Is this death?

Pain engulfed her body. A whimper slipped out as she tried to open her eyes. It took a nauseating minute for the world to come into focus.

The stars were twinkling overhead. The only witnesses to the death that awaited her.

A light breeze floated around her as if to usher her to the next life.

Slowly, the stars burned out, one by one.

13
EVIE

Evie awoke with a cry, arms swinging wide. Every instinct she had was on high alert, and the need to protect herself was severely overwhelming. There was so much pain. It threatened to send her back into the darkness.

Through her wild gasps for air and rising panic, she heard her dad's voice. "Shh, baby, you're okay." His arms carefully fought to catch her flailing arms. Calmness began to settle around her at the sound of his voice, and everything started to come into focus.

As things became clearer, her eyes fixated on her dad, sitting in front of her with a worried look on his face.

"You're safe, baby. You're safe," he told her, smoothing her hair down. His hands gently traveled her hair and arms, soothing and most likely, checking for injuries.

A beep filled the air, causing her eyes to dart around the room. She was no longer in the woods but in the hospital.

The memories of the night came rushing back in like freight train, driving all the fight in her away. The tears began to fall as she looked back to her dad, and all she could do was lean forward into his strong arms and sob. His deep voice murmured reassurances as he continued to stroke her hair, waiting for the sobs to subside.

Several long minutes later, the tears finally ran dry. After a couple of deep breaths, she tried to speak, but nothing would come out. Her throat hurt terribly and felt thick. Carefully, she ran a hand along it and wanted to cry all over again at the memory of Dylan's hand on her.

"How?" The question came out hoarse and a near whisper.

"It's okay, baby. Try not to talk," her dad implored her. "When you never came home last night, Lucy called me. I tracked your phone to the park." Aiden's eyes darkened in anger. "Dylan?" His voice was quiet.

Evie nodded.

Her father's fists tightened, and his jaw clenched. "I should've put him down a long time ago." His voice promised retribution.

Tears began to silently creep down Evie's cheeks again. She wished with everything in her that she had never met Dylan. That she could go back in time and stop herself. If not for herself, then for her dad. This was one burden she didn't want him to carry on his shoulders, and she hoped one day he'd forgive her for placing it there.

"None of this is your fault, Buttercup," he told her as he lightly touched her chin, making her look at him. "He is responsible for his actions. No matter what has occurred between you two, none of it warrants any of this." Aiden stood up and leaned down to place a kiss her on the head. "I'm just glad you're okay, Buttercup." His voice was thick with emotion. Last night must've scared him. He wasn't the kind of man to let his emotions slip through. "I'm going to go find the nurse, and we'll get you checked out."

"Wait." He stopped to face her. "Did he?" Her voice felt thick as she tried to ask what she really needed to know. "Did he?" She tried again, but the words kept getting caught. As she took a deep breath, her dad answered.

"No, baby. He didn't." Evie couldn't meet her dad's eyes. She wouldn't be able to bare seeing the pain in them at her question. A small sigh left her as her dad stepped out of the room. She didn't know if she should be thankful that he'd only beat her and not also sexually assaulted her.

It wouldn't have been the first time for either.

I'm okay. I'm breathing. I'm alive.

Lying back, she stared at the ceiling, chanting those three little sentences, praying for the nightmare to end.

Two hours later, her dad had convinced the doctors to let her check out and go home to rest. Thankfully, she only had some heavy bruising and a fractured hand. With a promise to come back if anything worsened, they headed to the truck to go home.

Evie was met with a warm inviting smell as Aiden opened the door to her apartment. "Oh my gosh! EJ," Lucy exclaimed as she came running out of the kitchen. Lucy wrapped her in a hug.

"I am so glad you're okay." The tears began to fall again.

Evie's dad ushered her and Lucy to the couch, and there they sat wrapped in each other's arms, crying. It wasn't the same as having her mom, but Lucy was the next best thing. Evie had thought about asking her dad to tell her mom to come down, but she didn't want to worry her.

Evie didn't know a whole lot about certain aspects of her mom's life, but she knew enough to know it was a burden worthy of lasting a lifetime. Evie wouldn't ask anymore of her, even if her mom begged. She'd already tethered her dad to this life with her; she couldn't do it to her mom.

A little while later, her dad brought both of them a cup of hot chocolate. Evie winced as the warm liquid burned her throat.

"Are you okay?" Lucy asked. Evie simply shook her head no. Everything about what had happened was not okay.

The illusion of being fine had shattered at Dylan's touch.

"I am here for whatever you need," Lucy told her with a squeeze on her arm. "I also made soup if you're hungry."

She loved Lucy's soups. They were always delicious and mending, like a hug in a bowl, but she didn't think she could stomach eating anything. "Thank you. Right now, I need a shower," Evie whispered.

Setting her mug on the coffee table, she headed for her room. As she passed the mirror in the hallway, Evie's feet came to an abrupt halt. She hadn't seen herself since the attack, and now, she wished she hadn't. Her face was bruised on the left side complete with a swollen black eye. Her left arm was also in a cast from where Dylan had fractured her hand. There were little fingerprint shaped bruises on her throat. Nausea crept inside of her at the sight.

Tears welled up in her eyes, but she kept moving to her room. A shower and sleep would go a long way in helping heal things.

After a quick shower, she collapsed on the bed as exhaustion took over and forced her into a deep sleep, but not deep enough to keep the nightmares from finding her.

14
EVIE

Evie woke up the next morning sore all over. She groaned and winced as she tried to roll out of bed. She sat on the edge of the bed, letting the nausea and pain subside before standing. Previous experience told her she'd most likely be lightheaded when she stood.

Walking out of her room, she found her dad sitting on the couch with a bowl of cereal, watching cartoons. "Morning, baby," he said over his shoulder to her. Evie walked up behind him and leaned over the back of the couch, planting a kiss on the back of his head.

"Morning," she croaked out. Her throat still hurt terribly, but at least, her voice wasn't a complete whisper like the night before.

"The swelling in your throat should go down soon," he told her. She nodded to him before heading to the kitchen.

Lucy was waiting for her with a mug of warm green tea. "Good morning," Lucy greeted sympathetically. "Why don't you go crawl back into bed, and I'll bring you some breakfast."

Evie shook her head. "I want normal."

"Normal is completely fine, but you also need rest and healing," Lucy lectured as she followed Evie to her room. "Mr. Aiden, can you talk some sense into her?"

"Do what you need to do, Buttercup."

Evie smirked at Lucy with a wince before shutting her bedroom door.

Normal was all she wanted. Maybe, if things continued on as normal, then it would be like nothing had ever happened. That nothing *was* happening.

That she was just a normal girl with average issues, living a boring life.

Deep down, she knew it wouldn't be possible, but she could try. As least, it would help to not get caught up in the fear. If she sat and rested at home all day, she wouldn't do anything but think about what happened and be scared, and she really didn't want to be scared anymore.

I won't be scared anymore.

No more.

No, she would face the day and keep moving.

That afternoon, Evie and her father were slowly making their way across campus. It felt good to be moving, despite being sore.

"You sure you're up to going to class?"

"Yes," Evie hoarsely whispered. Her dad gave her a skeptical look. She knew she looked horrible, and any sane person would've stayed home, out of sight from the public. However, she was Evie James, and she wouldn't be defeated. "You didn't have to come with me."

Aiden shot her an incredulous look. "Did you really expect me to just send you out into the world after being attacked, especially when I don't know where that little demon is hiding?"

"Fair enough."

"I *will* find him in whatever hole he crawled back into, though." Aiden's voice was filled with deadly venom.

Evie almost felt sorry for Dylan.

Almost.

Her dad could be a very scary man when he wanted to be, and she had no doubt Dylan would regret being born if her dad got his hands on him.

"I know you will."

Although she wanted to be tough and need no one, she was grateful for her dad, and that he was with her now. Even though she wanted normal, she'd been anxious about going back out alone. She was also anxious about seeing Andrew. There was no way to hide what'd happened. Makeup couldn't fix it, but she did put her ballcap on, pulling it really low in an attempt to conceal some of it; however, from the glances she was getting, she didn't think it was doing a good enough job.

Andrew had texted her, asking where she'd been the day before, but she hadn't replied. She didn't want to lie to him but also didn't have the words to explain.

How do you explain being beaten and left in the woods to die to someone?

Awkward.

He'd texted again this morning telling her that he had meetings on and off all morning and to not worry about office hours. Thankfully, it'd given her a few more hours to come to terms with everything and think about what she was going to tell him.

Maybe she'd get lucky, and he wouldn't notice anything was wrong.

Who am I kidding?

She'd been drawing people's stares from the moment she'd stepped foot out of her dad's truck.

Pausing in front of the language arts building, she took a deep breath, closing her eyes and sending up a silent prayer.

"It's going to be okay. I'm right behind you, kiddo." It was as if he could read her mind sometimes. He opened the door for her and waited. After one more deep breath, she stepped through the door.

"Do you want me to sit in the back of the room or in the hall?"

Anxiety was rapidly building. The walls of the hallway seemed to be closing in on her, causing her to feel as if she might pass out. She felt like a baby for even entertaining the idea of asking her dad to sit in the classroom with her but to heck with it. Sometimes, a girl just needed her daddy because some things were just too big to handle alone.

"Room," she whispered.

He put an arm around her shoulder and pulled her close. Kissing her atop the head, he said in a low voice for only her to hear in the crowded hallway, "Wherever you need me, Evie. I'm there. Always." She smiled up at him with tears in her eyes.

Walking into the room, she braced herself for the stares. The closer she got to her seat, the quieter the room became. Several audible gasps could be heard, but she kept her head down. Evie winced as her dad helped her slowly ease into her seat. After she was situated, Aiden gave her shoulder a quick reassuring squeeze and made his way to the back of the room to sit in one of the empty seats.

"What happened to you?" David asked with a mix of concern and shock on his face as he looked her over.

"I don't want to talk about it," Evie replied hoarsely.

"Are you okay?" Lizzie asked gently.

Evie only nodded. She didn't want to talk about anything, which was partly due to her throat still hurting.

Maybe this was a bad idea.

The door at the bottom of the lecture hall opened, and her heart started pounding as she heard Andrew walk into the room. Evie kept her head down and her ballcap as low as possible.

Andrew cleared his throat and brought the class to attention. His voice sounded off, and that's when she realized her arm had been lying on the table. She quickly slid her casted arm off the table and ducked her head lower.

Evie refused to look his way. She knew she'd fall apart if her eyes met his. However, she could feel Andrew's eyes on her throughout the entire class. They never seemed to leave her. Even still, she couldn't bring herself to so much as glance at him.

Coming to class was a bad idea.

How much longer?

She probably should've taken Lucy's advice and stayed home.

What kind of person comes to class after nearly dying?

Evie blew out a breath as class ended.

Finally.

She made it through without anything eventful happening.

Before she could move to get up, her dad was at her side, helping her up from her chair. She was a little embarrassed he was there, being overbearing. She could get herself up. She let out a loud groan as she tried and failed to stand, drawing the attention of everyone in the room. Clearly, her dad was smarter than her because she hadn't thought about what would happen after sitting still for so long. She'd forgotten.

I should've remembered. Dad did, clearly.

Gosh, Evie. Good job blaming him for being overbearing when he's only trying to be helpful.

Guilt was becoming her best friend.

"Crap," she muttered under her breath. Her cheeks heated in embarrassment.

"It's okay," her dad whispered, reassuring her. Aiden slid an arm around her and counted to three. She gritted her teeth has he hauled her out of the chair. "Good?" She nodded. He reached down and picked up her backpack, sliding it onto his shoulder.

"Come on. Your boyfriend looks like he's about to be sick from worry," he whispered in her ear.

Evie made the mistake of looking to Andrew. His face was filled with so much agony it tore her heart. Tears filled her eyes as she quickly looked away, letting her dad slowly steer her out of the room.

ANDREW

Andrew had walked into class excited to see Evie. Truth be told, he had missed her. There was a big difference being in his office with Evie and being in it without her. She made it come to life and filled it full of laughter.

He'd expected to see her smiling face but instead, found her broken and bruised. It'd felt like a punch to the gut when his eyes had landed on her. A visible shiver of rage had run through him when she'd turned her head, allowing him to catch sight of the fingerprints decorating her throat. Someone had tried to kill her, and his best guess was the ex-boyfriend she'd told him about.

It'd been hard to keep his feelings concealed during class, but when she put her arm on the desk, his words had faltered. Everything in him had screamed for him to go to her and offer comfort and protection.

Although he had a lot of negative and hard feelings from seeing her like that, he couldn't help but be proud. Proud of her for surviving. Proud of her for showing up to class, despite being so battered.

Andrew was also grateful for Evie's father, and his willingness to show up for his daughter. He didn't know why Aiden hadn't been able to stop whatever had happened, but he was relieved she had someone to be there for her.

He had hated having to stand by and watch as Aiden helped Evie to stand. His heart had nearly shattered when he'd heard her cry out in pain and struggle to get out of her chair. Breath had been hard to come by as he'd watched her grit her teeth in pain as Aiden pulled her to her feet.

When she'd finally looked at him for the first time since he'd come into class, there was nothing but defeat and terror in her eyes. If he could find her ex, he would slowly rip him apart, starting with the man's hands, and he'd enjoy every last second of it.

Since class had let out, Andrew had been trying to focus on grading some assignments; however, he couldn't get the image of Evie out of his mind. Tears started to fill his eyes, and he was taken aback to find his vision blurred. He didn't consider himself a crier or an emotional person. In fact, he hadn't cried in years.

The last time he remembered crying was when his parents had died. There'd never been anything that he loved enough to cry over since, not even his wife; however, he'd never admit to not crying over his wife, but the sight of Evie was enough to eviscerate him.

Realizing he was never going to get any work done, Andrew packed up his things and headed out for the evening.

Without putting much thought into it, he altered his route home. Ten minutes later, Andrew found himself standing at Evie's apartment door. He debated about whether to knock or just leave. This had to be crossing a line, but after seeing her today, he wasn't sure he cared about the line anymore. With his fist raised to the door, he paused, questioning once again if he should be there, but before he could talk himself out of it, he knocked.

A few seconds later, Aiden swung open the door with a pistol in hand. Andrew merely glanced to the gun and back to Aiden's gaze. Aiden slid the pistol back into his concealed holster on his lower back and stepped aside for Andrew to enter.

"Glock 9mm?" Andrew asked.

Aiden nodded. "What about you?"

"What am I carrying or what do I own?"

Andrew watched as Aiden sized him up. He had no doubt Evie's father probably thought an English professor didn't know anything about guns, let alone owned one. However, Andrew had grown up like most southern Carolina boys and had done his fair share of hunting and target practice. Owning and handling firearms was second nature to him at this point.

Before Aiden could respond, Evie wandered into the room. Andrew watched as she came to a stop when she saw him standing there. "Hey." Her voice was hoarse, but he didn't miss the question in her tone.

"Hi," he replied.

Aiden turned to Evie and said, "I'm going to run over to my apartment and get some things done. I'll check on you a little later."

"You're actually leaving me?" she asked in a slightly mocking tone.

"Yeah, you're in good hands here," Aiden answered. Evie simply raised her eyebrows.

Andrew knew he'd earned Aiden's approval if he was

willing to leave his daughter's wellbeing and safety to him, but Andrew also thought, maybe, it went a little more than that. At least, he hoped it did. He hoped Aiden thought him worthy enough to hold and protect his daughter's heart.

He knew Aiden would be extremely reluctant to trust anyone with her, considering everything Evie's ex had done to her, but he really hoped he could earn the honor.

"Alright, well, you two have fun," Aiden said as he left.

Surprise lit her tone as she said, "Wow, he really likes you."

"What? I'm not likeable," Andrew teased.

"No, you're very likeable, but my dad doesn't like many people, especially not guys who randomly show up to my apartment."

"Yeah, sorry," he replied bashfully. "I didn't mean to show up here unannounced. It was a last-minute decision."

"So why *are* you here?" she asked, walking a little closer to him.

"I had to see you," he told her, voice dropping. His heart was in his throat. His jaw clenched tightly as he took in her bruised face. It was worse up close and grieved him. "Are you okay?"

"I'll heal. I always do," she replied softly, looking away.

"Always do?" His stomach dropped at the thought. "So, this isn't the first time he has hit you?"

Always do?

Always do!

Andrew could feel the anger growing inside of him at the thought of this happening more than once, but he shoved it deep down. Evie didn't need another angry male around her. The last thing he wanted was for her to find comparisons between him and her ex.

She swallowed and nodded her head. He made his way

over to where she was standing by the couch. "I am so sorry, Evie."

Before he could stop himself, he gently reached out a hand and pulled her towards him. She stood stiff in his arms for a moment but gradually relaxed into his embrace, wrapping her arms around him. Peace finally enveloped Andrew as he held her—the peace he'd been spent three months searching for in Wyoming.

They stayed wrapped in each other's arms slowly breathing each other for what seemed like forever.

All too soon, she pulled back and looked up to him. "I am a lot better now that you're here."

"Me too," he told her, placing a kiss on her head.

"Do you want to stay and hang out for a little bit? Lucy is at study group this afternoon and probably won't be back until late or at all. If you ask me, anything that requires that much studying isn't worth it." Her brown eyes regained some of their sparkle as she talked, giving Andrew relief.

"So, I take it you won't be studying for my class?"

"Are you kidding me? There isn't enough time in the world to study everything I'd need to, to be able to pass your class. Why even try?"

He couldn't help but laugh. "What can I do to make up for ruining your life with all of this work?"

"You can make it up to me by helping me make hot cocoa and then, watching a movie with me."

"If I must," Andrew said in a tone that suggested she was forcing him to do something abhorrent. She let out a hoarse laugh and grabbed his hand, dragging him to the kitchen.

It was nice to be out of the school setting and doing normal things together. The thought of school filled him with dread, prompting him to quickly vanish the thought.

Technically, he wasn't breaking any rules, even though he knew how it looked from the outside. However, Andrew new the fragility of life, and Evie's current state served as a flagrant reminder. He refused to give up any more time to what he knew was his.

Forget decorum. Forget it all.

A little while later, they were seated on the couch watching *When Harry Met Sally*.

"I have a theory about this movie," Andrew told Evie.

"Oh, really?" she asked, turning towards him. He smiled at the look on her face. Clearly, she thought whatever he was about to say was going to be preposterous.

"I think Harry and Sally weren't actually meant to be. No one takes that long to decide if they want to be together or if they love someone." She quirked an eyebrow at him, and it was adorably cute. He continued before he could get too distracted by her. "No, I think they both finally gave up on love and decided being married to one another was better than nothing or at least, better than continuing on the dating scene at their age."

She rolled her eyes at him. "Andrew," she drawled.

"Evie," he replied back in a matching tone.

"Love isn't black and white. Sometimes, it doesn't make sense, and sometimes, people are blinded to it. I happen to think the best relationships start out with two people being best friends." She paused and seemed to ponder on something for a moment before fixing her eyes on him. "And, despite all of that, you're just wrong."

"I'm wrong?" he asked incredulously.

"Yes." She was very adamant with her answer. He snorted at her, making her to grin at him.

"It's because I am a guy. Isn't it?"

"Yep," she stated matter-of-factly, turning her attention back to the movie.

"Women know nothing," he sarcastically muttered under his breath.

"I heard that," she said without looking away from the tv.

Andrew watched Evie for a minute. Even broken and bruised, she was lovely. Her long brown hair loosely cascaded down her shoulders, covering the hideous fingerprints on her throat. Even with the bruises on her face, he could still make out all the features that made Evie, Evie. The little dimples that appeared on her face when she smiled were his favorite, and lucky for him, she smiled quite frequently.

Andrew loved being there with her, simply sitting on the couch and watching a movie after a long day at work. The absence of her had contributed to his long day. He'd realized halfway through his day that she made his days a lot brighter and more enjoyable. She didn't know it, but with every look, laugh, and moment, she was healing something inside of him. Something that had broken a long time ago.

He hoped and prayed one day he'd be able to come home to her every day after work, and that they would spend the rest of their lives doing things like sitting on the couch, watching movies. The fact that the possibility of a future with her had almost been taken away, that she had almost been taken from him, made it difficult to breathe. His chest grew tight at the thought.

"Hey," he said to get her attention. His voice came out quiet and somewhat rough from the emotions running through him, causing her head to immediately whirl towards him.

"Come here," he said, holding out his arm. Without hesitation, she scooted over on the couch and into his waiting arm. He adjusted until she was comfortably snuggled up next to him. Only then, did his chest finally begin to relax. Kissing the top of her head, he murmured into her hair, "I'm really glad you're okay."

15
EVIE

Evie was beyond grateful and happy Andrew had found himself at her door. Cuddling on the couch was the best thing to happen to her in days. She felt safe with him and having him close made her fears and anxiety fade into the background. It felt like she could breathe easy when he was around.

As the movie came to an end, her stomach rumbled. It'd been a while since she'd had a proper meal. She leaned her head back and looked up at him, asking, "Are you hungry?"

"I could eat."

"Pizza?"

"Sure. Do you want to go out or order it?"

"I don't really feel like going out," she replied quietly. "Do you mind if we order in?"

"Not at all." His fingers softly stroked her arm, reassuring her.

She hated having to uncurl herself from his side but needed to grab her phone to order the food. "I don't want to move," she admitted. She heard him chuckle and felt his arm tighten around her.

"You can come back. It's your spot."

Evie couldn't remember a time she'd ever been happier than she was right now snuggled up to Andrew Brant.

Who would've thought?

Reluctantly, she moved to get her phone and immediately settled back against him.

E: Can you pick us up a pizza?

"You're texting your dad to get us a pizza? He's going to think I'm not capable of feeding you."

Evie let out a hoarse laugh. "Maybe he won't."

"I'm serious." She quirked an eyebrow up to him. "Well, half serious."

"I texted him because, more than likely, he's already at the Pizzeria. It's where he typically hangs out when he's in town."

"Oh, yeah. You said your dad and Ed are old friends, right?"

She smiled up at him. "You remembered. Yes, they were Navy Seals together."

"So that's why your dad is so intimidating."

"Yeah, he definitely has a "don't mess with me" vibe, doesn't he?" A little laugh escaped her at the thought. "It has always made me feel safe to have him around," she thoughtfully added.

"I can see that. My dad had that effect on me too, but he was almost the opposite of your dad in physical appearance."

Evie didn't know anything about Andrew's parents, but she noticed his use of past tense and noted the sadness tinging his voice. "What was he like?" she asked.

"He was the nicest guy. He would help anyone, and everyone loved him. I once saw him literally give the shirt off his back to someone."

"Really?"

"Mhm. It was rare to see him angry. I don't think he and my mother ever fought, or if they did, it didn't happen around me or my brothers. I do know he loved my mother fiercely and would have done just about anything for her."

"He sounds like a good man."

"He was. I don't think I will ever be able to live up to him or that level of goodness."

Evie wondered if Andrew knew how wonderful he was or if anyone had ever told him. If no one had, she would because he deserved to know.

Placing a hand on his cheek, she looked up at him and said, "You are that good, Andrew and so much more."

He looked deep into her eyes as he told her, "You haven't known me for very long."

Something like regret passed through his eyes, but it was there and gone before she could get a good read on it. Andrew was very good at covering up what he was feeling, but Evie was getting good at reading him.

"No, but time doesn't make a difference. I don't need to have known you for a long time to know you. I know you're a good man with a good heart."

His eyes softened at her words. "Evie." His voice was low and thick with emotion. She let her hand fall from his face to his chest, and his free hand took it. His thumb lightly brushed the back of her hand. "I'm having a hard time not crossing this line."

She knew what line he meant.

It was the line that prohibited them from stepping from friends into something deeper. There was no official rule in the handbook about teachers and students dating; however, the idea of a professor dating a student was severely frowned upon and for good reason. Evie wasn't naïve enough to know why the "rule" existed, but she also knew the reason didn't apply to her or Andrew.

"I know," she whispered.

"For the first time, I don't know what to do. I don't want to jeopardize you or me, but I don't know how much longer I can keep this up," he quietly confessed.

"Me either."

The connection between them had been growing stronger by the day. Neither one of them had acknowledged it, but she knew they could both feel it. She'd often wondered what would happen when they finally reached the breaking point and could no longer deny or ignore it.

There had to be an exception to the "rule" for these unexpected and extraordinary circumstances. They hadn't asked for this or tried to make it happen. The stars had simply aligned and opened a path for them to convene.

Andrew adjusted, allowing them to separate a little and face one another.

"I want you to be honest with me, Evie. What do you want to happen? I know we talked about just being friends and figuring all of this out at the end of the semester, and if you ask me to wait, I will try my best. However, I'm no longer sure if I want to or can wait."

"I know. This thing between us is becoming too much. I've never felt anything like this before. To be honest, I didn't know it existed or was possible." There was a reverence to her voice. She didn't know what kind of connection they had, but she knew it had to be divinely appointed. There was no other way to explain it.

"Me either," he admitted.

"I don't want to have to wait, but I don't want things to become messed up at school. You have your job, and I don't want to jeopardize that. At the same time, it's becoming very difficult to ignore this pull I have to you, and it feels incredibly unfair to deny it."

He gave her long look before taking a breath and saying, "What if we don't deny it anymore? What if we were to go for it but keep school and personal life separate?"

Her heart started beating wildly. Everything faded away. There was only her and Andrew. And the loud drumming in her ears from her heart threatening to explode.

Is he really taking this to the next level? Right here? Right now?

With my bruised face and black eye?

At least I won't need to do cardio for the next five years with the way my heart is beating.

"At school, we are strictly Evie and Dr. Brant. After school, we are just you and me but privately. No matter how much I want to, I won't be able to take you on proper dates or show you off because no one would be able to know. Even though Beaumont is a good size town, it's still small enough that word would get around, and I don't want any rumors started about you. However, the minute I am free to do so, I will gladly show you off all over town. Heck, I'll march into town square and announce it for all to hear."

She couldn't help the smile on her face or the giggle that escaped at his words. "I don't think that'll be necessary, Andrew."

"What do you think?" he asked with a smile that matched hers.

Evie wasn't sure what to say. This was the last thing she'd been expecting today. She certainly never dreamed Andrew would be offering this while she was covered in bruises and hurting. He was offering everything she was longing for, and she desperately wanted to say yes. Her heart was already his, whether he knew it or not.

She could feel his eyes on her as she took her time to fully think things through. While she wanted him more than anything, she knew the dangers of rushing into something without thinking it through.

"There are two things I am confident of: I want this, and I want you. I just don't want things to be ruined before they're given a chance to really begin. Even though I'm only your grad assistant and student for the semester, I still have a year before I graduate. We were talking about pursuing things after the semester, but could we realistically do that before I graduated?"

"After this semester, I will speak to Dr. Hayesworth about us and explain things to her. I don't think she would take issue with us being together as long as we weren't working directly together. We only need to make it through this semester."

Evie nodded her head at his words as she contemplated everything.

"Technically, if we saw each other, it wouldn't be against the rules. We wouldn't be breaking the rules. I wouldn't even ask you to consider this if I thought we didn't have a future together, but I *can* see a future for us. It may be selfish of me, but I want that future to start as soon as possible."

Evie grabbed his hand, looking ardently into his green eyes as she said, "I can see a future for us too. I want to do this. I want us to begin now."

"You're sure?" he asked, searching her eyes for any hint of doubt.

"Yes." This was insanely fast, but it was the first time she'd ever been completely sure of something.

Evie knew what she wanted and what her heart held. She wanted him now and forever.

They were both grinning as Andrew said, "Just to confirm, we are going to see each other privately for the remainder of this semester, and then, we will pursue a more public relationship after."

"Yes. Sounds like we have a deal," Evie smiled broadly. She was so incredibly happy and blown away by the fact that this was even happening. Part of her couldn't believe it.

Is this really happening?

No one pinch me!

I swear I will riot if this is a dream!

"Yes, we do, but we will *not* be shaking on this one," he told her, a mischievous grin lighting his face.

"We won't?"

His faded into a tantalizing smile. "No."

"Oh," she whispered as he leaned in.

His lips met hers, and Evie felt the earth shift.

Mine. This is mine.

Andrew's lips were soft and warm, and they seemed to be molded just for her. The kiss was gentle and sweet until his hand found its way to her hair. Andrew slid his fingers into her hair, grabbing a fistful and tugging on it to tilt her head a little, deepening the kiss. There was a hunger in his kiss that matched hers.

A longing and belonging.

Finally, they parted, breathing heavily. Reluctantly, both opened their eyes and leaned back to find tears glistening in the other's eyes. A slow smile spread across their faces that rapidly turned into laughter.

"I don't know what's wrong with me. I never cry. But you, Evie James, are tearing everything out of me," Andrew admitted breathlessly. He grabbed her face and kissed her hard and fast on the mouth just as a knock sounded at the door.

Wiping at the tears spilling down her cheeks, she said, "That's probably my dad with the pizza."

As she went to stand up, Andrew put a hand on her arm, stopping her. "I'll get it." There was a seriousness now filling his eyes instead of the laughter from before, and she knew why he wanted to get the door instead of her.

The memories of that night flooded back in. Dread and guilt consumed her at the thought of Andrew placing himself between her and a deadly threat.

Andrew opened the door to find her dad with a goofy grin on his face, holding two boxes of pizza with a smaller box perched atop.

Her dad sauntered in, telling them, "Suzanne sends her love, and Ed sends his cannoli." Evie all but leapt off the couch and dived across the coffee table.

"Cannoli," she attempted to shout but immediately regretted it. Her hand shot to her throat. "Ow."

"Well, I see someone is feeling better," Aiden joked as she snatched the small box atop the pizzas. "Hey, hey! You need to eat something nutritious first," her dad said very seriously.

Evie paused and quirked an eyebrow at her dad. "Really? You think pizza is nutritious?"

He glanced at the pizza boxes and back to her. "Well, no, but it's higher up than the cannoli."

"Is it though?" she asked, settling back on the couch with the box of cannoli.

"Fine, do what you want but don't come complaining to me when your cholesterol is out of control," Aiden retorted.

Turning his attention to Andrew, he asked, "Everything good here?"

"Great," Andrew replied with a nod.

"Good," Aiden said, strolling over to Evie and placing a kiss atop her head. "Night, Buttercup. I'll pick you up in the morning for school."

"Dad, you don't have to do that. I'm fine." Immediately, she wanted to take the words back, just to never see that look on her dad's face ever again. It was a mix between horror and despair, chilling her to the bone.

"Two days ago, I picked your unconscious body up out of the woods, so yes, I *will* be escorting you to school." Her dad's face and voice were struggling to retain their usual mask of calm. There was a resolve of steel in his words, hollowing her from the inside out.

She hadn't thought of how everything might have affected her dad, but finding your daughter beaten and half dead in the woods was bound to affect even the strongest of men—and her dad was of the strongest and toughest.

The guilt weighed even heavier than it'd been before. It seemed to be growing rapidly, lately, and she was having a hard time managing the weight of it. If she hadn't made the decision to date Dylan and had listened to her dad in the first place when he'd warned her about him, then none of this would be happening right now. One day, when the dust finally settled, she'd ask for his forgiveness and spend the rest of her life making it up to him.

Setting her box of cannoli down, she stood up and wrapped her arms tightly around her dad. "I'm sorry. Thank you and thank you for always taking care of me."

She felt his hand tenderly caressing the back of her head. "It's not your fault. We all make decisions we have to live with, but he controls his behavior and emotions. It's not on you for how he chooses to behave, and none of what has happened is on you. You survived that night and did everything right."

Evie had replayed that night over in her head many times, and she always wondered if she could have done something differently—just like with every other time before.

Could I have stopped him?

"How do you know that? I could've done a lot more. I sensed something was wrong, but I kept running. I thought I was fine because I could see the end of the trail." She took a breath, trying to keep the tears at bay. "I didn't try that hard to fight back."

"Evie, I know because I was the one that taught you how to survive. Sometimes, not fighting back is the only option for survival. It takes more courage to remain calm and still in the face of a threat than it does to fight back." He softly tapped on the cast on her arm. "This right here proves you're a fighter."

The memory of Dylan stomping on her hand played in her head. He'd only done it because she'd started to fight back.

She nodded silently.

Aiden leaned forward and pressed a kiss to her forehead. "I love you, Evie."

"I love you too, Dad."

As Aiden left, Evie looked up to find Andrew staring at her with absolute devastation on his face. Realization dawned on her. He didn't know what'd occurred that night in the woods, and from the look on his face, she wasn't sure she wanted to tell him. She didn't know if she could bear causing him to live with this burden, like she was causing her dad, but if they were going to have a future together, she couldn't keep this from him.

It was a story she'd have to tell.

ANDREW

Andrew could scarcely breathe as he'd listened to Evie talk to her dad about her attack. Now, she stood across the room, staring at him, and he didn't have any words.

He watched as she took a deep breath and somberly asked, "Do you want to know?"

He knew he needed to know about what had happened that day and to know her full story. If this was going to work between them, he'd have to know, but he wasn't sure his heart was ready. However, if he could ease her burden by helping her carry this, then he would hear everything she had to tell him.

Andrew slowly nodded towards her.

She let out a small sigh before asking, "Okay. Do you want to know everything or just what happened the other day?"

He walked over to her, taking her hands into his. "I want to know you. The good and the bad. I want all of it. I will always listen to anything you wish to tell me."

A small smile appeared on her face, and she motioned to him to sit on the couch.

Once they were comfortable, she began. "Throughout most of my time in undergrad, my dad and I were at odds. He thought I was throwing my life away and would never be able to support myself with a degree in literature. He was really pushing me to get a degree in almost anything else, but there was nothing else I was passionate about." She took a deep breath before continuing. "That one argument snowballed from there. He and I spent most of those years fighting. As graduation approached, things between us grew immensely worse."

Andrew was a bit shocked at what he was hearing. He'd seen her and Aiden together. They were as close to a picture-perfect father daughter duo as one could get.

"My dad retired from the military around my senior year of college and was back home fulltime. It was a big adjustment for us all, and it really put fuel on the fire for me and him. At that point, I became uncaring. I was so angry at his refusal to watch me prove him wrong, so I guess, I decided to prove him right."

She looked away as a tear slid down her face. "So, I turned into his worst nightmare. I began going to local bars in town and drinking until someone would call him to come pick me up because I was too drunk to drive. It would make my dad livid to have to come pick me up."

There was some hesitation as she confessed, "Some nights, I drank so much I could barely walk. However, no matter how many times I walked into a bar, my dad would be there to carry me home." A small smile shown on her face, but it quickly disappeared. "The bar is where I met my ex."

Every muscle in him tensed.

"He was everything my dad hated and had always warned me to stay away from. He had long hair, tattoos all over, and a motorcycle. Go big or go home, right?" She huffed a little laugh. "At first, things were fine. He seemed nice and caring. My dad met him and immediately, told me to stay away from him. I can still remember my dad's face as he told me. His eyes were so full of sadness, and his face looked so broken and empty. It was the first and only time I've ever seen my father defeated."

Silent tears ran down her face. If Andrew knew her like he thought he did, he knew she was still carrying that guilt with her, and he wished he could take it from her. It was clear she had more than enough made up for it.

"Instead of seeing that my dad was just trying to keep me safe, I saw it as me gaining the upper hand." Andrew rubbed his thumb over the back of hand, reassuring her that he was there for her. "A few weeks into dating, if you could even call it that, things took a massive turn. My ex grew impatient and increasingly angry as I put off doing anything sexual with him. I got by with coming up with excuses for a while, but the excuses started to run out quickly. Finally, I was forced to tell him that I didn't want to have sex with him. I had a limit of what I was willing to do, and for whatever reason, that was where I'd chosen to draw the line." Evie took a slow deep breath before she said, "That was the first time he hit me."

Andrew's heart broke at her words. Yes, he was angry, but above all, he was sad. It was sorrow that gripped him the most, but the idea of a guy putting his hands on Evie because she didn't want to sleep with him made him want to put his fist through the brick wall in her apartment. He felt his free hand clench into a tight fist, but he quickly released it. He didn't want to make Evie feel any more uncomfortable than she already was.

"When he finally realized, he wasn't going to get what

he wanted from hitting and belittling me, he decided to just take what he wanted."

Everything stopped as he processed her words. Andrew thought he was going to be sick. He felt his blood run cold and drain from his body all at the same time.

"The first time it happened, I thought maybe I could just give in and give him what he wanted. Maybe it would've been okay, but I couldn't relinquish that side of myself to him. So, he just continued to take whatever he wanted and punish me whenever I showed any sign of hesitation." A lone tear slid down Evie's cheek. "I was able to hide it for a little while, but one day, my dad accidentally walked in on me in the bathroom, while I was trying to examine my very bruised back. That's when I broke down and told him everything. He just held me as I sobbed, and then, he went and unleashed utter hell on my ex."

The tears were streaming down her face, and Andrew could feel the tears in his own eyes, trying to spill over. "I'm sorry" didn't feel adequate in the moment, so he remained silent, holding firm to her hand.

"We thought that was it. Life would go back to normal, but then, the stalking began. It started with little notes, or he'd show up wherever I was. Things began to escalate when I went back to school to finish my last year. He'd show up every so often, finding me unaware. Most of the time, he'd physically hurt me to teach me a "lesson." He wanted me to know I couldn't get away with disrespecting him or keeping away what he considered his." Evie took a shaky breath. "The night I graduated, he found me and gave me what he said was my graduation present." Her eyes were distant as she told him, "That was an especially bad night."

Andrew couldn't stop the tears from spilling over at Evie's words. He quickly wiped them away before she could see them.

"He was so careful in everything that he did that there was no way to catch him. On top of that, it's so hard to get a rape kit tested that it all seemed so hopeless. After that night, I didn't see him for a while. I moved back home, and about a year later, I began hearing rumors that he'd found a new girl. I finally felt like I could breathe easy. I felt bad for his new girl, but at least, he was done with me. Eventually, I started living my life and trying to move on. I applied for grad school and moved here. Life seemed to be going back to normal, and everything was fine for a while. Then, around December, I ran into him in town. I spent so much time hoping and praying that it wouldn't turn into anything, but then, he started popping up here and there. The other night was the first time something has happened since he reappeared."

"What happened the other night?" Andrew asked softly.

Evie let out another breath and smiled at him. "Well, the day started out pretty fantastic."

He remembered that day well. He'd found her in his office, curled up in her chair asleep. His heart had swelled at the sight of her so comfortable and relaxed in his office. He'd hated to wake her but hadn't wanted her to miss her Shakespeare class.

"After class, I decided to go for a run to clear my head, and about halfway through, I started to get this anxious feeling, like something was wrong, but everything seemed okay. I kept checking my surroundings, but nothing seemed off or out of the ordinary. I should've turned around, but I kept going. As I neared the end of my run, something shot out from behind a tree, slamming me to the ground. I remember being so out of breath. No matter how hard I tried, the air just would not come." Her hand slid to her chest before falling back into her lap.

"Before I could move, he was on top me, holding me down. He told me I still had a lot to learn as he punched me in the face." She paused and glanced at him. "I haven't ever told anyone this, not even my dad. He always calls me Little Genny or Kitten. That's what he kept calling me the other night."

Andrew gave her hand another squeeze.

He hated this so much, but he was glad she was trusting him with it. Her free hand slid to her throat, brushing the bruises from her ex's hand. Andrew would like to wrap his own hands around her ex's throat.

"When I began to scream, he put his hand on my throat and squeezed, hard. I thought that was it. That was the moment it would all end for me. That he'd finally come back to finish what he'd started all those years ago." A sigh escaped her lips, sounding like defeat. "The only time he let his grip ease up enough to let me get some air was when he stomped my hand into the ground as punishment for trying to fight back." She gestured to the cast. "If you can call it fighting back. I wanted to, but I had nothing left to give at that point."

Resignation filled her voice. Defeat seemed to encompass her body, but Andrew only saw her as a fighter. Her endurance was admirable and unyielding. Above it all, he was impressed by her and so proud.

So that's what Aiden meant by her cast being proof of her fighting back.

My beautiful strong warrior.

"After that, he squeezed harder, and the world simply faded away. I woke up in the hospital."

Sadness gripped him. He couldn't begin to fathom the amount of hurt and suffering Evie was enduring. Anger and melancholy blended within him, making his chest tight.

How could anyone ever harm you?

Andrew tenderly placed his palm on the side of her face. "Evie, I am *so* sorry. I really don't know what to say. You are so much stronger than I ever imagined. Brave. Beautiful." He looked into her eyes, hoping he was conveying all the love he had for her. "Thank you for telling me everything. I hope you know you can trust me in every way. If there is anything I can do to make things easier for you, let me know. If I ever do something you don't like or are not comfortable with, please tell me."

"I do, and I will." After wiping the tears away, she gave him that gorgeous smile of hers, showing her dimples. "You have been the biggest and most unexpected blessing in my life."

Leaning in, he pressed her a soft kiss to her cheek. "The next time something happens, or you see him, call me. I know your dad is here and can put the fear of God into the devil himself, but I'm here for you too. Your safety and protection are top on my list of priorities. I know this thing between us is still somewhat new, but you are already very important to me."

"You're important to me too, Andrew, which is why I never want to put you in harm's way, even for me."

"I will gladly and without hesitation put myself into harm's way for you. You are worth more to me than I could even begin to describe to you, Evie." He said it so softly he didn't think she could hear him. The tears began to spill down her cheeks again, and he wiped them away as they fell.

Pulling her close, together they laid in silence, resting in the nearness of one another.

Please, let me be able to keep her safe.

Please, let me be enough.

16
EVIE

Evie felt as though a weight had been lifted from shoulders. She'd been nervous to tell Andrew everything, but she'd been able to tell him everything without holding back. She was also relieved he hadn't run out of the apartment, thinking her a crazy person. She knew her story and circumstances were a lot to hear and comprehend. It was a lot for her, and she was the one living it. Part of her wouldn't blame Andrew if he decided he couldn't handle the truth or didn't want to involve himself in an ongoing situation.

Though, right now, her heart felt full as she snuggled close to him, and nothing would top this moment for her.

His hand absentmindedly stroked her arm as they sat in silence, processing everything that'd been said.

"Are you okay?" she finally asked, cracking the silence.

"Yes."

Evie hesitated before nervously asking, "Are we okay?"

Andrew looked down at her with serious but loving eyes. "We are perfect."

Relief swamped her. Acceptance was all anybody

wanted in life, and for him to accept her and her baggage, meant everything and more to her.

As he pulled her closer, she let out a contented sigh. From the moment she'd laid eyes on him, she'd longed to be in his arms, and the feeling of being in them was more than she could've ever expected. Peace and security seemed to seep from the arms encircling her.

After a time, he murmured, "It's getting late." Andrew started to move, causing Evie to let out a soft whine and clutch onto him harder. A low chuckle sounded from him at her response. "I know, I know. I wish I could stay, but I have to go."

"Fine," she reluctantly conceded.

"I'll see you in like eight hours," he laughed.

She was disinclined to let him go, but she appreciated him respecting her unspoken boundaries. Evie slowly peeled herself away from Andrew and sat up, allowing him to do the same.

He leaned forward and placed a kiss her on the head before getting up and heading to the door. "I'll see you in the morning. Lock the door behind me." A smile filled his face as he shut the door, and if she hadn't been sitting, she would've fallen. As cheesy as it was, that smile of his always made her weak at the knees.

After locking the door and turning the lights off, Evie snatched up her uneaten cannoli and headed to her room. Even though the day had been wearisome, it'd also been completely wonderful.

Turning on a movie, she laid back on her bed and munched on her cannoli. From her first bite of Ed's famous cannoli to now, it'd been her favorite dessert. Cannoli were the perfect mix of creamy and crunchy.

This is pure bliss. Actual bliss.

Her phone dinged, sounding through her blissful thoughts of cannoli and Matthew McConaughey on her tv.

A: Can't wait to see you in the morning

E: Me too

A: Goodnight Evie

E: Goodnight Andrew

Evie was happier than she'd ever been in her life. She never wanted this blissful feeling to end, but all good things must come to an end. They always came to an end.

Not this time. This time it'll be different.

However, the doubt tingled in the far corner of her mind, whispering its truth. That was the thing about doubt. Sometimes, it would lie, but every now and again, it would speak truth.

17
EVIE

Evie woke up a little stiff the next morning but felt a lot better than the day before. Even though she was improving, the bruises still looked nasty, bringing memories of that night to the surface. Shoving them away, she took her time getting dressed, opting for her usual leggings and t-shirt.

She couldn't wait for the cast to be removed. It was more of nuisance than anything. There was no fixing her bruised face, so she skipped the makeup.

There was a knock at the door as she struggled to finish lacing up her sneakers. "Who is it?" she called through the door.

"Dad." She quickly unlocked the door and let him in. "Morning, Buttercup," he said brightly. There were two coffees in his hand.

"Morning, I hope one of those is for me," she responded with less enthusiasm, gathering her things.

"Bad night?" he asked, handing her one of the cups.

She took a sip before responding. "No, just a long one."

"Really?" he asked with raised eyebrows. It was the look

he used to give her right before she got into trouble for something. She rarely saw the look these days, but whenever he gave it, it always made her feel like a little girl again.

"Dad. It's definitely not what you're thinking. Just hard to sleep when you're all bruised and broken." She gestured to her arm and face. She could've sworn relief rippled over his face, causing her guilt to reappear.

"Oh. Okay, then. Well, how did things go with Dr. Boss Man?"

"Good," she evasively said.

"Mhm." His nonchalance caused her to glance up, finding him with an amused look on his face.

"Fine. It went very well. We have decided to start seeing each other privately."

"Privately?"

"For now, yes."

"Well, I like him. I'm not sure about the private part, but I like Andrew. He seems like a good man." Aiden grabbed her backpack from her and slung it over his shoulder.

She paused taken aback by her dad's reply. "Wow. I wasn't expecting that."

"What do you mean?"

"You don't like anybody," she said, walking past him and out the door.

"That's not true," he called after her, shutting the door. "I like a lot of people."

So not true.

Evie's dad insisted on walking her across campus, so she insisted he buy her another coffee.

"I can't help that the coffee you brought me was subpar!"

"Hey, I made that coffee with that fancy espresso

machine you told me I just had to get." Aiden mimicked Evie's voice, making it really difficult for her to conceal the grin forming on her face. She'd take these nonsensical arguments over the ugly ones they used to have.

Evie managed to keep a straight face and shrugged. "Should've read the instructions."

"I speak three different languages and served in the Seals, and nothing could have helped me understand those instructions, which only proves my point. My trusty old, one pot coffee maker is better than any of these new fancy machines."

Rolling her eyes, she told him, "This sounds like a "you" problem."

Aiden's eyes bugged out of his head at her. "Me?"

"Mhm," she responded, gesturing for him to open the door.

"Here you go, Princess." He held the door for her as she walked into the coffee shop on campus. "We will concede this argument for the moment. Vanilla cappuccino?"

"You know me so well," she replied, smiling.

"Well, you *are* my favorite daughter."

"I'm your only daughter," she laughed.

Her dad's phone started ringing, interrupting the moment. Reaching into his back pocket, he pulled it out and handed it to her without looking at it. Her mom's name was flashing on the screen, and she couldn't help but wonder how he knew it was her mom.

Wandering over to an open table by the window, she sat down, answering the call. It'd been a while since she'd chatted with her mom, so this call was very overdue.

"Hi, Mom," she answered with an almost squeal. Even though her dad was her favorite person, it didn't take away from her relationship with her mom. She absolutely adored her mom and missed her incredibly much. For most of her life, it'd just been her and her mom because of her dad's military career.

Knowing her mom as she did, she knew she'd probably waited as long as she could before calling, which was longer than Evie had expected. Usually, her dad was able to keep her mom from worrying about her too much. The one good thing about living so far away was the ability to downplay situations.

"Hi, Sweetie. How are you? Are you okay?" Evie could tell her mom was trying to remain calm, but she could hear the definite worry laced in her tone.

"I'm fine. Dad and I are getting coffee right now before I head to class," she told her, trying to keep things casual.

"You know that's not what I meant, Evie."

Evie could almost see her mom standing in the kitchen with her hands on her hips, giving her a look. She couldn't help the smile that formed on her lips. She really missed her mom and would give anything to be home, baking in the kitchen with her while they listened to music. That was something they'd done a lot over the years, especially when her dad was overseas. Since he'd retired, he would sometimes join them on baking days, which always resulted in the kitchen turning into a gigantic mess. One thing her mom could not stand was a messy kitchen, but she seemed to give Aiden a free pass.

"I promise I'm fine. It's not a big deal."

A lie.

"Don't downplay it for my sake, Evie. I know it's a big deal, and I'm really sorry this happened to you again. If you need me to come down, I can. Your dad snuck out of here, again, and left me here."

Aiden never wanted Elaine to worry about anything

and did his best to keep her out of the hard details of the evil that occurred, but Evie often wondered if it just made her worry more. Her mom had been through her fair share of traumatic events and could relate to Evie in a lot of ways, which was why Evie and Aiden had an unspoken agreement to leave Elaine out of the heavier details.

She felt the guilt weighing on her again. She'd started all of this and was the reason her dad was trying to protect his wife from carrying the burden of seeing her child broken and hurting.

I'm the gift that keeps on giving.

"No, no. It's fine, mom. I promise I'm fine. I'll call you later and tell you about the guy I met." Evie couldn't help the smile that danced on her lips at the thought of Andrew.

"A guy?" Her mom practically screamed with excitement, forcing Evie to pull the phone from her hear. "What's he like? What's his name? Is he handsome? How old is he? Give me grandkids."

"Mom!" A nervous laugh escaped Evie.

She needs to slow down. Things are going fast enough.

"Okay, okay, but I expect a full report. Call me tonight and tell me everything!" The joy in her mom's voice was comforting to Evie.

"I will. I promise."

Her dad walked over with their drinks, snatching the phone out of hand. "She's fine, Ellie. Stop stressing. I've got her."

She knew her mom spent most of her time worrying about her. If Evie was completely honest, she had more guilt about her mom than anyone else. It'd never once crossed her mind how her mom might be affected throughout her downward spiral, aimed at her dad. She loved her mom fiercely, and Evie hated herself for causing her mom a moment of unnecessary distress.

Evie smiled as she heard her dad say, "I miss you too. I'll be home as soon as our girl is safe. Love you."

Aiden hung up the phone and told her, "She's worried about you."

"I know," she said somberly. "I hate that I caused all of this. If I hadn't started down that path of retribution, then none of this would've happened."

"If it wasn't this, it would be something else. That's just how life works, Buttercup" She nodded at him. A smirk formed on her dad's face as something behind her caught his attention. "Dr. Boss Man is staring hard."

"What?" she asked in confusion.

Aiden motioned with his head. "He's sitting over there in the corner with some people, and he can't quit looking this way." Aiden turned his gaze on her. "What exactly happened last night? Poor guy looks completely smitten."

"Dad, stop." Evie watched in absolute horror as her dad gave Andrew a cutesy little wave. "Dad!" Mortified, she slumped low in her chair.

"What? I need to get to know this fella of yours."

"Keep your voice down and stop embarrassing me," she hissed at him. Her dad smirked again, thoroughly enjoying messing with her. "That's it. I'm leaving," she said, hopping up and grabbing her drink.

"Evie, come on," he pleaded. Although, his tone was nothing but pure amusement as he teasingly objected to her leaving. He was clearly enjoying himself a little too much.

Evie jumped up and hastily left the coffee shop without looking in Andrew's direction and paying absolutely no mind to her dad's fake pleas. Footsteps grew quickly behind her and knew her dad was roughly two steps behind her. She waited a beat before making her move. Quickly, she spun around and aimed her fist straight for her dad's right shoulder.

"Whoa," he laughed as he dodged her hand. "Still not fast enough for your old man." A smug look settled on his face as he threw an arm around her shoulders and kissed her on the head.

She just shook her head and smiled up at him. "Maybe one day."

"Buttercup, the day you get the drop on me is the day I'm dead."

Her laughter filled the air as they made their way through the campus square.

Since Andrew wasn't in his office yet, Evie and Aiden took advantage of the beautiful morning, sitting on a bench under a shady tree across from the building. They were chatting about nothing in particular when Andrew came strolling up.

"Good morning." His deep rich voice washed over her, causing goosebumps to pebble her skin.

How does he have this kind of effect on me?

Should I be worried?

Andrew held out a hand to Evie's dad. Standing, Aiden accepted it, giving it a firm shake. As she watched them shake hands, she realized the situation was weird for her. As far as memory served, her dad had never liked any guy in her life. That included her guy friends, but for some reason, Aiden seemed to really like Andrew. He also trusted him, which was mind blowing. Her dad had always been a good judge of character, but the statistics just weren't there for every man in her life to have been evil. And, for whatever reason, Aiden seemed to have no misgivings about Andrew.

I don't know whether I should be happy or not.

Cautiously optimistic, maybe?

Standing up, she cleared her throat and said, "Gentlemen, I hate to break up this love fest, but Dr. Boss Man here is about to be very late for work." They both checked their watches at the same time, and Evie was very taken aback. Maybe it was true what people said about girls choosing men like their fathers.

She could do a lot worse. In fact, she *had* done *a lot* worse. A shiver ran through her at the thought.

"I'll see you later, Buttercup," her dad told her with a kiss to her head. "Keep an eye on her for me, Dr. Boss Man?"

"Sure thing," Andrew replied.

Satisfied, Aiden took off to his truck, pulling out his phone to most likely call her mom back. Those two were mostly inseparable. Evie really hoped her future marriage would turn out like theirs. From what she knew, they'd had to fight to get to a good place, but now, they were best friends, enjoying life and each other.

Evie's heart sped up as Andrew turned to smile at her. "How are you this morning?"

"Good, you?"

"Good."

"Great." They both stood there, staring at one another absorbed with the other.

"I wish we weren't at school right now," he said softly.

"Oh? And why is that?"

"Because I really want to kiss you right now," he told her as his eyes dropped to her lips. She ran her tongue over them before biting her bottom lip. He let out a low growl for only her to hear. "You're going to be my undoing, Evie James."

"Good," she replied with a smirk as she walked off

towards the building, leaving him behind. A small giggle escaped her she heard him let out a rough breath and follow her.

Dating is so much fun.

Evie had been working for a couple of hours at her table in Andrew's office when a knock sounded at the door. Looking up, she found David standing at the door. "Do you need something, David?" Andrew asked.

Evie was mildly taken aback by Andrew's bored and dismissive tone.

"I actually came to see Evie," he replied. David turned his attention to her. "Can I talk to you for a second?"

"Yeah," she answered, getting up and following him out of the office. "What's up?"

"I wanted to see how you were doing." The concern was plainly written on his face.

She gave his arm a reassuring but mostly awkward pat. "David, I'm fine. I promise."

"I mean this in the nicest way possible, Evie, but you don't look fine."

"It looks worse than it is."

"Evie, clearly something bad happened." There was no mistaking the wince as he took in her black eye. Frustration was beginning to build up inside of her. While she appreciated the care and concern, it wasn't his position to pry.

"Yes, something bad did happen, but I don't really want to talk about it," she told him, trying to keep her reply gracious. David was a friend and meant well, but her story was one he'd never get to hear.

"You should talk to someone though."

"I have. Don't worry. I'm fine. Everything is under control."

"Well, if, you're sure." He gave her a studied look, which she didn't fully appreciate but decided to let it drop.

"I'm sure," she replied with a smile, hoping he would take her smile as a good sign. His shoulders relaxed just a bit.

Why can't people just take me at my word and stay out of things?

It was hard when people meant well, but it was even harder when they couldn't take no for an answer.

How many times will I say, "no" before someone hears it?

"Since you say everything is under control, do you think you'd like to go to dinner with me Friday night?" David looked at her with an expression that resembled a shy little kid. It was the first time she'd ever seen him look unsure. Usually, he was the picture of confidence, especially when talking to girls.

Evie blanked. Her mind went absolutely blank of everything. That uncomfortable and awkward feeling she hated washed over her.

Is he asking me out?

"Like on a date?" The question came out as a sputter, which only made her feel more awkward.

"Yeah, if you want to."

"I'm really flattered, David, but I sort of just started seeing someone."

"Oh." The disappointment was on his face, and she wished there was something she could do about it. However, she couldn't feel too bad since the reason she couldn't go was Andrew.

"But I really appreciate you asking." She felt a little bad about having to turn him down. David was a great guy, and once upon a time, she might've said yes.

"Yeah, no problem, Evie," he said with that charming

smile of his that showed off his perfectly straight white teeth. "See you in class tomorrow?"

"You bet." David gave her an awkward wave as he walked away. She watched as he walked down the hallway, thinking about how different life could've turned out if David had been a day sooner.

Timing plays such a massive roll in life.

Evie returned to Andrew's office and felt his eyes trailing her all the way to her desk. As she sat down, he swiveled in his chair to look at her, but she ignored his pointed stare. After she didn't say anything, Andrew finally asked, "So, what did David want?"

Evie shrugged. Keeping her voice as nonchalant as possible, she answered, "Just to check on me."

She couldn't quite meet his eye and knew he was picking up on it. Evie sunk a little lower in her chair and tried to hide behind her computer.

"Just to check on you?" He mused and was quiet again.

"Mhm," she murmured from behind her computer. The sound of Andrew's chair rolling closer to her filled the silence. A second later, her laptop slowly began to close, ridding her of her hiding spot.

"And?"

"And what?" she inquired innocently.

"He asked you out, didn't he?" His tone was slightly teasing.

"I believe he may have inquired if I happened to be free for dinner on Friday night." Evie's eyes circled the room before landing on Andrew.

"And what did you say?"

"I said I'd have to check my schedule," she quipped.

"I happen to know for a fact that you are busy Friday night."

"Am I?" She straightened up in her seat excited about having Friday night plans with Andrew.

"You are."

"Then, I guess I'll have to cancel with David. He'll probably be heartbroken."

"I think he'll be okay. I'll make sure he has plenty of homework to keep his mind off of it."

She snapped to complete attention at that. "Is that why I'm going to busy Friday night? Homework?" The disappointment and disbelief were evident in her voice, which only caused Andrew to laugh.

"Guess you'll have to wait and see." With a wink, he rolled back to his desk and got to work, leaving Evie with her mouth slightly agape.

He's messing with me.

Right?

18

ANDREW

The next day, Andrew walked into class to find Evie and David in a lively conversation. He felt a twinge of jealousy at the sight of them, even though he was sure of Evie's feelings for him. If he was being honest, he was mostly jealous of David being able to talk so freely and publicly with her. There was nothing he wanted more than to talk and laugh with her out in the open for everyone to see—for everyone to know she was his.

Even still, he wasn't a huge fan of David, crushing all over his woman, but there was only so much one could do about that.

Andrew set up for class and heard Evie's laugh fill the lecture hall. It warmed his heart to hear her laughing, especially after the last class; however, Aiden's presence didn't go unnoticed and only served as a reminder of the reality of Evie's situation. Although, he was pretty sure Aiden wasn't only sitting in the back of his class for Evie's sake. In some ways, it felt like an audition because Andrew knew Aiden didn't attend Evie's other classes. Andrew met Aiden's eyes, giving him a small nod.

Maybe, he only attends my classes because I don't have the nerve to kick him out.

Does anyone, though?

Wait, is he waiting on me to kick him out? Should I try?

Andrew looked to where Aiden was sitting in the back of the room, scrolling on his phone. His eyes popped up, boring a hole straight through him. Andrew tried to not flinch under his domineering gaze.

Nope. Definitely, not.

He can stay.

The man was scary, and Andrew had no issue admitting that. Evie had mentioned that her dad trusted him, and it was an honor that someone like Aiden James would trust him with his daughter's wellbeing.

His phone vibrated on the table next to his computer drawing his thoughts back to the present.

E: Hey, Hey

Andrew looked up to see Evie glance his way. It felt like his heart skipped a beat as their eyes met. It meant everything to him that she had taken time to text him while laughing and talking with her friends.

I must be on her mind as she is mine.

A: Hey yourself

He looked up just in time to see Evie smile at her phone. She kept talking to David and Lizzie as she texted.

E: Miss you

A: I just saw you like 20 mins ago

E: Your point being?

A: I miss you too

E: Good

E: You're going to be awesome today! You always are!

He'd never been a fan of being in front of people, but the years of teaching had helped to remove some of his apprehensions about being the focus of people's attention; however, it was nice to have someone's support and reassurances.

A: Nice to know I have a fan club

E: I'll be sure to bring signs next class

Looking up, he found her watching him and gave her a quick smile. Andrew started class with a renewing sense of calm and joy, knowing he did in fact have a fan. As long as Evie was with him, there would always be a smiling face, cheering him on.

Andrew gave out the next assignment to be completed over the weekend, and he felt, more than heard, the entire class groan their disapproval. He could definitely feel Evie's searing glare. He didn't dare look at her for fear of laughing if he saw those dark eyes of hers narrow at him in their best attempt to scare him with their fury.

Grinning to himself, he heard someone whisper, "He finds all of this funny."

Whoops.

The last thing he needed was students thinking he was celebrating in their misery.

After class, he heard several comments about him that were not pleasant. A couple of those came from Evie's friends, and for the first time, he felt bad that he didn't have a better reputation for her. When their relationship inevitably came out, she'd be known as the one dating the most hated professor. Being a man of few words would normally be acceptable but pair that with being a "demanding" professor, you become the most misunderstood professor. That was also the result of having arm length relationships with students. While that was the nature of the job, it did possess the ability to create animosity between student and teacher.

However, he couldn't question his teaching methods. He knew without a doubt they worked. The methods may be difficult, but they were crafted with the intention of bettering students. He knew it worked because he could always see a vast improvement in most students by the end of the semester. No, he would never compromise his students just to make himself more likeable.

E: Still your number one fan

Andrew was sitting at his desk quietly working when Evie sauntered in about an hour later. "How are you doing?"

"Me? I'm fine," he replied casually.

Dropping into her chair, she said, "Then why do you look like someone stole your special edition whittling tool?"

He gave her an incredulous look.

"Fine, your fishing pole that was given to you by old fisherman, Rick?"

A slight smile cracked at the corner of his mouth. "You're nuts."

"Thank you, so what's wrong?"

He watched Evie's eyebrows wrinkle with concern. He didn't want her worrying about him when she had so much going on in her life. "It's nothing," he replied, keeping his tone light and casual.

To his surprise, she only replied with, "Okay." He heard her digging through her backpack and knew she was looking for a book, which meant she was just there to keep him company. A fresh wave of guilt washed over him, but his heart simultaneously warmed at the idea of her just wanting to keep him company.

"You don't have to stay," he said quietly without looking at her.

"I know, but I want to." He heard her slowly get up and walk over to him. She touched his shoulder just long enough to let him know she was there. "What's wrong?" she asked him again, as she leaned against his desk, waiting.

Blowing out a breath and keeping his voice low so no one passing his open office door could hear, he said, "I just hate that you're with the professor everyone hates. When we eventually reveal to everyone that we are together, what is that going to say about you? That you don't have very good taste in men?" He winced as he realized what he'd just said to her. "I'm so sorry, Evie. I didn't mean that the way it sounded."

"I know." Her voice was so full of understanding and compassion. His chest felt tight from the onslaught of guilt and regret—regret for not only the comment but also, for not being enough for her.

I don't deserve her.

"I know what you meant. My only answer is that people who know me will know that I saw something beyond the exterior they see. That I looked inward and chose your heart, who you are at the core and not the man made up by rumors."

He looked up at her and saw the truth in her eyes.

She'd really chosen him. All of him. The him no one else could see. The one hidden beneath loss and insecurities.

Evie was the only one to see past the ugly façade that'd been painted on him.

After a moment, she said, "So, you really weren't

kidding about me being busy this weekend." He looked up to see a humorous look on her face.

"When I told you that earlier, I didn't mean the homework."

"Oh, really?" Her eyes lit with excitement, and his breath caught at the sight of it. To him, Evie was pure radiance.

So exquisite.

"Yes, really. I was planning on you being all mine Friday night," he said, grinning up to her.

"I'm sorry to tell you, Dr. Brant, but I am very busy this weekend due to a certain professor giving out way too much homework." She narrowed her eyes at him.

"If it helps Miss James, you are welcome to bring your homework along. I don't care what you do as long as you're doing it with me." He watched her as she contemplated his offer.

"Deal," she replied, extending her hand to him.

"Deal." His heart started to race as he held her hand. Clearing his throat, he said, "I've got some work to do."

"Anything you need me to do?" she asked, reluctantly slipping her hand from his. He savored every second of her soft touch before it vanished.

"Not today. You are free to hang out or do whatever."

He watched her flop down in her chair and open her book. Andrew couldn't help but smile at the sight of her comfortably reading in her chair. That moment in his office was small in the grand scheme of things, but the moment was perfect. If they never did anything else but exist comfortably in the same space, he'd be perfectly content.

19
ANDREW

Friday arrived a lot faster than Andrew had anticipated. He couldn't wait to have Evie all to himself. She was currently sitting in his office, grading papers, looking beautiful in her jeans and oversized cardigan. One thing he'd learned about Evie was she was almost always cold. It was rare for him to see her without a cardigan or jacket of some sort.

"Are you almost done?" he asked.

"Yeah, I'm finishing up the last one," she answered without looking up.

"Good." Andrew saw her look up and smile at him. He felt his heart flutter at the sight of it. He wondered if the effect she had on him would ever wear off but really hoped it wouldn't.

"So, what are we doing tonight?" Excitement lit her voice.

He shrugged at her. "I figured we would figure it out later." He lied. Zack was currently at his house setting everything up and getting the fire pit going.

"Okay, I'm fine with whatever," she absentmindedly replied, continuing to work.

"When you finish that, you can head home, and I will come pick you up."

"Sounds good," she said, giving him another one of those beautiful smiles.

If he was being honest, her smiles made his world go around. If Evie was happy, then everything was right, and her happiness was all he wanted for her.

Thirty minutes later, they were in his truck heading to his house. Pulling into the driveway, he heard Evie let out a small gasp. He looked over to find her gaping out the window at the mountainous landscape.

"This place is gorgeous." She was practically speechless as she stared out the window of his truck. It wasn't completely dark yet, so the mountains behind the house were still visible along with the small lake in front of his house. As he rounded the bend that opened to the house, Evie let out a squeal. "Andrew, your house is so cute, and not at all what I thought you'd live in."

A deep chuckle sounded from him. "Thank you. I think."

"It looks so cozy and like I need a cup of cocoa and a blanket."

"Nice description, and that can be arranged."

He looked over his small cottage home, trying to see it from Evie's perspective. It truly was the perfect little house tucked away at the base of the mountains, away from everything and everyone. Pulling into the parking spot in front of the little workshop, he turned the truck off and got out, walking around to open the door for her.

"It's so peaceful here. I don't know how you ever leave," Evie said in a reverent awe.

Pride filled him at her words. "I'm glad you like it."

Maybe, you can live here someday, too.

Whoa. Slow down, Brant.

Andrew led Evie down the little path to the back of the house to the stone patio that he'd designed last summer. The fire pit was lit, and the string lights above the patio were twinkling in the night sky. Zack had even gone ahead and set up the small pizza oven and all the necessary ingredients.

"What do you think?" he asked, stopping at the edge of the patio.

"It's perfect," she beamed up at him.

"So, I know you do this as a job, but I thought we could make our own pizzas tonight," he told her, leading her to the small pizza oven.

"Wait a minute. I thought you didn't have anything planned for tonight," she said, eyeing him suspiciously.

"I wanted it to be a surprise," he admitted a little shyly.

He didn't know how long it'd been since Evie had been treated properly on a date, and the thought made him angry. He wanted tonight to be a fun and romantic surprise for her.

Eventually, he'd give her the world, but for tonight, he'd give her the quiet of his home.

Evie's dimples were showing as she smiled up at him, causing his chest to tighten. "It's a good surprise."

"Good." Leaning down, he pressed a quick kiss to her cheek. "Start looking through the pizza ingredients, and I'll turn on some music."

The previous owners had installed an outdoor sound system, which Andrew thought he'd never use, but tonight was the perfect excuse. Two minutes later, 70's country music echoed softly throughout the backyard.

Andrew found Evie sipping a drink, waiting on him to return.

"I thought Zack would forget to stock the cooler, but I am left impressed," he said, grabbing a soda from the cooler.

"So, I'm thinking we should make this a competition. Your pizza against mine," Evie challenged.

"You think you can beat me?" He narrowed his eyes, sizing up his competition.

"I'm surprised you think I can't. You've seen my pizza making skills in action," she retorted.

"Wow, Miss James. That is rather haughty statement, is it not?"

"One, I know I have a special skill set, so no, it's not haughty."

"If you say so. What's the second thing?"

She stepped closer to him until they were almost touching and tilted her head back to look up at him. "Two, you're not allowed to call me Miss James when we are off campus."

"I'm not?"

"No, you're not. You can call me anything else but no formalities when it's just me and you."

Andrew was completely smitten with Evie. She was the most beautiful thing he'd ever beheld, standing there in the twinkling lights with those brown eyes looking up at him.

His eyes slid to her lips. They looked so soft and inviting.

"Deal," he whispered as he lowered his head to give her a slow sweet kiss.

Her lips conformed to his perfectly, and Andrew knew she'd been made just for him.

The faintest taste of soda was on her tongue as it

skimmed across his, and it left Andrew thirsty for more. Before he could get himself in trouble though, he withdrew.

"Alright, sweetheart, time for me to show you how to make a good pizza."

Her eyes sparkled as she said, "Whatever you say, love."

Something clenched in his stomach at hearing her call him, love. Andrew didn't think anyone would ever call him an endearing nickname again, but it'd been rare for Lily to call him anything other than Andrew. The relationship he had with Evie was moving so much faster than he'd anticipated, and it made him nervous. It seemed almost too good to be true. Life shouldn't be that good, that fast, and it left the possibility of it all imploding on him.

But, for now, he wouldn't think about that. He would focus on her. He would make pizza and spend time enjoying the woman he was falling madly in love with.

EVIE

"So, what's it going to be? Pineapple?" Evie asked Andrew as she added cheese to her pizza."Never, sweetheart. That's all you." He looked over, giving her a grin that made her knees weak. "I'm going with the tried-and-true pepperoni."

"How did I know?" She threw a smirk in his direction.

"Let me guess. You're going with the spicy sausage and pineapple." Andrew gave her an assessing look that dared her to contradict him.

Evie's eyes widened. "How did you know?" Shock filled her tone. Andrew finished placing pepperonis on his pizza and wandered over to her.

He leaned close to her and let his lips graze her ear, sending chills down her spine. In a low voice, he said, "You're not the only one who has been paying attention, Evie, dear."

Her voice was wobbly as she told him, "Andrew, I can't concentrate when you're this close."

"Oh, really?" Delight lit his voice. "That's very interesting." His slid a hand onto her hip as he closed the gap between them and peered over her shoulder to the pizza she was making.

"Andrew?"

"Yes, darling?" His voice was leisurely, like he didn't have a care in the world. Another shiver ran through her.

"What are you doing?" She did her best to keep her voice even and controlled, but it came out a little too airy for her liking.

Evie felt him shrug behind her. "Just observing your pizza skills."

"Could you, maybe, back up a little?" Clearing her throat, she came up with a lame excuse. "I need some room to work." The nearness of him was almost overwhelming. The smell of him consumed her, and she thought if he stayed that close for much longer, she wouldn't be able to breathe.

"Mmm, I don't think I can," he said low and close to her throat. As his hands squeezed tighter on her hips, Evie went rigid. Suddenly, she was no longer in Andrew's backyard but in a dark alleyway. It wasn't Andrew's hands on her hips but Dylan's.

Breathe. It's not real. It's not real. Breathe

Andrew must have sensed the change because he immediately let go and backed up a step.

Breathe. In. Out.

Slowly, everything came back into perspective. No longer was she trapped in the alleyway but in Andrew's backyard.

"I'm sorry, Evie. I didn't mean to." Andrew's soft voice crossed the void between them.

She turned to face him. Sorrow and concern were etched into his face. She knew he'd never intentionally hurt her. The things he'd been doing were completely normal things that were done in relationships. It wasn't his fault someone had ruined those things for her and in turn, for him, too. It would take time to heal, but everything could and would be mended.

"It's not your fault." She ran a hand through her hair, blowing out a breath. Meeting his eyes, she quietly admitted, "This is my first relationship since my ex. I don't know what it might trigger."

Andrew's eyes were full of compassion and understanding. "I understand. I never want to do something that is going to cause you pain or make you uncomfortable. If you ever need me to stop or to do something different, please tell me. Whatever you need, I will do."

"Thank you," she said, voice breaking. She couldn't stop the tear that rolled down her cheek.

It was such a wonderful feeling to have a man like Andrew. Someone who would love and protect instead of break and destroy. After years of torment and suffering, she'd finally found life again.

Before she knew it, Andrew was moving towards her, wiping her tears. "I am so sorry, Evie. If I could take it all away, I would. Believe me."

"I know. Believe it or not, these are happy tears."

Confusion filled Andrew's face, causing a giggle to escape Evie.

"Happy?"

Nodding her head yes, she said, "Happy because I'm here with you."

Andrew pressed a kiss to her forehead. "I'm happy too. Let's get these pizzas in the oven."

Five minutes later, Evie and Andrew stood, looking over their pizzas. Both pizzas looked equally good, which surprised Evie just a bit. She hadn't expected Andrew to live up to his big talk of his pizza skills.

"Well, yours certainly looks better than anticipated," she told him. He gave her a disbelieving look that made her laugh. "I'm just saying," she said, raising her hands in innocence.

Shaking his head, he told her, "Ye of little faith."

"I still have a lot to learn about you, apparently."

"Yes, you do. Now, let's try these and determine a winner." Andrew cut the pizzas, and they each took a bite of their pizza. "Mine is definitely good," Andrew stated.

"Mine is equally as good if not better."

"Let's see. Here." Evie turned to face Andrew and found him holding a slice of his pizza up to her mouth. Leaning forward, she took a bite. Normally, the idea of someone feeding her would have left her feeling disgusted, but with Andrew, it her gave her butterflies. He made the entire situation so charming that the feeling of disgust was nowhere to be found.

Andrew's pizza wasn't half bad. Actually, it was really good, and she was impressed. "Not bad, Brant."

"That's all I get? A not bad?"

"For now," she laughed, grabbing a slice of her pizza. She held it up to him as he'd done for her. His eyes met hers and held her gaze as he took a bite. Evie was sure she was going to melt and become one with the stone patio.

Eating pizza should not be this sexy.

Am I drooling?

She couldn't help but imagine what else his mouth could do as she watched him.

Genevieve James. Not the time or place.

He was still watching her as she cleared her throat. "Well?" she urged, desperate to get her mind off his mouth.

He swallowed and grinned at her. "Not bad." She rolled her eyes, making him laugh. "Call it a tie?"

"If I must," she replied.

"We can have a s'more building competition later to break the tie. How about that?"

"Deal." Her fist shot into the air, ready to conquer the competition.

Andrew's laugh filled the night air. "Oh, Evie. Life with you is going to be anything but boring."

Thirty minutes later, Evie and Andrew were deep into a serious s'more building competition. The goal was to see who could make the tallest s'more. Evie was currently losing. She couldn't quit eating her ingredients.

"Evie, you are making this too easy for me," Andrew said as he roasted another marshmallow.

"This competition is very skewed. I can't say no to a nicely toasted mallow or chocolate." She popped another piece of chocolate in her mouth. "You tricked me."

Andrew's face was filled with pure amusement. "You caught me. I know you have a weakness for sweets and used that to my advantage."

Evie dramatically gasped. "Andrew, I am shocked. I'm calling this a forfeit."

"It's not my fault you have no self-control."

"Maybe not, but it *is* your fault for providing me with delicious food," she replied, eating the toasted marshmallow off the end of her stick. After a moment of contented silence, Evie said, "This is perfect."

It really was a perfect night. Being under the stars listening to the fire crackle with the faint sounds of the lake behind her was beyond peaceful and relaxing. Spending it with Andrew made it all the better. Things had happened so quickly between them that it almost seemed unreal at times. It wasn't supposed to happen like that.

But I'm glad it did.

"I have a question that is somewhat cheesy," she said quietly.

"Okay," he replied, setting his roasting stick down and looking at her. A light breeze blew by at the same time Andrew looked at her, and she wasn't sure which had caused the shiver that ran along her skin.

"Will you dance with me?"

"Always." Standing, he held out his hand for her and led them over to an open space a few feet away from the fire. They stood closely wrapped in each other's arms, swaying to the soft music playing in the background.

His arms were quickly becoming her favorite place to be.

Safe. So safe.

Evie leaned her head on his shoulder and breathed him in. The smell of cedar and fire smoke mingled around her, persuading her to relax further. It'd been months since she'd felt that relaxed and safe. The comfort of it all was almost enough to put her to sleep.

"You still awake?" His deep voice murmured from above her.

"Barely," she confessed. "I haven't been this relaxed or comfortable in a long time, and I guess it's trying to lull me to sleep." Looking up at him with a warm smile, she said in almost a whisper, "It's like coming home."

"I know exactly what you mean," he told her, holding her a little tighter.

"I don't want tonight to end," she whispered. She felt his laugh more than she heard it.

"Just imagine how much better tomorrow could be if this is our today."

She smiled at his response. It seemed impossible for things to get any better, but she hoped she was wrong in her thinking.

"I hope you're right."

"Trust me. I am." Now, it was her turn to laugh. "What?" he asked.

Evie looked up at him and teased, "You must think very highly of yourself to be so sure."

"If I don't think highly of myself, then who else is going to?"

"That's true," she shrugged.

"Stepped right into that one, didn't I?" His quiet laugh filled the night air around them.

"Yeah, you did."

He looked at her intently for a minute before speaking again. "I like you," he declared.

"I like you too."

A smile spread across his face just before he leaned down and kissed her. Evie's breath caught as his lips met hers. The hand that'd been on her back found its way into her hair. Evie's her free hand gripped the front of his shirt, tugging him closer.

However, Andrew abruptly stopped and stepped away.

"I can't," he said.

Evie's stomach plummeted at his words. That was the last thing she had expected.

"Can't what?" She wasn't sure she wanted to know but needed to ask, either way.

"Keep kissing you. You're doing things to me, Evie. You taste so good, and if I keep kissing you, I'm going to drag you into that house, rip all your clothes off, and have my way with you." His eyes were wild. Normally, it would scare her, but she understood him completely.

She didn't know what to say to him. All words and thoughts left her.

"I want to do this right and not rush this any faster than it's already going. So, I need to know what you want. Do you want me to drag you in the house or do you want me to stop?"

This was a conversation they probably should've had before the kissing began because logical thinking and reasoning had all but left the situation at that point.

Evie took a deep breath. She wasn't quite sure how to respond. There was so much she was feeling and wanted as well, but he was right. They didn't need to rush. "Well, I think the better question is what do I need? Because what I want and what I need are two different things right now. What I want is for you to drag me into that house, but what I need is for us to go slow."

He nodded. "I can wait, but it's going to be mighty difficult."

It shouldn't be so shocking to hear a man say he would wait, but when you've never heard it, it was earth shattering.

The love she had for Andrew began to bloom into something more beautiful than she'd ever known, burying its roots deep into her soul.

"I know. I'm sorry." She ran a hand through her hair as she let out a sigh. "There's been a lot taken from me, stolen from me, and I want to be back to 100% before I give it."

"You don't have to apologize for that, Evie. Don't ever apologize. It's yours to give and not mine to take. I don't want it, unless you're giving it willingly and freely." There was such a tenderness to his words that her heart ached.

I love this man so much. How could he be any better?

"You'd be okay waiting no matter how long it takes? Because if I'm being completely honest, I'm not sure I want to be with someone again until I'm married." She looked at him as he took in what she was telling him. "The security of forever might be what I need."

Evie waited for him to answer. The seconds ticked by, increasing the anxiety within her.

Something flickered across Andrew's face as if he'd come to some sort of decision, and he took a step towards her, closing the gap between them. Both hands came up, cradling her face. "I would wait an eternity for you. Your body is not what I'm after. You. You are what I want."

Evie felt the tears begin to slip down her cheeks. She'd always longed for a man who would respect and wait for her with a love unimaginable.

This was it. This was everything she'd ever wanted.

This is him.

This is my forever.

His thumbs lightly wiped the tears away as they fell. "I know the guidelines for a typical relationship say to go to bed as soon as possible, and don't get me wrong, I really want to; however, nothing has been typical about us so far, and I'm fine with this not following the usual ways either. I just want you, Evie. Part of you or all of you. Whatever you're willing to give me, for however long."

Evie was shocked and falling so hard and fast for him she thought she might break apart, as if her body wouldn't be capable of containing all the love. The feeling was new and all encompassing.

This was a good man.

To his very core, Andrew Brant was a good man.

"Thank you," she whispered. She felt him kiss her forehead as his arms wrapped around her, holding her close.

ANDREW

Andrew and Evie chatted comfortably on the drive back to her apartment. He hadn't expected the night to go as well as it had. His heart was already wholly hers, and he was willing to do just about anything for her, including waiting to sleep with her. It hadn't been a complete surprise that she had wanted to wait, but he hadn't expected her to want to wait until she was married. However, he could and would respect her wishes. If they did end up married, they'd have forever to be together.

Besides, it wouldn't kill him.

I think.

The desire and need to have her was so overwhelmingly strong, which, if he were honest, was a relatively new feeling. It felt amazing to have a burning, consuming passion for someone. His love for Lily had turned platonic very early on in their marriage. Andrew wasn't the kind of man to renege on his word or vows, so he'd stayed and cared for his wife, giving her what he had to give.

However, the things he felt for Evie were nowhere near anything he'd ever experienced. If she asked, he'd lasso the moon and give it to her. She could ask him for the most ridiculous things, and he'd make a fool out of himself to make them happen.

He'd run to the ends of the earth without looking back.

Give life and breath.

Greet death with a smile.

As he pulled into a spot and turned his truck off, Evie broke through his thoughts, saying, "I had a very lovely time tonight. Thank you."

"Me too. I'm glad I could spend time with you." Looking at her smiling face, all he felt was gratitude. How had he gotten so lucky as to find Evie James at his literal feet?

Andrew walked Evie to her door, bid her goodnight, and waited for her to lock her door before heading back to his truck. Nothing could bring down the high he was currently riding, until the hairs on the back of his neck stood, halting his steps.

Someone was watching him.

That eerie feeling had him checking over his shoulder before he continued walking to his truck.

Pausing by his truck, he scanned the parking lot and surrounding areas. There was nothing or no one in sight, but he knew he was being watched. Squaring his shoulders and rising to his full height, he opened the door. He would not be intimidated or show any sort of weakness or fear. He knew who was watching, and it was time Evie's ex started to learn just who he was up against.

Andrew climbed in and locked his truck doors as he pulled out his phone. He may not be intimated, but he wasn't stupid either.

A: I don't want to frighten you but do not go outside again tonight.

He didn't want her to worry or lose sleep over that

snake, but he also didn't want her to accidentally happen upon him.

The worry grew as Andrew drove home. It had been twenty minutes, and she still hadn't responded to his text. As he pulled into his driveway debating on whether or not to call, his phone pinged with a text.

E: I'm guessing he's outside

A: I don't know for sure, but my instincts say someone was there

E: Great. Am I supposed to spend the rest of my life watching my back, hoping he doesn't attack me again?

A: I promise this will all come to an end one day

A: I texted your dad to let him know

E: You have my dad's number?

A: Yeah, we are best buds now

E: No. Stop. Please

A: Never! :) Please stay inside and keep the doors locked

E: I will. Goodnight, Andrew

A: Goodnight, Sweetheart

Andrew didn't know how he would stop her ex, but he knew in his gut the time would come when they would eventually face off; however, that time didn't appear to be happening anytime soon, which Andrew was thankful for.

20

The weeks and months passed peacefully without any sign of her ex-boyfriend. The long reprieve from her ex had allowed Evie to relax a bit, which made Andrew more than relieved to see. Things were going very well between them, and they'd gotten to know each other deeper during the months that'd followed them becoming official, spending time together whenever they could.

Evie continued to heal as time passed. She'd gotten her cast off and began to settle into life, as the absence of her ex continued. Aiden had even left to go back home to Kentucky for a while, leaving Evie in Andrew's care.

Life was good and oddly, quiet.

The leaves had officially changed colors, and the air had a chill in it. Death clung to the bitter air, ushering in the changing of the seasons, and the shadows lurked silently, watching from afar.

Biding their time.

21

ANDREW

Next week was Thanksgiving break, and Andrew wasn't excited about not being able to see Evie for most of that time. She was going back to Kentucky to spend time with her family, and although he was going to miss her, he wouldn't begrudge her that time with her parents. Luckily, his brothers and their families were coming to his house the day before Evie left, and she'd agreed to come spend time with them before she left for the week.

"Are you still good to come over on Sunday?" he asked her as they walked to their cars that Friday afternoon after work.

"Yeah, I'm looking forward to it." A grin lit her face as she looked up at him.

Opening her car door, he said, "Me too." "And you're sure you can't do anything tonight?" he asked almost pleadingly.

She huffed a laugh. "Yes, love. Lucy and I are having a girl's night before we both leave to go home." Andrew gave her his best puppy dog look. The look quickly turned into a smile as he saw Evie copy his look. "You'll be okay for a night or two," she told him sympathetically.

Although they saw each other almost every day, the amount of alone time they had was relatively low. Between friends, family, and work, it'd been difficult to schedule time for just them. Hopefully, all of that would change soon.

"Fine, but I won't like it."

"Good," she replied, giving him that look that made him want to devour her. He looked around to make sure no one was looking before he leaned into the car, kissing her quickly but soundly on the lips.

Before pulling away, he whispered against her lips, "I'm really not going to like it."

"I'll make it up to you," she whispered back. With a groan, he straightened up out of the car.

"I'll call you later," he told her, closing her door.

Evie James was going to be his undoing, and he didn't mind it in the slightest.

EVIE

Evie nervously pulled into Andrew's driveway Sunday afternoon. She was excited to meet his family, but there were a thousand thoughts pushing what felt like a brick into the bottom of her stomach.

What if they don't like me?

What if I can't talk?

What if I fall into the lake?

That last question was very unlikely to happen since she'd likely be nowhere near the lake.

But still.

She turned the car off and took a deep breath. After several more deep breaths, she got out and made her way to the door.

Evie could hear laughter coming from inside the house before she could reach the front door.

That's a good sign. Everything will be fine.

What could possibly go wrong? It's just lunch.

Evie let herself in as she had many times before and hung her coat on one of the hooks. As she rounded the corner into the main room, she was greeted by the smell of food cooking and two gorgeous women.

The woman to her left let out a loud squeal, and a pair of arms came around her very quickly, "Hi! Sorry, I'm just really excited to meet you." The tall blonde woman smiled broadly at her before letting her go. "You *are* Evie, right?"

"Yes." Evie smiled back.

"Oh good," the woman breathed. "That would've been very awkward if you weren't."

"Nicole, give the woman some room," said the other woman walking towards them.

"Hi, I'm Lacie, and this crazy lady is Nicole." Lacie was a little shorter than Nicole and had black hair, while Nicole's hair was almost white, blonde. They seemed complete opposites but fit so well. They were both smiling at her and seemed very happy she was there.

"It's nice to meet y'all." Evie already liked them. She was also thankful for them because they had helped her to relax. With the social anxiety nearly gone, she could finally enjoy herself.

Lacie noticed the bottle of wine Evie was holding. "Ooh, now, the party can begin," she said, grabbing the bottle.

Nicole echoed Lacie's sentiments. With the bottle in hand, Lacie rummaged through Andrew's cabinets looking for wine glasses. After pulling three out, she turned back, looking for a corkscrew. "Does anyone know where he keeps his corkscrew?"

"Drawer to the left of the dishwasher," Evie responded.

Nicole and Lacie turned to her with stares. Both, gave her an amused, knowing look.

"Spend a lot of time over here?" Nicole smirked at her.

Evie returned her smirk and fired back, "Sure do."

Lacie handed out the wine glasses, and all three took a

sip and sighed at the same time, causing them to fall into a fit of giggles. Evie didn't have any siblings, but this was what she supposed it would be like. It made her happy to the core to be a part of the moment.

"You're going to fit right in," Nicole said through a giggle.

The girls chatted as if they'd known each other for years. They sat on the floor of the living room around the cleared off coffee table, now holding many snacks and a half empty bottle of wine. Evie was enjoying herself so much she'd completely forgotten about Andrew.

"Oh my gosh," Evie suddenly exclaimed with a gasp.

"What?" Lacie asked as Nicole paused with her hand in the bag of chips. Both looked very concerned.

"I completely forgot about Andrew."

Nicole and Lacie burst into a fit of laughter, and Evie quickly followed with her own. They were out of breath when the back door opened, and Andrew walked in with a platter of steaks, followed by two of his brothers and their kids.

"What are y'all laughing at?" one of the brothers asked, walking over to them.

Evie thought he was an older and bigger version of Andrew, which was saying something since Andrew was already a big man. Two little girls hung about his legs, looking apprehensive but curious about Evie.

"Nothing," Lacie replied.

"Mhm, sure," he said before walking to the kitchen. The little girls stayed where they were as their dad walked off.

"That was Connor, my husband, and these two are Ella and Olivia," Nicole told her. The girls looked to be about four and six. Both had light brown hair and beautiful blue eyes. Evie thought they were almost picture perfect, especially in their little pink dresses.

"Hello, it's nice to meet you guys," Evie said cheerfully.

Ella and Olivia must have decided Evie was okay because they walked over and sat on the floor next to her. Nicole gave her a thumbs up; she must've passed an unspoken test with the girls.

"The other big guy with the baby strapped to him is David. The cute little fella strapped to him is Dakota," Lacie told her.

"You two sure have some cute kids." The baby fever started to grow in Evie.

Not good. Calm down.

"Thank you," Nicole said.

"Don't worry. You and Andrew will make cute babies too," Lacie quipped at her, causing Evie to choke on her wine.

"Lacie, too much," Nicole halfheartedly warned as she laughed. Lacie patted Evie sympathetically on the back.

"What? I'm just stating facts," she said innocently.

"Y'all already trying to kill her?" Andrew asked, frowning at Evie coughing and Lacie patting her.

"No. Just speaking some surprising truths to her," Lacie replied very sweetly.

Andrew arched an eyebrow at her and squatted down next to Evie.

"You good?" he asked.

Evie nodded and smiled. She looked at his very handsome face and those dark green eyes and knew Lacie was right, no matter how shocking the truth might be.

He'd make very pretty babies.

Genevieve James! What is the matter with you?

Must be the wine talking.

Evie took a breath. "Yep, I'm good, but Lacie did in fact try to kill me."

A loud dramatic gasp came from behind her. Nicole failed to conceal the laugh she was trying poorly to hide.

"I knew it," Andrew said, leveling Lacie with an accusing look.

"I could never," Lacie boldly stated.

"She sure did. I saw it with my own eyes," Olivia told Andrew. Lacie gasped again. Evie saw Olivia elbow Ella in the side.

"Me too," Ella chimed in.

"Girls, how could you betray me?"

They both shrugged, and Olivia said, "We like Evie."

"Sorry, Lacie," Evie said, giving her a sympathetic look and patting her on the shoulder.

Andrew chuckled and kissed Evie on the head before standing, filling her with all the warm fuzzy feelings.

"Food's ready," he said, reaching a hand down to help Evie up. Pulling her close, he whispered, "You look beautiful."

Evie felt shivers rush down her body at the feel of his breath against her ear. His arm lingered around her waist. Even though neither one of them had confessed their love to the other, their eyes spoke it loud and clear.

David cleared his throat from behind them and asked, "Are we going to eat or are you two going to make googly eyes at one another all day?"

"Shut up, David," Andrew said in brotherly irritation and humor.

Evie felt her cheeks slightly warm from being caught in such an intimate moment but was also sad the moment hadn't lasted longer. She often wondered when they would confess what they felt for one another. They both knew it was there, but neither felt in a hurry to put it into words. The words seemed to fall short of what they felt for one another, but even still, there was something deep within her that kept those words locked up.

Andrew led Evie to the big round table in the corner of the room that was surrounded by windows. She'd always admired this spot. The natural light was unmatched, and it always felt warm and inviting. She'd spent a lot of time at the table, working on homework or work. It'd kind of become her spot in Andrew's house. It also helped that the table was big enough for her to spread all her work out.

Andrew had built the table by hand many years ago. He'd told her that he wanted a place where his family could all dine together and face one another. There was enough space for them all to sit comfortably and for more people to join.

Evie sat down between Andrew and Lacie. Their backs were to the rest of the room, which meant they could see part of the lake through the window. Even though it was cold and drizzling outside, Evie appreciated the look it gave the lake. It was slightly eerie but inviting.

Everyone seemed to be enjoying themselves as they ate and chatted comfortably. The Brant family had a way of being loud and overwhelming but also very intimate. There was so much joy in their family.

I love it here.

Evie noticed there was one spot left open across from her. Connor must've seen her looking at it because he said, "Our younger brother was supposed to come today, but he seems to be running late per usual."

David chimed in, "Scout has never been on time a day in his life. It's a wonder he made it through the military."

Everyone laughed and added their agreement to David's comment.

Just then, the front door opened and closed. Heavy footsteps slowly approached.

"Speak of the devil," Nicole said.

"Y'all started without me?" a voice asked from behind them.

Evie froze as the voice registered in her ears.

Panic began to seep in from all directions. It couldn't be.

Not possible.

It's fine. I'm just being dramatic.

The voice is merely familiar.

She couldn't bring herself to look up as the man made his way around the table and slid into the seat across from her. Tattooed arms came into view as the man slid them onto the table.

Her stomach sank as her breath quickened.

No. No. No.

Please, no!

Evie's very worst nightmare had just come to life.

Ever so slowly, she raised her eyes and met Dylan's, watching her from across the table.

The predator had found its prey.

"And who do we have here?" Dylan asked slyly with a vile smile that made her stomach turn.

Evie wasn't sure if it was Dylan's tone or the way she was sitting frigidly stiff, but she could feel the shift in the room. From the way everyone had greeted him, she was sure no one there knew about Dylan's true self.

Andrew's hand found its way to her thigh, giving it a gentle squeeze as he told Dylan, "This is Evie, my girlfriend."

"Beautiful," Dylan responded, like she was a prized calf

up for auction. Leaning back in his chair, he let his eyes drift over her in an inappropriate and sensual way.

Evie recognized the look for what it was.

Hunger.

Without a doubt, Evie knew Andrew was beginning to pick up on her distress and knew it was only a matter of time before he pieced together what was wrong. However, she didn't know if she wanted to be around for that moment or not.

How do I get out of here?

Deep down, she wasn't fully certain Andrew would do anything, given it was his brother, and if he did do something, she didn't want to be the reason the Brant family broke apart or knew the truth about their immoral brother. Despite what Dylan was to her, he seemed to be a valuable part of the family.

"It's nice to meet you, Evie." Dylan's voice slithered across the table, causing her to visibly flinch.

There was no way Andrew had missed it or anyone at the table for that matter.

Dylan quietly chuckled at her, clearly enjoying the sick and twisted game he was playing.

"Are you okay," Andrew quietly whispered in her ear.

"Oh, she's fine, Andrew," Dylan drawled. "You always did worry too much."

"Do you two know each other or something?" Connor asked, looking between her and Dylan.

"No, she's just falling for me and my magical hair," he joked lightheartedly.

"Oh, shut it, Scout," David replied.

"Yeah, and you really should cut that long hair of yours. Man buns are out," Nicole quipped.

Thankfully, the attention had passed from her and back

to the normal conversation of the table. Evie had lost her appetite and wanted nothing more than to crawl under the table and hide. She needed to get out of there, but there was no way to do that without raising suspicion. With no present options, Evie focused on her breathing.

She was stuck between two brothers. One was concerned, and the other was waiting. They were two sides of the same coin.

Saint and sinner.

Angel and devil.

Love and hate.

Life and death.

And Evie didn't know which side would prevail.

Thankfully, lunch ended without disaster and with only a few uncomfortable comments from Dylan. Evie breathed a sigh of relief as soon as she was able to move from Dylan's direct gaze, which had lingered on her throughout lunch.

As she stood at the edge of the kitchen, deciding her next plan of action as everyone finished cleaning up from lunch, Andrew approached her with worry written all over his face.

"Are you okay? I know something weird happened at that table, but I don't know what." He ran a hand down her arm in a gentle caress. "Did something trigger you?"

"I'm fine," she answered, trying to give him a smile.

"Evie, you're not. I know Scout is a bit of a roguish handful, for a lack of better words, but he wouldn't hurt you."

His words were like a slap in the face and stung more than he'd ever know, but she couldn't be angry with him. He didn't know.

Despite it all, she felt sorry for Andrew. It would kill him to know the truth.

I need to get out of here.

To air. To safety.

She nodded and said, "I need to run out to car and get my phone."

"Do you want me to go get it?"

"No, you stay with your family. I could use a bit of air anyways." She knew her voice was a bit shaky, but she hoped Andrew would write it off as her being triggered. She didn't know how long she could conceal the truth from him. They'd grown too close over the past couple of months for her to be able to hide something like that from him.

Even though she could tell he was still worried and wanted to say more, he merely replied, "Okay."

Thank you.

She breathed a silent breath of relief that he wasn't going to press the issue. Sadness creeped in because she knew she couldn't stay there or with his family. The only way to leave would be to make a run for it.

Thank you for being everything I could ever need or want.

Evie kissed Andrew on the cheek and headed to the door, snatching her coat off the hook and running to the car. Thankfully, her dad was in town to escort her back to Kentucky. She'd reach safety soon.

She was almost to her car when she heard him.

"Still so predictable, Kitten." Dylan's malevolent voice came from behind her. Evie spun around to find him leaning against a tree. "Always needing some air."

"Can you not leave me alone? I thought you had a new girl to torment."

Dylan slowly raised up and stalked towards her, stopping mere inches from her face. She could feel the warmth of his breath on her cheek, causing an involuntary shudder.

"No, Little Genny, I can't. You're dating my brother, and you know I don't like sharing what's mine."

"I'm not yours, Dylan," she firmly stated.

"You're mine until I say you're not," he snarled.

"That's not how it works, and I refuse to play these demented games of yours any longer," she gritted out. Evie could feel her hands shaking and balled them into fists. She knew he couldn't hurt her with Andrew right inside, but the thought didn't put her at ease. This was becoming a bigger mess by the minute, and she needed to get out of there.

"Now, Genny, you know better than to refuse me."

"You're not going to hurt me outside your brother's house."

"Maybe not, but you won't always be outside his house." He leaned forward, bracing his hands against the car on either side of her head. "Will you?"

"You need to get away from me," Evie stated, doing her best to stand her ground and not give into fear.

He chuckled sinisterly in her ear and ground out, "What have I told you about trying to go against me? I would've thought you would've learned your lesson by now."

He pulled back to stare down at her. His black eyes were filled with nothing but threats; however, she refused to back down and returned his stare. A slow smirk formed on his mouth. "I see my brother has been teaching you some bad habits, Kitten. I guess I need to give you a new lesson."

"No." Her word was adamant and unrelenting. Anger flashed through his eyes. He didn't like being told no, and he definitely didn't like seeing the power he held over her slipping from his grasp.

Ignoring her, he said, "Lesson number one, this is my family. Not yours." He slid a hand down to her neck and gripped it before continuing. Desire poured off of him, causing nausea to rise in Evie. "Do you really think they're going to believe you over me? Do you honestly think they'll think me capable of anything you could tell them? They love me."

She tried not to show any emotion, but she knew he saw the quick flash of doubt that crossed her face.

"Good," he cooed, as if he were praising a puppy. "Second lesson, I know you may think you and Andrew have something special, but one word from me and it will crumble. Hard and fast. Andrew is weak, gullible. Do you honestly think he stands a chance against me?" His revolting words hung in the air between them as he waited for her to respond.

"Is that a threat? You wouldn't honestly hurt your brother." She couldn't believe what she was hearing.

"Wouldn't I? He took what's mine." Dylan was more psychotic than she thought, and that was saying something.

"You can't hurt him," she whispered in a plea.

"Why not? Shouldn't he be punished just like you? Hm, Kitten? Should I show him what happens when someone touches what's mine?" The hand on her throat left, but it only moved to allow his finger to trace the outline of her lips.

"No, Dylan. No," she pleaded, sounding more desperate than she wanted, but she'd throw herself at his mercy to keep Andrew safe.

Evie glanced towards the house. No doubt, Andrew was beginning to wonder where she was and would come looking for her soon. He was good, and she refused to let him be dragged into the turmoil with her.

"What do you want?" She was scared to hear the answer, but she already knew it.

To be his. His and his alone.

Evie felt utterly sick. If this didn't end soon, she'd throw up all over Dylan, unleashing a new level of hell from him.

"I want what's mine," he hissed.

She watched as his dark eyes flickered towards the house and back, settling on her. He let his arms casually drop from the car and gave her that endearing smile that he'd won her over with the first time they had met. Although now, she knew it wasn't real.

Evie's stomach dropped as the realization hit her just as Dylan's lips crashed into hers.

Andrew is watching.

Dylan pulled back just enough to look her in the eyes. His breath curled around her lips. To anyone looking, they would appear as two lovers having an intimate moment.

Forgive me.

"I want you to get in your car, leave, and never return. Do that, and I promise I'll leave him alone."

"And if I don't?" The question was barely a whisper.

His eyes darkened as he growled low, growing irritated. "Then, I will shove my gun down his throat and not hesitate to pull the trigger."

The blood drained from Evie's face. If she knew anything about Dylan, it was the fact that he did not make idle threats. He may seem like he loved his family, but there was too much evil and selfishness within him to keep him from harming them—killing them.

A finger lifted her chin, forcing her to look him in the eye. "In your car. Now," he demanded, stepping back to give her room. Evie hesitated, looking back towards the house, but when she saw Andrew standing at the door, she turned and opened the car door. "Good, girl. I'll see you soon, Kitten," he said, shutting the car door and sauntering back to the house.

Tears rapidly fell down Evie's face as she started her car. She watched as Dylan turned to look at her, making sure she was leaving. He gave her a flash of a smile and a wink that made her stomach turn.

As she backed away, she dared to look at Andrew's face. It was a mixture of hurt and confusion. Who knew what Dylan was going to tell him?

She was going to be sick.

Forgive me, love.

As she looked in her rearview mirror one last time, she saw Andrew step off the front step and onto the gravel driveway. It took more strength than she had to keep driving. The hurt on his face broke her heart into a million pieces. She prayed he would understand and not believe a word Dylan told him.

Despite the horrible things Dylan had said, she knew Andrew. He was stronger and smarter than given credit for, and he knew her.

He knew her heart, and that was the only thing she had to cling to now.

22

ANDREW

"What was that?" Andrew demanded, following Dylan back into the house.

Everyone fell silent at the sound of Andrew's tone. Anger rushed through his veins. Every step towards his brother threatened violence. He always tried to keep his anger hidden and locked up around Evie, but *for* her, he would unleash it.

"What was what?" Dylan asked back casually, as if he didn't have a care in the world.

"You know what," Andrew bit out.

At the sound of his voice, Nicole and Lacie began herding the kids out of the room, as David and Connor watched warily from the far side of the living room.

"I honestly don't know what you're talking about."

Andrew didn't care for his indifferent tone.

Something was severely wrong, but he couldn't put his finger on it. It was driving him mad not to know. She'd been upset with Scout's presence, and then, Scout had kissed her.

Kissed her!

Andrew began shaking in anger. He didn't know how long he could keep his emotions in check.

"Why did you kiss her?" Andrew demanded.

A loud intake of air and gasp came from Connor and David's side of the room, but he kept his eyes focused on Scout.

A smug smile formed on Dylan's face. "So, you did see."

Why does that make you happy? Did you want me to see?

"Of course, I saw. You knew I was watching," Andrew said dangerously close to yelling. He rarely lost his temper and hated to, but the situation warranted it.

Dylan didn't say anything.

"I'm only going to ask one more time. Why did you kiss her?"

Dylan shrugged nonchalantly. "Felt like it."

"That's not good enough, Scout. You didn't just feel like it. I don't see you randomly kissing Nicole or Lacie, so why did you feel the need to kiss my girlfriend?" Andrew saw something change in Dylan's demeanor as he referred to Evie as his.

Is he jealous?

"You can't have everything Andrew," Dylan replied, visibly annoyed.

"I can if it's already mine." Dylan's eyes flashed with anger as he called Evie his again, but he only huffed a laugh at Andrew's words. Anger boiled within Andrew. "This isn't funny, Scout. Evie has been through more than any woman should, and kissing her without her consent is not okay under any circumstance; it's especially not when I'm dating her."

The anger slashed through Dylan's eyes again. Andrew didn't know what it was, but something was beginning to connect in his mind.

"How do you know I didn't have her consent? Did you ever think that she asked me to kiss her?"

"I know you didn't, and I know she didn't. I know her." Andrew was firm in his words. He would never waver in the truth of knowing Evie.

Dylan slowly stalked closer to Andrew, quietly chuckling.

"How well do you know her, Andrew? Do you know what she feels like?" Dylan spoke slow and deliberately. "What does she sound like as she's finishing?" Shock and disgust rocked through Andrew. The corner of Dylan's mouth turned up in a half smile. "No, you don't know her. You don't have it in you to slide all the way home."

"That's enough," David said from behind them. Dylan laughed again.

"I'm just messing around." Andrew's fists were clenched so tight his fingernails were cutting into the palms of his hands. Dylan turned to walk away. "Besides, Genny just isn't my type."

The world slammed to a halt as everything clicked into place.

No. No. No.

Please, no.

The blood drained from Andrew's body as he remembered Evie's words. The only person to call her Genny was her ex.

"Who's Genny?" Connor asked. Dylan stopped walking.

"What did you call her?" The words were barely audible.

He prayed he was wrong.

That his own brother was not Evie's ex. That he had not laid his hands on her and broken her in more ways than one.

Dylan was utterly silent and still.

"What did you call her?" Andrew demanded once more. His deep voice filled the room.

"Isn't her name Genny?" Dylan asked innocently, turning to face Andrew.

Andrew shook his head. "No, but you know that don't you?" When Dylan didn't say anything, Andrew yelled, "Don't you?"

"Look, I don't know what you're trying to imply, but I just mistook her name," Dylan replied calmly, too calmly.

"Don't lie to me. I know it's you," Andrew said, stepping closer to him.

"And what if it is me? What are you going to do? Nothing." Dylan spat his words at him in mockery. "You're not a man of action. Never have been, and that's why she will always moan my name and not yours."

The restraint on Andrew snapped.

Before he could say anymore, Andrew slammed his fist into Dylan's face. A satisfying crunch filled Andrew's ears as his fist connected with his brother's nose. Blood poured down his face as he dropped to the ground, holding it.

Andrew grasped a handful of his hair, tilting his head back to look up at him. "I will do whatever I have to, to protect her." Pure venom dripped from his words, promising death to anyone who dared to touch her, his very heart. "I know what you think of me, the weak English professor, but there is no length I will not go to for the people I love, the woman I love." He let go of Dylan's hair and let his fist fly into his face again.

"Okay, guys. That's enough," Connor said, moving towards Andrew and Dylan with David trailing behind.

"No, it's nowhere near enough," Andrew snapped back.

"I didn't say I did anything to her." Dylan winced in pain.

Good. Let's turn the tables.

"You didn't have to," Andrew hurled back at him.

David gently pushed Andrew back and asked, "What is going on?"

"He beat, raped, and nearly killed Evie! That's what's going on." Andrew was beyond irate at his brother. The fact that his brother was even capable of doing such a thing to a woman was sickening, but for him to do it to the woman he loved was a complete other.

"Are you sure? That's a big thing to accuse someone of, especially your own brother," Connor said calmly.

"Yeah, and it's Scout. He's our brother. He wouldn't do something like that," David responded.

"Yes, I'm sure." Andrew began to pace. If he didn't do something with the energy coursing through him, he was sure he was going to kill Dylan. "She told me her ex was the only person to call her Genny." Pointing at Dylan, he continued, "He called her that a little too easily. Not to mention, I saw him kissing her just before she drove off." Bile rose up the back of his throat at the memory of what he had witnessed.

What did I do? What did I do?

I failed her.

I absolutely failed her.

Connor and David looked between the two men and at each other. David broke the silence. "Scout, what do you have to say about all of this?"

"Yes, Genny and I used to date." Andrew's fist curled tightly at Dylan calling her Genny. "But I never did anything to her that she didn't ask for. It's not my fault if she prefers me to him." Andrew rushed Dylan and got one good hit in before Connor and David pulled him back.

"Settle down," Connor insisted.

"Didn't do anything she didn't ask for? Really? I saw her, Dylan. I saw her the day she limped into my classroom, beaten and broken. Saw the fingerprints around her throat. The cast on her arm. You're telling me she asked for that?"

His voice was thunderous throughout the room, but he didn't care. He had unknowingly invited Evie's abuser into his house. He had placed her within his reach, and Dylan had taken advantage of her once again, as he had watched.

Andrew was shaking with rage and guilt. He hoped she'd forgive him, even though he didn't deserve it.

"Yeah, she did ask for that. She didn't listen and had to be taught a lesson, but she's better off for it," Dylan finally admitted.

Silence filled the room at his confession. No one said or did anything until Andrew rushed at Dylan again, and this time, neither Connor nor David stopped him. Andrew pounded Dylan until there was nothing left but a bloody body on the floor. Dylan had managed to get two hits in on Andrew, but he hadn't even felt them. There was nothing but red blinding rage.

Dylan's face was almost unrecognizable from all the blood smeared on it. The man bun was long gone. Breathing hard, he tried to get off the floor but couldn't get his feet under him.

Andrew hauled Dylan to his feet and said in an unrecognizable voice, "I do not want to see your face ever again. You're no longer welcome in my house. If I ever catch you near Evie again, I will not hesitate to put you down, like the filth you are." Andrew shoved him hard towards the door and prayed Dylan had enough strength to get to the door because if he stayed, he might very well kill him now.

Hearing the front door shut, he walked to the kitchen sink to wash the blood off his hands. He didn't know what else to do in the moment. He was so incredibly angry at Dylan but mostly at himself.

He should've known.

Should've protected her.

It's on me. This was my fault.

All my fault.

"Wow," David breathed out from behind him. "I don't even know what to say."

"No kidding," Connor said just as shocked. "What do you say when you find out your little brother is an abuser and rapist?"

Andrew was shaking so badly he had to brace his hands on the edge of the sink.

"I need to find Evie," Andrew announced.

"Yeah, man. Go," David said.

Andrew quickly dried his hands and grabbed his keys. He had to make sure she was okay and apologize for putting her in this nightmare.

He'd had one job, to protect her. That's what he'd promised her and her dad, but instead, he'd miserably failed. Instead of protecting her, he'd unknowingly led the lamb to slaughter, and he'd never forgive himself for it.

Andrew raced across town to Evie's apartment, blowing through a couple of stop signs. The truck was barely in park before Andrew was out of the it, running across the parking lot and up the stairs to her door. Chest heaving from exertion, he tried to calmly knock.

It felt like an eternity before he heard the lock on the

door turn. All he wanted was to see Evie's face but instead, was met with the ice-cold death glare of Lucy.

"She isn't here." Normally, Lucy was a bubbly kind-hearted person, but right then, she was a stone wall. Clearly, she'd spoken to Evie, and he deserved every ounce of anger shown to him right now.

A slight panic went through him. If she wasn't there, where was she? "What do you mean she's not here? Where is she?"

"She left with her dad for Kentucky."

"How long ago?"

Her eyes promised death as she said, "Right after leaving your house. Thirty mins or so ago."

"Thanks, Lucy." He stepped away from the door, feeling nothing but defeat.

The door shut with a resounding thud that he felt throughout his entire body.

How did I let this happen? I should have just killed him and put an end to this nightmare.

My baby brother.

Andrew trudged back to his truck, feeling numb. Climbing into his truck, he pulled out his phone and dialed Evie. Each ring was agony. She had every right not to speak to him, but he really needed to talk to her and at the very least, apologize.

The call rang and rang until he got her voicemail. Loss encompassed Andrew. He didn't blame her for not answering. He wouldn't have answered either, if he was her.

I can't lose her. Not like this.

Instead of trying Evie again, he found himself calling Aiden.

"Andrew," Aiden answered on the first ring with a voice colder than Lucy's. Being on the receiving end of Aiden's anger was not something Andrew ever wanted to experience, but there he was, doing just that.

Because I'm a fool.

"I didn't know," Andrew said very quickly. If anything came of the call, he needed it to be that—for Aiden to know he hadn't known the truth.

"I know, but you still put my little girl in danger. I trusted you with her, and you served her up for lunch to that demon. Brother or no. Whether you knew or not, she didn't deserve that, Andrew."

"I know, and I will never forgive myself for it." He meant every word. He wouldn't. Not for as long as he lived.

Anger seeped from Aiden's voice as he said, "And where were you when he kissed her? If you saw what was happening, why did you not step in to stop it?"

I failed her in every way imaginable.

Andrew didn't have an answer. "I honestly don't know. I think I was confused by what I was seeing and trying to process it. It's no excuse though. I should've stepped in, and I will forever regret just standing there. I failed her. It was my job to step in and protect her, and I wasn't there when she needed me." His voice broke, but he didn't care. "I'm so sorry, Aiden, and I just want a chance to apologize to her."

Aiden was quiet for a few minutes, and Andrew wondered if he was even still on the phone.

A deep sigh came through the phone before Aiden asked, "Did you really not know?"

"No. I didn't have a clue. Evie never mentioned her ex's name, and my brother has never shown any sort of behavior that alluded to him having a dark side. If it counts for anything, he left my house a bloody mess."

"It does." Another pause in the conversation. He knew Aiden was weighing and assessing the situation, and he wouldn't blame him if he told him to never speak to Evie again.

Andrew broke through the silence. "Is she okay?"

"She will be."

"I need to talk to her," Andrew said a little too desperately.

"Give her some time. She'll call when she's ready."

"Just let her know how sorry I am."

"I'll let her know."

"Thank you." Andrew heard a click, and the line went dead.

Slamming his fists on the steering wheel, Andrew let out a cry full of rage and misery.

He was to blame for all of this and at what cost? With each mile, Evie slipped further and further away, and who knew how much more trauma his inaction had caused her?

Andrew rubbed at his aching chest. There was no fixing it. There was no coming back from knowing his little brother had hurt and raped the love of his life.

How does one move on from this?

Andrew slid his truck into drive and took the long way home. He knew Connor and David would have questions, but he wasn't ready to talk. It all hurt too much.

23
ANDREW

The week passed by slowly. Andrew tried to follow Aiden's advice and give her time, but the silence was killing him. The connection between them felt as if it was holding on by a mere thread. Without her, emptiness was his only companion. It was eating at him to know how she was doing.

Monday morning eventually came, and Andrew rushed to campus eager to see Evie. It'd been a week of silence, but now, he could see her face-to-face. The minutes turned into hours as he watched his office door.

It was mid-afternoon, and Andrew was staring woefully at the empty chair in the corner. Everything was as she left it—her book lying on her table, and oversized cardigan draped across the back of her chair.

He missed her so much it hurt. What wouldn't he give to hear her voice and see that smirk on her face when she sassed him? It was funny how little time it took for someone to make a deep and lasting impression. Evie had marked his office, his life, and his heart.

A knock sounded at his door, and he looked up, hoping

it was Evie. Instead, he found Lucy standing in the door-way, watching him. "Yes?"

Lucy walked into the office before saying, "EJ asked me to pick up the work she has left for the semester. She and father decided it would be best if she finished out the semester in Kentucky."

Andrew's heart fell to the floor. "She's not coming back?"

Something akin to pity formed on Lucy's face. "I don't know. For now, she's not, but if it makes you feel any better, she didn't tell me she's planning on moving out of our apartment."

"So, you've spoken with her? Is she okay?" Jealously inched its way through his body. He wanted so badly for her to talk to him. It hurt that she was ignoring him, but he couldn't blame her for it or hold it against her.

I deserve it.

It was good she was talking to someone though, even if it wasn't him.

"She's a little shaken and trying to process everything."

Andrew could only nod at Lucy as he began to put the work together for Evie.

As Andrew was digging through his bag, Lucy said, "I can't believe you actually used the bag."

He looked up confused. "Someone left it for me as a gift a couple of years ago." Lucy got a funny look on her face. "What?"

"You don't know?"

"Know what?"

"It was EJ that gave you the bag. She noticed your old one had broken, and you were having to carry everything around. She had her dad make that one for you."

Shock hit Andrew. That was the last thing he'd ever

expected to hear, but he should've known. "EJ. Evie James," Andrew mused.

How did I never put that together?

Lucy nodded, "She didn't want you to know it was from her. Hence, the card signed EJ." Andrew was stunned and didn't know what to say. He found the paper he needed and added it to the stack of work before handing it to Lucy.

As Lucy turned to go, she paused before telling him, "You know, I think she fell in love with you the moment she laid eyes on you two years ago, and I don't think she'll ever stop, no matter the time or space."

Her words took a moment to fully register, but once they did, shock rocked into him, leaving him stunned. His voice was barely steady as he asked, "Why are you telling me this?"

"So, you don't give up on her. EJ deserves happiness more than anyone. One mistake isn't worth losing that over, as long as you don't plan on making the same mistake again." Her eyes narrowed at him.

"No, I don't."

"Good."

After dropping that bombshell, Lucy turned and left the office, leaving Andrew astonished. Evie had gifted him the one thing that'd become a constant for him during such a horrible time in his life. She'd always been there, loving him.

He really hoped Lucy was right because he knew one thing with absolute certainty.

He would always love Evie James, no matter the time or space.

24
EVIE

Evie stared out the window of her childhood bedroom, overlooking the barn and cow pasture.

How did everything go so horribly wrong?

A sigh escaped her as she stared silently out the window. She missed Andrew terribly and longed to be with him. She'd clung to his text message and voicemail like a prayer. He'd found out about Dylan and knew everything and was beyond sorry for everything that'd occurred.

She didn't blame him though.

It wasn't his fault.

Everything that had happened that day was on Dylan. While her dad was angry with Andrew for not intervening, she was grateful. Who knows what Dylan might've done if Andrew had stepped in to stop him? He didn't know what his brother was capable of, but she did.

The only thing that stopped her from going to Andrew that very second was Dylan and his threat to kill Andrew.

I miss you so much.

She sent her thought out into the void, hoping it would

somehow find its way to Andrew's heart, letting him know she was his, no matter how far away she might be.

A noise drew her attention to the driveway below. Her dad was back from meeting Lucy to get her things and work from school. The desire to be curled up in her chair in the corner of Andrew's office and living life like normal was almost unbearable.

Stupid Dylan. I hope you rot in a field, as the birds feast upon your innards.

Letting out another sigh of discontentment, Evie peeled herself from the window and headed downstairs to greet her dad.

"Hey, Buttercup," her dad said, as he came in the back door. She smiled at him in return. Aiden held out the leather tote bag for her. "This is all your schoolwork. Lucy was fairly certain she'd packed everything. If something is missing, let her know, and we'll get it for you."

"Thanks, Dad," she told him, taking the bag. As Aiden passed by her, he dropped a kiss on the top of her head. He'd been giving her space since everything had happened, but she wished he would give her some of that sage wisdom of his that would fix everything. "Dad?"

Aiden paused and turned to face her. Evie started to speak, but the words wouldn't come out. Sensing what she wanted to ask, he answered, "Lucy said he seems to be doing okay but looked miserable. She caught him staring at your spot in his office, like a lost puppy. Her words, not mine." Evie merely nodded not knowing what to say.

Tears welled up in her eyes, and she looked away, willing them not to fall. Aiden crossed the kitchen in two strides and wrapped his arms around her. "This is all going to work itself out. It may take a while, but it will." The anxiety inside subsided just enough to get a breath of air down. "And, if it's right and true, then he'll be there at the end of all of this."

Evie nodded into her dad's shoulder. She knew he was right, but it was always easier said than done.

But, will it ever be okay with Dylan alive?

After a few moments, Aiden let her go and started to walk away before telling her, "You should call him. I know what Dylan said, but there are ways of doing it without him knowing. Just let me know if you want to make a call."

"Okay."

Evie dragged her bag upstairs and dumped the contents of it onto her bed. As she skimmed through all the work she had to catch up on, a folded piece of notebook paper fell from one of the books she'd tossed to the side. Her heart caught in her throat as she opened it.

Dear Evie, My Heart,

I can't apologize enough for everything that happened. If I had known for a second about Dylan, I would never have let him near you. I hope you can forgive me for putting you in harm's way and making you endure even one second around him. I don't know what he said to you that caused you to leave, but whatever it is, I do not care. Whatever it is, we can work through it. We can overcome anything, Evie, if you'll only talk to me.

I miss you. Please come back to me.

Love,

Andrew

Tears streamed down her face as she closed the note. Not everything could be overcome.

Death couldn't be overcome, and she wasn't prepared

for a world that didn't include Andrew. Even if they couldn't be together, the connection between them remained because he remained.

Without him, her heart would cease to exist.

Realizing what she needed to do, she rushed out of her room and onto the balcony, overlooking the living room.

"Dad," she called down.

"Yeah, baby?" Her dad looked up from where he was sitting on the couch, watching tv.

"Can you set that call up for me?"

"Sure thing," her dad replied, getting up from the couch and heading to his office.

Ten minutes later, the phone was ringing, and Evie thought she might pass out with each ring.

ANDREW

Andrew was working at his desk when his phone started buzzing from an unknown number. The only person he knew who called from unknown numbers was Dylan, which should've been a clue. Andrew decided to ignore the call and continued working.

I have nothing to say to you, Scout. Absolutely nothing.

The unknown number called back, and something urged him to pick it up. However, the thought of hearing Dylan's voice was revolting, so he ignored it once again.

A minute later, his phone buzzed again, alerting him to a voicemail. Andrew hesitated to listen to it, but for whatever reason, he did.

His breath caught, as regret found him, once again.

"Hey, I figured I would've caught you between classes, but you must be busy. I found your note today, and that's the reason I'm calling. First, you don't have anything to apologize for. Dylan's actions are his own, and him being your brother doesn't matter. I don't blame you, Andrew. Secondly," Andrew heard her voice falter. "I want to come back to you. I want nothing more than that." He could tell she was crying, and the sound broke his heart.

"But I can't. Dylan made it very clear what he'd do if I didn't stay away from you. That's also why I left that day." Anger rose in Andrew at the thought of Dylan threatening her. "He *will* kill you, Andrew. If I come back, he will, and I won't let him. If I have to spend the rest of my life away from you to keep you safe, then I will. I need to know you're out there somewhere. It doesn't matter how long or how far we are separated. I am yours now, tomorrow, and forever. My heart belongs to you. It always has and always will. I pray and long for the day we might be reunited, but for now, this is goodbye."

Andrew felt tears, fighting their way into his eyes as the voicemail ended. He loved Evie James more than words could ever express, and he wanted nothing more than to tell her. They belonged to one another, and he refused to allow Dylan to be the one to stand in the way of them.

He ran his hands through his hair trying to think. Frustration, anger, and love coursed through his veins all at the same time. The last time he'd felt this much at once was when Lily had died. However, he hadn't been in love then, and now, love might be the thing that got him killed. Enough was enough, and he was going to figure this out no matter what it cost him.

Andrew turned to his computer and quickly sent out an email, canceling his classes for the next day before rushing out of his office. As soon as he got home, he threw some clothes into a bag and whatever else he might need.

A couple of hours and one errand later, Andrew was on the road, heading to Kentucky. It might've been a mistake, but he couldn't let the last time they saw each other be the last. Nothing was more important than them. He'd finally found the place where his heart belonged, and he wasn't going to let his little brother keep it from him.

It was almost midnight when Andrew pulled onto the gravel road to Evie's home. He was shocked by the amount of land her father owned. He'd driven for a good two minutes before the house came into view. It was a beautiful white farmhouse with a huge front porch surrounded by two large oak trees. It was one of the most picturesque homes Andrew had ever seen.

Before leaving South Carolina, Andrew had texted Aiden he was coming. There was no way he was showing up to Aiden James' home unannounced. The lights were still on inside, where he assumed Aiden was waiting for him.

Maybe, he won't kill me and bury me somewhere out here.

He pulled in next to Aiden's truck and took a deep breath, praying he was doing the right thing. He didn't want to push Evie, but he also didn't want her to pull away from him out of fear.

Before Andrew could knock on the door, it opened. Aiden's large form filled the doorway.

"Let's talk out here before you come in," Aiden said quietly, stepping outside and shutting the door.

They walked towards the small garden area off the side of the house and sat down at the small table. The night air bit through Andrew's jacket, but he didn't mind. It was the first time in days that he felt somewhat at peace.

Aiden took time to light the outdoor heater that instantly lit up the table and began warming the area. Andrew watched Aiden ease into the chair and sit back comfortably before saying, "So, before I let you see Evie, I want to know why you're here. I know *why* you're here, but what made you come?"

Andrew took a breath and told him, "Because I love her with everything I am, sir. I'm not going to let Dylan take her from me, especially not by scaring her with threats."

Aiden nodded silently, taking time to think over Andrew's words.

After a minute, Aiden asked, "Are you sure? Because you need to be sure. I can't let you come into my house, tell her things like that, and put her in danger only for you to break her heart in the end. I guess what I'm asking is, are you in this for the long haul?"

Andrew held Aiden's gaze. "Yes, I am in this for the long haul." Andrew reached into his pocket and pulled out a small black box. As he set it on the table, Aiden drew in a sharp breath. "The other reason I came was to ask for your blessing to marry your daughter. I know she and I haven't known each other very long, but when you know, you know. Although, I don't plan to ask her for a while. At least, not until all of this is settled. I don't want to put her in more danger by asking her, and I don't want anything influencing her answer."

Aiden picked up the box and examined the ring. "Well, it's perfect, and she'll definitely love it."

"Is that a, yes?"

"It is if you can promise me three things. First, I want you to promise that you will *always* fight for her. No matter what. Next, I need you to promise that you will never leave her. Divorce is never an option. If you have a problem, you work through it, fighting for each other. Lastly, I want to know that you're never going to leave her in harms away again. If you see her in a compromising situation, I want to know you won't leave her to face it by herself." His eyes stared very intently at Andrew. "If you can promise me those three things, then you can have my blessing." Aiden closed the box and slid it back across the table to Andrew.

Picking up the box, he mulled over what Aiden was asking him. It was easy to say you would always fight for your marriage and never divorce, especially at the peak of being love. It was always in the low points people forgot why they loved one another. However, Andrew knew deep in his soul he'd been meant for Evie. That he'd been born for her. It'd just taken a while to find her, his heart and his purpose.

Andrew felt his head slowly nodding before saying, "Yes, I can promise you those things. I vow to always fight for her and to never leave her. As for the last thing, I will *never* do that again. No matter what or who. If I see she needs me, I will act."

"Then, you have my blessing, Dr. Boss Man," Aiden told him, grinning. "I don't think I could've chosen any better myself."

Andrew smiled, feeling full of pride at Aiden's approval. He wasn't an easy man to impress, and he'd just entrusted his daughter's life and future to him.

A renewed sense of determination welled in Andrew. He hadn't expected to ever find Evie, let alone so soon after his wife's death, and he knew he couldn't let her escape him. He wasn't just grasping for her. He was taking hold of his purpose.

Aiden led Andrew into the house and told him how to find Evie's room. Slowly, he made his way up the stairs and stood outside her closed door, feeling nervous and anxious but also excited. He hadn't seen her in days, and despite everything bad that had occurred, he was excited to see her.

Taking a deep breath, he quietly turned the knob, pushing the door open. Sliding his jacket off and placing it in the chair behind the door, he quietly walked to the edge of the bed. Evie looked so peaceful and beautiful sleeping in the moonlight shining through the window onto her bed. He hated to wake her, but they needed to talk.

He knelt beside the bed and smoothed the hair off her forehead.

"Hey," he whispered. Her eyes slowly fluttered open.

Confusion filled her face as her eyes focused on him. "Andrew?"

"Yeah."

She reached out and touched his face, causing a small sigh to leave him. Her touch felt like returning home.

Finally.

He turned his head and kissed the palm of her hand.

"Is it really you?"

He softly chuckled, "Yes, it's really me."

She sat up, asking, "What are you doing here?"

Andrew sat on the bed next to her and explained, "I got your voicemail and didn't want things to end like that. In fact, I don't want to end things at all."

Evie began shaking her head. "Andrew, Dylan told me he would kill you if I returned. I can't put you in danger like that." She took hold of his hand, as if she were clinging to his life, trying to keep him from disappearing into the night.

"Evie, I can't let Dylan be the reason we end. It's not a good enough reason."

"Your life isn't a good enough reason?"

He shook his head no. "No, sweetheart. It isn't. Besides, I'm not living if you're not with me. Dylan can threaten all he wants, but that doesn't mean he will be able to follow through with it. I know him. I've known him for a lot longer than you, and if there is one thing I know for certain, he underestimates me. He found that out that day before leaving my house."

"But Andrew, you didn't even know who he really was until that day at your house. If I hadn't been there, you still wouldn't know. Maybe, you underestimate him too."

"I am prepared for anything, Evie," he confessed, squeezing her hand.

"Well, I'm not." She pulled her hand away from his. "I'm not prepared to lose you permanently or to live in a world where you don't exist. I can't do that, won't do that."

Andrew cupped the sides of her face and with a voice full of emotion, said, "Evie, I love you. I love you more than my own life. I love you with everything I am and everything I hope to be. I can't be the reason we aren't together. I would rather live with the possibility of dying than live separately from you. I need you." His thumbs swiped at the silent tears, sliding down her cheeks. "I need you to trust me, baby. We can get through this, but I need to know you're with me. Can you do that? Trust me to see you safe and to get us through this mess?"

Andrew's heart felt like it was going to beat through his chest. He loved this woman with everything he had, and he prayed she would take a leap of faith and trust him. None of it would mean anything if she wasn't with him.

He felt her hand slip into his and saw her slowly nod. "I can do that but on one condition."

"Anything."

"You cannot die."

"Deal." A small smile formed on her lips as he leaned forward.

"Deal," she whispered as Andrew's lips met hers.

Pulling back, he said, "It's late, and you need some sleep."

As he started to stand up, Evie grabbed his hand, holding on tightly. "Don't go."

Andrew hesitated, weighing the odds of Aiden shooting him for sleeping in his daughter's bed, but given the circumstances, he decided to take the risk.

Andrew slid his boots off as Evie scooted over to the other side of the bed, making room for him. He took his flannel shirt off but left on his pants and undershirt. Sleeping in her bed was a big enough risk already, and he didn't feel the need to make things worse by taking his clothes off.

Lifting the blankets, he slid into the bed and reached for Evie. As she nestled up to him, they both let out a sigh of relief. Andrew couldn't help breathing her in. The sweet flowery scent of her began lulling him to sleep. Everything about her calmed him.

He pressed a kiss to head before closing his eyes.

As he was drifting to sleep, Evie's soft voice called, "Andrew?"

"Hm?"

"I love you too."

Andrew's arms tightened, pulling her closer.

25
EVIE

Evie's eyes fluttered open, and for just a moment, she didn't know where she was. There was a warmth surrounding her, making her feel safe and secure, and all she wanted was to melt into it and let it consume her. A light snoring sounded from behind her, jolting her senses awake. A small panic began before she remembered the cause of the cocoon of warmth.

Andrew.

They must've not moved at all last night, which explained why she felt so stiff. However, she'd slept like a rock, and for the first in a very long time, she hadn't had a nightmare. In fact, she hadn't dreamt at all. All was right in the world, but deep down, she knew it was only a matter of time.

Eventually, the bubble would burst. They were merely living on borrowed time. As much as she'd like to deny it, she couldn't.

Evie hated to move from Andrew's arms, but she desperately needed to stretch her aching limbs. She'd barely moved an inch when Andrew's arms instinctively tightened around her. Smiling, she ran her fingers down the arm wrapped around her waist. At her touch, the arm instantly relaxed. Even in his sleep, Andrew reacted to her touch, and it was fact Evie relished.

It seemed impossible to Evie that they could have this kind of connection. She knew her parents had a soul tied connection, but she'd always believed they were the exception. Evie firmly believed that if it could be read about in books, then it wasn't destined to be real. Not to mention, she never thought she was the kind of person that could have someone anchor to her soul, but there he was, snoring softly behind her.

Andrew Brant was so intertwined with her soul and heart she knew she'd never be able to separate herself from him.

No matter how hard she might try.

No matter the miles or distance.

No matter the time or space.

This is forever.

It was barely dawn, so she still had a little time to spare before getting up to go feed the chickens and milk the cow. Being back in her parent's house meant back to farm chores, but she didn't mind. In fact, she quite enjoyed working on the farm. It felt good to be doing something physical, and it helped to keep her mind off things.

Gently, she rolled over to face Andrew. She couldn't help but trace his face with her fingertips. As her finger slid over his square jawline, it didn't escape her at how good looking he was, so she took full advantage of him being asleep to simply gaze at him.

Ever so slowly, his eyes opened, and those beautiful

dark green eyes settled on her. A smile found its way onto both of their faces.

"Good morning," she said quietly but gleefully. Evie wasn't a morning person by any definition, but her heart was happy to wake up in Andrew's arms. And her heart was even happier that he was now awake.

"Morning," he said, squeezing her hip.

"Sleep good?"

"Mhm. You?" She nodded at him. "Good." He pressed a kiss to her forehead. "I could get used to this," he whispered as he nuzzled her face with his.

"Me too," she sighed. They lay entangled for several minutes, taking in the moment that was sure to not happen again for a long time. "As much as I want this moment to last, I have things to take care of."

"At this hour of the morning? It's barely light outside."

"Yes. If I don't feed Matilda, she will be very angry with me. Not to mention, I can practically hear Clarabella making a fuss because I'm late," she stated matter-of-factly, detaching herself from Andrew and climbing out of bed.

"Who are Matilda and Clarabella?" Andrew asked, sitting up. Evie stopped looking for her clothes and turned to look at him.

"The chicken and cow, of course. Who did you think I was talking about?"

"I forgot this is an actual farm," he sighed, rubbing a hand down his face.

"Give me two minutes, and then you can take a turn in the bathroom," she smiled at him as she walked into the ensuite bathroom and shut the door.

Several minutes later, Evie opened the door to find

Andrew buttoning his flannel shirt. She paused before continuing into room.

Is this what it's like? To live life with Andrew?

Would it be like this if we were married?

Andrew looked up to find her staring. His eyebrows went up in question.

"This all feels very domestic." When a quizzical look passed over his face, she clarified. "This. Me. You. Getting up and getting dressed. Doing normal things."

A knowing smile formed on his face as he asked, "Does that bother you?"

As she continued into the room, she answered, "Quite the opposite actually." Tossing her pajamas on her bed, she gave him a quick kiss on the cheek and went to open her bedroom door. "Aha! I knew it."

"What?"

"Here," she said, turning around with his bag. "I thought I heard Dad creeping outside the door earlier."

"I didn't hear anything, and I'm usually a light sleeper."

The floor outside her door was especially squeaky, but her dad had always made it his mission to sneak by without her knowing.

Evie sat on the edge of the bed, dividing her hair into two sections to braid.

Something on her face must've changed because Andrew asked, "What?"

"What, what?" Evie asked back.

"You know what?"

She tied the elastic around the end of her braid and looked at him. "I feel a little silly admitting this but hearing my dad walking around and going about his business makes me feel safe. It always has. He was gone a lot when I was growing up, but when he was here, I knew if he was going about his regular routine, then everything was fine and nothing bad could happen. I haven't had that kind of security or reassurance since I moved out."

"There's nothing silly about needing your dad, Evie. No matter how old you are. I wish I still had my dad around to run to when things get messy or just for reassurance in life."

"How old were you when he died?"

"Nineteen."

"I'm sorry," she told him softly.

"It's okay." He walked over and kissed her on the head, setting his bag on the bed. As he dug through his bag, he kept glancing at her.

After three glances, Evie finally asked, "What?"

"What, what?" He smirked at her.

Evie couldn't help but roll her eyes, causing Andrew to laugh.

"Why do you keep looking at me?"

He found his toothbrush and paused before turning to go to the bathroom. "It just makes sense now." He told her, like she should know what he was referring to, but she was lost.

"What does?"

"Your style. You always seem comfortable and relaxed in what you wear. Don't get me wrong, I like it, but it's not what most of the girls in Beaumont wear. Seeing you here, it makes sense. You're a farm girl."

An unladylike snort came from her as she quirked an eyebrow at him. "It took you that long to figure out?" She looked down at her work leggings, wool socks, and old hoodie and realized it was pretty much her normal attire.

Maybe, I should change things up a bit.

"Yeah, it did, but like I said, I like it. Give me a second, and I'll come help you with your chores."

Evie hopped up and searched for her beanie. It had snowed during the night and would no doubt be freezing outside. It wasn't where she'd left it, but she knew it was in her room somewhere. She was crawling on the floor, looking under the bed when Andrew came out of the bathroom.

"What are you doing?"

"I can't find," her voice trailed off as she hopped up and opened the drawer to her bedside table. "Found it," she shouted triumphantly. She pulled her beanie on and asked, "You ready?"

Andrew stared at her, clearly perplexed, but his eyes were shining with what looked an awful lot like unfiltered love. "Have I told you that I love you?"

Every part of her warmed at his words. Three little words from his mouth had the power to make her melt.

Is love supposed to be this cheesy?

"Not recently."

His arms came about her waist as he leaned close to her face and said, "I love you."

Her arms circled his neck and rested there, returning the sentiment. "I love you too."

It was all the invitation he needed as his lips met hers. A low sound came from the back of his throat that made Evie feel like she was on fire. After a moment, they finally broke apart.

"We should go," Evie said breathlessly. Any longer in that room with him, and they were going to have to call the fire department to put out the flames from her inevitable combustion.

The house was quiet as they walked downstairs to the mudroom attached to the kitchen. Evie pulled on her boots and grabbed her heavy work jacket. She zipped it up over her hoodie as they walked outside. "It's freezing." Her teeth were chattering uncontrollably.

"I can't believe it snowed," Andrew mused, walking beside her.

There was a light dusting on the ground. Thankfully, it wasn't more because she didn't want to face her dad's wrath by not doing her chores, and that's exactly what she would've done, if there'd been more on the ground.

"I've always loved the snow, but I'd rather enjoy it from inside by the fire." She tucked her frozen hands in her pockets, seeking the slightest bit of warmth.

Andrew laughed as he looked around, taking in the scenery. "Are we the only one's up?"

She shook her head. "Dad has been up for hours. He's probably out checking cows with the cowhands, Davey and Pete."

"Only two cowhands?"

Evie opened the barn and stepped inside before saying, "Despite the size of the land, the amount of actual farming is relatively small. My parents have always loved being able to live off the land, but they never wanted to go commercial with it." Evie grabbed two baskets and two buckets from the shelf in the back.

Andrew took the two buckets from her and asked, "Where is your mom? I haven't met her yet."

"Mom has her virtues but waking up at the butt crack of dawn is not one of them."

Andrew laughed, "I didn't think it would be your thing either."

"Oh, I can assure you it most certainly is not. However, I have a retired Navy Seal for a father, so when he says go, I just start running. Don't even bother asking how far."

"I see," Andrew replied, amused.

"I don't mind the work, but it would be better if it wasn't freezing and barely morning." Evie paused to make sure they had everything. "Ready to work, cowboy?"

"Cowboy? I like it." Andrew's chest puffed up at being called cowboy.

Evie could only shake her head at him. "I'm sure you do. Come on."

26

EVIE

Evie and Andrew worked side-by-side, getting the morning chores done. An hour or so later, they headed back to the house with fresh milk and eggs. Walking into the kitchen, they found her mom rolling dough for biscuits.

"Morning, Mama." Evie walked over to the counter and set the basket of eggs down, all while failing miserably to stifle a yawn. Her mom looked down at her feet, and Evie grimaced. Her mom had a strict no boots in the house policy, especially in her kitchen. The kitchen was her mom's domain, and she had strict rules for it.

"Take those dirty boots off right now, young lady. No boots in my kitchen," her mom fussed. Evie turned to go but was stopped by a hand on her arm. "Wait, come here." Before she could move, her mom pulled her in for a tight hug, giving her a big squeeze.

Andrew came in the kitchen in his socks with the pails of milk. "Where would you like this, Mrs. James?"

"Call me Elaine," she said, waving a hand at him. "You can set the milk on the island."

"Yes, ma'am," Andrew replied, walking to the center of the kitchen and setting the pails down on the counter.

Elaine turned her attention back to Evie and said, "Boots, now, missy." Evie huffed as she turned to go to the small mud room by the back door. She plopped down on the wooden bench and yanked her boots off, dropping them with a thud by the bench.

Tossing her jacket on the peg on the wall over the bench, she heard Andrew ask her mom, "Is there anything else I can do for you?"

"Have you ever made biscuits?"

"Yes, ma'am," Andrew replied, surprising Evie. She leaned against the doorway and watched as Andrew crossed the kitchen to where her mom was standing.

"You must have some good women in your family."

A small pang of sadness shot through her chest at her mom's words. Andrew had lost both of his parents, and she knew how much they had meant to him. To lose a parent was unbearable, but to lose both, took more strength than any one person had.

"Yes, ma'am. They made sure I knew how to feed myself and others."

"Feeding others is a delight of the soul. At least, it's that way for me."

Andrew smiled at her. "I've never heard it put like that, but I concur with that statement."

"Well, this is mostly finished. The dough just needs to cut and placed on the baking sheet."

"Alright. I think I can handle that," he told her, stepping back to the sink to wash his hands.

"You get going on that, and I'll get the bacon and eggs going."

Evie had always enjoyed watching her mom working in

the kitchen. Elaine was independent, fierce, and extremely tough, but she was also a gentle homemaker. She always said it was because Aiden had softened her by giving her a safe place to exist.

Evie couldn't remember a morning when her mom hadn't been in the kitchen, making breakfast. She was almost always barefoot, but on cold mornings like that one, she had her wool socks on. This morning, she had her dark hair pulled back with a small blue clip that matched her blue eyes almost perfectly.

Joy always exuded from her parent's house, and it was mostly because of her mother. She made the house a home and made it come alive. Without her, everything would be very dull and despondent.

Before she could ponder anymore on the topic, Elaine's voice broke through her thoughts. "Well, Eve's, are you going to stand there all day, or are you going to help?"

"Sorry," she murmured, dragging her way across the large kitchen.

"Will you strain the milk, please?"

"Yes, Ma'am," Evie replied, bending to open the large cabinet on the bottom of the oversized kitchen island. She brought out two large glass jars and set to straining the milk into the jars through cheese cloths. The sounds of the kitchen filled the background, as the three of them worked.

She was almost done with the milk when her mom walked up beside her and whispered, "I like him."

"Me too," she whispered back.

She and her mom turned to look at Andrew as he finished cutting the last of the dough into biscuits. His back was to them, but he must've sensed someone staring at him because he suddenly turned around.

A smile slowly formed on his lips as he asked, "Am I the only one working this morning?"

Evie and her mom dramatically gasped at the same time. "Are you kidding me?" "He's joking right?" They spoke at the same time and turned back to their work, muttering about Andrew to themselves and one another.

Andrew's deep laugh filled the gaps of their muttering.

"What did you do, Dr. Boss Man?" Evie turned to see her dad's enormous frame, filling the doorway to the kitchen.

"Got them working," he replied, as if he'd gotten an army into shape by himself.

His answer sent Evie and Elaine into a new round of comments about his audacity as they flew about the kitchen, getting breakfast ready, while Andrew and Aiden watched and laughed together.

"You'll fit right in," Evie heard her dad tell Andrew as she passed by them. Evie couldn't help but think about how true her dad's words were. Everything felt natural and right about having him there. He fit in seamlessly with her family. It was like placing the final piece in a puzzle. Except, she never knew she had been missing a piece, until then.

Andrew felt right.

He felt like home.

He was home.

A little while later, breakfast was on the table, and they were seated.

"Well, I believe that was the fastest breakfast has ever made it to the table," Aiden teased.

"Don't you start Aiden James, or it'll be the last breakfast you ever have," Elaine warned.

Aiden laughed and leaned over to kiss Elaine on the

cheek. "I meant thank you, honey. Breakfast is especially delicious this morning."

"What am I going to do with you?" Elaine asked, shaking her head at Aiden.

"Love me to eternity."

"And beyond," Elaine finished.

"Get a room," Evie hollered. "Bleh."

Her dad started laughing and said, "Speaking of rooms."

Evie glanced at Andrew and found him glancing back at her. Aiden's gaze narrow and hardened at Andrew.

"Nothing untoward happened last night. I swear," Andrew said hastily. All of their eyes were on Andrew, and he looked ready to make a run for it.

"Stop giving the boy a hard time, Aid," Elaine said, nudging him with her hand.

"It's my job. She's my only daughter, so it's the only time I have to put the fear of God into someone," he pleaded to Elaine.

Evie leaned forward on her elbows, narrowing her eyes at her dad. "He knows nothing happened."

"What makes you think that, Buttercup?" Aiden switched his narrow gaze to Evie.

She matched his gaze and said, "Because if you had suspected the slightest whiff of something untoward happening, you would've ripped him out of my room in a heartbeat. Not only that, but you left his bag outside the door."

"How do you know that was me? Your mother could've left the bag," Aiden countered.

Evie leaned a little further towards her dad. "One, Mama doesn't get out of bed that early. Two, the sound of the footsteps. It's cold this morning, so there was just the slightest bit of a hitch in your step from where that old gunshot wound was bothering you."

Aiden sat back satisfied with a bit of smug look on his face.

"You've taught her well," Elaine told him.

"That wasn't anything but basic observation," Evie said, waving her mother off.

It was a game she and her dad had played since she was little. It'd been his way of teaching her to pay attention to her surroundings. He'd ask her questions about different things, and she'd have to give an account. Most of the questions had been easy, like the color of the house they'd passed on the way to town. As she'd gotten older, he'd taught her to learn the differences of people and to take note of them. Did they have tattoos? Did their voice have any noticeable characteristics? Evie had practiced by listening to her parents and learning to tell them apart without thought.

"Yes, but you were confident and sure of your answers," Aiden argued. "That means more than you think it does."

"Again, basic information from knowing you for so long. It's not going to be lifesaving by any means."

"Well, maybe not, but you two are going to take up training again. You're growing better and stronger by the day," her mom told her.

"It's not enough," she muttered.

Aiden reached out and grabbed her hand that rested on the table. "We're going to get there, Buttercup. I'm not going to let you go back out there unprepared."

"Really? Isn't that what you said last time? When you sent me to Beaumont?" Evie snapped back at her dad. "I wasn't really prepared the day Dylan knocked me to the ground and choked the life out of me nor was I prepared for when he showed up at Andrew's and forced himself on me while Andrew watched."

She pushed back from the table, standing. With a shaky breath she said, "I feel like I'm just waiting for the day when he finally loses all control and kills me or someone I love, and I don't know how much longer I can handle living with that, looming over me."

With that, Evie left the table. She was shaking as she left the room. She hadn't spoken to her father like that in years, and she hadn't meant to express so much of what she was desperately trying to keep hidden inside.

Heading to the front door, she yanked her dad's spare work coat off the hook by the door and ran outside. She was breathing hard as she reached the rope swing, hanging from the big oak tree in front of her house. Evie's chest tightened as she tried to force air into her lungs. She hadn't had a panic attack in months, and honestly, this one was overdue.

Evie's eyes were squeezed tight as she tried to shut out every intrusive thought, rapidly passing through her mind. Leaning forward, she grabbed at her chest, gasping for air. A large hand pulled her clenched hands from her chest as another one gently but firmly pressed on her chest. Her eyes opened to find Andrew standing in front of her.

A look of wariness was on his face, but the sight of him provided the comfort she so badly needed. He pressed her still clenched hands on his chest and softly said, "Breathe with me."

Evie could feel his chest, rising and falling beneath her hands and began to match his breathing after a few desperate tries. Peace began to flow through her, like a warm light invading the darkest of nights.

"You're safe, Evie. *We* are safe," Andrew told her in a low soothing voice.

Tears began to fall at the comfort his voice and words offered her. The tears turned into agonizing sobs as she finally broke from the weeks of suffering and hurt Dylan had caused.

She felt Andrew's arms envelop her, pulling her close. "It's okay, sweetheart," he murmured into her hair as he held her. "It's okay. I've got you."

Gradually, her sobs began to subside. Evie sniffed, wiping her eyes. "I'm sorry."

"There's no need to apologize. None of this is your fault. You've had to deal with a lot lately, more than anyone should. If you need to cry, scream, or hit something, then do it. The only thing I ask is that you do not run away from me. Let me in. Let me be there for you and share in your hurt." As she looked into his dark green eyes, she found solace and a safety she'd never known. She didn't know when it had happened, but Andrew had become her home. He'd become her protector and safe place to run. She feared what might happen in the future, but no matter how far she ran from him, it wouldn't be far enough to untangle herself from him. Andrew was etched into the deepest parts of her very being.

So, she promised him a lifetime with her words. "No more running." Even if the world burned down around them, she would still cling to him.

"No more running," he echoed, kissing her forehead. Brushing escaped strands of hair from her face, he asked "Are you okay?"

Evie nodded as she blew out a hard breath, wiping her face some more.

"Good. Now, let's go back inside and eat. I'm starving."

Evie laughed at that. "Of course you are. You eat like a teenage boy."

Andrew slung an arm around Evie's shoulders, and they made their way back inside.

Breakfast passed uneventfully as they all chatted and laughed comfortably with one another. Despite the panic attack, Evie was happy and for the most part, content.

Maybe, this was how it was always supposed to be? Maybe, I was always waiting for him.

As they finished eating, Aiden slapped a hand on Andrew's shoulder and said, "It's you and me today, Dr. Boss Man. Let's go." Aiden rose from his chair, taking his plate and glass over to the kitchen sink.

Andrew raised his eyebrows, giving Evie a questioning look. Evie merely shrugged and gave him a sympathetic look. She watched as he stood and gathered his plate. Before he followed her dad, Andrew bent and kissed her on the head.

"Love you," he whispered for only her to hear.

Everything about her seemed to warm at his touch and words. Being loved by Andrew was by far the best thing she'd experienced.

27
ANDREW

Andrew stepped out the backdoor of Evie's parent's house and was met by cold air. He'd never minded the cold and sometimes welcomed it; however, he wasn't sure what Aiden had in store for them today, and he was sure whatever it was might go somewhat smoother if it were a little warmer outside.

Blowing a breath out and watching it curl around the air in front of him, he began to make his way to where Aiden was waiting for him by the barn.

"Ready to go, Dr. Boss Man?"

Andrew nodded, following Aiden around the back of the barn to where two ATV vehicles were waiting.

"Know how to drive one?"

"Yes, sir."

"Good. Hop on and let's get going." A loud rumble came from Aiden's ATV as he cranked it to let it warm up. Andrew climbed up and did the same.

They spent the next several minutes in silence, waiting for the ATVs to warm up. Andrew took the time to let the cold seep into his veins and further awaken him, while he observed the farm around him. It was still early in the morning, but there was now enough golden light to get a good look at things.

The fields were vast and spotted with black cows. In the distance, Andrew could make out the ridge of a mountain. They weren't quite as big as the ones surrounding his house, but he still appreciated the view.

Pair the fields and mountains with the wooded area towards the back of the property, and it was almost perfect. Not to mention, the gorgeous yards surrounding the house. Andrew couldn't help but wonder what it looked like in the Spring when everything was alive and thriving. Hopefully, he would get to see it one day and experience it with Evie. He hoped they'd have many experiences together. Perhaps, they were at the beginning of the road for new adventures.

The revving of Aiden's ATV brought him back to reality. He looked over to find Aiden signaling for him to follow. Andrew and Aiden followed the driveway past the back of the house and onto a small dirt road. They drove down the road past several large fields before the road ended. Aiden turned to the right, heading towards a trail that ran through the woods.

Andrew and Aiden had been driving for about ten minutes before Aiden came to a stop and turned his ATV off. Andrew followed suit. He turned to look at Andrew before gesturing towards the area in front of them and saying, "I like to check the property lines at least every couple of days, but I always have an eye on everything through the cameras posted every 100 yards or so."

"How many acres are there?"

"500. It's hard to keep it all monitored. I used to keep a check on things by myself, but ever since Dylan came into the picture, I've also had Davey and Pete monitoring things. I'll let you meet them later."

Andrew nodded, surveying the area. They were in a heavily wooded area. Even with the trees empty of their leaves, it was dense. As he looked around, he noticed a camera in one of the trees to his right. It was pointing at a spot that looked like it had been disturbed by a large animal of some kind. "I'm assuming we stopped here because of whatever the camera caught coming through there," Andrew said, gesturing to the spot.

Aiden stood up and made his way over to the spot. Andrew followed him, and they both began to survey the area. Aiden put his hands on his waist and sighed through his nose. Andrew had a sinking feeling in his stomach as he watched Aiden's breath turn into a swirling cloud of smoke.

"I asked you to come with me today for a reason. I haven't told Ellie or Evie about this yet, and I'll hear you out on what you think might be best in that regard."

Andrew felt like a brick had wedged itself in the pit of his stomach.

"Two nights ago, the camera went off. By the time I got here, he was gone. I haven't seen any sign of him since and none of the other cameras have gone off. Davey and Pete also haven't seen any signs of someone being on the property."

Andrew took a deep breath and blew it out. Dylan had followed Evie back to Kentucky and was making his presence known.

"Are you sure it was him?" Andrew really hoped Aiden was mistaken, but he knew a man like Aiden was rarely mistaken.

Aiden's face was grave when he answered. "Yeah, I'm sure. He had plenty of time to figure out Evie had left town and headed here, so he's doing what any confident psychopath does."

"Letting you know he's here and waiting," Andrew responded somberly.

"That's my thinking. He only wanted to make his presence known this time; however, that only means he's biding his time, and who knows what he'll do when he does make a move?"

They were both silent for a moment before Andrew spoke. "I'm sorry, Aiden. I wish I'd known he was like this. If I had even a hint of his true nature, I would've tried to put an end to it a long time ago and get him help. I truly had no idea until he was in my house with her."

A wave of guilt and nausea hit Andrew as the memories of that day flooded in. He'd nearly killed Dylan, and for the span of a heartbeat, he thought he really might. And although he hadn't, he'd really wanted to, and that scared Andrew, a lot.

If his own brother was capable of raping women, what was he capable of, and how far could his anger carry him if he let it? He'd never experienced the kind of rage he had that day, as he had beaten Dylan. Even though it'd been in defense of Evie, it still worried him. He'd never considered himself the violent type, but when he had realized what had happened to Evie, he was ready to obliterate everyone and everything in his path.

"It's not your fault. I don't blame you," Aiden said, slicing through his thoughts. Sincerity filled his voice. Andrew had been worried Aiden would blame him and not give him his approval, but as their eyes met, Andrew only found trust and forgiveness.

With a deep breath, he asked, "So, what do you want to do about this, or what are you doing about this? Not to mention, if he's this close, then he will figure out I'm here. If he doesn't already know."

"I think we should keep this from the girls for now. There's no need to worry them." Andrew nodded his agreement. He didn't want Evie having any extra anxiety in her own home. "I've explained things to Davey and Pete, and they're in the process of moving the cows to the pasture closest to the house. That will put them nearby in case anything happens."

"You trust them?" Andrew hadn't met them, and he was positive Aiden wouldn't hire people he didn't trust. However, he had to ask for himself. Worry would follow him if he didn't at least ask.

"Yes. They both served with me, and I know them well. If I'm not around, they're the only two I trust with the safety of Ellie and Evie." Aiden stuffed his hands into the pockets of his jacket and rolled his shoulders back, as if he was shoving the cold off of him. "I'll introduce you to them later today, and you can decide for yourself."

Andrew let out a small laugh. "I don't think there's anything to decide. If you trust them, then I trust them."

"You might be right about that," Aiden grinned. "However, I understand the need to make your own judgments when it comes to the protection of the ones you love." Aiden gestured over his shoulder to the ATVs. "Let's go find some heat, and we can figure out the rest."

Andrew and Aiden were standing around the fire pit outside the bunkhouse, warming up when Davey and Pete came riding up on a utility vehicle. A large blonde-haired man with a scruffy beard got out first and asked, "Is this Dr. Boss Man?"

Aiden clapped Andrew on the shoulder and proudly answered, "The one and only."

Andrew smiled and stuck his hand out to the man. "Andrew," he said.

"Pete," the man replied.

"Don't you mean, whipped little sapsucker?" The other man loudly asked in a joking manner. He was clearly the oldest of the group, but despite his age, it was obvious from his muscular frame that he was still very much in shape. Unlike Aiden and Pete, he had gray hair and a gray beard.

"Leave him alone, Davey," Aiden warned in the same tone.

"I'm just messing," he said, grasping Andrew's hand. "It's a pleasure to meet you." A genuine smile was on his face.

"You too," Andrew told him with his own smile.

He already liked Davey and Pete. Andrew had been expecting two very serious and scary men, but Davey and Pete were almost the opposite. If he hadn't already known they were former Seals, he would never have guessed.

As they gathered around the fire warming their hands from the cold air, Aiden took the time to get the morning rundown from the guys. "How're the cows?"

"They didn't seem thrilled to be losing their field, but we eventually got them all moved to the upper pasture," Pete answered.

"Would've been easier with some extra help," Davey chimed in, eyeing Aiden and Andrew.

"At least you get paid," Aiden quipped back.

Davey waved him off. "Yeah, yeah."

"How about I make it up to you by taking you over to the range after lunch?"

"Heck yeah," Davey and Pete yelled at the same time.

Eagerness seeped from Pete as he told them, "I've been wanting to try out my new Ruger SR 1911."

"I need to give my 44 Magnum a clean and shoot it. It's been a while," Davey echoed Pete's sentiments.

"I've always wanted to shoot a 44 Magnum," Andrew told Davey. Excitement filled him at the thought of shooting the same gun Dirty Harry had used.

"You're welcome to it if you want," Davey told him.

"Wow," Pete responded incredulously.

Clearly, he had missed something. "What?"

"Davey won't let Pete touch it," Aiden answered.

"Not after he dropped it and nearly killed me," Davey nearly shouted.

"That's not what happened, and you know it," Pete protested.

Aiden was trying to stifle a laugh but was failing miserably. Andrew felt a laugh beginning to rise within himself, as he watched Pete and Davey argue over what really happened. He never imagined he would be standing on Aiden James's property, laughing with him over two former Navy Seals arguing. There'd been a lot of hardship lately, but in that moment, everything felt good. It felt really good and right.

"Alright you two. Why don't we go to the range right now and see which one of you can shoot straight?" Aiden's deep voice cut through the shouts.

Davey and Pete only paused long enough to hear what Aiden was saying before starting a new argument over who was the better driver. They climbed on the utility vehicle and headed off; their voices lingering in the air.

"Are they always like that?"

Aiden let out a low chuckle. "Yeah, but they're brothers. I've only seen them get into one serious argument. They're more like an old married couple, bickering for the sake of bickering."

Andrew laughed and got on his ATV to follow the guys to the range.

This is turning out to be the best day yet.

Andrew and Aiden had been taking turns, shooting several of Aiden's guns on the range located near the back of Aiden's property. The range had six open stalls. Two of the stalls included concrete tables for benchrest shooting. At the back of the range was a large backstop wall, and throughout the range were several randomly spaced targets.

They'd been at the range for about thirty minutes, and for the entirety of that time, Davey and Pete had been arguing on and off about who was the better shot. Aiden and Andrew took turns interjecting their thoughts into the argument, which only served to add fuel to the fire and amuse Andrew and Aiden.

Andrew felt the bond growing between him and Aiden as they joked with Davey and Pete. It'd been a long time since he'd had an older male's presence and perspective in his life. A wave of sadness washed over him, as he realized how much he missed his dad. He tried not to dwell on the fact that his parents were gone, but there were moments, like that one, where it was unavoidable.

"I wasn't too sure you'd be a good shot. Glad to see you proved me wrong, Dr. Boss Man," Aiden told him in between shots.

"What? An English professor can't be a good shot?"

Aiden let out a small laugh. "The likelihood of an English professor being a good shot is slim to none."

"Feeling a little better about your daughter dating me now?" Andrew gave him a sideways look. He knew Aiden had been waiting for this moment. He may trust Andrew with Evie, but he'd been waiting for Andrew to prove his skills. Maybe he should've been more nervous to prove himself in front of Aiden, but he'd be lying if he said he hadn't been waiting for the moment himself.

Aiden raised his hands in surrender. "Fine. You caught me on that one, but yes, I do feel better about it."

Andrew couldn't help but laugh before turning serious. "Can I ask you a question?"

"Sure," Aiden replied, setting his gun down and turning to face Andrew.

Andrew did the same.

"Why did you give me your blessing if you weren't sure I'd be able to take care of her?"

"I wouldn't have given you my blessing if I thought you couldn't. I wouldn't have left her with you that night in her apartment if I wasn't sure."

Andrew thought back to the night he'd gone to her apartment after her Dylan had attacked her. He'd been surprised at Aiden for leaving him with her. Aiden was very protective of his daughter and to leave her in his care had meant something.

"Okay, fair enough. However, you did have some reservations." Andrew pushed Aiden a little further.

Aiden faced him head on before replying, "At the end of the day, I knew it was right. I knew the kind of man you were and are; however, even though I knew it was right, I needed to know for certain what skills you possessed. I need to know that the person my daughter will marry is capable of protecting her, as I would. That he can meet her needs beyond the basic necessities. That if push comes to shove, he can and will shove harder."

Aiden picked up his gun and reloaded it as he continued. "So, even though I know you'll care for her, I needed to know you could execute that care. You may be able to carry a gun, but do you know how to use it? Would you be able to hit your target without killing her? A lot of men go into relationships and marriage with the idea of caring for their woman, but at the end of the day, they have no idea how to execute that care. I know you had the foundation, but do you have the skill? You being able to hit the target was the last thing I needed to know about you, and if you couldn't, well, I would've made sure you did before we left today."

Andrew slowly nodded, taking in Aiden's words.

"And, just to be clear, you being an English professor isn't an issue. As long as you're able to provide for her financially by honorable means, then I don't care what you do. I only care about who you are as a man."

Aiden's eyes grew intense and narrowed slightly. Setting his gun down, he made his way around the table, prowling closer to Andrew. Everything about his body language emanated intimidation and a fierceness that promised violence. "However, there is one more thing I need to make extremely clear. I'd like to think I know what kind of man you are and that you would never do anything to intentionally hurt her." Aiden's voice dropped low and deadly as he promised, "But if the day should ever come where that changes, I will end you. I won't make the same mistake as before nor will I give you the chance to hurt her twice."

Andrew swallowed as he stared into Aiden's dark eyes. He felt two feet tall with Aiden towering over him. He cleared his throat. "Yes, sir. Agreed."

Something cleared in Aiden's eyes, and Andrew swore he saw relief fill them. They were all feeling the weight of Dylan's actions, not just him and Evie. She and her family had been bearing this burden for a lot longer than he had, and it was easy for him to forget that.

He had the sudden urge to kick his brother's butt from end of the country to the other, but he pushed the urge aside as he addressed Aiden.

"I promise, Aiden, that I will do my best to care for her, but if that day should ever come, heaven forbid, I give you full permission to end me. I'd rather be dead than cause Evie even an ounce of pain." He meant every word. If he ever turned into a fraction of the monster Dylan was, he didn't want to live. There was no world in which he would want to be anything like his brother. If there was even a minuscule chance he could hurt Evie or anyone in that way, then he didn't deserve to live.

Didn't *want* to live.

Aiden clapped a hand on his shoulder and gave it a light squeeze before going back around the table to pick up his gun. They returned to shooting just as Davey and Pete finally gave up on arguing who was the better shot. As far as Andrew could tell, they were pretty much the same shot, so the argument had become a moot point.

The guys were almost out of ammo when they heard a rumbling coming from the distance. A few moments later, someone on a purple dirt bike appeared. The dirt bike stopped a few feet away from them, and the driver cut the engine off.

It only took a second for Andrew to study the driver before he became thoroughly impressed. Long brown hair cascaded down as she took her helmet off, and then those familiar brown eyes met his. Just the sight of her set his heart soaring.

A loud whoop sounded from behind him. He turned to see Pete take off in Evie's direction, yelling, "There's my girl!" Pete swooped in, picking Evie up and spinning her around. Evie let out a giggle, igniting a spark of jealousy in

Andrew. As he watched the situation unfolding in front of him, there was something about it that didn't sit right with him.

Before he could think things through, Andrew started after Pete, asking, "Who's girl?" The casual tone he aimed for came out surly and strained. He wasn't trying to be possessive or act as if he had some sort of claim, but regardless, he figured Pete needed to know where things stood.

However, Pete ignored him, keeping his eyes on Evie. "What are you doing down here?" Pete asked as he slowly let go of her.

Andrew thought it was much too slow, and he was sure Pete's hands had lingered on her waist.

"Bringing y'all some lunch," she smiled up at Pete.

A lustful look passed over Pete's face before he flirtatiously told her, "I hope it's as sweet as that smile of yours."

That was enough for Andrew. He took one stride and was at Evie's side, pulling her to him as he scoffed, "Cheesy."

Evie had been smiling at Pete, but her face completely lit up when she saw Andrew. "Not everyone can be a hot shot professor," Evie said, as she looked up at him. Andrew rolled his eyes at her. She gave him a quick hug and kiss on the cheek. "Having fun?"

"What do you think? ATVs. Guns. What more can a man want?"

Evie laughed. He loved the sound of her laugh. It filled him with joy to know he was the one that could make her laugh and cause the world to be filled with its beautiful sound.

"I'll take that as a yes," she replied.

"Hey, Buttercup," Aiden hollered from his spot at the range. Evie walked toward the stall her dad was occupying.

Aiden took the backpack from her shoulders and kissed her head. "What do you have in here?" Aiden held the backpack up, testing the weight of it. "It feels like it's filled with lead." With a dramatized grunt, he set the backpack on the table.

"Just the basic necessities," she replied, as Davey came up and gave her a quick side hug.

"Basic necessities," Aiden mused to himself as he opened the backpack. Food and drinks poured out onto the table. Aiden gave her a look, and Evie just shrugged.

"Mama wanted to make sure y'all had enough to eat."

"Us and what army? This is enough to feed a whole platoon," Aiden gawked.

Davey and Pete began to snatch up food. There was an assortment of sandwiches, chips, fruit, and cookies. Andrew bent and snatched up a bottle of water that had rolled off the table onto the ground.

"Well, with those two, I think it'll be gone in a hurry." Andrew joked, gesturing to Davey and Pete.

"You're probably right," Aiden said. "Thanks, Buttercup." Aiden slung his arm around Evie's shoulders and tucked her to him. Andrew watched as Evie relaxed into him. He was glad she and Aiden had managed to repair their relationship after everything that'd happened. It would've been easy for Aiden to blame her and shut her out, but he'd opened his arms and welcomed her home, the moment she had needed him.

"Do you want to stay and shoot a round or two?" Aiden asked Evie.

"I wish, but I promised Mama I would come back and help her make bread and watch a movie." Aiden let her go to grab one of the sandwiches. Evie came around to stand by Andrew, wrapping an arm around his waist as Andrew's arm went around her shoulders.

He leaned down and whispered in her ear, "You look cute in those boots and that helmet." She'd replaced her work boots with riding boots. It was another look that fit Evie. Andrew felt her hand tighten on his waist in reply.

"Walk me back?" she asked, nodding towards the dirt bike.

"Always." He gave her a quick kiss on the head before dropping his arm from her shoulder and grabbing her hand. She gave his hand a light squeeze that made him feel loved. Pete may have been flirting with Evie earlier, but she had chosen him.

Loved him.

Owned him.

As they approached the dirt bike, Andrew told her, "Drive safe on this thing." He eyed it warily and was a bit concerned about Evie riding on it, especially with the distance she had to cover to get back to the house.

"I always do," she replied flippantly. Her response did nothing to ease Andrew's worries. If anything, it only amplified them.

"Just promise me you will. I don't need you breaking your neck," Andrew replied dryly, which elicited a snort from Evie.

"I'll be fine. I've been riding on a dirt bike since I could walk." Andrew gave her a stern look that made her laugh. He couldn't help but smile at the sound of her laugh; however, he was serious about her being safe. The thought of her hurting herself or worse on that thing made him extremely nauseous.

He must've looked like he felt because Evie stopped laughing and grabbed his shoulders, as she looked at him and promised, "Andrew, I promise I will be very safe. Don't worry."

"I will always worry, Evie. Even if you're wrapped in a bubble, I will worry. It's my job."

"If you say so, Mr. Big Shot Professor," she said, giving him a little smirk.

"So many nicknames around here." Evie shrugged and picked up her helmet. "I wasn't lying about you looking cute in that helmet," he told her quietly so no one else could hear.

She smiled up at him and teased, "I guess I'll have to add it to my daily wear."

"Well, I don't know about that, but you could add it to your nightly wear," he replied, giving her a suggestive look. The words were out of his mouth before he could stop them.

"Andrew Brant!" She hissed somewhat playfully. "You can't go around saying stuff like that, especially with my father a few feet away."

Andrew's smile grew as she went off on him. She was cute when she was getting onto him, and he liked it.

He couldn't help himself as he leaned down close to her ear and whispered, "What if I whisper it real quiet for only you to hear? Then, can I go around saying stuff about what I think you should be wearing to bed?" He straightened up and looked at her. Pink stained her cheeks as she avoided his gaze.

She took a deep breath and turned to meet his gaze. Her bottom lip was between her teeth, as she seemed to contemplate saying something just as tantalizing to him; however, she opted to douse the flames. "You're going to make this very hard for me, which is why we are going to set some ground rules. Tonight. You, me, and ground rules."

"I can do ground rules. Set as many as you want," he challenged. He would. As much as he'd like to take her to bed, he would abide by whatever rules she set. They'd been taking it slow since their first date at his house, and he had no plans to stop, despite his words.

"Good. I will," she told him, lifting her helmet to put it on. Andrew leaned down to kiss her cheek before she pulled it down. Right before his lips met her cheek, a loud bang sounded, causing them both to jump.

"Sorry! Misfire," Pete yelled at them.

Andrew glared over his shoulder and spotted Pete with his hands up like he didn't know what had happened.

"Misfire my foot," Andrew murmured. He looked back to Evie and found her grinning at him. "What?"

"I think it's cute that you're jealous."

"I'm not jealous," Andrew huffed. However, his words lacked any surety.

"Sure," she said, pulling the helmet down over her face.

"Remember to drive safe on this thing," he reminded her as she climbed on.

"Babe, stop worrying. I'll be fine. I'll see you later this afternoon," she told him before cranking the dirt bike.

Before she could drive off, Aiden came jogging over. "No jumping, Buttercup."

"You two really need to stop worrying." Evie speedily took off, causing Andrew to throw his hands in the air in disbelief.

What am I going to do with this girl?

"I mean it! No jumping!" Aiden shouted after her. Evie only revved the dirt bike and drove a little faster in response.

"And slow down!" Andrew shouted. He knew she couldn't hear them, but he was sure she knew they were shouting at her.

After she was out of sight, Andrew turned accusingly to Aiden. "A dirt bike? Really?"

"What? You're blaming me?"

"Yes, you bought her that thing."

"Look, she has had one since she was little, and she's usually safe on it."

"Usually?" Andrew asked warily.

"Sometimes, she has a tendency to go a little wild and jump things with it."

Andrew gave Aiden a look that said he couldn't believe what he was hearing. He didn't want to end up with a girlfriend who had a broken neck from being reckless on a dirt bike. It would really put a damper on things if she was dead.

Aiden threw his hands up. "I warned her."

Andrew leveled him a look as they headed back to the stalls.

The more he was there on her family farm, the more he discovered about Evie. She was a farm girl at heart and had a tendency to be reckless on a dirt bike. He didn't know if he was more impressed or more concerned. Secretly, he loved that she rode a dirt bike and didn't fear doing things on it that pushed the boundaries of being safe. Of course, he'd never admit to liking her a little careless. He didn't want to encourage her reckless side, but he did find that wild side of her very attractive.

Lily had never done anything remotely careless or ever gone wild. One time, he'd tried to get her to go skinny dipping in a creek, but it'd only led to a fight. They had fought so much during those last couple of years together. It wasn't that he'd grown tired of being with her, but he'd grown somewhat bored as the years had gone by. They had quit growing together soon after marrying. Looking back, he knew it hadn't been either of their faults. They'd just been two very different people. He hadn't realized how different they had been until they had married, and by then, it was too late.

Andrew had never been one to believe differences between spouses mattered, but Lily had been unwilling to compromise or meet him in the middle. Therefore, they'd slowly and painfully grown apart.

Pete walked over to where he and Aiden were standing. "Y'all need to go easy on her. She's a big girl."

Andrew had liked Pete when they'd first met, but his behavior towards Evie was beginning to rub him the wrong way.

"She's my girlfriend, and I will worry about her however I want," Andrew replied curtly. He may have put too much emphasis on "my" because out of the corner of his eye, he saw Aiden's eyebrows shoot up.

Aiden surprised Andrew by saying, "Pete, I think I have to agree with Dr. Boss Man on this one." Aiden clapped Pete on the back before walking off without another word.

Andrew hit Pete with a fixed stare as he waited for him to reply. He could see Pete trying to decide what to say, but ultimately, he decided to walk away without saying anything, which seemed the best course of action at that point.

Unrequited love appeared to be Pete's problem, and Andrew could even sympathize with it. If he lived in a world where Evie didn't return his feelings, he'd flirt and attempt to deter any potential suitor too, but Evie did return his feelings. Therefore, Pete would just have to learn to live with it in a more agreeable manner. If he couldn't, then Andrew would deal with it.

The afternoon passed uneventfully. Everything had

settled back into a normal rhythm, and there was no awkwardness between Andrew and Pete. Even though Andrew was having a great time with the guys, he was eager to get back to the house and see Evie. He missed having her around and needed some time with her.

Andrew and Aiden rolled to a stop behind the barn, parking their ATVs. The sun was beginning to sink low in the sky, and the air had a chilling bite to it. Thankfully, the afternoon had warmed up some, so they hadn't been completely miserable at the shooting range. Overall, it'd been a great day, and Andrew looked forward to the next on the James' farm.

As they took their time walking to the house, Andrew said, "Thanks for today, for making me feel included."

"You're family, Andrew," Aiden stated matter-of-factly.

Andrew felt the weight of his statement. Despite having only known him for a short period of time, Aiden had accepted him into his family, and Andrew knew that was no easy thing to accomplish. There was a lot of hurt surrounding the James family. A lot of hurt caused by his own family. Andrew didn't take it lightly that Aiden had accepted and trusted him. The man had absolutely no reason to and had every right to judge him solely off his family, but Aiden hadn't. And for that, Andrew would be forever grateful.

"Besides, I don't think I had much of a choice. Evie seems to have decided to keep you."

Andrew let out a low laugh. "I hope you're right."

They walked in the backdoor and kicked their boots off before entering the kitchen. Neither one wanted to invoke the wrath of Elaine by walking in her kitchen with dirty shoes. The heavenly aroma of food filled the air. Andrew felt his stomach rumble at the scent of whatever was cooking.

Aiden was a lucky man to come home to this every day, and he prayed he might be as lucky one day.

"Hey, you two," Elaine greeted them.

"What's for dinner? It smells delicious," Aiden told her, as he wrapped his arms around her waist and kissed her cheek.

"Shepherd's pie, roasted vegetables, and homemade bread that Evie made."

"Sounds good," Aiden said, peeking in the oven.

Elaine lightly slapped his hand. "Close it, or it'll never finish cooking." Her eyes flicked to Andrew. "Evie is upstairs working on some schoolwork. Will you go get her for me?"

"Yes, ma'am," Andrew replied.

Andrew was glad Elaine had suggested he go get Evie. He longed to be alone with her.

To breathe in her scent and hold her.

Even if it was for a minute, he would cherish it. Cherish her.

As he reached the top of the stairs, he saw Evie's door was ajar. Gently, he pushed it open to find Evie in the window seat, writing notes in the margin of a book.

"Dinner's ready." His voice broke through the peaceful quiet of her room. Her head popped up. A sparkle filled her eyes as they landed on him.

"Hey," she said cheerfully. Then, her smile fell away. Andrew instantly went on alert. Before he could ask what was wrong, she said, "This book sucks." She held up the book, and he instantly recognized it as one of the assigned readings for his class. He couldn't help but laugh because the book really did suck.

He shrugged. "I know."

"You know?" She practically yelled at him, clearly exasperated.

He strolled across the room and sat on the side of the bed closest to her. "I like to assign at least one "unhappy" book in each class."

"Why? For torture purposes? To keep your status as Dr. Hard Butt?"

Andrew laughed. Evie made him so happy and filled him with such an indescribable joy, even when she was calling him names.

"No, but it helps," he teased.

"Well, it doesn't help your students, so I think you might need to reevaluate your thinking."

He felt himself smiling broadly at her.

"Why are you smiling? This isn't amusing. This is a legitimately terrible and sad novel. Everyone keeps dying."

"I know, but you make me incredibly happy. Spending even one second around you raises my mood exponentially." Andrew saw her face go blank. She clearly hadn't been expecting that response.

After a moment, she let out a slight huff. "Well, I can't stay upset with you when you go and say stuff like that."

"Good," he told her, standing up to sit opposite of her on the window seat. He picked up her feet, placing them in his lap. "I assign one terrible book a semester for several reasons. Mainly, I do it because there is always something to be learned from it. If you look, truly analyze it, you'll see that it's not that the book is poorly written. The story is just hard to digest. No one wants to read books with hard stories, but they're some of the most well written novels out there."

Evie pondered on his words for a minute before saying, "I guess you're right about that."

"Also, most people don't want to read books they don't

relate to or that don't end happily. It's good to step outside of that comfort zone every now and again."

She studied him before asking, "How are you always right?"

Andrew chuckled and said, "I'm not. I've just been teaching for a while, and as your professor, I think you should finish that book. Don't just google it and get enough info to pass a quiz on it."

Evie gasped dramatically and placed a hand on her chest. "I would never, Dr. Brant. What kind of student do you think I am?"

"One who hates what she is reading and would do anything to get out of it."

"I would never do that." He raised an eyebrow at her. "I would never do that more than once." He gave her another look that said she was lying. "Twice." Andrew stared and waited. "Fine. I do, do that, but what student doesn't?"

He grinned at her and continued rubbing her feet. "Just promise me you'll finish that one."

"Andrew, I'm going to be really honest with you right now. I don't think I can promise you that."

"Evie James, I am your professor. You can't tell me things like that."

"I feel like I'm being tricked here."

"The struggle of dating your professor," he told her.

"Next time, I'll know better," she teased.

"Next time? I'm sorry to break it to you, but you're stuck with me."

While he may have been teasing her, there was a seriousness underlying his tone. They both felt it and gazed at one another with a thousand silent messages. They may be teasing one another, but the truth was this was it for them.

They both knew it. It was only a matter of time before they made it official.

I'm ready to put this ring on your finger, sweetheart. Just a little longer.

Andrew never thought life or love happened that quickly, but he was beginning to stop questioning it. It may not happen that fast for some, but he'd always been told "when you know, you know."

And he knew.

He knew deep in the quiet part of his soul.

The very marrow of his bones whispered her name.

Evie quietly broke the silence. "We should probably go downstairs before they send a search party."

Right as Evie got the words out of her mouth, Aiden shouted from downstairs, "Where are y'all? I'm hungry."

Evie and Andrew both laughed.

"Let's go," he said, pulling her up and drawing her in quick for a kiss. "I've been wanting to do that all day."

"I've been waiting for you to do that all day," she confessed.

Grabbing her hand, they made their way downstairs.

28

EVIE

After dinner, Evie snuck out the back door while everyone pitched in to help her mom clean up the kitchen. She made her way down the small path in the backyard to the sitting area that her dad had built her mom. The patio area was covered with a pergola that had thick vines encompassing it. In the spring, it would be beautiful with the budding flowers.

Evie lit a fire in the small brick fireplace at the end of the patio and turned on the twinkle lights strung across the top of the pergola. There was an outdoor couch in front of the fireplace and several outdoor chairs placed throughout the area. A huge bed swing hung off to the side. The space was very cozy and quite warm even in the dead of winter. The fireplace provided a lot of heat, but her dad had also placed two outdoor heaters on the opposite side of the patio for extra heat.

She spent a lot of time out there no matter the weather or season. Most of the time, she would go down there to read, but other times, she'd go down there to think. It was close enough to the house that she felt safe, but far enough away to give her space to think without interruption. Tonight, she thought it would be a good place to spend some time with Andrew.

Making her way back to the house to get Andrew, something rustled in the bushes several yards away to the left of the house. It was enough of a noise to make her pause and listen. The hairs on the back of her neck rose, but she didn't hear anything else. She tried to keep the rising panic at bay.

It's probably my imagination or just an animal.

Her thoughts drifted to the last time she didn't think there was anything wrong. Evie didn't want to become a paranoid person, but she also didn't want to ignore something that could turn out to be a real threat.

Hastily, she made her way back to the house. In the kitchen, her mom and Andrew were tag teaming the dishes. "Where's daddy?" she asked, interrupting their conversation.

They both looked up at her. She must've not looked as relaxed as she thought because Andrew's face wrinkled with concern.

Her mom spoke first, asking, "Everything okay, sweetheart?"

"Yeah, it's fine."

"You sure?" Andrew asked this time.

"Yes." Looking back to her mom, she asked again, "Where's dad?"

"He snuck off to his office. Don't think I didn't notice you two ran off and avoided dish duty." Evie smiled at her mom and headed to her dad's office.

Knocking on the door, she opened the door before her dad could answer. He was sitting at his desk next to the window that overlooked the wooded area of the yard. She'd always loved her dad's office. It was the darkest room in the house with dark wooden furniture and dark green walls, which she noted looked like Andrew's eyes. To the side of his desk was a large floor to ceiling bookshelf filled to the brim with books about anything and everything. They had a small library in the house, but these were her dad's personal collection.

Like father, like daughter.

"What you need, Buttercup?" he asked, spinning in his leather office chair to face her. She stepped in the room, shutting the door behind her. "Everything okay?" Concern filled his voice. She could tell he was instantly on alert by the way his body tensed ever so slightly. Most people wouldn't be able to note the subtle change, but she'd always been able to read her dad very well.

She paused before saying anything. If this turned out to be paranoia, she would've worried everyone for nothing, so for a second, she truly questioned whether she should say something or not. However, her dad had always taught her to follow her instincts.

"I don't know. I feel like I'm being paranoid. I don't want to begin to question every little thing, but I heard something when I was leaving the patio." Her dad immediately turned to face his desktop computer, pulling up the camera feed. "It sounded like loud rustling. As if someone were in the bushes and lost their footing. I stopped to listen, but I didn't hear anything but the wind."

"It may be nothing, but it's always good to check regardless," he said, watching the computer screen.

She crossed the room to his desk and watched the video feed from over his shoulder. Everything looked clear on the footage, but there was a blinking red light on the upper right video feed. Evie felt her stomach drop as her dad picked up the two-way radio and said, "Davey, the camera tripped in the southwest field. Can you two check it out?"

"Sure thing, boss."

Aiden scanned the footage a few moments longer before looking over his shoulder saying, "It could be an animal, but I'll go have a look around the house to be sure."

She nodded, stepping aside to let her dad stand up. Evie knew it wasn't an animal. Her dad had purposefully not pulled up the southwest field feed, even though the camera was currently active.

She watched as he walked over to the large gun safe hidden behind a panel on the far side of his study. He attached a pistol to his side and grabbed his rifle. Nothing about this should make her worry. This was normal for life on a farm. If there was a large predatory animal nearby, he would need those things; however, she was almost positive her dad had seen something on that screen—something only his military training had allowed him to quickly see before her civilian eyes could catch up.

Deep in her gut, she knew the truth, but she refused to admit it. Instead, she forced herself not to think about it, following her dad out of his study and to the kitchen.

"So, everything wasn't okay," her mom stated, giving her an accusing look after seeing her dad carrying his rifle into the kitchen.

"Everything is fine, honey" Aiden told her mom.

"Then why do you have your rifle?"

"Just a precaution. We *do* live in the country with wild animals," he said, handing the rifle to Evie to hold. He shrugged into his jacket and pulled his boots on. "To the left of the house?" he asked her lowly.

She nodded.

He looked over her head to where Andrew was standing. "Keep an eye on things here, Dr. Boss Man?" Even though his voice was casual, a serious understanding passed between them.

"You bet," Andrew replied just as casually, but his eyes told another story. With that, her dad opened the door and disappeared into the night.

"Just so everyone knows, no matter how flippantly you speak, I know when it's not nothing," Elaine said somewhat annoyed.

"I'm sure he just doesn't want you to worry," Evie said.

"Why didn't you say anything?" Andrew asked.

He and her mom both looked at her, waiting. She hadn't technically lied to them, but she had avoided saying anything.

"I didn't want to cause a stir in case it was nothing. There was no point in getting everyone worried."

"What happened?" her mom questioned.

Evie recounted the events of what had occurred and about her dad radioing Davey to check the southwest pasture.

"So, he's here," her mom quietly stated. Her mom rarely got angry, but Evie could see the anger radiating off her. Elaine was a gentle soul, but if someone messed with her family, she'd go nuclear.

"Probably," she mumbled. Guilt seeped into every pore of her body. If she'd only made a better decision years ago, none of this would've happened.

One decision.

One choice.

One.

Evie closed her eyes and let out a sigh.

Her mom's attention snapped to her. "It's not your fault, baby."

"I know."

It is.

Almost an hour later, her dad came back in the house. Evie, Andrew, and her mom were in the living room, watching a cooking competition. Aiden walked in solemnly and stopped at the edge of the living room. His face was a slab of stone, hard and cold. It was obvious he was trying to keep a hold on his emotions. If her dad was struggling to keep his emotions at bay, then it must be bad.

Despite the fire, the room went cold. The weight of whatever Aiden was keeping in fell heavily on the room.

Andrew stood and broke the tense silence. "What did you find?"

Aiden only shook his head silently and pulled his hand out of his jacket pocket, revealing a pair of lacey pink underwear.

Evie gasped.

She knew them well. They were the pair Dylan had stolen off her the first time he'd raped her. She desperately tried to shove the memories back behind that locked door in her mind, but they flooded in despite her efforts. Tears filled her eyes, but she refused to give a single tear to that foul being.

A heavy silence filled the room once again. Aiden strode over to the fireplace and tossed the underwear in the fire. Evie watched as the orange flames consumed them, as if attempting to erase a part of that horrific night for her.

Aiden faced the fireplace until the last thread was incinerated before slowly turning to face everyone. He cleared his throat and said, "I found them lying on the bed swing." They all knew who had put them there and why. There was no need to ask. Dylan knew Andrew was there, and he was leaving a reminder of who he believed Evie belonged to.

"I'm assuming he's gone." Andrew's voice was thick with emotion.

Aiden nodded. "I was able to follow his tracks to the southwest pasture. He isn't even trying to hide his presence anymore, which is good."

"How is that a good thing?" Evie asked.

"Because it means he's getting desperate. The more desperate a man becomes, the more likely he is to mess up. Trust me, he's going to mess up, and I'm going to be right there when he does." There was a vehemence to his words that caused Evie to shiver.

"In the meantime," he continued. "I don't want you or you," he said, pointing to her and her mom, "going out of this house alone, and no one out past dark. Is that understood?"

"Yes, sir," Evie said.

Elaine nodded her agreement, looking somewhat pale.

Aiden turned his attention to Andrew. "What day do you need to head back?"

"Sunday, or I can leave out early Monday morning if needed."

"Tomorrow, I need to set up some extra cameras and alarms around the property along with Davey and Pete. If you can keep an eye on things here at the house while I do that, I'd appreciate it."

"Yeah, whatever you need."

"And I know this goes without saying but keep the doors and windows locked," Aiden said before heading out of the room to put his rifle up. Elaine followed behind him, closing the door to his office. Evie was sure her mother wanted to talk things through with her dad.

Andrew sat down on the couch next to her. "Are you okay?" Quiet concern filled his voice.

This was hard for her, but she couldn't imagine what Andrew felt.

Evie kept her eyes on the fireplace. Her voice was little above a whisper when she spoke. "Those were from the first night he raped me. He told me they were his to keep just as I was." Evie heard Andrew suck in air. "I just want this to be over," she admitted. "I'm not even scared anymore. I'm just frustrated that this seems to be never ending. He's the only one playing this demented game, and he doesn't even realize it."

She looked up at him. His dark eyes were filled with so much emotion. "I should've smothered him as a child." Evie burst out laughing. Andrew wrapped his arm around her, hugging her close. "You think I'm joking, but I probably should have."

"Probably," she grinned at him. "Are you okay though? I can't imagine what you're feeling."

Andrew took a second before he answered her. "Honestly, I'm angry and devastated. Devastated that someone could hurt you the way they have, and that of all people, it was my little brother causing such pain." He slid his arm from her shoulder and picked up her hand, lacing his fingers through hers. His deep voice was grave and quiet as he confessed what he'd been feeling inside. "It scares me, Evie. I've never had this much anger bottled up inside of me before. I didn't tell you, but I nearly killed him that day after you left my house."

His voice was a near whisper. "There was so much blood. I couldn't stop."

Evie held his hand tightly as she listened to him. Her chest was hurt so badly. She'd caused all of this, and now, Andrew was another victim of her poor choice.

"I've never felt that much rage before. At some point, I

stopped seeing him as my brother and saw him only as your abuser. I had the man that had violated and tortured you in my grasp. The only thing I could think in that moment was that I needed to protect and avenge you. This primal instinct to protect overwhelmed every other sense I had. It was pure unadulterated rage at what he'd done to you that compelled me into that level of violence."

Andrew lifted his eyes to meet hers, and there was nothing but fear and dismay in them—fear of becoming a monster like his brother. With her free hand, she reached up and cupped his cheek. Her thumb gently brushed across his warm skin.

Looking deep and intently into his wary eyes, she said, "Andrew, you are *nothing* like your brother. Nothing. I don't fear your anger or the fact that you possess the ability to be violent. Every human possesses those things, but it's how you handle them that marks you." His eyes began to clear and soften at her words. "You are a good man, Andrew Brant. A very good man. To the very core of you. Dylan is dark and marred at his core. His anger and violence are the characteristics of his person, but they're not yours. You are kind, caring, and compassionate. While Dylan only carries animosity, you carry love."

Evie let go of his hand and brought her hand to hold the other side of his face, leaning little closer to him. "Do not *ever* compare yourself to him. Ever. Do you understand me?" Her voice was intense and thick with emotion, but she didn't care. She wouldn't have Andrew thinking himself anything like his brother.

She wouldn't stand for it.

Andrew turned his head to kiss the palm of her hand, resting on his face. "I understand. I love you so much."

"I love you too," she whispered before leaning forward

and placing a tender kiss on his lips. "Now, let's get back to the cooking competition."

Evie turned the volume up on the tv as they snuggled together. Neither of them willing to let Dylan steal anymore of their thoughts and time.

They were both on their second bowl of ice cream and fifth episode of the food competition show. Time had slipped away from them, but they didn't care. Staying up too late and eating too many snacks with your best friend and love was the best part of life.

"No," they both yelled at the tv as one of the contestants dropped their pot of soup on the floor.

"There better be some left in the bottom of that pot. I know that had to have tasted bomb," Andrew exasperatedly said.

"Did you just say bomb?"

Andrew looked at her, staring at him. "What? I'm not allowed to say bomb?"

"Aren't you a little old to be saying things like bomb?" she asked teasingly.

"Old? I don't know if I should be offended or not. I'm only thirty-five."

She grinned at him. Evie loved teasing Andrew. Sitting on the couch, eating ice cream, and watching tv was the perfect night to her. There was nothing special about it, but they were together. And that was all she could ever want.

"You should definitely be offended."

"Well, I am officially offended." They smiled at each other, and it was clear he was just as content and happy to be sitting with her as she was with him.

"Do you want to make brownies?"

His eyes widened, causing Evie to giggle. "We just had *two* bowls of ice cream."

"So?"

"If this is what life is going to be like with you, I am going to end up incredibly fat."

Evie rolled her eyes at him. "First of all, I've felt those abs. Do you really think you're hiding them from me beneath that shirt? You're basically all muscle, so let's not pretend you're going to get fat. Secondly, do you want to make brownies with me?"

Andrew let out a laugh. "Fine. I give up. Let's make brownies."

Evie let out a squeal, dragging Andrew off the couch.

As she led him into the kitchen, she asked, "Should we make this a competition?"

"I don't know, James. My grandmother taught me to make brownies, and her recipe is award winning."

"Oh, really?"

Nodding, he answered, "County fair. Won the blue ribbon."

"Impressive, but I have my mom's recipe."

"I know your mom is a fabulous cook, but what makes it special?"

"They made my dad fall in love with her," she told him, stopping in the middle of the kitchen and turning to look at him.

"Impressive," he said, copying her response. He stuck his hand out to her and said, "May the best recipe win."

She grasped his hand, giving him a deadly stare. "Deal." They shook on it and spread out to begin baking.

They took up spots on opposite sides of the kitchen. That way no one could see what the other was doing. However, that wasn't about to stop Evie. About halfway through, she tiptoed across the kitchen and tried to sneak a peek over Andrew's shoulder.

She'd barely gotten a glimpse before Andrew said, "I believe you are in violation of the rules, Miss James."

Evie quickly sank back onto her feet and sulked back to her side of the kitchen. She couldn't believe he'd caught her looking, but then again, she could. She'd never been the stealthiest walker.

A little while later, Evie was lost in the momentum of her own baking. "Nice," a deep voice said very close to her ear. Evie let out a scream and jumped, causing the bowl of extra flour in her hands to fly everywhere. She was covered in white when she turned around and gave Andrew the meanest look she could muster. Andrew started laughing as he told her, "Hold on. Stay right there."

Before Evie knew what was happening, he pulled out his phone and snapped a picture of her.

"Andrew Brant, you delete that right now," she demanded.

"I don't think so," he said, still laughing. He turned the phone around to let her see it. A picture of her covered in white flour filled his lock screen.

"Andrew," she growled.

Just as she reached for his phone, her dad and mom came barreling into the kitchen. They both slammed to a stop as they surveyed the flour on Evie and all over her side of the kitchen.

"We heard a scream and came running," Aiden said. Her dad stood there, looking ready to kill someone in his Santa boxers and gun in hand.

"Why on earth is there flour all over my clean kitchen?" Elaine surveyed the mess with hands on her hips. She looked a little more put together with a robe on over her flannel pajamas.

Evie pointed at Andrew and said, "Ask him." Her parents turned to look at him.

"I only told her, her brownies looked nice," he stated innocently with hands raised in the air.

"Don't act all innocent. He snuck up on me and said it right in my ear, scaring me half to death. Hence, the mess," she explained, gesturing to herself and the kitchen.

"Well, I don't care whose fault it is. You two are going to clean it up," Elaine replied.

"Yes, ma'am," Evie and Andrew said at the same time. Elaine turned and left the kitchen. Aiden gave them a smirk, turning to follow her.

After her parents were gone, Andrew and Evie turned to one another and burst out laughing.

Evie couldn't breathe from laughing so hard. Tears rolled down her face, leaving streak marks through the flour as she tried to catch her breath. Andrew looked almost as out of breath as her.

"Oh my gosh. Did you see my dad ready to take someone out in his boxers with Santa Claus plastered all over them?" Evie let out another giggle as she wiped the tears from her face.

"I think I was more scared of your mom. She's serious about her kitchen." A broad smile filled Andrew's face as amusement shone in his eyes.

Evie's breath caught in her chest as she looked at him. No one ever witnessed this side of him, and she was beyond grateful to be the one to see it.

If only everyone knew you weren't the broody professor, they believe you to be, but this wonderful, delightful man that loves to laugh and joke and bake.

"I'll clean this up. Go take a shower and get cleaned up," Andrew told her.

"Good idea," Evie said, looking down at all the flour on her. As she took off her apron, a clump of flour fell to the floor, causing her to let out a small snicker at the added mess. Looking up, she found Andrew watching her with a grin on his face.

"I love you," he said.

Evie's heart skipped a beat at his words. She didn't think she'd ever get used to them.

"Good because I love you too." She pressed a quick kiss to his cheek and headed upstairs to clean up.

29
EVIE

Thirty minutes later, Evie was showered and dressed. A soft knock sounded on her door as she toweled her hair. "Come in," she said quietly so not to wake her parents again. Andrew popped his head in the door.

"Hi," he said, smiling at her. He stepped in the room, carrying two plates. Each plate held one brownie. "I went ahead and baked them, and before you accuse me of cheating, I looked at your mom's recipe and baked it according to the instructions."

Setting the plates in the middle of the bed, Andrew took up a spot at the end and leaned back against the iron bed frame as he waited for Evie. She tossed her towel in the bathroom and made her way over to the bed, taking a seat opposite of him. "These look good," she said.

Andrew picked up his brownie and held it up for her to take a bite. Evie noticed the way his eyes seemed to glimmer in the dim light coming from the lamp by her bed. She'd always found him very attractive but seeing him in various settings always revealed a new way of experiencing him. In those moments, it was as if she were seeing him for the first time.

She leaned forward and took a bite of the warm, gooey, chocolatey goodness. A small moan worked its way up her throat as she chewed Andrew's brownie.

"That good, huh?" His voice sounded thick and rough.

"So good," she told him, picking up her brownie and holding it up for him to try. Life seemed to slide into slow motion as he leaned forward to take a bite. The bite was more seductive than it should've been, or maybe, it was just her imagination. Evie watched as his tongue snuck out to get a bit of brownie that had decided to linger on his bottom lip. The moment felt charged, and she needed to splice through the electricity before she wound up in a situation, she wasn't fully ready to be in.

Evie had wanted to change the direction of the moment, but what came out of her mouth told a different story. "You are so incredibly hot."

Andrew looked slightly taken aback, and Evie felt her cheeks grow warm. She hadn't expected those words to come out of her mouth. She and Andrew had talked about a lot of things and were connected in some weird supernatural kind of way, but she'd never audibly told him what she thought about him physically.

Andrew's face softened. "Thank you." He reached forward, picking up her hand and bringing it to his mouth. Evie felt that electric charge spark again at his touch.

"Andrew," she said somewhat breathlessly. His eyebrows went up in response. She cleared her throat, trying to tamp down some of the emotions, attempting to burst from her. "I think we need to set some ground rules."

"Might not be a bad idea," he said with a low chuckle. "I want you to feel comfortable and safe around me—no matter how hard it may be for me to contain myself around you."

Evie's heart felt as if it was trying to literally take flight and leave her body. She'd never had a man so concerned with her in that way before. The last man only took what he had wanted, never looking back.

"I know I've said before that I want to take things slow, and I do. It's just becoming harder and harder to do that, and as much as I would like to strip you of your clothes and take a close look at those abs you're hiding from me, I don't think I'm ready for us to do that. Not that I would regret being with you in that way, but I want to be very sure of myself and us before doing that." Evie knew Andrew had previously agreed, but that didn't mean he hadn't changed his mind or wanted it to remain that way.

He slowly reached his hand out and cupped her face. "I understand, sweetheart. I can wait however long you need me to. I'm in this with you. What do you need?"

Evie let out a sigh of relief and felt the love she had for him grow just a little more.

"No more comments about taking clothes off. It leaves me feeling a little too much if you know what I mean," she said, fanning herself.

Andrew laughed. "Okay, no more comments about taking your clothes off."

"I don't think I could cut kissing." She looked away as she quietly added, "I may be addicted to kissing you."

"Good." His eyes grew dark with desire. The look on his face said he wanted to devour her right then and there.

"Andrew," she said accusingly. The hunger vanished from his face.

"What?"

"None of those looks either. They're deadly."

"I'll try my best." Although, he sounded anything but convincing.

"Back to what I was saying earlier, we should keep the kissing to places where there is no opportunity for clothes to come off." She glanced down at the bed. "So, maybe, no kissing on the bed or with the door closed."

"Okay, no kissing in opportune places. What else?"

"I think that's it," she said. Evie hated that she felt somewhat scared to tell him that this was an absolute thing, and she felt even worse about giving him a timeline. She knew he was waiting for her to finish telling him what she wanted, needed, but she couldn't do it.

Finally, his voice broke through the heavy silence. "For how long?" She took a slow deep breath and looked at him but remained silent. "For how long, Eves?" His voice was firm but gentle. He was going to make her say it.

They were her rules, and it would be her choice.

"I don't really know." They both knew it was lie. Her eyes slid away from his as she pulled her knees to her chest.

Andrew stood up, picking up the plates and placing them on the dresser. Evie heard him set the plates down and walk back to her. He sat down a little closer to her this time and gently pulled her ankles until her legs stretched out across his.

"Evie, look at me." Very slowly, she lifted her eyes to meet his. "I'm not him," he stated firmly. "I don't want you to be afraid to tell me what you need because you think I might get angry with you. I don't want you to curl into yourself to protect yourself from me. I promise there is nothing you could ever say or do that would make me mad enough to hurt you. Don't hide from me. Never from me." Deep emotion filled his voice as he spoke. "I love you from the darkest depths of my heart, Evie. You light up the darkest corners of me. I'm yours and am in this with you. I'm not here to get something from you. Just you. Only you. Always you." His hand came to her face and cupped it as he whispered, "I love you so very much."

His voice exposed the depth of his emotion. Evie felt his words run through her, filling in some of the cracks Dylan had left behind. Andrew was asking her to trust him, and if this was going to work, she was going to have to take that leap of faith and trust him as well.

Her voice was barely above a whisper as she said, "It's really hard for me, Andrew."

"I know, sweetheart. I know," he told her, his voice just as quiet as hers and filled with such tenderness that it squeezed her heart.

The tears in her eyes spilled over and ran down her cheeks. No one truly knew the depth of damage and destruction Dylan had done to her. There were some things she would never dare utter aloud.

"Andrew," she whispered through the silence. His eyes were watching her, waiting. "I want to trust you with every part of me. I want nothing more, but years of his abuse has left me more broken than I will ever be able to admit to."

Andrew picked up her hand and squeezed it. "I won't pretend that I understand what you feel, but I can accept it, Eves. If I have to prove myself to you and remind you every day that you can trust me with yourself, then I will. What-ever it takes, I will do. Whatever you need."

Evie didn't know what she'd done to deserve him. He was beyond good to her, and she hated that she wasn't whole enough to fully appreciate him.

But, one day, she would be. One day, she would repair everything Dylan had broken.

"There is one thing I do need to from you right now

though," Andrew said, watching and waiting. She knew what he wanted, but there was a small voice that whispered he was going to be angry and lash out at her.

But that voice was a liar.

Andrew was good. He was safe, and Evie knew that deep down in her soul.

Evie nodded at him and sat up a little straighter.

"How long do you want to keep the ground rules in place?" His voice was so gentle and kind as he asked. She searched his eyes, looking for any hint of waiting anger. Dylan's eyes always looked like they were a simmering fire, waiting to go ablaze at any second. Andrew's eyes were dark and cool, like the lake in front of his house.

What Dylan set on fire, Andrew extinguished.

Evie took a deep breath and blew it out. "Until marriage." She subconsciously braced herself for the first blow to come, but nothing happened.

"Evie open your eyes," Andrew told her softly. His words surprised her. She hadn't realized she had closed her eyes. Slowly, she opened them and saw him looking at her with a mixture of concern and love. "You okay?"

She studied him for a moment, looking for signs of irritation or anger, but she didn't find anything. There was nothing but love in his expression.

"I'm okay." Her voice was a bit shaky but confident.

"Good," he said, letting out a small breath. He must've been as tense as her. "I need you to know that I am completely okay with waiting for marriage. If that is what you need, then it's what I need. I don't want any part of you that you aren't willing to freely give to me. If waiting is what you need in order to do that, then I am very okay with it."

Deep down Evie knew that was how it was supposed to

be, and that she shouldn't be so shocked at hearing his words; however, she felt like someone had knocked the air out of her.

How did I get so lucky to find him in the middle of this mess I'm in? How are he and Dylan even related?

"Thank you," she told him. "Thank you for loving me."

"Baby, you don't have to thank me for loving you. I don't think I could stop even if I tried."

Evie knew she was smiling like a fool in love, but she couldn't help it.

"I know. That was very cheesy to say," he said with a small laugh.

"Yeah, it kind of was, but I loved it."

He leaned close to her and asked, "So when do these ground rules start?" The desire was evident in his eyes, and Evie felt her own desire growing.

"I think we can give it a few minutes," she replied.

A heart-stopping grin formed on his face as he leaned in a little further until their lips met. Every thought in her brain vanished as his tongue skimmed her bottom lip.

Bliss. Utter bliss.

30
EVIE

The next morning, Evie sat in the window seat of the library, looking out the window towards the pastures. A smile lit her face as memories of the night before floated to the surface of her mind. Andrew had kissed her gentle and slow as if he'd been savoring every second of her. It had been more intimate than any of their other kisses, and Evie had felt the bond between grow in a deeper and stronger way. It wasn't just that they were in agreement on the boundaries they had set, but it was the promise of a future. A future they were both running towards. They still had a lot to overcome and conquer before that future could begin, but for now, the hope of it was enough for them.

Evie turned her head from the window and tried to focus on her book. She and Andrew were in the library, trying to get some work done. She had a lot of schoolwork to finish before the semester ended, and Andrew had a lot of papers to grade.

She glanced over her book at him and wondered if he was having as hard of a time as she was at concentrating.

Her thoughts were constantly circling back to him. She'd been perched in the window seat for two hours now, and those two hours had been very long and unproductive as she kept glancing over her book to where he was sitting at the desk.

Evie looked back out the window and watched the cows off in the distance and attempted to calm her thoughts, but it was no use. There was a lot she wanted to know and ask him, but she didn't want to make things awkward; however, he knew a lot about her, and it was only fair that he showed her his metaphorical scars. He had asked her to trust him, so he was going to have to trust her with himself at some point. They had talked about a lot of things, but he'd yet to talk about his wife.

Evie felt a small sting of jealousy at the thought of his late wife. It seemed wrong to be jealous of a dead woman, but she'd seen more of Andrew than Evie had.

Not just physically. She got to see and experience all of him in every way.

Andrew had shared a life with her and let her see himself in a way no one else had—the intimate things that can only be shared with a spouse.

She glanced back over to him. His head was bent in concentration as he looked at something on the computer screen. She couldn't help but admire the way his gray shirt hugged his biceps. Andrew wasn't bulky, but he was very well sculpted.

As if sensing she was watching him, his head popped up, and those dark green eyes looked at her intently. "Need something, sweetheart?" His deep voice filled her with warmth, and she felt her cheeks warming from being caught staring at him.

Gawking is more like it.

Closing her book, Evie cleared her throat and sat up straight. "Well, since you asked, I have a question."

"You can ask me anything. You know that." Andrew sat back in the chair, giving her his full attention.

Before she could chicken out, she quickly asked, "How did your wife die?"

Smooth, Evie. Way to be awkward.

Andrew's eyes widened as he went rigid and very still. Clearly, he hadn't been expecting her question. He took a deep breath and opened his mouth to speak but nothing came out.

Maybe, I shouldn't have asked, but no take backs! I need to know.

Clearing his throat, he finally said, "That wasn't what I thought you were going to ask."

Evie noted he'd avoided answering the question right off and knew he was stalling. She could give him a minute or two if he needed one, so instead of pushing, she said, "I know, and I'm sorry if I caught you off guard. However, it's an important part of your life that we've yet to discuss. You asked me to trust you with the hardest parts of my life, so I'm asking the same of you." Before he could respond, she quickly added, "I won't push you about it if you don't want to talk about it, but it's a part of your life I would like to know about."

Andrew was silent for a moment. He nodded and stood, gesturing to the small sofa on the other side of the room. "Can we sit on the couch?"

"Sure," Evie replied, putting her book down and walking over to the couch. They sat on opposite ends of the small couch, facing each other. The sofa was small enough that their legs were almost touching but big enough to grant the space needed for a serious conversation.

Evie sat quietly, waiting for Andrew to take the lead whenever he was ready.

With a deep breath, he said, "Cancer." He didn't say anything after that, and Evie wasn't sure how to fill the silence. She had thought it might've been something along those lines, but she was at a loss as to how to respond.

"She was diagnosed with stage 3 breast cancer about a year before she passed away."

"I'm so sorry, Andrew." She truly meant it. Even though she loved having him to herself, she wouldn't wish that on him or his wife. "What was her name?"

"Lily."

Evie felt a bit strange at hearing her name. It was as if it made it all a little more real.

Before going forward with more questions about Lily, she asked, "Are you okay talking about her?"

Andrew looked at her, giving her a small smile. "Yeah, I am. I said you could ask me anything, and I meant it. I don't have any secrets from you."

With that, Evie asked, "What was she like?"

"She was tall. She had sandy blonde hair and the bluest eyes. They always reminded me of the Caribbean Sea," he grinned at the memory. Evie felt another jolt of jealousy but hurriedly stomped it down. "Lily was beautiful. She had a way of capturing everyone's attention when she walked into a room. In fact, the first time I ever saw her, I walked straight into this display of magazines at the mall and thoroughly embarrassed myself by knocking it over."

A laugh escaped Evie's lips. "Sorry," she murmured.

"No, you're not. You would've laughed," he replied, eyes sparkling with humor.

"Yeah, you're right," she smiled. "But what did Lily do?"

"She felt bad for me and tried to help me clean up the

mess, which proved to be more than either of us could handle. When the employees told us to leave it, I asked if she wanted to get a coffee with me, and for whatever reason, she agreed."

"That is like the perfect meet cute," Evie said completely in awe. She had tripped and fallen flat on her face at Andrew's feet. There had been nothing cute about that.

"It was almost too perfect," he said more to himself than to Evie.

"What happened after that? I'm assuming it went well since y'all were married."

Andrew chuckled. "Yeah, it went well. We had been dating for a little over a year when I proposed. She was busy with her interior design business, and I was fresh out of grad school and starting as an assistant professor at Beaumont. We saw each other as often as we could with our busy schedules and living two hours away from each another. But the time we did spend together was always good."

"That sounds normal and good, so why am I sensing a but?" Evie watched as he shifted uncomfortably.

There's definitely more that he's not telling me. What are you hiding, love?

"Things were always good with us, too good. It was almost perfect. We hardly disagreed on anything. If you saw us together, it looked as if we were the picture-perfect couple, but I think that was part of the problem. We were together almost three years before living near one another. I guess I thought things would be like they were when we spent time together, but I don't think either of us thought about how the other was living when we weren't together. Does that make sense?"

Evie tucked her feet beneath her before saying, "It does. There is a lot of life missed when living apart like that, and when you finally come together, there is a bit of pressure to remain on your best behavior."

Andrew nodded at her words. "Exactly. We never truly got to know one another during that time, but I never understood that until after she had died."

Evie could tell there was a lot more to unearth there but could also sense Andrew needed a breather, so she redirected the conversation.

"So, what kind of wedding did Dr. Andrew Brant have?" Evie couldn't help herself. She had to know what that day was like for him. She could imagine him waiting at the end of an aisle for her but not for someone else. If he and Lily were as perfect as he said, she could only imagine the wedding was too.

Andrew chuckled and grabbed her hand as if he needed to be connected to her. "It was a wedding that I never saw myself in. It was huge. I remember there being so many people and a ton of white roses. It felt more like an event than a wedding."

"I'm assuming this was a black-tie affair," she said, trying to picture him in a tuxedo. He was very dashing in the image in her head.

He nodded. "It was the picture-perfect wedding. Lily came from a very rich family, so there was nothing that was skimped on."

"I'm having a hard time picturing you in a scene like that. It seems so out the ordinary for you."

"I was definitely a fish out of water."

She gave his hand a little squeeze. She hated the thought of him feeling awkward or out of place at his own wedding.

He smiled at her and returned the squeeze. "Her parents bought us this massive house, and everything seemed good for a while."

"What happened after a while?"

"About a year or so into the marriage, we started drifting apart. Lily wanted to do things like go to brunch with friends or go golfing every weekend. All of which, I was happy to participate in, but eventually, it seemed like all we did was what she wanted to do. If I ever asked if she wanted to do something that I wanted, she would come up with an excuse as to why she couldn't. I would want to go hiking, but she would already have plans to go get manicures with one of her friends. Between working and having different hobbies, it became easy to spend time apart."

Evie was having a hard time picturing Andrew living a life alone.

"Eventually, we started doing things separately, and we began spending more and more time apart. We told ourselves it was good because we each got to do what we wanted, but it got to the point that we hardly saw one another anymore. We had basically become roommates."

Evie's heart squeezed. She couldn't imagine being married to Andrew and not wanting to be around him. If she was being honest, it made her a little mad at Lily for being uncompromising and unwilling to meet Andrew halfway in the things he had wanted.

"Did you think about leaving?"

"I'd be lying if I said it hadn't crossed my mind once or twice. I didn't want to live in a marriage that wasn't really a marriage, but I also didn't want to leave without trying to fix it. We had a long discussion about everything, and things seemed to change for a little while. However, eventually, she quit trying, and then, I quit. We continued to live that way until her diagnoses."

"I'm sorry, Andrew. I can't even imagine."

He took a deep breath and let it out. "It's okay. I wouldn't be the man I am today if I hadn't lived through that season of my life, and to some extent, I don't blame her. We were two different people, and my lifestyle didn't match hers."

"Well, if it's any consolation, I like who you are today." He gave her a grin and kissed the back of her hand.

"We had been married for three years when she was diagnosed," he told her, running a hand through his hair while sighing. Evie could tell he was tense and ran her thumb across the back of his hand. "For a little while, the treatments were mild and seemed to be working, but then, things took a turn. My time became split between Beaumont and the hospital. I was barely keeping it together," he quietly admitted.

"I know," she replied almost inaudibly.

She did know. The whole English department had known. Evie had watched as he had become an empty shell of a person. She remembered the dark circles under his eyes and how his mood had gone dark. They had never interacted until she had become his graduate assistant, but Beaumont was a small university. Everyone knew everyone in their respective departments.

Andrew squeezed her hand and stared at her for a moment. He started to say something but stopped. He hesitated before finally whispering, "I was relieved when she finally died." Evie's heart broke for Andrew. The weight of having to handle all of that and to feel relief at an inopportune moment, like death, was more than any normal person should handle. "I've never admitted that to anyone." She could see the guilt eating at him, but before she could respond, he said, "She died at the beginning of November of last year. I finished the fall and spring semesters and took the summer off."

"What did you do during the summer?" Evie asked.

"I bought a house and moved. Then, I flew to Wyoming and spent most of my time reading, hiking, and fishing."

"Sounds relaxing and nice."

"It was for the most part, but it was hard to not reflect on the past. I spent a lot of time thinking and realized a lot more than I ever wanted to," he admitted a bit stiffly.

Evie wondered if he had spoken to anyone about any of it. She didn't want him to feel uncomfortable, but if he was willing to talk, she was willing to listen.

No matter how dark or ugly.

"What did you realize?" she asked gently.

He took a breath and blew it out.

Looking at her, he said, "I made a lot of mistakes in my marriage. There is a lot that I've learned and grown from. I need you know that before I continue." He seemed almost desperate for her to understand. Evie was growing more anxious by the minute.

She squeezed his hand tightly before telling him, "I know the man that you are, Andrew. Nothing you tell me is going to make me think differently of you."

Evie knew her words had hit home because he relaxed almost immediately. "I realized that I never truly loved her. I had never truly loved my wife. I dated, married, and lived life with a woman I was never in love with." He let go of Evie's hand and leaned forward, bracing his arms on his legs. His head hung low between his shoulders as he let out a deep sigh. "It was unfair to her. I should've left her. She might've been able to find true love and have someone who felt that for her at her side when she died."

Shock hit her square in the chest. Evie couldn't imagine the weight of carrying that revelation around. Now, she knew why there was so much guilt written all over his face and body language.

Oh, my love. How big your heart.

Evie scooted close to Andrew and placed a hand on his shoulder. "Maybe, but she had you. I know you, and I know you cared for her in the best way possible until the very end. I know she felt loved. There's no way she couldn't have with you around. It's just the kind of person you are Andrew. I don't think there could've been a better person to hold her hand through all of that." Evie pressed a kiss to her shoulder and laid her chin on the spot. "And even if you weren't in love with her, you still had love for her. You wouldn't have stayed and cared for her if you hadn't."

Andrew's hand covered the one she had wrapped around his arm. "Thank you, Evie," he said in a gravelly voice. His shoulders shook once, and he let out a small sound that shattered Evie's heart. Wrapping her arm around his broad shoulders, she pulled him to her.

After several moments, he sat up and pulled her into his arms. They stayed that way for a long time. "I love you," she whispered to his chest. His arms tightened around her, and she felt him press a kiss on top of her head.

"I love you too," he whispered back.

31
EVIE

A little while later, Andrew broke the comfortable silence by saying, "I need to get back to work." Evie groaned in response, causing Andrew to let out a low chuckle. "I know, baby. I wish I could stay cuddled up to you all day long, but I don't think Beaumont will pay me for that."

"They might. You never know," she replied hopefully.

"Doubt it, but how about we make a deal?"

"My favorite thing to do," she exclaimed, sitting up to face him.

"How about I go get us some snacks, and then, we work for another hour. After that, you and I can do whatever you want. Deal?"

Her eyes widened in excitement as she quickly nodded and said, "Deal." Andrew laughed, pulling her towards him and kissing her.

Reluctantly, he let her go and said, "I'll be back in a minute."

"Hurry back," she told him, tugging him back for another kiss. With a smile, he headed out the door.

Evie headed back to the window seat to get her book. She was determined to finish reading it before the day was out, but it was slow going. Her phone buzzed next to her book, drawing her attention.

A: Meet me outside on the patio for a surprise

Evie was surprised Andrew was texting her to come outside since they were supposed to be working, but she'd rather have a surprise than read. She dropped her phone on the cushion and headed to the backdoor.

Slowly, she pulled on her boots, pondering Andrew's text and what kind of surprise he could have for her.

Excitement filled her.

Should I bring my book? I could read by the fire outside. No, I can always come get it if I want.

Evie stood up and decided against wearing her heavy work coat. It was sunny and a little warmer outside than it'd been all week. Before opening the door, she unlocked the small gun safe on the shelf by the door and pulled out the Bodyguard 380. She hooked the holster on the band of her leggings and pulled her sweatshirt over it.

Stepping out into the sunshine, she took a deep breath, breathing in the cool air. It felt good to take a breath of fresh air after that heavy conversation with Andrew. She didn't know how it was possible, but she loved him more than she had before. It only solidified her belief of him being a good man.

Evie made her way to the patio, wondering what Andrew's surprise might be. She stepped onto the patio, but Andrew was nowhere in sight. She turned back to look at the house, and the hair on her arms stood on end. She spun back around to find Dylan's sinister face smiling at her.

"How did you?" She stammered out.

"Impressed, kitten?"

Evie's heart pounded in her head. There was a rushing in her ears, warning she was near passing out.

You will NOT pass out. You will NOT.

Her hand slid to hip, remembering the gun holstered there.

"Go ahead." There was a mocking laughter in his voice.

"What?" Her voice shook. She hated that it was shaking. She didn't want to give Dylan the satisfaction of knowing she was scared, but there was nothing she could do about it.

He nodded to where her hand was on her hip. "Pull it out." His voice was demanding and very controlled as he dared her to pull the gun on him. If he wanted her to pull the gun on him, then she would. She had no problem pulling the trigger on him. However, she knew Dylan and knew he had ulterior motives. He never did anything without a plan or motive.

Evie removed the gun from the holster, wondering how long it would take Andrew to notice she was missing. Her dad was out, setting up the new cameras with Davey and Pete, and her mother was in town. Andrew was all she had in that moment, and somehow, she knew Dylan was going to use it to his advantage.

Dylan made a sound of disapproval as she pointed the gun at him. "Little Genny, I thought I'd taught you better."

"Guess not," she responded, sounding a little more confident than before. Rage flickered across his face as he pounced forward and disarmed her.

Evie didn't know when he had moved. It'd all been a literal blur.

Now, she stood helpless and defenseless.

She watched as he unloaded the weapon and tossed it aside.

Bile rose in the back of her throat as the panic began swelling inside of her.

What am I going to do now? Has Andrew realized I'm missing?

Dylan strode up to her until he was mere inches from her face. He loomed over her, but she refused to tremble in front of him. His voice was low and deadly as he said, "I'm so very tired of having to teach you the same lessons over and over. What did I tell you was going to happen if I found you with him again?"

Evie stood silent, hoping and praying Andrew had noticed she was missing by now and was coming to look for her.

"Answer me," he demanded.

"You'd kill him," she reluctantly answered. Her words were little above a whisper.

"That's right, kitten. Good girl," he praised, running his hand down her left arm. Very slowly, he brought her hand to his mouth and sniffed it. His eyes burned in rage at the scent. "I smell him on you," he spat out. Disgust filled his face.

He folded his hand over her fingers, lifting her index finger. "I think you need to be punished for betraying me, kitten." He forced her to hold his gaze as he slowly slid her finger into his mouth. His mouth felt warm and wet, reminding her of warm honey. Dylan lightly sucked on it, causing her to shudder in disgust; however, she didn't move to pull away. One, she knew it would only anger Dylan further, and two, she would put up with it to bide time for Andrew.

Dylan's teeth grazed along her finger as he sucked and

kissed his way along it. He was taking his time, enjoying teasing his prey. Evie was wondering why he was sucking on her finger when she heard a crunch. Blood spurted from between Dylan's teeth just as a bloodcurdling scream ripped its way out of her throat, splitting the air like a lightning bolt.

Evie's knees buckled under her as spots blotted her vision. She hit the ground hard but could feel nothing over the pain in her hand. Cradling her bloody hand to her chest, she couldn't bring herself to look at it. Blood pooled on her chest, gushing from between her hands.

Blinking the spots away, her eyes drifted up to Dylan, watching as he sucked the blood off her detached finger, cleaning it spotless. After he was finished savoring his kill, he tossed the remnant onto the bed swing.

Evie swayed sideways, nearly hitting the ground.

"Oh no you don't," Dylan said, hauling her to her feet and over his shoulder. "I'm not finished with you yet."

Blood trickled down the back of Dylan's shirt and onto the ground from Evie's limp hand, but Dylan didn't seem to care or notice. Evie raised her head just enough to take one last hopeful glance toward the house, longing to see Andrew, but alas, her time had run out.

Lowering her head, she watched the blood splatter onto the bricks below her, just as the world grew dark.

This is making a mess. Glad it's not the kitchen.

ANDREW

Andrew felt like a weight had been lifted from his shoulders after telling Evie about his marriage to Lily. It had been hard to dredge up the past and relive some of those harder moments from his time with Lily, but he was glad Evie now knew about his marriage and about Lily. There was nothing looming between them any longer. They both knew the others deepest secrets, and it felt good to have that vulnerability and bond with her.

Coming out of the bathroom, Andrew headed to the kitchen to get the snack he'd promised Evie. He loved being at her parent's house. The house itself was a good size, but it still felt very cozy and warm. He could easily picture living in a similar house with Evie and eventually, with their children. The idea gave him hope and joy for the future, which was something he hadn't had in a very long time.

If only we could get through this mess with Dylan, then I can give her this ring that is burning a hole in pocket.

Andrew walked into the kitchen and began looking through the variety of snacks Elaine kept in the fridge and cabinets. Finally, he decided to put together a makeshift charcuterie board. He knew Evie always liked a variety of food to snack on, and he always made sure he had plenty of options when she came over to his house. Sometimes, she'd rather snack than eat a full meal, and who was he to deny her?

My little snacker.

He pulled a small platter out of the cabinet and began layering it with different fruits, vegetables, and nuts. When he was satisfied with his assortment, he headed back to the library to present Evie with his creation. He was rather proud of himself because he had somehow managed to make a little flower out of some of the fruits.

Walking in, he immediately noticed Evie was gone, but if he was being honest, he knew she was gone before he'd walked through the door of the library. It was weird how he always knew if she was near or not.

Andrew placed the plate of food on the table next to the couch and turned to go look for her when his phone pinged. Crossing the room in three strides, he picked it up to find a text from Evie.

E: Headed upstairs to take a quick shower. Be back in 20

He thought it was a little weird she was showering in the middle of the day, but it wasn't uncommon. Andrew felt a bit uneasy but couldn't find anything out of the ordinary. There was no reason to be paranoid; after all, she was still in the house. Realizing he was being paranoid, he decided to give her at least five minutes before he went to check on her.

Why wouldn't she just tell me? Why text?

I'll give her five minutes.

Andrew spent a total of thirty seconds, trying to

concentrate but couldn't move past Evie's text. As he pulled up the text to check it again, he was abruptly and very rudely interrupted by silence.

There was no noise.

No running water from the shower.

No movement from someone upstairs.

No Evie.

Andrew's stomach sank to his feet as he shot up out of his chair, knocking it over. Just as he made it to the library door, he heard her scream, slicing through the eerie quiet. Terror invaded every area of his being, propelling him out of the room and through the house.

He sidestepped the living room furniture as if he had lived there his entire life and knew the layout by heart. He was through the living room and into the kitchen within seconds.

As he bolted into the kitchen, he snatched up the two-way radio on the counter in one swift motion. He didn't slow as he ran across the kitchen to the back door. Pressing the button on the side of the radio, he yelled, "Black Heart, Black Heart."

Andrew and Aiden had spent the early morning hours going over all the safety procedures for the house. Aiden had shown him where all the weapons were hidden in the house and had given him a rundown of all the security cameras on the property. They had come up with a series of code words for various situations to help eliminate time and confusion. Black Heart was a phrase meant only to be used in the direst of circumstances. It meant everyone was to drop what they were doing and immediately come running to whoever called it.

Andrew hadn't needed to assess the situation to know. Evie's scream was proof enough.

He didn't stop to put his boots on before yanking open the back door and running out into the cold. He didn't feel the pebbles digging into his socked feet as he ran.

There was nothing but Evie.

Her scream ricocheted off the corners of his mind, pushing his feet faster.

Andrew hadn't been sure where the noise had come from, but he knew she was somewhere in the backyard. Since Dylan was last seen near the patio, that's where he headed. As he rounded the corner, he heard an ATV rev up about seventy yards to his right. Andrew reached into the back of his shirt and pulled his gun out of the holster on the small of his back. He didn't want to kill his brother, but if it came down to Dylan or Evie, he would choose her.

He would always choose her.

Andrew adjusted his course and bypassed the patio, heading to the woods towards the ATV. His chest was burning, and he was breathing heavily as he finally reached the spot where he'd heard the sound coming from. However, the sound of the ATV was little more than a whisper on the wind, and that's when he knew.

He was too late.

The absence of her was palpable. Everything within him went silent at her absence. He heard nothing as reality slammed into him like a train. He was vaguely aware of Aiden yelling instructions and questions through the radio.

He swallowed heavily before saying into the radio, "She's gone."

32
ANDREW

Andrew's vision blurred as every emotion raced through his body all at once. He was angry at himself for not being there when it had counted, again.

Angry at Dylan for playing him once more.

Angry at the fact he couldn't keep her safe.

The fear felt all consuming. Images of what Dylan might do to her danced through his mind. He tried to push them from his mind, but it was near impossible.

After taking a few deep breaths to calm his mind and body, Andrew slowly began to make his way back to the house. His socked feet trudged through the mixture of left-over snow and mud, but he didn't even notice. Dread had become nearly all-encompassing. He was lost in his thoughts that he nearly missed the small drops of blood at the edge of the patio.

Andrew walked over to examine the spot and noticed a trail of red, leading to the middle of the patio. His stomach lurched as his mind finally caught up to his eyes.

The trail ended in a small puddle of blood—not enough to be fatal but enough to signal something had gone very wrong.

Please let it be his and not hers. Please, God, please.

Looking around for more clues as to what had happened, Andrew's eyes came to a curt stop, landing on the bed swing. Lying in a splatter of red was a small finger.

"Please, no," Andrew whispered.

With a shaking hand, he reached down and picked it up. Turning it over, he saw the blue painted fingernail and knew.

The blood was hers.

The finger was hers.

He cut off her finger.

Her finger?

The corners of his vision began to darken as his breathing quickened. He dropped the finger back onto the swing bed and stumbled to the edge of the patio before throwing up in the grass.

Andrew had always believed he could handle anything. He knew he was stronger than most and was rarely bothered by anything, but the moment was proving to be more than he could stand.

It wasn't surprising that someone could do something so heinous to another individual, but it was surprising that his own brother could do that to the woman he loved.

Wiping his mouth, Andrew straightened up and squared his shoulders. Evie would need him at his best. This was all the time he would afford to being scared and weak. Now, it was time for him to step up and to be the man Evie believed in and loved. Failing again would be unacceptable. With a determination that could not and would not be stopped, Andrew headed back to the house to grab his jacket and shoes.

After putting his boots, Andrew stepped outside on to find Aiden and the rest of the guys pulling up on their ATV's.

"What happened?" Aiden angrily yelled, hopping off his ATV.

"I don't know. I really don't," Andrew replied, sounding defeated. Aiden was fuming, and he didn't blame him one bit.

"Tell me what you do know," Aiden bit off.

"We were in the house working. I got up to go to the kitchen. When I returned, I had a text from Evie saying she was going to take a shower. I didn't think much of it until I noticed the house was quiet. I started to get up to check on her, and that's when." His voice broke as he remembered her blood chilling scream. It still rang in his ears, sending a chill down his spine. "When I heard her scream. I immediately radioed you and ran outside to where I thought she might be. As I reached the patio, I heard an ATV crank up a little ways away, but by the time I got there, they were gone."

Aiden ran a hand down his face and looked around. "That's all? Nothing else? No warning or signs of anything wrong?"

"Yes, sir, nothing else. No alarms went off. No cameras tripped. No warning of any kind." Aiden had set his phone up to receive notifications of any alarms or motions detected on the cameras. He also had access to the camera feeds, but there were no notifications.

"Let me see the text she sent you," Aiden said, holding his hand out for Andrew's phone.

Andrew reached into his back pocket, pulling his phone out. Handing it to Aiden he said, "I have no clue why she went outside."

Aiden looked at the text and said, "I have an idea, but I'll have to get Pete to run analysis on the text first." He handed the phone to Pete and said, "Can you trace the origin of the text? I know it's from her number, but I'm going to guess she didn't send it. And if she didn't send it, then I'd guess Dylan also sent her a text, luring her outside."

Pete took the phone and rode off to the bunkhouse to do his part of finding out what had gone wrong. Andrew knew it was foolish to hope he could find anything helpful, but he hoped, nonetheless.

"There is one other thing," Andrew said hesitantly. He didn't want to show Aiden what he'd found on the patio, but it wasn't something he could keep hidden.

"What?"

"There's evidence that Dylan hurt her before taking her." A shudder ran through him as he remembered the feel of her severed finger between his.

"What kind of evidence?" Aiden ground out.

"It's on the patio."

Aiden didn't wait for Andrew to explain further. He promptly turned and headed for the patio with long strides. Andrew knew Aiden had probably seen way worse during his time with the seals, but he wasn't sure how he'd handle seeing his only daughter's finger, lying in a puddle of her blood.

Davey and Andrew followed Aiden to the patio and nearly collided into the back of him as he skidded to a very abrupt halt. Andrew felt his stomach lurch again at the sight. However, he refused to vomit in front of Aiden. He'd had his moment earlier to feel what he needed to, and now, he would be strong for Evie and her father. Andrew looked over and saw Davey cover his mouth with his hand and look away. Aiden on the other hand hadn't moved since he came to a stop.

"I am going to kill him in the slowest and most painful way possible," Aiden threatened in the darkest voice Andrew had ever heard. He knew he meant every word.

Andrew didn't know whether to feel bad for Dylan or not because he was sure Aiden would do nothing short of filleting the skin off his body.

Andrew was struggling with his own feelings. He'd never felt the need to cause harm to another human being before but looking at Evie's severed finger brought up a very deep and raw need to destroy anyone and anything that had harmed her. He wasn't so sure he wouldn't help Aiden torture Dylan to death, and he might even enjoy it a little bit.

Aiden walked over and carefully picked up the finger, examining it. What he was looking for, Andrew didn't know, but he knew it was nothing good when Aiden let out a slow breath.

In a cold distant voice, Aiden told them, "Looks like the finger was bitten off."

A rigid silence fell among the group as they absorbed his words.

Finally, Davey broke the silence by asking, "He bit it off?"

Aiden nodded. Anger radiated off him, but sadness filled his eyes. There was a brokenness there that Andrew had never witnessed before, but one he was becoming very familiar with.

Helplessness laid heavy within him, and he knew Aiden felt it too.

There was no turning back time to stop the pain; however, a time of mending and healing was coming.

They just had to reach it, and to do that, they had to reach Evie.

33
EVIE

Evie slowly came to. Her head was pounding, and everything was a blur.

With a groan, she tried to sit up, but immediately fell back onto the bed from the pain shooting through her hand. Looking down at her damaged hand, the memories slowly began to rise to the surface.

Images from the moment on the patio began to take shape, causing her breathing to become shallow and rapid, but she shoved desperately at the rising panic. There was no way she would survive if she began panicking. That was one of the first things her dad had taught her during one of his Survival 101 bootcamps. It was as if he'd known this day would come and wanted her to be prepared. A shiver ran through her at the thought, but she didn't have time to focus on it.

Survival rule number 1. Do not panic.

She took several deep breaths and concentrated on calming her tattered nerves.

2. Assess the damage.

Evie held her left hand up, finding a white bandage on

it. It'd been dressed and taken care of since the incident. She curled away from her hand as the memory of Dylan sliding his mouth over her finger and biting it off filtered into her mind. Disgust snaked through her, making her shiver.

At least, I can take taking care of my bleeding hand was off the to do list.

3. Figure out where you are.

Evie rubbed her eyes, trying to help clear them. She was groggy from whatever Dylan had given her to keep her asleep. The room was cold and dark.

No wonder I keep shivering. It's freezing in here.

Feeling around the side of the bed, she found a lamp, but it wouldn't turn on.

He must've cut the power to wherever we are.

A psychopathic maniac bent on freezing to death. Great.

Panic started to rise again at the thought of being alone in the dark, but she took a deep breath and let it go.

Carefully, she pressed her feet to the floor to stand, fighting through the pain and dizziness. She had to take several deep breaths before she felt like she could steadily move. Stumbling around the room, she finally found the door, and to her surprise, it was unlocked.

As quietly as she could, she opened the door and discovered a dim light, filling the hallway. It was obvious the light was coming from the down the stairs, which meant Dylan was most likely down there waiting for her. Nausea threatened to overtake her at the thought of having to face him again.

Not now. What's next on the list?

4. Use every context clue to fill in the blanks of what you don't know.

The light from downstairs flickered just as the smell of

smoke hit her nose. There was no power, but Dylan must've lit a fire for light and heat, which also meant he was definitely downstairs. Who knew what he had planned next? As much as she really didn't want to, Evie had to decide whether to go downstairs and face Dylan or remain upstairs and hope for the best.

5. Try to find a way out.

She let out an internal groan.

Since she was upstairs, the only probable exit was down the stairs. Without power, it would be hard to find a window to climb out of up there. Not to mention, she'd have to attempt to climb out of a second story window with an injured hand and make it to the ground without breaking her neck. That only left one option.

With a deep breath, Evie slowly began making her way downstairs.

Each step down the stairs was agony. She wasn't ready for whatever would come next, but like a lot of times in life, she didn't get a choice.

A small gasp escaped her lips as she stepped off the last step and straight into Andrew's living room.

"You're up," a dark voice greeted her. Dylan stood from where he'd been sitting on the couch with his back to her. As he turned to face her, it took everything in Evie to remain calm.

His eyes slid to her hand. "Awe, kitten. I'm sorry about your hand. Do you need some medicine for the pain?" He came around the couch to her. Nothing but concern filled his dark eyes, and his voice sounded thoroughly sincere and caring. Rage seethed in her, but she smothered it. It was obvious Dylan had moved to the next step in his deranged game, but at least, for now, it didn't seem like he was going to hurt her.

However, one wrong move from her, and she knew that would change.

6. If you can't escape, play the game and bide your time

The game was changing, and she needed to adapt or risk dying.

Evie cleared her throat and replied, "Yes, please." She let some of the pain and neediness come through in her voice, which only seemed to enhance Dylan's pleasure.

Dylan led her to the kitchen counter where he had prescription pain meds, waiting. Evie picked up one of the bottles and saw her name on the label.

How did he get these?

I don't even want to know.

She figured it didn't really matter in the long run. It wasn't like the answer was going to help her in her current state.

Dylan handed her a glass of water.

"I'm not sure about taking these." She noted the anger that began to simmer in his eyes and quickly added, "Prescription pain meds make me sick." The anger was almost immediately replaced with concern. Evie tried not to sag in relief.

"Why not start with half and see if that's okay. If not, I can get you something else." He broke one of the tablets in half, handing it to her. Evie took it from him and hesitated before swallowing it. She was taking a gamble on Dylan not wanting to harm her.

He gave her a nod of approval.

No, Dylan wouldn't harm her unless she stepped out of line or angered him in some way. Dylan always took care of what he possessed, unless that possession stepped out of line. As long as she along, everything would be fine.

As she swallowed the pill, she looked around and

slowly began to put the pieces together. All of this was Dylan's way of playing "house" with her.

He doesn't just want me. He wants what Andrew has.

Dread hit her. There'd be no easy way out of the situation.

Evie thought she'd be sick when the next thought popped in her head. If Andrew showed up there, Dylan would kill him. There was no way Dylan would let Andrew take her again. She knew deep in her gut this was the end of the game.

Dylan's final move.

7. Switch to offense when the time is right

If she was going to keep Andrew safe, she was going to have to turn the tables and play a game of her own.

Evie smiled sweetly at Dylan and asked, "Are you hungry? I don't know if we have anything to fix, but I could order a pizza." Evie was careful with her wording, making sure she always implied it to be their house and not Andrew's.

"Pizza sounds great, Genny," he replied with a smile.

"Why don't you go sit down. I'll call in the order and bring you a beer." She kept her voice even and pleasing. If it was going to work, she'd have to pretend to be the adoring and attentive girlfriend. She would have to pretend to be his. The thought induced vomit, but the need to keep Andrew safe outweighed everything else.

I can endure anything for a little while.

"I think the game is on. I'll turn on the generator and power up the tv." Dylan kissed her on the head and handed her his phone.

"Great. I'll watch with you." Evie said as she dialed the pizzeria. Suzanne answered the phone.

"I need to place an order," Evie said with a steady voice.

"Evie, honey? Is that you?" Confusion and shock flowed through Suzanne's voice. Her dad had probably already called Ed and let him know she was missing.

"Yes." Evie's voice shook slightly.

"Tell me, Sweetie."

"I need one large pepperoni and a large cheese."

"Anything to drink?"

"No, just the pizza. Can you deliver it please?" Evie rattled off Andrew's address to Suzanne. She and Ed had come up with the pizza code in case there was ever an emergency. Evie would be able to alert Ed or Suzanne without raising suspicion, and they would be able to tell her dad where she was.

Before she hung up, Suzanne said, "We've got you, honey. Just hold tight."

Evie hung up the phone, fighting the tears that were desperately trying to spill over. She prayed Suzanne would get the information to her dad quickly. She knew she would but prayed anyways. She needed all the help she could get.

Blowing out a breath, she opened the fridge to find Dylan a beer. The power hadn't been off long because the fridge was still cold. She couldn't help but wonder how long it would take her dad to get to her. She just wanted to go home, but there was no sense in longing for something that wasn't happening.

With a sigh, she headed to where Dylan was sitting. Handing the beer to him, she sat down and turned her attention to the television.

Let the games begin.

34
ANDREW

Andrew was busy loading his truck up when Aiden came jogging over to him. "Thanks, Ed. We'll be there soon."

"Does Ed know something?" He hated the desperation in his voice, but he truly was desperate for any sliver of information.

Aiden pocketed his phone. "Yes. Evie called Suzanne at the pizzeria and ordered using a code, letting her know she was okay. She was able to get the address of Evie's location."

"Where is she?" Relief should be flooding through him right now, but Aiden didn't seem happy.

"Your house."

"My house?"

Aiden nodded his head solemnly.

"Aiden, I'm not understanding. What's the problem with my house? If anything, that seems like an advantage?"

"Before we leave, I need to ask you a question, and I need you to be very honest with me." Aiden's tone was deadly and grave, which left Andrew with a load of concern.

He wasn't sure he wanted to answer whatever he was about to ask, especially since Aiden had avoided answering his questions and was asking his own.

"Okay. What's your question?"

"Are you willing to kill your brother?"

Aiden stared him down, searching his face. Andrew paused. He'd never really thought about it before. Sure, he'd kill anyone for Evie, but the possibility of him killing his brother had never been a reality until then.

Despite it all, Dylan was his little brother.

Would I kill him? Could I?

Cautiously, Andrew asked, "Why are you asking me this?"

"I'm not an expert on kidnapping or insane men for that matter, but this looks like it's shaping up to be your brother making his final stand. He wants what you have. All of it. Your house. Your woman. Your life." Andrew took a deep breath as Aiden continued. "There's only one way he achieves all of that. With you dead. I'd bet a lot of money he's waiting on you to show up, so he can take you out."

Andrew was having a hard time processing everything Aiden was saying. He knew Aiden was right. It all made complete sense, but he had no clue how they'd ended up there. His little brother kidnapping the woman he loved, and said brother being so envious and possessive that he wanted to kill him.

They had grown up together. They'd road bikes in the summertime and played baseball together. There was a lot of good memories mixed in with bad ones.

Where did it all go wrong?

What happened to my baby brother?

Why does he want to kill me?

Can I kill him?

Aiden interjected into his racing mind. "So, I'm going to ask you again. Are you willing to kill your brother? Because I'm not going to send you in there to rescue her if you're going to hesitate, should the moment arise." Andrew opened his mouth to answer, but Aiden stopped him with a raised hand. "I know you love her, and I know I gave you my blessing. But this is different. I can't risk her life. I *won't* risk her life."

Andrew didn't know how Aiden was able to remain level-headed throughout everything. Maybe, it was the years as a Navy Seal, but whatever it was, he was compartmentalizing all the emotions and information. If Andrew had any hope at surviving the day and ending the nightmare once and for all, he was going to have to take a cue from Aiden.

Hurriedly, he began separating thoughts and emotions until he was left with nothing but clarity. Andrew took a second to process all the information he knew and had before looking Aiden in the eyes with complete certainty.

"Yes."

"Yes what? I need to hear you say it." A warm fatherly look formed on Aiden's face. It hadn't escaped him about what he was asking Andrew. He knew what it would cost. "*You* need to hear you say it."

"Yes, I am willing to kill my brother if it comes to it. If it's a choice between him and Evie, I choose Evie. I'll always choose her." His words were firm. He solidified his choice within himself and moved on from it. This was one decision he wouldn't be able to dwell on. His little brother had made his choice, and now, he had made his.

Aiden clapped Andrew on the shoulder. An understanding passed between them. Andrew knew Aiden didn't want to kill his brother any more than he wanted to, but sometimes, people went beyond redemption. Sometimes, people were past saving. If his brother wouldn't willingly give up, then there'd be no chance of salvation.

Andrew looked over Aiden's shoulder to Davey and Pete, loading something into Aiden's truck. "Is that C4?"

Aiden gave Andrew's shoulder a pat as he said, "Don't worry about it."

Five hours later, Andrew pulled over on a cut off road about a mile from his house. Ed was already waiting for them when they arrived. Andrew climbed out of the truck and immediately asked him about Evie. Ed had delivered the pizza to his house about thirty minutes after her call and had been able to see her for himself as he'd assessed the situation.

"I only caught a glimpse of her. She was on the couch, watching the ballgame. Dylan answered the door," Ed explained grimly. "She did hold her arm up when he wasn't looking. It's heavily bandaged. I'm guessing Dylan took care of her hand. She gave me a thumbs up, so I think she's okay for the moment. All things considered."

Relief swamped Andrew as he listened to Ed recount the interaction. Despite everything, it was a blessing Dylan didn't appear to want to hurt Evie any further. Andrew didn't think it would be possible to find anything positive about the situation, but there they were with a small ray of light, illuminating through the cracks of the darkness. Knowing Evie was cared for, would ease all their minds and make the situation more manageable.

Aiden walked up asking, "Did you see any weapons?"

"No, but he's armed. The power is off. The lights were off, and the house felt cold from where I was standing. He does have a fire going, though, and a small generator is plugged up for the television and probably the fridge as well."

"We might have the element of surprise with the security system down," Andrew offered.

"Perhaps, but that means everything will be very quiet. They'll be able to hear us coming, and Dylan is waiting on you. He's probably estimating us to be here right about now." Andrew realized Aiden had already thought through everything and worked out how to go about saving Evie.

"What are you thinking?" Andrew asked.

"I'm thinking we wait." Andrew opened his mouth to object, but Aiden continued. "Dylan is expecting us. He's not stupid, but he's probably expecting us to rush in as soon as possible. The longer we wait, the more on edge he'll become, which may help us out in the long run."

"We also risk Evie the longer we leave her in there." Andrew couldn't help the anger and desperation that tinged his words.

"It's a risk we'll have to take. I don't want her in there with him anymore than you do, but I'm also betting that he's not aiming to harm her. After all, she gave Ed a thumbs up. She wouldn't have if she thought she couldn't handle whatever is going on in there."

She shouldn't have to handle whatever is going on it there, whether she can or not.

Andrew's anger continued growing until he spat out. "He bit her finger off." Aiden, however, didn't so much as blink at his words. Andrew locked down on the anger and murmured, "Sorry."

"I get it. Trust me. That's my baby girl in there. I've loved her for a lot longer than you have and will only ever do what I think is best for her. I have more experience in this area than you do, which is why we're going to do it my way." Aiden's words were firm and final. There was nothing Andrew could do but nod.

Davey and Pete pulled in behind Aiden's truck. When everyone was gathered around, Aiden began laying out the plan and giving out instructions.

At 2am, they'd make their move.

EVIE

The rest of the evening had gone okay. She and Dylan had eaten pizza and watched the football game. They'd even chatted a little about nothing in particular, which had taken every bit of effort she'd had to sound her regular self. While Evie was forcing herself to play a part, Dylan appeared to be enjoying a normal evening at home. It made Evie sick at her stomach to think about his nonchalance for the entire situation. He was even more delusional and insane than she'd initially thought, which didn't bode well.

Evie was getting tired when she finally dared to ask Dylan what his plan was. "Dylan?"

He made a sound of acknowledgement without taking his eyes from the television screen.

"What are we doing?"

His eyes slid to her with a predatory glint. She knew she was treading in very dangerous waters, but she couldn't keep silent anymore.

"What do you mean?" He cocked his head sideways as if daring her to challenge him.

She swallowed before answering. "I mean what is your

plan?" She kept her tone soft and unthreatening. "How long are we going to be here?"

"As long as we want, kitten. This is our home now." His eyes narrowed at her, causing them to darken. Evie knew she shouldn't, but she shoved ahead and asked anyways.

"What about when Andrew comes home?"

Dylan tensed. She could see the anger, burning throughout him as he stood and came to stand over her. Reaching down, he smoothed her hair before snatching a tight fistful of it.

Evie yelped as he pulled her head back to look up at him.

"I won't punish you for this, even though you should know better, kitten. Do not mention my brother's name to me again. But since you asked so sweetly, I'll reward you. If he dares to show his face, then I plan on it being the last time we see it." His voice was full of hate for his brother. "I'm going to put a hole through that perfect face of his, marring it beyond recognition. With any luck, our parents won't even recognize him in the afterlife.

Dylan tugged harder on her hair, while gently caressing her face with his free hand. "Understand, little Genny?" Evie tried nod. "You're mine. Not his." Evie nodded again. "Say it."

Evie swallowed, wanting to throw up. She'd rather cut her tongue out than say those words, but if she didn't, Dylan might very well cut it out.

Keep playing the game.

"I'm yours," she said with as much confidence as she could muster.

"Yes, you are," he replied insatiably. He pulled her head back even further as he leaned down and slammed his mouth on hers. His tongue darted into her mouth, trying to claim what wasn't his. A dirty smirk was on his face as he pulled back. "I plan on my mouth doing a lot more later in a lot more places." His eyes hungrily roved over her body before he let her hair go, returning to his place on the couch opposite of hers.

It took everything in her not to look repulsed. As much as she didn't want to close her eyes, she couldn't help it. Between the pain meds and everything else that had happened, she was exhausted. Evie grabbed the blanket from the basket at the end of the couch and curled up under it as sleep overtook her weary and fragmented body.

Several hours later, Evie awoke to loud bang.

35
ANDREW

"Do not hesitate." Aiden's words replayed over and over in his mind as Andrew approached his house. The entire situation felt surreal. He'd used the past several hours waiting, trying to come to terms with everything. The only thing he knew for certain that Evie was innocent. She'd been used and abused by his brother for years, and it had to end. The other thing he knew with absolute certainty was he would do anything to ensure her safety, so there he was, coming to make that happen. He'd once promised her he would put an end to all of it, and that's what he was going to do.

Despite being practically unarmed, he felt confident. The guys had decided if he appeared armed, Dylan would start shooting before Andrew had a chance to open his mouth; therefore, Andrew had one gun in a holster at the small of his back. The plan was to get Evie to a safe part of the room, let Aiden get her out, while Andrew dealt with his brother. Davey and Pete would provide backup if necessary. Aiden said the less people involved the better, considering the law hadn't been informed of the situation yet.

Andrew figured he'd already beaten his brother once. He could do it again.

Andrew slowly walked to the front of his house.

It was his house. His woman.

And he was there to claim them.

With a deep breath, Andrew released the hold on his anger and kicked the front door off its hinges.

"I'm home," Andrew yelled in a voice he didn't recognize.

It was in that moment, as he surveyed the cold dark home, he realized he had just enough evil within himself to be just as terrible as his brother.

If his brother wanted to play evil, Andrew would become evil itself.

Andrew walked into the living room to find Evie sitting on the couch wrapped in a blanket, looking dazed. He held in his relief and turned his attention to his brother. Dylan stood across from Evie, pointing a gun at Andrew.

"Brother." Andrew bit off to Dylan. It was the first and last greeting Dylan would be receiving from him.

"What are you doing here, brother?" Dylan asked, returning the greeting.

Andrew raised his eyebrows and gestured to the house. "This is my house."

"No, I don't think so. Not anymore." A nasty smile formed on Dylan's face. He was going to enjoy making Andrew watch and suffer as he took what was his.

"Going to kill me for it?" Andrew's tone was casual but challenging.

"Oh, I am, and I'm going to enjoy every second of making you pay for touching what's mine."

A small whimper came from Evie. Andrew's heart

threatened to crumble at the sound, but he kept his unfaltering gaze on Dylan.

"So, how do you want to do this, brother?" He practically spat out the word brother, as if it were the vilest word to exist. Dylan had stained it with the blood of Andrew's very heart.

"I'm thinking execution style. I want you on your knees, begging." Dylan's face grew crazier with each word. Andrew concealed the shiver that wanted to crawl all over him at Dylan's words and face. He didn't recognize the man in front of him. His little brother was depraved and beyond saving. He didn't know what had happened to him, but he didn't have time to figure it out.

"Okay, but can you let Evie leave the room first? I think it might a little much for her." Andrew dared a glance at her. Her eyes were wide with fear. He wished he could reassure her, but he needed to get her out of alive first. Then, he'd hug and kiss her as much as she would let him.

She'll be lucky if I let her out of my sight after this.

Dylan seemed to ponder Andrew's request. "No, I think she should watch." Evie let out a sob at Dylan's words. "It'll be okay, kitten. I'm doing this for us, and once it's over, I'll make you forget all about him. It'll be like he never existed."

"I don't want you to do this for us. No one needs to die for us to be together," Evie said, rising from her spot on the couch. She walked around the large coffee table to Dylan. Everything in Andrew screamed to grab her, to stop her from getting too close to him. He watched as she placed a hand on Dylan's raised arm, speaking to him as if they were the only two there.

"You don't have to kill him. I'll stay with you," she whispered.

Andrew knew she was only trying to diffuse the situation, but he thought she might really mean what she said. Deep in the back of his mind, he knew she would stay with Dylan if it meant he would live. Even though his stomach clenched at the thought, his love for her only grew. She was the most selfless woman he'd ever known, and she deserved the absolute world. If they made it out of there, he'd give it to her.

"Evie, this is between me and Dylan." There was a dominant authority in his voice, prompting a look of confusion from Evie as she turned to look at him. Andrew pointed to the far side of the room by the staircase. "Can you go over there and wait?" He'd never used such a commanding tone with her before. He hated using it but needed her to know it wasn't a suggestion.

"Finally, something we agree on." Dylan's eyes moved from Andrew to Evie. "It's okay, Genny. I'm going to deal with my brother, and then, you can go back to sleep." Evie nodded and started to move around him, but Dylan suddenly grabbed her by the throat, pulling her to him and kissing her hard enough to bruise.

Hot blinding rage shot through Andrew's veins as he watched his brother violate Evie, yet again. He didn't let out the breath he was holding. He wouldn't give Dylan the satisfaction of knowing just how much he was getting to him. It took everything in him, but he managed to conceal every emotion waging a war within him.

Seconds later, Dylan let her go and sent her to the other side of the room with a slap on the butt. Andrew made sure Evie was safe across the room before he turned his attention back to his little brother.

"Ready for this brother?" Dylan strode towards him, motioning with the gun for him to get on the floor. "On your knees."

"You know what? I don't think so. I think I'm ready for a nap." Andrew looked hard at Evie, praying she understood.

"Goodnight, brother."

Andrew dove behind the couch just as the far wall behind the dining table blew open with a deafening sound. Chunks of dry wall, wood, and other debris hurtled throughout the room, landing all around them. As the dust settled, he looked up to see Evie curled into tight a ball on the floor.

Thank God.

Andrew got his feet under him and took off, running for Evie.

Just as he reached out to grab her, a pair of hands locked onto his shoulders, yanking him backwards. He landed on his back with a thud, forcing the air from his body. As he looked up, Dylan's fist flew towards his face. Andrew awkwardly blocked the punch; however, it didn't stop Dylan from connecting with the side of his face, but it had lessened the impact. He managed to roll away, getting to his feet before Dylan could advance on him again.

Before he could make another move, Aiden rushed in behind them and snatched Evie up off the floor, heading for the massive hole in the side of his house. Dylan paused, seeming torn between getting Evie or finishing Andrew off.

He opted for the latter.

"I am going to kill you." Dylan bit off each word as he stomped towards him.

Andrew held his ground and waited. Dylan swung, and Andrew ducked, driving his fist into Dylan's stomach. Much to Andrew's surprise, Dylan absorbed the punch. As Dylan's left hand slammed into his cheek, he realized Dylan was thinking ahead and plotting how the fight was going to go.

Harder than any punch was the realization that Dylan

had let him beat him that day at lunch. Dylan had been playing a longer game than anyone had thought to realize. The confidence quickly drained out of Andrew. He'd always thought his brother had underestimated him, but it was *he* who had underestimated his little brother.

How am I going to get out of this?

Dylan landed another hit, forcing him to stagger back against the couch. Before he could hit him again, Andrew stumbled around the side of the couch, trying to get his bearings back. Stars were dancing in his eyes, but he didn't dare stop moving. Dylan advanced on him, like a predatory animal waiting to make its kill. He backed further until his legs met the broken coffee table.

There was debris all around him. Wood and plaster littered the floor. The blast from the explosion must've been worse than he'd thought because pieces of stone from the fireplace were also scattered about. Hastily, he reached down and picked up a piece of stone. He waited as Dylan made his way closer and then, hurled the stone at him, sending up a quick prayer for accuracy.

Thanks to his former years a baseball player, the stone found its mark. Andrew launched himself at Dylan just as he lost his balance from the hit and shoved him solidly toward the fireplace. Dylan fell hard onto the stone hearth. Before he could move, Andrew was there. Fist flying into his face. Blood spewed from Dylan's nose and mouth. He got two hits in before Dylan blocked his next blow, knocking Andrew's feet out from under him. Andrew smacked the hardwood floor with a groan.

He was trying to avoid shooting his brother at all costs. If he could subdue him, he could hand him over to the police, but in order to do that, he needed a new plan. Eyeing the opening in the wall, Andrew decided to make a run for it. With the guys around, it would be harder for Dylan to succeed.

As he stood to run, Dylan slammed into his back, shoving him back to the floor. This time, Dylan was on top of him, and the air was out of him. Dylan grabbed his shoulder and rolled him over, pinning him to the floor. His fist pounded into Andrew's face. Blood streamed into his mouth, filling it with a coppery taste.

Dylan paused his fist just long enough to wrap his hands around Andrew's throat. Fighting through his clouding vision, Andrew moved his arms through Dylan's and shoved out hard and fast, causing Dylan to lose his balance. Roughly, he shoved him off the top of him. Andrew slid back, reaching behind him for the gun at the small of his back.

Before he could grab it, Dylan dove back on top of him. Hands slammed onto his throat again with a vengeance. With his arm wrapped awkwardly beneath him, Andrew strained hard for the gun. Dylan tightened his grip just as Andrew's fingers grazed the grip of the gun.

A low laugh rumbled out of Dylan. "I don't think so big brother. Today is your day of death. Not mine." Blood coated his depraved smile.

Darkness was creeping in, and death was lurking in the shadows. It was now or never. Andrew strained for the gun once more. Fingers wrapping tightly around the grip, Andrew pulled his arm quickly from beneath him.

There was no hesitation as he pointed the gun and pulled the trigger.

Surprise lit Dylan's face, as blood rained down onto Andrew's face. The grip on his throat loosened as Dylan slumped to the floor.

Andrew closed his eyes and took a breath.

It was over. The threats to Evie.

The stalking. The fighting. The violence.

All of it was finished.

His brother was dead. By his own hand.

He sat up and opened his eyes to look at his brother's limp body on the debris ridden floor. Numbness fell over him as he took in the scene. Blood was pooling on the floor under his brother's lifeless body. Memories from years gone by shuffled through his mind.

Somehow, in the middle of everything, he'd forgotten the joy he and his little brother used to share. From riding bikes to baseball games. Their laughs. Their tears. It was all there and gone within minutes; however, Andrew knew deep down that little boy had been gone for a long time.

Grief and sadness swamped him as he stared at the life he had taken.

Boots crunched on the rubble of his living room, drawing his attention from the lifeless body. Aiden knelt beside him, laying a hand on his shoulder.

The weight of what had occurred blanketed the room. Andrew's shoulders began to shake. He couldn't stop the sob that escaped his tight lips. He couldn't help the tears that fell for his brother—the life he had taken. Aiden's arm slid around his shoulders, holding him through the waves of grief and tears. Andrew wept over the months of worry and hurt for Evie, for the absence of choice, and the loss of life.

It all poured from him in aching sobs.

After several minutes, the tears subsided, and he rose to meet the consequences. Aiden steadied him as he swayed on his feet. Sirens wailed in the distance.

Time seemed to blur.

Everything slowed.

He was so incredibly tired.

As he began to make his way through the ruins of his house, a small sound drew his attention to his brother's body.

There he was. Eyes open.

Gun drawn.

Andrew heard the shot before he felt it. He hit the ground just as Aiden fired his gun, hitting Dylan square between the eyes.

The world stilled and cooled. Peace blanketed him as he floated between space and time. Somewhere above him, Aiden was shouting at someone, but it didn't register. He was too far from the surface.

Evie.

36
EVIE

Evie chewed on her nails as she waited for her dad to go get Andrew. They'd heard a gunshot followed by deafening silence. Her dad had immediately left her to go see about him. She should've been feeling relief, but she wouldn't breathe easy until she saw Andrew's smiling face and Dylan's dead body.

Ed squeezed her shoulder, "Relax, honey. It's over now."

Evie nodded, but she couldn't shake the uneasy feeling that had taken over. Anxiety clawed at her from the inside out.

Something isn't right.

Just as Ed went to reassure her again, two gunshots rang out into the night air, ridding her of the drop of hope she'd been clinging to.

A hollowness consumed her, numbing her to everything. Her whispered pleas drifted into the cold night, returning unanswered.

Her feet moved of their own volition, running for the hole in the wall—just as her dad began yelling for help.

No. Please! Please, let him be okay. He has to be okay.

Her legs burned as she ran as fast as she could. Her socked feet thudded on the gravel driveway and across the yard to the missing wall. Reaching it, she could see her dad, standing there, looking panicked. Evie had seen many looks on her dad's face before, but panic had never been one. She had a feeling it would forever be scarred onto her heart as a reminder of the night.

"Evie," her dad choked out as he quickly knelt in front of the couch.

She dashed across the room, not caring about the debris under her feet.

"Where is he?" she cried.

Just as she rounded the corner of the couch, her world came to a screeching halt.

There before her were two brothers. Each lying on the floor in a puddle of their own blood.

Finally, equal in life and death.

Death had no winners. Everyone always lost against it, including the living.

Evie opened her mouth, but nothing came out. Her knees crashed to the hard floor beside Andrew, but she didn't feel it.

Looking to her dad, she yelled, "Why aren't you applying pressure?"

Scrambling for Andrew, she placed both hands on the hole above his heart, pushing down hard. The gauze on her left hand quickly soaked up the warm blood.

"Do something!" She quickly looked to her dad for help, but only found him staring wide eyed at her. "Daddy, do something! Help him!"

"Buttercup," Aiden started in the softest tone his deep voice would allow.

"No! Do *not* say it!" Evie's eyes drifted down to Andrew's cooling body. She pressed harder onto his chest, ignoring the pain in her hand. "Don't you dare leave me. You made me a promise. We had a deal."

Blood slowly seeped between her fingers. The bandaged on her hand was completely red from her blood mingling with Andrew's. Her knees were wet from the blood pooling beneath him, but she didn't notice.

In the haze of the moment, Evie could just make out the sirens from the ambulance. Help had finally arrived; however, hope was still noticeably absent.

"This isn't how it ends. It can't end like this. Please," she pleaded with anything and everything around her.

The thump of Andrew's heart grew slower with every passing second, causing her to put more pressure on his chest, using her body weight. She had nothing left to give, but she'd give him her nothing.

"I love you," she whispered to him just as his heart beat for the last time.

"No! No! No!" She screamed, quickly gathering the blood from the wound and pushing back towards the hole in his chest. A guttural cry came from deep within her, from the darkest corners of her. A cry that could only come from the tie of two souls being severed.

A heavy hand fell on her back, trying to stop her from putting the blood back into Andrew's slain body. "No, he'll be fine." The hand grabbed her, pulling her away. "No, let me fix him!" She thrashed about, blindly punching at the person holding her.

"Stop, baby. You have to stop. The EMTs are here. Let them help him," Aiden gently said into her ear as he held her tightly against him.

She stilled long enough to see two men, kneeling over

Andrew's lifeless body. One began CPR, while the other began pulling out supplies.

Tears were a steady stream down her cheeks as she watched. As the seconds dragged, her breathing quickened. Her eyes flickered to Dylan.

"You," she spat before shoving out of her dad's arms and heading to Dylan's dead body. "This is all your fault." Tripping over a piece of stone, she fell next to him. Reaching out, she grabbed ahold of his shirt, violently shaking the limp body. "It's all your fault! You did this! You stole, killed, and destroyed everything! Everything I am, and everything I loved! You took it!" Evie dropped the body to the floor with a thud before lifting her fist and punching him. Her arms pounded repeatedly on the dead body, until her dad was there, pulling her away.

"Evie, you have to calm down," he said, hauling her to her feet.

"I can't," she wailed. "I can't. He's." She couldn't bring herself to say it.

Aiden hesitated before cupping both sides of her face with his red stained hands, "I know, baby. I know."

A sob ripped from her at her dad's words.

Don't admit it. Don't let it be true. Let me wake up.

Aiden pulled her into his arms, holding her tightly. The only sounds were those of the two men, working diligently on Andrew, but Evie knew it was a fool's errand. She had felt his heart stop beneath her shaking hands. It had been minutes. No one survived a wound like that.

"I've got a heartbeat," one of the men said from behind her. "It's weak, but it's there. Let's get him loaded, quickly."

Evie's world began to spin again as she took in the man's words.

A heartbeat.

There, in the dead of night, like a flicker of hope was a heartbeat.

37
EVIE

Aiden helped Evie out of his truck. They had followed the ambulance to the hospital, but Evie didn't remember much of the ride. The night was beginning to weigh on her.

Rushing through the doors of the emergency room, Aiden went straight for the desk, asking after Andrew. A gasp sounded to her left. Her head turned to see a nurse, moving towards her. Looking down, she realized just how much blood she was covered in, but it was hard to tell with how blurry her vision was becoming.

"Daddy?" Her voice was thick. The world began to dim just as everything tilted.

"I got you," her dad's voice said from somewhere above her.

Once again, she met the darkness, but this time, she welcomed it with open arms.

The next morning, Evie woke up to the sun, streaming through the window. A steady beep sounded somewhere behind her. A fog filled her mind, causing her thoughts to jumble. Looking over, she saw her mom and dad, sitting together on the small couch by the window.

"Hey, sweet girl. I'm glad to see you're finally awake," her mom said, standing and coming over to her bed. "Feeling okay?"

"Yes," she replied. "I'm okay." She felt anything but fine, but she wasn't about to let her mom know. Or anyone for that matter. She wanted to curl into the numbness a little longer. It was safe there, and she needed a moment longer before she could face the truth.

Her mom sat down on the edge of the bed before saying, "Well, I know that's a lie."

Aiden's large frame cast a shadow over her, "Yeah, we both know it is, but we'll let it pass for now."

Evie was scared to ask or even think about Andrew.

As if reading her mind, her dad told her, "He's alive, but he's still unconscious in the ICU."

Tears filled her eyes, but she willed them not to fall. She was so tired of crying and worrying. The tears wouldn't fix anything at that point, and she'd cried enough to fill a river. For now, she would breathe and focus on what was.

Andrew was alive, and so was she.

It was enough.

It has to be enough because we don't have anything left.

38
ANDREW
TWO WEEKS LATER

He'd had enough of that hospital room. It'd been two agonizing weeks of lying there, staring at the ceiling. He was ready for his own bed—if he could even go home.

Thank you, Aiden.

Aiden had blown almost the entire front side of his house off, and he didn't know how he was going to get it fixed. He hoped his insurance covered explosions.

The door to his room opened, and he hoped to see Evie, standing there. His brothers had told him she'd come to see him while he'd still been unconscious. He swore he'd heard her, beckoning him back to the light. He'd only been out of the ICU for four days, and he thought she would've come to visit him by then. Connor had told him she'd gone back home to Kentucky after she'd been released from the hospital, which worried him.

He didn't blame her for escaping back to her home after everything, but he had a sinking feeling something had changed between them. He didn't know what, but he felt it deep in his chest.

Looking up, he saw Aiden, filling his doorway. The hope flickered out as the door shut behind him.

"Hey, Dr. Boss Man. Looking good for a dead man," Aiden said, making his away across the room.

"Ha" was all Andrew could muster. Laughing hurt like the devil, due to the stitched-up hole in his chest, serving reminder as a constant reminder of that night.

"How are you feeling?"

"Better than my house." Andrew narrowed his eyes at Aiden. "What happened to a small distraction?"

Aiden slid into the chair beside his bed before answering, "Now, Andrew, did you really think I was going to let go of you not protecting my little girl?"

The memories of Thanksgiving at his house filled his mind.

Of course he wouldn't.

Andrew shook his head, smiling. "No, I guess not."

"I won't hesitate next time," Aiden warned.

"Understood."

"Good, and I'll help you rebuild it."

Shocked by his response, Andrew asked, "Really? Why would you do that?"

"Because the lessen is learned, and no one should be left to pick up the pieces alone."

Clearing his throat, he asked, "Is she picking up the pieces alone?" Andrew was nervous as he awaited Aiden's answer. He didn't think Evie had gone back home to simply go home or to even run away.

She was gone. Gone from him.

He just needed Aiden to confirm what his gut had already told him.

Aiden cleared his throat. "Do you want the truth?"

Andrew only nodded.

"To be honest, I don't think she's picking up the pieces at all. I think she left them lying on your living room floor that night." Aiden's voice was quiet with worry. "She's very quiet these days, and you know Evie. She's always talking."

A small smile pulled at Andrew's lips because he did know. It was one of the many things he loved about her.

"It might take more time this time." Aiden paused, trying to find his words. "This last round with Dylan took more from her than it ever has before, and it'll take her some time to come to terms with it."

"Is she coming back?" Andrew's voice was a near whisper as he asked.

"Eventually. She's going to be back in January to finish out the semester."

"Good." A tiny bit of the anxiety eased in Andrew's chest.

Aiden rose from his chair. "I've got to get going, but I'll be back in a couple of days to check on you and to get started on repairing the damage."

"Thank you, Aiden, but you don't have to do that."

"No, but I want to," he said, placing a hand on his shoulder. "In the meantime, this is for you." Aiden reached into his back pocket, pulling out a small envelope. "I'll see you soon, Dr. Boss Man."

"See ya."

Andrew felt sick as he saw Evie's handwriting on the envelope. He didn't know what was inside, but he thought it might as well have been a Dear John letter.

Pulling the letter out, he blew out a breath before reading it. He already knew what it said, but he wasn't sure he was ready for it to be real.

· · ·

Dear Andrew,

I don't know where or how to begin this letter. First, let me tell you how sorry I am for not being there in person. I know you probably don't like me for running off on you again, but I don't have the air to breathe. I couldn't breathe that night at your house or in the hospital. Truth be told, I'm still struggling to breathe here on my parent's farm.

One day, I hope to be whole. I hope to be enough, more than enough for you. I hope you will forgive me for what I'm about to write. I love you with my entire heart, and I always will. Nothing will ever change that, but for now, I need for us to end. I need a break. I'm so tired, Andrew. So very tired. And I don't think I can carry this for both of us. I've got to figure myself out. I need to deal with the past, so I can attempt to have a future. I'd like a future with you, but I need to heal before we can reach it. I hope you understand.

Please, forgive me for any pain I have caused you and for everything that happened that night.

Love,

Evie

Andrew closed the letter, letting out a rough, shaky breath. He knew. He'd known the moment he'd woken up in the ICU. He wasn't surprised, but it still hurt worse than the bullet hole in his chest. The worst part was he did understand her. There was a lot of water under the bridge. They'd both lost a lot that night, and he still had demons he needed to confront. They both needed to work on themselves for a brief time, and then, they could reconvene stronger than before.

Even though it wasn't what he wanted, it might be

what they both needed. He'd see her in a month, and they could figure things out then.

Shutting his eyes, Andrew laid back, awaiting tomorrow.

I'll worry about it then.

39
EVIE

Christmas break had passed uneventfully. She and her mom had spent a lot of time baking cookies and watching Christmas movies while drinking hot cocoa. The holiday season had been peaceful and comforting, especially knowing Dylan wasn't out there anymore, watching and waiting for her. With the threat of stalking and violence gone, she felt lighter, but her heart ached with longing for Andrew.

Too much had happened for them to continue with their relationship. If Andrew and Dylan hadn't been brothers, then maybe they could have survived together. The guilt of what Andrew had, had to do remained deep inside of her. Evie didn't know if it would ever fully go away, and she knew it wouldn't if she remained in a relationship with him.

Her heart would always remain with Andrew.

How can it not?

He'd sacrificed everything for her and had paid a difficult price to get her back.

"I love this movie," Lucy said with a sigh as the credits

for *While You Were Sleeping* rolled. Even though Christmas was officially over, she and Lucy were still celebrating with Christmas movies and cocoa.

"Me too." Her voice was devoid of feeling.

"You could call him," Lucy gently suggested.

Evie shook her head. "No, I can't." She'd told Lucy everything when they'd both gotten back from Christmas break. Lucy was only trying to help, and if their positions were reversed, she'd tell her the same thing.

Lucy reached over and squeezed her hand. "How about I refill our mugs, and you pick the next film?"

"Sure," Evie replied.

Lucy stood and picked up the mugs, heading to the kitchen. Evie let out a discontented sigh and shuffled through the Christmas movie section on the tv. It didn't really matter what they watched. It only served to pass the time. Nothing had felt or been right since that night at Andrew's house. A shudder ran through her at the memory.

She'd nearly vomited on the floor as she'd run back into the house after hearing her dad yelling for help. The sight of Andrew on the floor barely breathing had nearly killed her. Subconsciously, she rubbed her knees as the memory encompassed her. Her knees had been bruised for two weeks after, from where she'd fallen so hard to the floor by his side.

She'd been so covered in blood that they'd had a difficult time at the hospital, discerning between her and Andrew's blood. Some nights, she woke up breathless and sweating with the feel of his blood on her.

A hand drifted to her throat as she remembered the razor-sharp burn from the scream she'd let out as she'd felt his final heartbeat. The agony of losing him had been unbearable as she'd screamed and pleaded with his lifeless body.

It had taken the EMTs minutes to get his heartbeat back, and as she had watched their efforts, she'd felt her heart shatter in an unrepairable way. Andrew had spent three weeks in the hospital before he'd all but discharged himself. Evie had only seen him once since that fatal day.

If she regretted anything, it was not breaking things off in person. He didn't deserve a crappy letter, but it was all the strength she'd had left. There'd been nothing left, and now, she was left with an emptiness that she couldn't seem to fill.

She knew her decision to take a break had been right. They both had healing they needed to do, and she knew she couldn't heal with him. The guilt inside of her needed to find a way to dissolve before she could face him again.

Plus, she needed to be on her own for a while and figure out how to do life without having to look over her shoulder. To stand on her own and be okay. If she didn't, she'd never truly know if she could and would always have it looming over her.

Dylan had stolen a lot from her, and she needed to reclaim some of it before she could be whole enough to be with Andrew. She wanted him. She wanted him so badly it hurt, but she wanted to be her best for him even more. He deserved her at her best.

He deserves everything and more.

Evie clicked on one of the Christmas movies and let it play. She and Lucy spent the rest of night drinking hot cocoa and watching movies in companionable silence. They both knew what tomorrow brought, but neither would bring up the subject. It wouldn't change the fact that Evie would have to begin her final semester of grad school in the same building as Andrew. Luckily, she was no longer his grad assistant or taking his class, but it still didn't make tomorrow any easier.

Eventually, Lucy and Evie fell asleep on the couch. Luckily, Lucy had set an alarm, even if it had nearly given Evie a heart attack when it went off. Quickly, she ran to her room to hop in the shower and get ready for the last first day of her college career.

Evie came out of her room to find her dad sipping coffee and chatting with Lucy. "Dad, what are you doing here? I thought we talked about this."

Her dad had offered to take her to school, but she had refused. She no longer needed his protection from Dylan, and as much as she loved her dad, she needed to be able to stand on her own.

"I know, but I figured I would at least offer you a ride," her dad told her, giving her a smile.

"Fine, but only a ride," Evie replied with a slight glare. She knew she was lucky to have a dad who was so invested in her life and should be more grateful for him. However, that didn't mean she wanted him to baby her.

"Want some coffee?" Lucy asked from the kitchen.

"Yes, but I can get it. Shouldn't you already be gone? You're going to be late."

Lucy waved her off. "It's fine. I wanted to see you before I left. Professor Addison won't mind if I'm a little late."

Evie walked into the tiny kitchen and pulled a mug out of the cabinet, pouring herself a cup. She inhaled the scent of the dark coffee and sighed. Coffee could make anything better.

Today will be fine. Everything will be completely fine.

Evie turned to find Lucy standing behind her but not close enough to freak her out. "What?"

"If you need me today, just call. I will come running, and we can have a girl's day or do whatever you want."

"I truly don't deserve you as a best friend," Evie told her, turning to set her mug on the counter.

"Yes, you do," Lucy said as they hugged. "You're going to be just fine, EJ."

"Okay, enough before I start crying again," Evie said, pulling away.

Lucy headed into the living room and gathered her things. "Remember, just one call away," she hollered, waving her phone at Evie.

Evie nodded her head. "Have a good first day."

"You too," Lucy called as she stepped out the door, blowing her a kiss.

"She's a good friend," Aiden said as Lucy closed the door.

"Don't I know it," Evie replied. "Let me get my things, and then you can *drive* me to school." She put emphasis on the word drive, because she knew her dad would want to walk her to the door. The number of dads walking their daughters to class was guaranteed to be zero, and Evie didn't want to add to it.

Twenty minutes later, Aiden pulled his truck into a parking spot on campus and turned the engine off. Evie didn't move. She didn't know if she was breathing, but she knew her heart was beating because it was pounding in her ears.

Her dad let out a small chuckle. "It's okay, Buttercup. Just one foot in front of the other. This will get easier."

"What if I see him?" Her voice was shaky. She hadn't spoken of Andrew since the day she'd given her dad the letter to give to him.

"Seeing him won't be as bad as you've made it out to be

in your head, but eventually, you'll have to see him. Need to see him." She felt her dad's strong hand lightly cupping the back of her neck, slowly massaging, and soothing the stress and anxiety away.

She took a deep breath and let it out. "Will you walk me to the building?"

Her dad smiled at her. "Sure, but let's get a coffee first. You have some time before your first class, right?"

Evie nodded.

Ten minutes later, Evie was armed with a vanilla cappuccino in her right hand and her dad on her left. She couldn't help but notice the missing index finger on her left hand. Of all the things Dylan had stolen from her, her finger might've been the worst.

They stopped in front of the English building, and Evie froze. "The longer you wait, the worst it's going to be. Just rip off the bandage, Buttercup," Aiden told her, squeezing her hand.

"You going to walk me in?" she asked, looking up at her dad with pleading eyes.

He slowly shook his head. "Not this time. You can do this. One foot in front of the other and keep going." His voice was deep and reassuring.

Evie slowly let go of her dad's hand and started walking to the door. Her dad's words rolled through her mind like a chant. "One foot in front of the other and keep going."

She made it to her first class without seeing Andrew and managed to focus on what Dr. Carson was saying. As the morning progressed, she felt herself beginning to relax and fall back into the academic rhythm of things. Despite everything, Evie loved school and learning. A large part of her was happy to be back in class and back to a normal routine.

Evie was making her way down the hall to leave when she felt Andrew. She didn't know how, but she felt him. Deep in her gut, she knew he was near. Evie froze, causing a slight disturbance in the flow of students in the hallway. Her heart was threatening to beat its way out of her chest, and she was unsure if she was about to spew coffee and chocolate all over the floor from her nervous stomach.

Evie kept her eyes straight ahead and didn't move until the feeling in her gut had subsided. With a deep breath, she remembered her dad's words and took one step and kept going. The ache in her heart hurt worse than before, and she wondered if it would ever get easier.

No because he holds the other half of my heart.

40

ANDREW

Andrew had been anxious all morning. He knew she would be there and was desperate to catch a glimpse of her. Things hadn't been right since she'd written him that letter. There had been no way to smooth everything over or pretend everything was fine because it wasn't. He'd killed his brother to save Evie, the woman who held his heart. It was something he was still reconciling within himself, and even though he didn't like being separated from her, he understood the need. In the meantime, he would wait however long it took for her to come back to him.

Andrew was rushing through the hall to his next class when he spotted her, causing him to nearly stumble. The sight of her had caught him and his heart off guard. She looked better and healthier than he'd ever seen her. The dark circles under her eyes were gone, and she had filled out, from no longer losing sleep and living in a constant state of fear and anxiety. His heart swelled at the thought of her being happy and healthy. It was all he could ever and had ever wanted for her.

She turned the corner of the hallway, heading away from him. He knew he shouldn't, but he wanted to go to her. As he took one step towards her, she froze. Andrew immediately stopped. She knew he was there. He didn't know how, but he was sure she knew he was there. It gave him hope that the connection between them was still there, existing in the void.

Andrew felt lost in time as he stared at the back of Evie. The world seemed to pause long enough for him to drink in the sight of her. Someone's phone rang, jerking him back to reality. With one last longing look, he tore himself from the sight of her and made his way to class. He absentmindedly rubbed at the pain in his chest that had taken up permanent residence there, and it had nothing to do with the scarred over bullet hole. Andrew had never felt emotional pain in a physical way before, but it had become part of his day-to-day life.

Life was made better with Evie. Without Evie, it was excruciating.

He didn't know what the future held, but he knew it would be with her.

He was sure of it.

41
EVIE

Evie took a deep breath as she stepped out of the library. After a couple of hours of reading and studying, it was nice to breathe fresh air. The air was crisp and cold, but her favorite thick green sweater kept her warm. She took her time making her way to Beaumont Pizzeria. Downtown wasn't a far walk from campus, and even though it was cold outside, she enjoyed the walk because for the first time in years, she felt free and safe.

As she pushed open the door of the pizzeria, she was greeted with the warmth and smell of pizza. Suzanne looked up from the counter and gave her a big smile. About twenty second later, Evie was being squished by Suzanne and Ed in a big group hug.

"We've missed you," Suzanne told her.

"What took you so long to come in?" Ed asked, talking over Suzanne. Evie couldn't help but smile. Ed and Suzanne had always treated her like family and had always gone above and beyond to take care of her.

"I just got back into town yesterday. I came as soon as I

could," she promised. Evie glanced at the back of the restaurant to see if her dad was there yet.

"Aiden is over by the window. I'll get you something to eat. Go sit and enjoy," Suzanne said, squeezing her arm gently before turning to head to the kitchen. Ed kissed her on the cheek and followed Suzanne. Evie smiled as they started bickering before reaching the kitchen.

Turning to find her dad at one of the window tables, Evie stopped cold. There, sitting across from her dad, was the one person she hadn't been expecting to see. Her heart sped at the sight of him as if it was being called by his own.

Home.

He was her home.

However, she had to remind herself that their home was broken and needed to be repaired. It needed to be made whole before it could be livable.

Taking a deep breath, she made her way over to the table. Andrew rose as she neared. Out of the corner of her eye, she saw her dad anxiously awaiting their interaction. Evie was definitely going to have a few choice words for her dad when she got through this moment.

Traitor.

"Hello, Evie," Andrew said in that same still deep voice, causing chills to skitter along her skin. His dark green eyes were clear and hopeful and above all, beautiful.

Evie cleared her throat. "Hi, Andrew." She saw an almost imperceptible shift in him at her words. He thought she wasn't going to speak to him. Little did he know, there was nothing on earth that could keep her from speaking to him. Not even herself. There was nothing in her that could ignore or be intentionally hurtful to him.

"I was just leaving." He shifted to the side, gesturing for Evie to take his seat. She remained frozen, unable to move.

Andrew reached out a hand to Aiden. "Next week? Same time?"

Aiden clasped his hand and replied, "You bet. See you then."

Evie was trying to process what was happening when Andrew turned to her. She looked at him as he paused. He seemed to be trying to figure out what to say to her.

"See you on campus?" Hope once again filled his eyes.

Evie could only nod.

"Good," he replied softly. Stepping behind her to head to the door, his hand slid along the small of her back. It was a motion he'd done a million times to her, but that one touch seemed to be charged with a thousand lightning bolts. It seared through her sweater to her skin. She subconsciously leaned into his touch as his hand seemed to linger. As he continued walking, she was left empty and cold.

Lost.

The moment felt like it had lasted an eternity, but it'd merely been seconds. It left a hunger for him that she wished she could quell.

Sitting down, she turned her attention to her dad. "What was that?" she snapped.

"What was what?" her dad asked innocently.

"You and Andrew. Why are you having lunch with him? We broke up. Normally, parents do not continue to hang out with their daughter's ex-boyfriend." She sounded exasperated and nearly deranged. Clearly, her run in with Andrew had affected her more than she'd thought.

I need to calm down.

"No, not usually, but just because you and Andrew broke up doesn't mean he and I did." She knew her father's tone. It was the tone he used when he would *not* be budging on something. To her dismay, it meant he would be keeping his lunches with Andrew.

"Are you telling me you two have been hanging out? This wasn't a first-time offense?" Evie felt slightly betrayed. Her dad knew how hard it'd been for her to let Andrew go. She knew it wasn't fair to ask her dad to not have contact with Andrew, but nothing about the situation was even remotely normal, which made her feel somewhat justified in her feelings of betrayal.

"I'm sorry, Buttercup. I know none of this has been easy, and you shouldn't have had to deal with any of it." He said it with such gentleness that Evie's heart broke just a little more. She hadn't been the only one to suffer, and so often she forgot that. It was easy to focus on only what she was feeling and had lost, but her dad had always been walking alongside her. Then, Andrew had come along too. They'd both lost something that day. They all had.

Before she could tell her dad what she was thinking, he said, "But, I think it's a bit unfair for me to write Andrew off because you need a break. I fully support what you need to do, but Andrew and I had begun building a relationship too. I think part of him needs me just like you need me."

Evie agreed with her dad. "I know dad. I know." She let out a sigh before continuing. "It's just hard. I'm still trying to figure everything out, but I can't do that if I'm going to constantly be running into him with you."

"I understand. From now on, I'll be sure to do my best to make sure your paths don't cross."

"Thank you." Evie reached across the table, grabbing her dad's hand. "I mean it dad. Thank you for everything."

Giving her hand a reassuring squeeze, he replied, "Always, buttercup."

Suzanne and Ed made their way over to the table with a pineapple pizza and raspberry sweet tea.

It was the best Evie had ever had.

42
EVIE
FIVE MONTHS LATER

Evie strained in her seat to look behind her to where her family was sitting in the bleachers of the gymnasium of Beaumont University. Graduation had finally arrived, and Evie was more than excited for that moment. She deserved it after everything she'd endured the past year.

While she was excited, she was also a little sad for that season of life to be ending. She hadn't told anyone yet, except for Lucy, that she'd accepted a job in South Carolina. The job was in a little beach town at a community college as an English instructor. She'd also made friends with Anne Prittchet, the local bookstore owner. Anne was in her early seventies and loved all things books and flowers. She and Evie had become quick friends during her stay there over spring break. Before she'd headed back home, Evie had found herself with a parttime job that would help to pay the rent on the cute seaside cottage she'd signed the lease for while there.

She knew her family would be happy for her, but there was one person Evie was anxious to tell. She dreaded what the news was going to do to Andrew. They'd been cordial to one another throughout the semester, and Evie never missed the hope that remained in Andrew's eyes. He was waiting for her, and in some place deep inside, guarded from the hurt, she was waiting to find her way back to him.

Two hours later, with her diploma in hand, Evie made her way among the sea of students and families to find hers. Her parents were waiting with Suzanne and Ed under a tree on the far side of the quad. Elaine and Suzanne both squealed and rushed to hug her when she came into view.

"Alright you two. Y'all are going to smother her," Ed said, trying to break up the love fest of tears and happiness. When they finally let go of her, Ed stepped in for a hug, pulling her off the ground.

Evie laughed, "Who is doing the smothering now?"

"Proud of you, kiddo," Ed told her. Unshed tears glistened in his eyes.

"My turn," Aiden said, opening his arms. She stepped into his strong arms and felt like a little girl again. He'd always been her safe place to run to, and some part of her was glad he always would be. Wherever she went, she knew he'd always be her shadow, watching and guarding. "I'm so incredibly proud of you," Aiden quietly told her.

If he didn't let go of her soon, she was going to begin crying, and she hated crying more than anything. "Dad?"

"Just a little longer." His hold tightened.

"Who wants food?" Elaine asked, breaking through the wave of the emotions flooding out.

"Me," Evie said as her dad finally released her.

"Tacos or sushi?" Suzanne asked.

Evie laughed at the look on her mom's face. She could handle the tacos, but her mom detested sushi.

"Tacos." Everyone laughed as relief flooded her mom's face. "I'll meet y'all there. I need to do something first."

"Sure thing, kiddo," Ed said, grabbing Suzanne's arm to lead her to the car.

"See you there, Buttercup," her dad said, kissing her on the head.

Elaine pulled her in for one last hug. "Congratulations, baby girl."

Evie watched her family walk off before turning to go find Andrew.

After searching the main areas of campus with graduates, Evie decided to check Andrew's office. Her heart pounded as she made her way down the familiar hallway. "One step in front of the other and keep going" had become her motto over the past several months, and it was what she quietly chanted to herself as she made her way to his door.

With a fist raised to knock, she paused.

How am I going to tell him this?

What she had to say was not what he was going to want to hear, but she hoped he would understand. She hoped she was doing the right thing for herself and him. There was no hope for them if she didn't learn how to stand on her own and find out who she was without Dylan lurking over her.

With a deep breath, she knocked on the door.

"Come in." His deep voice made her heart flutter, and she prayed she'd always remember the feeling.

May we find our way back together, no matter the time or space between us.

"Hi," she said quietly, stepping into his office.

"Evie." He sounded surprised to see her standing there

just as he had been the first day she'd stepped into his office.

"I came to say goodbye." Sadness filled her voice. She hadn't meant for it to, but it was hard to keep it out.

"Heading home?" Andrew stood and came around the desk to stand in front of her. Out of the corner of her eye, she saw her table and chair in the corner. It was still there, just as she'd left it. Ready for her to come back whenever she wanted.

Clearing her throat, she said, "Not exactly." She closed her eyes briefly and sent up a quick prayer that she was doing the right thing.

"Evie?"

"I haven't told anyone yet because I wanted you to be the first to know. I felt I owed you that much with everything you and I have been through, and I didn't want you to think that I was running away from you." His eyes went on alert with that last statement. She knew it was beginning to click into place, and she dreaded her next words.

Before he could say anything, or she could lose her nerve, she said, "I'm leaving for Hemingway, South Carolina tomorrow. I accepted a job at Seaside Community College as an English Instructor."

Evie watched Andrew's face as he processed her words. There was a mix of hurt and confusion but also something else. A slow smile formed on Andrew's face.

"Congratulations, Eves. That's really great." His words were genuine. He was truly happy for her. They might not be together, but they still had love for one another.

"You're okay with me leaving?"

He paused, choosing his words. When he spoke, his voice was quiet and filled with emotion. "No, I'm not okay with it. Hemingway is what? Five or six hours away?"

Evie nodded.

"I'm not okay being that far from you. I know we aren't together right now, but I like knowing you are near. However, I would never begrudge you the opportunity to go somewhere new." Before she could respond, he said the one thing she'd been hoping he wouldn't. "I had hoped we could work through all of this before the decision of job opportunities came up, but we've hardly spoken all semester." Sadness lined the edges of his voice.

"I know, and that's my fault." She didn't want to have this conversation, but she didn't know when they'd be in the same room together again. "After that day, I didn't want to think about any of it. I kind of just shoved it deep inside and hoped it would go away. I thought with finding my freedom I would also find healing, but it didn't happen that way." Andrew leaned back against his desk and listened intently to what she was saying. She had always appreciated that about him—the way he made her feel heard.

"I buried myself in schoolwork this semester. I just kept telling myself that if I got to the end and graduated, it would all be fine. But the end arrived, and nothing was fine, is fine."

Taking a breath, she confessed. "I still have nightmares." She glanced down at her hands, wondering if she'd find blood on them. "I find myself looking over my shoulder more times than I should. The guilt of what happened and what you had to do eats at me constantly. I need to get away from here and learn to be on my own. To know what it's like to not have to constantly look over my shoulder and wonder if he's there watching me. To not have to rely on my dad to come save me or have an apartment across from mine. I've never truly been on my own, and I need to figure out how to do that. Alone."

Andrew nodded slowly, taking in her words. "You know I don't blame you for what happened? I would do it over again in a heartbeat because I love you. I understand you needing to stand on your own two feet and feel secure again. I respect that and want that for you. I just wish you weren't doing it so far away, and I really wish I could be there for you while you do it because I do love you, Evie. No matter how much time and space passes between us, that will never change."

Evie could feel the tears trying to well up in her eyes. "Andrew, I can't ask you to wait for me, and I can't give you a timeline of how long it will take before I am ready to be in a relationship again. It's not fair to you to wait on me. I'm not worth waiting on. I've put you through more than one person should."

Andrew closed the gap between them. "Yes, you are Evie James. Yes, you are." His voice was firm and unrelenting. "I love you, and I would wait a thousand years and more just for a moment with you." He took her hands in his. "One day, you will no longer be hurting and will be ready for us, and I'll be standing there waiting. No matter how long it takes. I am yours. Now and through the years ahead, I am yours." A finality filled his voice.

Evie couldn't breathe. She hoped she would be worthy of his love one day.

He leaned down, pressing his forehead to hers and whispered, "You hold my heart, Evie. You have it. It's wholly yours. It has been from the moment you fell at my feet."

They stood close, breathing in one another until Evie's phone rang, bursting the bubble. "I have to go," she whispered.

"I know," he replied reluctantly, pulling away from her. "Promise me one thing."

"Anything."

"Keep in touch with me. Let me know how you're doing every now and again. That you're safe."

"Deal," she promised.

A ghost of a smile flickered across his face. "If you ever need me, do not hesitate to call me. I'll be there. Whenever. Wherever. Doesn't matter. I'm yours." His dark green eyes were filled with nothing but love for her.

Andrew picked up one of her hands and pressed a kiss to it. "Goodbye, Evie."

"Goodbye, Andrew," she said as the tears started to fall down her cheeks. She slid her hand from his reluctant grip and quickly left the room. She didn't dare look back. If she did, she knew she'd never leave.

They would find their way back to one another. One day, when she was finally healed and put back together, she would find him, and he would be waiting for her.

But for now, she would put one foot in front of the other and keep going.

NOTE FROM AUTHOR

Thank you so much for reading my book! I absolutely adore Evie and Andrew, and I really hope you did too. If you're left longing for more, don't worry. I have more Evie and Andrew coming soon.

ACKNOWLEDGMENTS

To my best friend and husband, thank you so much for loving me and financing this expensive hobby of mine! I hope to pay you back for the ink cartridges.

To Beverly, thank you for being the first to take a chance on me and for praying for me along the way! Fingers crossed we hit that bestseller list, and yes, I am working on book 2, especially for you.

Sarah, Girl! We did it!! Without you, this never would have happened! Thank you for shoving me out the door and forcing me to step outside of my comfort zone! Forever grateful for you! Now, we gonna let it settle!

I couldn't have done this without my church family. Y'all have been absolute rockstars in supporting and praying for me. I hope y'all love this book!

Last and certainly never least, thank you to my Lord and Savior for giving me this story and for putting the right people in my path to make this happen! I hope I honor and bring You the glory.

ABOUT THE AUTHOR

Kate Embers is an indie author from Alabama, where she lives with her husband and two kids. She has two degrees in English and loves all things words and books. She is also obsessed with cooking and Turkish soap operas.

www.ingramcontent.com/pod-product-compliance
Lightning Source LLC
Chambersburg PA
CBHW020012120726
47903CB00004B/1250